W9-BTO-180

Fitz's heart stampeded against his ribs as he centered his cross hairs on a red speedboat racing toward the island.

It plowed through the water, waves cresting its bow. Two men decked out in camo stood at the helm, but they didn't look military. At least not anymore. Zooming in, Fitz saw two filthy faces and thick beards.

"Looks like a civilian boat," Beckham said. "Radio it in, Chow." He patted Apollo's head and knelt next to the German shepherd.

As the vessel got closer, it slowed, then coasted to a stop about two thousand feet out. The driver pulled out a pair of binos and centered them on the island.

"Got a bad feeling about this," Chow said. He plucked a radio off his vest and said, "Central, Ghost Two. Civilian craft with potential hostiles. Over."

Corporal Maggie Hook replied instantly. "Copy, Ghost Two. Tower Eleven and Tower Twelve have eyes. Stand by. Over."

Fitz glanced over his shoulder. Those towers were on the north side of the island. He turned to the others, but Chow was two steps ahead of him.

"Command, we are on the *south* side of the island. Repeat, south side," Chow said.

There was a pause and a flurry of static. It cleared, and Hook said, "Copy, Ghost Two. You have permission to engage if target displays hostile behavior."

"What do you think, Beckham?" Chow asked.

Fitz magnified his scope on the driver. A middle-aged man with a graying beard and a forehead smothered with grime stared back. Their gazes seemed to meet. Fitz was the first to look away. He watched the boat with naked eyes as it turned and sped off.

"Fuck," Chow said. "They were scoping us out."

Books by Nicholas Sansbury Smith

THE EXTINCTION CYCLE

Extinction Horizon
Extinction Edge
Extinction Age
Extinction Evolution
Extinction End
Extinction Aftermath
"Extinction Lost" (An Extinction Cycle Short Story)
Extinction War (Fall 2017)

TRACKERS: A POST-APOCALYPTIC EMP SERIES

Trackers
Trackers 2: The Hunted
Trackers 3: The Storm (Fall 2017)

THE HELL DIVERS TRILOGY

Hell Divers
Hell Divers 2: Ghosts
Hell Divers 3: Deliverance (Summer 2018)

THE ORBS SERIES

"Solar Storms" (An Orbs Prequel)
"White Sands" (An Orbs Prequel)
"Red Sands" (An Orbs Prequel)
Orbs
Orbs 2: Stranded
Orbs 3: Redemption

EXTINCTION
EVOLUTION

The Extinction Cycle
Book Four

NICHOLAS SANSBURY SMITH

www.orbitbooks.net

This book is a work of fiction. Names, characters, places, and incidents are the product of the author's imagination or are used fictitiously. Any resemblance to actual events, locales, or persons, living or dead, is coincidental.

Copyright © 2015 by Nicholas Sansbury Smith
Excerpt from *Extinction End* copyright © 2016 by Nicholas Sansbury Smith
Excerpt from *The Corporation Wars: Dissidence* © 2016 by Ken MacLeod

Author photograph by Maria Diaz
Cover design by Lisa Marie Pompilio
Cover photo by Blake Morrow
Cover copyright © 2017 by Hachette Book Group, Inc.

Hachette Book Group supports the right to free expression and the value of copyright. The purpose of copyright is to encourage writers and artists to produce the creative works that enrich our culture.

The scanning, uploading, and distribution of this book without permission is a theft of the author's intellectual property. If you would like permission to use material from the book (other than for review purposes), please contact permissions@hbgusa.com. Thank you for your support of the author's rights.

Orbit
Hachette Book Group
1290 Avenue of the Americas
New York, NY 10104
orbitbooks.net

Previously self-published in 2015
Originally published in ebook by Orbit in February 2017
First Mass Market Edition: August 2017

Orbit is an imprint of Hachette Book Group.
The Orbit name and logo are trademarks of Little, Brown Book Group Limited.

The publisher is not responsible for websites (or their content) that are not owned by the publisher.

The Hachette Speakers Bureau provides a wide range of authors for speaking events. To find out more, go to www.hachettespeakersbureau.com or call (866) 376-6591.

ISBNs: 978-0-316-55811-2 (mass market), 978-0-316-55812-9 (ebook)

Printed in the United States of America

OPM

10 9 8 7 6 5 4 3 2 1

For our wounded warriors.
Strong, brave, and heroic—thank you for your service.

"Intelligence is based on how efficient a species became at doing the things they need to survive."

—*Charles Darwin*

Prologue

Marine Staff Sergeant Jose Garcia flipped his night-vision goggles into position and watched as the half dozen outlines of the *George Washington* carrier strike group grew distant. That was home now, had been since the hemorrhage virus outbreak started over a month before. The *GW* was the last intact strike group in the world, with a nuclear-powered aircraft carrier, two Ticonderoga-class guided-missile cruisers, two Arleigh Burke–class guided-missile destroyers, a submarine, a Lewis and Clark–class dry-cargo ship, and a Pathfinder-class oceanographic survey ship. The strike group was the best and last chance the American military had of stopping the Variants.

Garcia's six-man Force Recon team cruised over the choppy waters of the Florida Keys in a nimble Zodiac. Somewhere to the east, the USS *Florida* lurked beneath the waves.

Thin clouds rolled across a jeweled sky of brilliant stars. Out here, he could almost forget the world was gone.

As the green-hued shapes of the *GW* strike group disappeared on the horizon, thoughts of Garcia's family worked their way into his mind. His wife, Ashley, his daughter, Leslie: They were gone now, like most of the world, nothing but flakes of ash in the cloud of death that had swept across the landscape.

Shit wasn't supposed to go down this way. He should be rocking his six-month-old baby girl to sleep on the porch of his country home in North Carolina, listening to the peaceful chirp of crickets at dusk. It was the home he and his wife had always dreamed of, the type of place you could only get to by back roads. Where no one bothered you. He'd been planning to retire there—raise his family, maybe keep some horses.

Garcia gripped his suppressed M4 and ground his teeth together. All he had left of his wife and daughter was the picture taped to the inside of his helmet, leaving him nothing but a shattered dream of what could have been.

Modern warfare had taught him there were lines *most* men wouldn't cross. There were international laws against torture, rules that governed war, courtesies that allowed the enemy to clear the injured off a field after a battle. But when was the last time the enemy passed up a chance to kill America's soldiers? War against the Variants was no different. Garcia had served in the Marine Corps for twenty years and seen some awful things—real-life nightmares. He had faced Al-Qaeda and the Taliban in the War on Terror, enemies who lacked all aspects of humanity. He thought he knew what monsters were, until he came face-to-face with the Variants.

This new enemy followed no rules and extended no courtesies. The human race was fighting tooth and nail for its very existence. He knew the value of life and how easily it could be taken away. The only respite in the dread that owned him now was his faith in God. He knew he would see his family again. Until then, his plan was simple: Fight and die well.

Garcia wasn't the only one suffering. Every man on

the Zodiac had lost someone. He flipped up his NVGs to conserve battery and took a moment to scan his team. Their faces were all covered by camouflage and shadow, but Garcia didn't need to see their features to know they were ready for whatever came next.

Sergeant Rick Thomas and Corporal Jimmy Daniels sat on the port side with their suppressed M4s angled toward the water. Like Garcia, they both had olive skin, short-cropped hair, and dark mustaches. Garcia privately thought they all looked like old-school porn stars. Knowing Thomas and Daniels, he figured they'd probably take it as a compliment.

On the starboard side sat Corporal Steve "Steve-o" Holmes. He was a quiet man with an honest face, Dumbo ears, and an M249 Squad Automatic Weapon with an Advanced Armament Corp. silencer cradled across his chest. In the stern, Lance Corporal Jeff Morgan and Corporal Ryan "Tank" Talon manned the motor. Morgan carried a suppressed MK11. He was thin, fast, and agile—the reasons Garcia had assigned him as point man. Tank, on the other hand, was a hulking African American with lumberjack arms and a barrel chest. The team's radio operator, he carried a suppressed M4.

These were the marines of the team code-named the Variant Hunters, or VH for short. Some scientist ten times smarter than Garcia had jokingly called them the Monster Squad, but Garcia didn't like that. Sounded too much like a B movie.

Tonight, their mission wasn't to exterminate Variants. It was simply to locate and observe the monsters in Key West. Recent intel indicated they were changing, maybe even evolving, at alarming rates. Garcia's role was to confirm this and document how, *scientifically*, the beasts were adapting.

Fuck science.

He didn't give a shit about what mutations the Variants were undergoing or what the lab jockeys were doing to stop it. He had his own cure—a suppressed M4 with a magazine full of 5.56-millimeter rounds. Each engraved with the initials of his daughter and wife.

Waves slapped against the sides of the Zodiac as they shot toward Key West. Garcia's senses were on full alert, taking in all his surroundings: the salty scent of the warm water on the breeze, the hum of the Zodiac's motor. The dull buzz of excitement pumped through his veins and made the spray of water on his skin sting.

On the horizon, the islands came into focus in the glow of the moonlight and glistening stars. He held up a hand to motion for Tank to ease up on the engine. They coasted until they were five hundred feet out.

Their final gear prep made little sound over the choppy waves. Garcia dismantled his NVGs and put the optics in a cascade bag. He stuffed it into his main pack and sat on the starboard side of the boat to put on his fins. Before he put on his scuba mask, he said, "Radio discipline when we get shoreside. Keep an eye out for anything on the way in. You all know those freaks can swim."

There were five nods, then Morgan dropped backward into the water. The others followed, one by one, with Garcia diving last.

As soon as he was submerged, he pulled his blade and finned after the others. The marines broke off into pairs and fell into a modified sidestroke, their heads just above the water.

Garcia couldn't see shit. There was always a small stab of fear that came with the underwater darkness. As a kid, he'd hated swimming in murky lakes. When he enlisted in the marines, that fear mostly subsided but never totally went away. Knowing the Variants could swim didn't help.

All it takes is all you got, Marine.

The motto always helped remind him what he was made of. How much he could take. Mental and physical pain were just temporary distractions. He took in a breath every other stroke and glided through the choppy water with ease. Every hundred feet he took a second to sight, scanning the water and island beyond for contacts. They were halfway to Smathers Beach, where the branches of palm trees shifted in a slight breeze.

When they reached the surf, Daniels held security while Garcia retrieved his NVGs, changed into his gear, clipped his fins to his bag, and jammed a magazine into his M4. Then they switched. The other men all did the same. Garcia used the stolen minutes to scope the terrain.

The pink Sheraton hotel towered over Highway A1A beyond the beach. Derelict cars were scattered across the road. Umbrellas and plastic chairs jutted out of the sand in every direction like unexploded missiles. A gust of wind sent trash shifting across the ground. Paradise had transformed into hell.

The beach looked like a war zone.

"Sarge," Daniels said over the comm, "you see that?"

Garcia followed the muzzle of Daniels's M4 to a pair of corpses stranded in the surf about one hundred feet to the right. Tendrils of ropy seaweed surrounded the bodies.

"Looks like we have casualties," Garcia said. He mounted his NVGs and flipped them into position. The small corpses came into focus through the green hue. His calm heart sank at the realization they were children.

Garcia flashed a hand signal, and the six-man team waded through the surf. A draft of air carrying a putrid scent hit Garcia as soon as he reached the loose sand. The stench was a cross between a slaughterhouse and a backwater swamp in the steaming heat of summer.

Garcia ignored it and hustled across the beach, his team spreading out in combat intervals.

He stepped over a broken bottle of Bud Light and motioned for three of his men to take up position near a concrete wall running along the entrance to the beach. Then he followed Daniels and Morgan to a tiki bar for cover.

It was quiet, but Garcia imagined the phantom sounds of what it had been like just over a month ago—the shouts of drunken vacationers, the growl of expensive cars prowling the strip. He never understood why people wanted to live in places like this. Maybe he was old fashioned, but he liked his peace and quiet. And now he had it. Only the faint whistle of the breeze and the whisper of the surf sounded in the distance.

The calm wasn't reassuring. The longer Garcia stood there, the more he felt as if they were being watched, as if someone or something had the drop on him. He scanned the beach, the road, and the Sheraton for a third time. The slimy feeling passed, and Garcia glanced back at the corpses.

Something didn't add up. The Variants rarely left meat behind. There wasn't a single rotting body anywhere else on the beach, so why here? Variants typically took their prey to their lairs or tore them apart where they killed, leaving nothing but bones. These bodies, while mangled, showed no sign of the bite marks or deep lacerations Garcia was used to seeing.

He pointed at his eyes, then to Morgan and Daniels, then to the kids in the surf. Garcia swallowed as he followed the marines to the corpses. Both were boys no older than eight or nine, wearing shorts and what looked like torn-up swim shirts. Their legs were tangled in seaweed, and they lay facedown in the wet sand as the waves beat against their small bodies. He flipped up his

NVGs and used the toe of his boot to push the first boy onto his side. In the glow of the moonlight, he examined the body.

"Holy shit," Garcia whispered.

The boy wasn't human. He was a Variant, with swollen lips and wide yellow irises where his innocent eyes should have been. Bulging blue veins crisscrossed his stomach and chest.

Discovering the corpses were monsters made Garcia feel better about what he was about to do.

He reached for his medical pack and pulled out a vial. The lab jockeys loved flesh samples. Fresh or rotten, they didn't care. He grabbed his knife and prepared to cut a piece from the boy's chest when he saw something that made him pause.

Leaning in, he pushed at the kid's neck with the blade to expose what looked like gills under his left ear.

"Morgan, check this shit out," Garcia whispered. .

The marine hurried over and crouched. Garcia used his gloves to spread the pink, meaty gills apart. Water squished out of them, making an awful sound that caused his stomach to churn.

"Do we tag and bag?" Morgan asked.

"No. Can't bring 'em with. Take pictures and a sample." Garcia stood and handed him the vial. He jogged over to Daniels while Morgan worked. The other three marines held their position at the retaining wall three hundred feet away.

A few minutes later, Morgan returned with the sample. Garcia put it in his medical pack and motioned for the team to advance to the highway. This was exactly what they were here for, but they needed more than a sample or two to please the higher-ups. They needed further documentation of how the monsters were changing, and why.

Somewhere overhead, he heard the *chop chop* of a drone. The reassuring sound of American military muscle reminded him there was a team monitoring them, watching his men advance. Help was only minutes away if they needed it.

Of course, out here minutes could separate life and death.

Garcia shouldered his M4 and worked his way across the beach. The other marines fanned out, keeping their heads low. There wasn't much cover, and Garcia wanted to get out of the open as quickly as possible. He followed Morgan onto the highway, toward an F-150 on a lift. Daniels took up position behind an abandoned cargo van with Steve-o and Thomas. Tank crouched behind a Mini Cooper, but the car was hardly big enough to hide him. His helmet crested the top like a turret. They all paused to listen and scan for hostiles.

Morgan glanced back at Garcia for orders, but Garcia held steady for a few extra seconds. His gut still told him something was off, even if his eyes and ears showed nothing out of the ordinary. There was no sign of the Variants.

Garcia finally nodded at Morgan and shot an advance signal. The team pushed forward at a slow jog, hunched and close to the vehicles for cover. Sweat dripped down Garcia's brow, but he didn't bother wiping it away. He swept his M4 over the terrain.

Midstride, Garcia caught a whiff of sour, rotting fruit. A sudden wave of anxiety rose in his stomach. He froze, then took a knee. The other men followed suit.

Something was watching them. He felt it.

His instincts had saved the lives of his men before, and he wasn't going to ignore them. They were compromised. He couldn't see the Variants, but they were watching. Additional intel wasn't worth the lives of his men.

Garcia flashed a retreat signal. Morgan narrowed his eyes as if he was going to protest. The moment of hesitation passed, and he was moving a second later. The team had made it only a few feet when a frantic female voice pierced the quiet night.

"Help!"

Morgan's hand went up into a fist before Garcia had a chance to search the streets. The entire six-man team crouched and took cover behind the nearest vehicle. Garcia looked over the hood of a blue BMW before moving to the driver's-side door of a minivan for a better look.

"Somebody...please..." The woman's voice was hoarse and crackly, as if she had chain-smoked her entire life.

Garcia cringed at her pleas for help. If they weren't compromised before, they sure as hell were now. He flipped his mini-mic to his lips and broke radio discipline. Stealth didn't matter now. The woman had blown their cover. Every Variant in Key West would have heard her. They had two options: help the woman and retreat to the Zodiac—or retreat without her.

Cursing to himself, Garcia ordered his team into action. "Daniels, grab her. Morgan, Steve-o, you're with Daniels. Tank, Thomas, you hold security, then we fall back."

The three marines fell into a crouched trot and vanished behind a donut delivery truck. Garcia moved to the front of the minivan and saw her. The woman dragged her body across the pavement, blood streaking behind her mangled feet.

"Help me..."

Morgan approached the woman and squatted by her side, his weapon still angled into the darkness. He put a finger to his lips with his other hand while Steve-o slung his SAW over his back and crouched on her other side. Daniels reached down to grab her with his left arm, but the woman swatted at him, groaning and screeching in a voice so loud it made Garcia wince again.

Shit. Shit. Shit.

"Let's move," Garcia said. He didn't like this one damn bit. How in the hell had this woman survived out here in enemy territory? Especially with feet that looked like hamburger meat?

The sensation of being watched hit him again. He could almost feel eyes burning through his back. The acid in his stomach churned. He twisted away from the road, raised his rifle, and arced the muzzle across the white balconies on the ocean side of the Sheraton. There, standing in the doorway of a unit on the third floor, was a lean figure draped in shadow. It slipped back inside the open door a second later.

"Move your asses!" Garcia shouted. "It's a fucking trap!" The words sounded strange, and he almost couldn't believe them. Variants didn't set traps.

Rising to his feet, Garcia watched anxiously as Morgan and Steve-o hoisted the woman up and helped Daniels sling her over his back. Tank and Thomas were already running toward the beach. Garcia checked the Sheraton one last time before he turned to run.

The high-pitched roar of a single Variant rose over the screams of the desperate woman and Daniels's futile attempts to calm her. The shriek ebbed and flowed into a whine that made Garcia's heart kick. He bolted through the maze of cars, flinging glances over his shoulder every few steps. A flash of motion from the parking lot of the Sheraton stopped him midstride. The clatter of clicking joints confirmed the screeching monster wasn't alone.

The distorted shadows of long limbs and withered bodies shifted across the concrete. Three Variants galloped into the green-hued darkness a beat later. The monsters used their back legs to spring forward like rabbits.

There was no way the Variant Hunters could outrun them. Garcia switched the selector on his M4 to single shot, aimed, and opened fire as the creatures dashed onto the highway. He clipped one in the shoulder and another in the leg before they darted behind a vehicle. Pivoting to the right, he fired a short burst that punched through metal and shattered glass, killing the injured Variant as it leaped onto the hood.

Daniels lumbered away from the beasts as Morgan and Steve-o stopped to provide covering fire. The crack of Steve-o's SAW broke out, and 5.56-millimeter rounds cut through the two beasts. Even with the AAC silencer, the gunfire was loud, but their dying shrieks were louder. He cut the creatures down in seconds. Scarlet blossomed across the street as the bodies crashed to the pavement.

The dying beasts were just the advance guard. The main horde swarmed from the open windows of the Sheraton like an army of enraged ants spilling from an anthill. They leaped off balconies and skittered down the sides of the hotel. Others squeezed from sewer openings and poured into the street faster than Garcia could flip magazines.

"Run!" he shouted. "Fall the fuck back! Tank, radio Command!" Garcia rushed toward the entrance to Smathers Beach, his lungs burning for air.

"Command, Victor Hotel Actual. We have a survivor and are being pursued by Variants. Need extraction, ASAP!" Tank said over the comm.

Garcia's earpiece crackled, and a voice hissed into his ear. "Roger, Victor Hotel Actual, eye in the sky has confirmed your location. Delta Four, Five, and Six are en route to your insertion point."

"Copy that," Garcia replied. He halted in the sand and waved frantically at his men. Tank and Thomas joined him near the tiki bar, but Daniels, Morgan, and

Steve-o were still running down the highway. Three dozen Variants darted after them, leaping on top of cars, sprinting down the sidewalk, and emerging from the fronts of surf shops.

They were everywhere, and Garcia watched the hungry maws chomping behind swollen sucker mouths in a state of horror. He was used to seeing Variants with long, muscular limbs, but now their stalklike arms seemed withered, almost frail, and their horned nails were even longer. They charged, scrambling over vehicles and darting on all fours across the street, claws scratching over metal and concrete.

"Covering fire!" Garcia yelled. He switched the selector on his M4 to automatic, shouldered the rifle, squared his boots the best he could in the loose sand, and sent a burst of fire at the onrushing horde. Rounds lanced across the beach at the tidal wave of pallid, veiny flesh. His foot slid in the sand as he fired, bullets ripping through car doors and breaking windows before he found a target. One of the rounds took off the top of a female Variant's skull. It skidded across the road, brain matter spilling onto the asphalt. He dropped four more of the creatures before his magazine went dry. The monsters continued to bleed onto the street, relentless and undeterred. By the time Daniels reached the entrance to the beach, there were hundreds of Variants pursing the team.

"Changing!" Tank shouted.

"Fire in the hole!" Thomas shouted back. He lobbed an M67 grenade across the beach. It landed in the street and rolled under the F-150 on a lift. Two agonizing beats later, a mushroom of fire blasted into the air, sending shrapnel whizzing into the heart of the monstrous horde. The explosion gave Daniels, Steve-o, and Morgan a chance to escape to the sand.

"On me!" Garcia shouted. He ran toward the surf, but

stopped when his boots were submerged. They were out of room, and there was no way in hell they could make it back to the Zodiac. Even with their fins and their training, the Variants could swim faster.

Not to mention they had gills now.

Daniels set the woman on the sand and raised his rifle. She was mumbling between her pained moans.

"We can't," she hissed. "*Please*, we can't."

"We're getting you out of here, ma'am," Daniels said.

"No," she groaned. "You don't understand. They won't let us leave. They *won't*!" She collapsed to her back, her words slurring between each breath.

Garcia caught a glimpse of her in the moonlight. She was young, maybe college aged, with her blond hair in ragged braids, probably a student on vacation before the outbreak. It only took a glance to see she was in bad shape.

Both of her feet were cut to pieces, flesh hanging loosely from the bones. Her youthful blue eyes were vacant and fixated on the moon above. The marines formed a perimeter around her, guarding her life with theirs. The team hadn't found a survivor for a week. Every remaining human soul was precious.

Injured Variants staggered onto the beach, shrapnel wounds gushing blood. They skittered across the sand and fanned out, their emaciated bodies stretching in the moonlight and yellow eyes homing in on the Variant Hunters. Garcia had to remind himself that he and his team were the predators, not the prey.

Daniels tossed a grenade and then bent over the woman to shield her body. A geyser of sand and body parts gushed into the sky, but the monsters still came, charging straight into the marines' gunfire.

Garcia's earpiece crackled over the noise. He only caught a piece of the transmission before the chaos drowned it out.

"Victor Hotel, watch your ..."

In the distance, Garcia could make out the faint mechanical roar of choppers. The reassuring sound of salvation prompted another shot of adrenaline through his veins. He didn't take his eyes off the horde in his cross hairs, mowing down creature after creature with short bursts. If he had turned, maybe he would have seen the Variants swimming under the waves and their pale, naked bodies leaping across the surf as they emerged from the ocean.

Maybe he could have saved Daniels and the woman before the beasts dragged them into the water.

Garcia's heart flipped, the rush of relief transforming into the stab of fear and shock. By the time he grasped what was happening, Morgan was gone too, half of his face ripped off by a set of talons. A dozen of the creatures had flanked them from the ocean, swimming unseen beneath the waves.

He ducked down as rockets streaked overhead from an Apache helicopter. Two Black Hawks closed in, spraying sand and death into the sky from door-mounted M240s. For Morgan, Daniels, and the woman, the birds had arrived a minute too late, but for the rest of the Variant Hunters the helos were salvation.

Rounds slammed into the sand around Garcia, Tank, Steve-o, and Thomas. They huddled together to avoid the spray. Diseased limbs and chunks of gore tumbled across the beach around their phalanx.

Garcia glanced over his shoulder to watch the birds circle. Green rounds tore through the water, turning the Variants into little more than floating meat in the crimson tide.

Another salvo of rockets hissed away from the Apache toward the street. Variants galloped away in retreat, screeching and squawking.

In minutes, it was over. The bark of the guns died,

replaced by the howls of dying monsters. Smathers Beach was truly a battlefield now, pockmarked with smoking craters and mangled, grotesque bodies sprawled across the sand.

Garcia took in deep breaths filled with the scent of charred flesh. Dazed, his ears ringing, he slowly stood and searched the water for his lost men and the woman they had tied to save. The Black Hawks continued to circle and fire at twitching Variants below while the Apache headed west to take care of any survivors.

As the Black Hawks finally lowered to extract Garcia and what was left of his team, all he could think about was how wrong he'd been. If he'd paid more attention to science and studied the adaptation of the creatures, his men would still be alive. The monsters had used the children in the surf and the woman on the road as bait. The deaths were on him, and he had to live with them, just like all of the others.

Fucking bait.

1

Three Days Later

The divine glow of a brilliant sunrise crept across Plum Island. On the walkway outside Building 5, twelve Medical Corps soldiers in black fatigues knelt with their hands tied behind their backs. Master Sergeant Reed Beckham walked the line and stopped to point the barrel of Lieutenant Colonel Ray Jensen's Colt .45 Peacemaker at the bowed head of the closest soldier.

Beckham didn't know the man's name—hell, he didn't even know his rank—but he was one of the late Colonel Wood's henchmen. It seemed only fitting Jensen's gun should kill them.

The soldier glanced up, his long chin wobbling. "Please. Please don't shoot me. I was just following orders."

Beckham resisted the urge to pistol-whip the man right then and there. If he had a bullet for every soldier who had used that line, he would have enough ammo to kill every Variant left in New York. On a deployment in Iraq, Beckham had helped disarm more than one hundred Iraqi troops during the fall of Baghdad twelve years ago. Many of those men had used that same line. It didn't excuse them from sectarian violence or killing Kurdish women and children.

These men were soldiers, but even soldiers had a choice. The Nazis had a choice. The Taliban had a choice. Osama bin Laden's men had a choice. When shit hit the fan, there was always a choice. Beckham had disobeyed orders in Niantic to save a stranded family, and he'd done so again when he killed Colonel Wood's men the night before.

"I say we drop them off in New York City and let the Variants have at 'em," Staff Sergeant Parker Horn said with a snort. "Although that would be a waste of fuel." The Delta Force operator's right bicep was still dripping blood, but he didn't seem to notice the pain. His eyes blazed. Corporal Joe Fitzpatrick and Staff Sergeant Jay Chow flanked him, their rifles all aimed at the Medical Corps prisoners.

Major Sean Smith was there too, arms crossed, supervising the scene. Given the state of the world, Smith had elected to give Beckham free rein to deal with Wood's soldiers however he saw fit. He hadn't done so without objecting, though, and his final words on the matter rang in Beckham's mind: *It may be their funeral, but it'll be your conscience.*

On the lawn behind Beckham stood a team of Army Rangers and marines—fourteen battle-hardened men, all stationed at Plum Island since the early days of the outbreak. Staff Sergeant Alex Riley sat in his wheelchair next to Meg Pratt, the firefighter they'd rescued from New York. She was propped up on crutches. It felt good to have a small army at his back, but the longer Beckham listened to the sound of the crowd, the more he realized how fucked things really were.

"Kill them," one of the marines barked.

"Shoot 'em!" yelled another.

Beckham was still fuming over Lieutenant Colonel Jensen's death the night before, but this wasn't right. His men were better than this. They weren't executioners. Civilization was gone, but Beckham wasn't going to let justice go with it.

"Get up," Beckham said. He motioned with the muzzle of Jensen's Colt .45.

The Medical Corps soldier struggled to his feet. He squinted in the morning sun, his youthful features scrunching together. He couldn't be more than twenty years old.

"What's your name, kid?" Beckham asked.

"Keith," he replied, his chin still trembling. "Keith Sizemore. I'm sorry, Master Sergeant. I'm sorry about Colonel Wood. I didn't know..."

"Shut the hell up, Sizemore," one of the other prisoners said. Beckham strode over to the man, a sergeant named Gallagher according to his uniform. He was the highest-ranking soldier of the group.

Beckham grabbed him under the arm and jammed the revolver into the man's back. "On your feet, Sergeant."

"Tough guy with a gun," Gallagher said. "Once they find out what you did to Colonel Wood, you're all going to wish you were dead. They're going to send an army after you fucking traitors."

The door to Building 5 creaked open. Doctor Kate Lovato and Doctor Pat Ellis stepped out onto the landing. Kate gave Beckham a critical look and slowly shook her head. The simple act washed away whatever bloodlust was still swirling inside of Beckham. He took in a breath and holstered his new Colt .45. Then he pulled his knife and cut the ties binding the sergeant's wrists.

"What the..." Gallagher said.

"No gun," Beckham said. He sheathed the blade and added, "No knife. Just me... and you."

Gallagher's cocky smile revealed a mouthful of

crooked teeth. He massaged his wrists in turn, then balled his hands into fists. In two swift motions, he planted a boot and threw a punch that sailed past Beckham's right eye.

Beckham hardly had the chance to move out of the way. Gallagher grunted, regained his balance, and swung again. He was fast, but Beckham was more agile. He grabbed the sergeant's arm, twisted it, and shoved him. Gallagher crashed to the grass.

"Take him, boss!" Riley shouted.

"Son of a bitch!" Gallagher yelled. He spat, wiped his lips with a sleeve, and pushed himself to his feet. As soon as he was standing, he launched another fist.

This time Beckham pivoted to the right. Gallagher's fist whizzed by his chin. Out of habit, Beckham stepped back, braced his left boot, lunged forward with his right, and used all the forward momentum to throw a punch that connected with the side of the sergeant's left cheek.

A bone-shattering crunch sounded over the shouts of the marines and Rangers. Blood exploded from Gallagher's mouth, a tooth flying out in the mist. He spun and crashed face first to the ground.

Gallagher crawled a few feet before collapsing to his stomach. There was a moment of complete silence, broken only by the chirp of a bird in the distance.

"Anyone else still loyal to Colonel Wood?" Beckham asked.

Not a single one of the Medical Corps soldiers said a word.

"Good, because I'm going to make this really simple. You're either with us or you're against us. This is the apocalypse. Things don't work the way they used to, but we all still have a choice. And I'm offering you all a very simple one—either you join us or my friend Big Horn will give you a ride to New York and you can fight the

Variants on your own." After a pause to let the prisoners digest his words, Beckham said, "Any questions?"

President Nate Mitchell started his twenty-first day as president of the United States with a cold cup of coffee. He brought the Styrofoam cup to his lips and eyed the muddy liquid. It was a far cry from the steaming Starbucks venti white chocolate mocha that used to be waiting on his desk in his private Senate office every morning.

Mitchell imagined sitting in the Oval Office, discussing the current jobs report or the War on Terror with his staff. That was what presidents did.

But this? He looked around the dimly lit conference room in the bowels of Cheyenne Mountain and took a sip of his coffee. It tasted like shit. Vice President Josh Black sat across the table, decked out in his perfectly pressed army uniform. He studied a pile of reports while scratching his halo of gray hair. Every few minutes he would lick his right finger, peel back another page, and then go back to scratching. It was annoying as hell, and Mitchell wondered if it was part of the reason Black didn't have a fourth star on his chest. Then again, looks didn't seem to matter in the military, as they had in Washington.

Nobody cared what you looked like at the end of the world. Men and women were judged on their ability to survive. That's how things should have always been, Mitchell thought, but it took the apocalypse for the playing field to even out. That was why Mitchell had appointed Black as his vice president. He was one of the highest-ranking soldiers left, and with martial law in effect, he had also been the perfect liaison to General Kennor.

With Kennor dead, Mitchell wasn't sure what was going to happen.

"You got the backup Central Command recommendations for me yet?" he asked.

The vice president closed a folder and placed it back into the pile. "I don't like any of the available options, sir. The Variants have found ways into almost every single one of our facilities: Raven Rock Mountain Complex, Langley Air Force Base, Offutt Air Force Base, the PEOC…"

Black winced, clearly realizing his mistake. Mitchell's wife, June, had died in the Presidential Emergency Operations Center two weeks after the first case of the hemorrhage virus appeared. He and June had been whisked away when one of the Secret Service guards began displaying symptoms, but she never made it out.

Mitchell closed his eyes, blocking out the memory of the gunshots that took her life as she reached out to grab him. "You're telling me we're out of options?" He snapped his eyes open and exhaled.

Black folded his hands on the table. "No, sir, I'm telling you we need to abandon dry land."

"And what? Circle the earth in Air Force One?"

The sides of Black's dry lips trembled slightly, as if he wasn't sure if he should grin. "I've been looking over our current assets on the sea, and it looks like the *George Washington* carrier strike group may be the perfect option for Central Command. They returned to US waters during the outbreak and are currently sailing off the coast of the Florida Keys. It's the last strike group still intact." He paused for a moment to lock eyes with Mitchell. "I'm also advising that we abandon Cheyenne Mountain. It's only a matter of time before the Variants infiltrate this facility."

Mitchell leaned back in his chair. He had never really liked the ocean, but it sure as hell beat this damp underground city built into the mountain. A rap on the door sounded before he could respond. Chief of Staff Brian

Olson walked into the room wearing the same pin-striped suit he'd had on since they entered the facility weeks before. The expensive suit made him feel normal, he'd told Mitchell.

"Mr. President, Mr. Vice President," Olson said. He reached up and fixed the side part in his thin black hair. The glow of the overhead lights illuminated his pale features and the bulging vein running from his forehead to his scalp.

"Jesus, you look like shit, Olson. Didn't you sleep last night?" Mitchell asked.

"Not a wink," Olson replied. "Was dealing with the fallout from yesterday's attack on Central Command. Speaking of, that's why I'm here. There's good news and bad news, sir."

"Start with the good," Mitchell said.

"Several of General Kennor's staff made it out of Central Command before it fell. General George Johnson is now temporarily in charge of the military. He's been taken to the *George Washington* carrier strike group."

"Smart man," Black said. "Another reason to move Central Command there."

Olson handed Black and Mitchell manila folders stamped TOP SECRET.

"The second piece of good news is that the first stage of Operation Extinction has been a success. Our teams collected more than enough chemotherapeutics. Inside these folders, you will see the four locations assigned to the development of Kryptonite. They're all using genetic modification to speed up the production of the antibodies. Three of those four have already started the process. Kryptonite should be ready in two weeks."

"What's the bad news?" Black asked, seemingly unconcerned with the science.

"Central Command itself is a complete loss. The

facility is off-line, and I wouldn't advise investing any resources in taking it back."

"I agree," Black said. "But if General Johnson is in charge, then it will be up to him."

Olson continued as if he hadn't heard the vice president, addressing Mitchell directly instead. "There's something else, sir. Apparently there has been an incident on Plum Island."

Mitchell finished off his coffee and said, "Isn't that where Secretary of State Ringgold is?"

"Yes, sir, it is. She's fine, but we received a report that Colonel Wood and several of his men have been killed."

Mitchell recoiled, although he wasn't sure if it was because of the coffee or the report. It was the second time in as many days that Plum Island had been attacked.

"Were they able to hold back the Variants?" Mitchell asked.

"Sir, Colonel Wood and his men weren't killed by Variants. There was some sort of altercation among the forces stationed there. We aren't sure what happened. General Johnson is still looking into the matter, but after the loss of Offutt, he's been preoccupied with more pressing issues."

"Humans killing humans," Mitchell said, shaking his head. He sank in his plush leather chair. "Just when I thought things couldn't get any uglier."

"That changes everything," Black said. "Colonel Wood was overseeing Operation Extinction."

"He will be replaced," Olson said. "The war will continue without him."

Black ran his index finger across a bleeding crack on his bottom lip. "You obviously know nothing about the military, Olson. Wood isn't the type of man who's easily replaced. From what I know about him he is—*was*—the fearless leader we needed to defeat the Variants."

Mitchell rose to his feet and palmed the table before Olson could offer a retort. He looked at his vice president and chief of staff in turn. Exhausted eyes stared back at him under the weak glow from a bank of overhead lights. He shifted his gaze to the concrete walls of the bunker that had been built to protect them from a nuclear impact.

"How'd it come to this?" Mitchell asked, bowing his head. His wife, his friends, and most of his staff weren't the only things he'd lost since the outbreak. The passion and killer instinct that had helped him climb the ranks of the Senate was gone too, eradicated by the fear he now lived with every minute of every day.

But what ate at Mitchell even more was his complete lack of power. He'd signed it all away to General Kennor in the hopes of taking back the streets from the Variants. It was his last move as a politician. Now he was just a lame-duck president in an empty suit.

"Is that all?" Mitchell asked. The words lacked emotion, and he hardly recognized his own voice.

The only response that came was the shuffling of papers. Black licked his right finger and began flipping through his folder. Mitchell glanced at his chief of staff. Olson had helped him win five elections. Over the years they had earned a nickname from his opponents he had secretly loved—the "Lions of Capitol Hill." Now there would never be an election again.

That was one of the hardest things to stomach. Democracy was gone, along with the promise of hope and freedom. Central Command was destroyed, General Kennor was dead, and now Colonel Wood, the architect of Operation Extinction, was too.

A loud knock on the door rattled Mitchell from his thoughts. Marine Lieutenant Caleb Stanton entered the room. He was chief of operations for Cheyenne Mountain and had kept the bunker safe—so far. His eyes were hidden under the shadows cast by his helmet, but Mitchell could tell something was wrong.

"Mr. President, Mr. Vice President," Stanton said. "I'm sorry to interrupt, but we have a situation. Several packs of Variants have been spotted along a frontage road that leads to a backup entrance to the facility."

Mitchell was no soldier, but he was smart enough to know that Stanton wouldn't interrupt if the threat wasn't serious. A chill ran down his legs.

"Pull the patrols back inside and post every available soldier to sentry duty," Black said.

"Already done, sir," Stanton said. "They won't get into the facility. I assure you." He stepped into the light, and Mitchell finally saw his eyes. They were strong and confident, but Mitchell didn't trust the lieutenant to keep him safe. Truthfully, he didn't trust anyone with that job.

As Stanton left the room, Mitchell faced Black and Olson. "Tell General Johnson I'm requesting Central Command be moved to the *GW* strike group. Olson, start packing. We're leaving this shithole and heading to the Florida Keys."

Kate slipped on the helmet of her CBRN suit and reluctantly entered the BSL4 lab. There was work to do, but her heart and mind were still on the tarmac where Lieutenant Colonel Jensen had been gunned down.

"You sure you're okay?" Ellis asked.

Kate nodded and pulled a stool over to her station. "I'll be fine," she lied. "Right now we need to focus on the second stage of Operation Extinction. Have we identified the other facilities participating in the production of the antibodies?"

"Major Smith went through Colonel Wood's files earlier this morning. The three facilities with bioreactors are located in Texas, Oregon, and Florida. Colonel Wood authorized production at all three facilities. They're using the same genetic modification as us to speed up the antibodies, but it appears there was no effort to contact other countries."

Kate wasn't surprised. She thought of her parents in Italy. Her hope that they had survived dwindled every day. For the longest time, she had felt isolated and unable to do anything for them. Now, with Wood out of the picture, she could finally do something to help the rest of the world.

"As soon as we get the reactors online, we need to find a way to reach other labs," Kate said. "Places in other countries. We can't produce enough antibodies with only four sites. They might cover the States, but that's nowhere near enough to cover the world."

"I know. Problem is, no one seems to know what's going on or who to talk to."

The wall-mounted intercom chirped. Major Smith and a neatly dressed African American woman stood behind the observation window at the far end of the lab.

Kate stiffened in her suit when she realized who the woman was.

"Doctors, as you already know, this is Secretary of State Jan Ringgold," Major Smith said. "I've spent the past hour explaining the work we do here and the incident last night."

"I'd like to ask you some questions," Ringgold said. Her tone was casual, but serious.

"Certainly, Madam Secretary," Kate replied. "Please give us a few minutes to get changed out of our suits."

"That won't be necessary. We can speak through the intercom."

Kate exchanged a glance with Ellis, who nodded back.

"You'll have to forgive me, Doctors, but I've been stuck under a rock for the past month, so to speak. Fortunately, Major Smith has brought me up to speed on VariantX9H9 and Kryptonite. You're both to be commended for your work, and I thank you."

Kate had expected to have to defend her role in the events of the previous night. Instead, she felt a tingle of pride. The feeling was unusual, and it quickly dissipated at the thought of the monsters VX9H9 had created.

"I wish that was all I needed to talk to you about," Ringgold continued. "Unfortunately, there are more pressing matters at hand. After witnessing the violence last night, I've been trying to piece together what little information I have to go on. And frankly, I don't trust *anyone* on this island."

Kate had known it was coming, but the words still made her feel slimy. As if she was part of the corruption. Then again, she wouldn't trust anyone either if she was in the secretary of state's shoes. Major Smith fidgeted and pulled at the cuff of his uniform. He raised a brow at Kate as if to say, *You better make this good.*

"I don't blame you, Madam Secretary," Kate said. "For the past month, Doctor Ellis and I have been working in fear of the men supervising this facility—first Colonel Gibson, the architect of VX-99 and the hemorrhage virus, and then his longtime colleague, Colonel Wood. The very building you find yourself in now was built to research VX-99 long before the hemorrhage virus made it out of a top-secret lab on San Nicolas Island."

"You're telling me Colonel Wood was involved too?"

Kate nodded. "The paper trail continues to climb the ladder. We can prove that General Kennor knew about Colonel Wood's involvement and that he continued to allow him to supervise the science division of Operation Extinction."

All trace of civility disappeared from Ringgold's face. She narrowed her eyes and glanced at Smith, who shook his head and said, "I'm sorry, Secretary Ringgold."

"Madam Secretary, I can assure you of one thing: Master Sergeant Beckham and Team Ghost have done everything in their power to stop the Variants since day one. Many of them have given their lives to save our country and protect Plum Island," Kate continued.

A moment of realization passed across Ringgold's dark brown eyes. "Master Sergeant Beckham saved me from Raven Rock...But he's still part of the military that brought our country to its knees. If what you say about General Kennor is true, then the new commander, General Johnson, could be just as dangerous."

Kate recalled the name. He was the general who had explained Project Earthfall. He had also been one of Kennor's confidants.

"Madam Secretary, if I may," Kate said.

"Go ahead, Doctor."

"General Johnson could very well be in on the VX-99 program, but we're running out of time to defeat the Variants. I need help coordinating the production of Kryptonite with other countries. That means contacting other labs and having access to confidential information. You heard Colonel Wood on the tarmac. He didn't want to deploy the weapon worldwide."

Ringgold nodded. "I remember."

Kate took a moment to think. There had to be someone out there they could trust. "How well do you know President Mitchell?"

"My experience with Mitchell has always been from the other side of the political aisle. He's a difficult man to deal with, but maybe I can talk some sense into him.

Problem is, he isn't in control of the military, or Operation Extinction." Ringgold looked toward the ceiling. After a brief pause, she added, "I need some time to analyze this information. This is a lot to take in."

"Wait, Madam Secretary," Kate said, raising a hand. "I know what it's like to feel as though you can't trust anyone. I've been there, but I promise you, you can trust us. And you can trust Beckham and his men. We're almost out of time to save the human race, and I desperately need your help."

Ringgold held Kate's gaze, searching for something. Kate wasn't sure if she found what she was looking for.

2

Fitz slept fitfully that day. He woke at three in the afternoon to what sounded a lot like a gunshot. Sitting up in his bunk, he rubbed at his eyes, then scanned the mostly empty room. The muscular outlines of several marines and Rangers slept in bunks across the barracks. After so much violence the night before, the silence was eerie.

Chow sat on a bed a few feet away, chewing on a toothpick and cleaning his scoped M4.

"Did you hear a gunshot?" Fitz asked.

Chow stopped chewing and flicked the toothpick to the other side of his mouth. "When?"

"Never mind, must be hearing phantom noises again."

Chow went back to cleaning his gun, and Fitz took a trip to the bathroom. When he returned to his bunk, he changed into his uniform and grabbed his MK11. His orders were to man Tower 4 for the afternoon and evening. There were more battles to be fought today, but the firefight with Wood's men had taken another piece of Fitz. He was still in a mild state of shock. That was to be expected; after all, he had taken the lives of four men. Colonel Wood deserved what he got, but what about the other soldiers? It wasn't the death penalty for killing an officer that Fitz was worried about—it was the thought that maybe the other Medical Corps soldiers hadn't deserved to die.

"You good, bro?" Chow asked.

The irony wasn't lost on Fitz. Three days ago, he had asked Chow the same thing. They'd both lost brothers, and they'd killed to protect the lives of the innocent, men and women like Dr. Ellis and Dr. Lovato. Everyone in this new world needed forgiveness for something, but Fitz had a lot to ask for, from the lives he had taken in Iraq to the men he killed on the tarmac. In the end, his fate was in God's hands.

"Just a bit rattled from last night," Fitz finally said. He slung his rifle over his back and reached down to rub his thighs. "I'll be fine."

Chow stopped to pat Fitz on the shoulder, but then continued on without uttering another word. The simple touch reminded Fitz he wasn't alone. Across the room the doors opened, and Beckham entered with Horn. Fitz finished rubbing out the knot in his upper right leg, then stood to greet his brothers.

"Fitz," Beckham said. His voice woke several of the marines and Rangers. Their heads popped up like prairie dogs, all of them still on alert from the night before.

Beckham whispered something to the marines and waved at Fitz and Chow. They met on the landing outside the building, where Apollo sat waiting. His tail whipped back and forth when he saw Fitz.

"Haven't had a chance to thank you, yet again, for saving our asses," Beckham said as soon as the doors closed. "You're one hell of a shot, Fitz."

"You're a hero," Horn added.

Fitz shook his head. "I'm not a hero. I couldn't save Lieutenant Colonel Jensen."

Beckham's eyes darted down to Apollo. The German shepherd whined as if he could sense his handler's pain.

"Neither could I," Beckham said in a hushed voice.

A moment of silence embraced them, but Fitz pushed it away. He was starting to hate the quiet.

"I should get to my post," he said.

"Right," Beckham said, snapping from his trance. "Let's get moving."

"I'll meet you on the beach, boss. I need to stop by the medical ward and have Doctor Hill check my arm again," Horn said. "You should have him check out your shoulder."

Beckham shook his head. "Nah, I'm fine, man. Besides, you're the one that got shot."

"It's nothing. Doesn't even hurt. The bullet only clipped me. I'm good to go, boss."

Beckham eyed Horn's bicep skeptically. "Let's let the doc be the judge of that."

"He's just a physical therapist."

"Then have Kate look at it," Beckham said. "And let me know what she says."

Horn snorted and walked away.

Beckham watched him go, then motioned for Chow and Fitz to follow him to the beach. Apollo ran ahead, sniffing the dirt path. The short walk was a powerful reminder of how low the island was on human resources. Each tower was manned, but Fitz didn't see a single patrol.

"You're really going to let Wood's men fight with us?" Fitz asked. He still wasn't keen on the idea of arming the Medical Corps. He also didn't like questioning Beckham, but the absent troops gave Fitz a bad feeling. He felt exposed, naked. *If the Variants...*

"It's a double-edged sword," Beckham said. "Without them we're at risk of another Variant attack, and I'm not sure we could stop it. But with them we risk sabotage. For now they're staying locked up until I make a decision."

"Maybe Gallagher is right. Maybe whoever is in charge will send some pogues to arrest us," Chow said. "Or worse."

"I'm hoping they have bigger fish to fry, especially with the loss of Central Command," Beckham replied.

Chow pulled a tree branch back to let Fitz and Beckham past. "We should plan for the worst. Wood was in charge of Operation Extinction."

Beckham drew in a long, deep breath as they continued through the wooded terrain. He slowed his pace but didn't reply. The men emerged from the thick underbrush in silence. They stopped on a ridgeline overlooking the western beach. The surf swished beyond the electrical fences, and a breeze whistled through the canopy behind them. Fitz wasn't deceived by the calm. He'd seen it before—and each time it had been shattered by the monsters.

Chow stepped to the edge of the bluff. "I still say we take our chances without Wood's men. Maybe Major Smith can get us some fresh blood from another post."

"Wouldn't count on it," Beckham said, "unless Ringgold can pull some strings. We don't know if General Johnson is one of the good guys. Judging from experience, he's probably not."

"That's why we should hunker down and reevaluate our defenses. If Johnson sends his dirtbags to take the island, we need to be prepared," Chow said.

"If they come," Beckham said, gripping the stock of his rifle so hard his knuckles popped, "we stand down. I won't risk the safety of the civilians here in another firefight."

"But—" Chow began to say.

"That's an order, Chow. I pray it doesn't come to that, but if it does, our only hope lies with Ringgold. We saved her from Raven Rock, and she knows the truth about the VX-99 program now. Hopefully that's enough to show her we're the good guys."

"She's a politician, man. Most of them don't care who the good guys are. They only care about their interests being served—in this case, preserving her life. Johnson can protect her. We can't."

"She's different. I saw it in her eyes at Raven Rock."

Chow shook his head and looked out over the water. "They're all the same in my book, brother."

Fitz held his opinion for later. He was busy scoping the horizon. A glint of metal flickered in his sights.

"Not Ringgold. She's different, man, I know it," Beckham said.

Chow changed the subject. "I should have given you these a long time ago, but they were buried in my rucksack from Bragg."

In Fitz's peripheral vision, he saw Chow digging in his bag, but his attention was focused on the gleaming metal in his scope. It moved toward the island at top speed.

"I grabbed these patches a few days after the outbreak started," Chow said. "Found some for Team Ghost."

Fitz kept his eye on the scope. "Guys," he said.

Beckham was thanking Chow for the patches, the two of them paying Fitz little attention.

"*Guys*," Fitz repeated. "I think we got incoming."

Chow and Beckham instantly stepped closer to Fitz and shouldered their rifles.

"Talk about déjà fucking vu," Chow said.

Fitz's heart stampeded against his ribs as he centered his cross hairs on a red speedboat racing toward the island. It plowed through the water, waves cresting its bow. Two men decked out in camo stood at the helm, but they didn't look military. At least not anymore. Zooming in, Fitz saw two filthy faces and thick beards.

"Looks like a civilian boat," Beckham said. "Radio it in, Chow." He patted Apollo's head and knelt next to the German shepherd.

As the vessel got closer, it slowed, then coasted to a stop about two thousand feet out. The driver pulled out a pair of binos and centered them on the island.

"Got a bad feeling about this," Chow said. He plucked a radio off his vest and said, "Central, Ghost Two. Civilian craft with potential hostiles. Over."

Corporal Maggie Hook replied instantly. "Copy, Ghost Two. Tower Eleven and Tower Twelve have eyes. Stand by. Over."

Fitz glanced over his shoulder. Those towers were on the north side of the island. He turned to the others, but Chow was two steps ahead of him.

"Command, we are on the *south* side of the island. Repeat, south side," Chow said.

There was a pause and a flurry of static. It cleared, and Hook said, "Copy, Ghost Two. You have permission to engage if target displays hostile behavior."

"What do you think, Beckham?" Chow asked.

Fitz magnified his scope on the driver. A middle-aged man with a graying beard and a forehead smothered with grime stared back. Their gazes seemed to meet. Fitz was the first to look away. He watched the boat with naked eyes as it turned and sped off.

"Fuck," Chow said. "They were scoping us out."

"Was only a matter of time before someone found us," Beckham replied. He stood and kicked at the dirt. Apollo looked up, sensing his handler's frustration. "The Variants aren't the only ones migrating. Survivors must be too, looking for safe havens like Plum Island."

"I'd hardly call this place safe, but it sure as hell beats the cities," Chow said.

"I didn't think there were many survivors left," Fitz muttered. He remembered the USS *Truxtun* barreling toward the island. Everything became a threat in the apocalypse. He'd always loved being a marine because he always knew who the enemy was. But now, at the end of the world, there were enemies on all sides. It wasn't just the Variants. It was men like those in the boat and fellow soldiers like those he'd killed the night before.

Beckham whistled at Apollo. The dog was sniffing a bush a few feet away. He came running back to the operator and sat down.

Looking back over the water, Beckham said, "I hope to God Secretary Ringgold has some allies left in the world, because we sure as hell could use some right now."

An emergency alarm reverberated through the beehive that was the command center of Cheyenne Mountain Complex. President Mitchell stood frozen just inside the entrance. All around him, staff worked at their stations, undeterred by the electronic discord. If the mountain had a central nervous system, it was this room.

Over the blaring alarm, he could hear someone shouting at him, but he couldn't make out the words. He was too focused on the wall-mounted screens. He took a step closer and squinted at the visuals. The displays monitored air defense over the United States and Canada. But these screens weren't tracking missiles or satellites in space; they were tracking a pack of Variants prowling Pike National Forest, right outside the bunker. At least they *had* been tracking them. The monsters had vanished into thin air.

Six miniature displays showed the green-hued view from a squad of marines wearing NVGs with built-in cameras. The images on each monitor bounced up and down as the men hauled ass back to base.

"How could they just disappear like that?" Vice President Black asked. "It makes no sense."

Of the forty-plus command staff, no one had an

answer. Most of them looked to be as much in shock as Mitchell. The Variants had finally found Cheyenne Mountain. Mitchell had feared this day would come from the moment he set foot in the aging facility.

"Is it possible they're tunneling underground?" he asked.

Black started to shake his head, but stopped short. "That would actually make sense. Someone get me a sitrep."

Officers, civilians, and enlisted soldiers who were staring at the monitors went back to work. Fingers pecked at keyboards, and chatter broke out all around Mitchell. Over the panicked voices came that of the only man Mitchell trusted.

"Mr. President, Mr. Vice President, we need to move both of you," Chief of Staff Olson said.

Mitchell's eyes flitted to the briefcase in Olson's right hand. For a second, things didn't seem to make sense. It was a product of shock—the same feeling Mitchell had had every damn day since the outbreak started.

How can this be happening?

The case Olson carried had a lot of nicknames: the atomic football, the black box, the president's emergency satchel, or simply the button. In Mitchell's mind, none of them effectively represented the package. Inside were the codes to launch America's nuclear arsenal. If ordered, the attack would obliterate both Variants and humans alike. The launch codes Mitchell had memorized surfaced in his mind.

Not yet. That's a last resort.

Over the alarms and shouts came the pounding of heavy boots. A detail of armed marines filed into the room. They weren't Secret Service—they were better. These men had fought and killed Variants. Marine Lieutenant Stanton hurried over with his rifle lowered at the ground. His features were smashed together in a snarl.

"Mr. President—"

"Cut the formalities. What the hell is going on?" Mitchell snapped. He took a step toward the marine so he could hear his response over the alarms.

Stanton pointed at the screen. "I ordered all of our patrols to pull back, but Bravo squad is still stuck in the field. The Variants have vanished. We're not sure where the hell they went. But one thing is certain. They seem to know we're here, sir."

Mitchell narrowed his eyes. "How is that possible, Lieutenant?"

"My guess is they've been watching our patrols," Black replied.

"We need to evacuate," Olson said. "Get POTUS and VPOTUS out of here."

"I wouldn't recommend that," Stanton said. "Not right now, at least. We're safer inside. Every entrance is sealed."

"Do I need to remind you the Variants found their way into Offutt, Langley, and countless other 'secure' facilities?" Black asked.

"No, sir, but with all due respect, Marine One and the squadron of Sea Kings and White Hawks are on the heliport a half mile from the front entrance. I'm the head of security here—"

"And I'm a goddamn lieutenant general, acting secretary of defense, and the vice president," Black grumbled.

Stanton held his gaze. "I'm sorry, sir, but if we move now, we risk . . ." His voice trailed off as an NCO shouted from the front of the room.

"Sir, thermal scans from our drones are picking up heat signatures in multiple locations."

"Show me," Stanton said.

The NCO, a short man with glasses, gestured at a female officer sitting in front of a sixty-inch display. She typed a command into her computer, and a map of the area emerged on-screen.

"Bravo squad is here," she said.

"And what is that?" Stanton asked. He pointed at a cluster of red dots on the map.

"I'm not sure, sir, but Bravo squad is moving right toward them."

"Holy shit, did you see that?" someone shouted.

Mitchell followed Stanton across the room to stand behind a gathering cluster of staff members. The soldier on Feed 1 had stopped at the bottom of a ridgeline. He stood there for several moments, his helmet roving from left to right. At the top of the hill, the ferns at the base of a stand of ponderosa pines shifted in the wind. Limbs covered in needles reached toward the marine. The low branches suddenly moved the other way, exposing the trunks of the trees. All at once, a dozen slitted eyes flipped open where there should have been bark. Stalklike limbs extended from the trunks, and the withered bodies of Variants peeled away from the trees and scattered in all directions.

"What in God's name—" Black said.

"It's an ambush!" Stanton shouted. He pulled his vest-mounted radio. "Bravo One, get the *hell* out of there!"

Mitchell resisted the urge to grip his sour gut as he watched. The marine in Feed 1 staggered backward, tripping over something out of view. He pushed himself to his feet and took off running away from the beasts. Ahead of him, something meaty and muscular darted across the camera's view and vanished into the underbrush. In the distance, a pair of dark figures scrambled up the base of a tree. The other five members of the squad were bolting through a grove of pines. Low evergreen branches hit them as they moved, obstructing the video.

"We have movement on Feeds Three and Five," a staffer said.

Stanton brought his radio back to his lips. "Bravo One, do you copy?"

The only response was the hiss of static, but Mitchell was hardly paying attention. He watched the six monitors with a sense of awe that only live battle could produce.

"Bravo One, return to home plate. I repeat, return to home plate. Do *not* engage. Over." Stanton turned and shouted at a marine across the room. "Where are they?"

"West side of the mountain, sir!" the marine cried back.

"Damn it," Stanton muttered. He pushed his way closer to the monitors.

The squad was spreading out through the tall, thin trees. Their rifles searched the branches and rocky terrain for contacts as they moved.

A flash of movement suddenly broke across Feed 5. The marine turned to the right just as a Variant came barreling over a boulder. He fired a burst that sent the creature smashing into the rock. It slumped to the ground, blood smearing across the smooth surface of the boulder.

"Bravo One! Do *not* engage!" Stanton repeated into his radio, his voice rising.

Again, the only response was static.

The marine in Feed 5 backpedaled away from the dying creature. He turned to run but crashed into a Variant that had flanked him. The impact knocked them both to the ground. In a blink the creature was on him. It slashed at the marine's neck with both hands, eyes bulging with bloodlust. Blood peppered the cam, but through the blurred feed Mitchell saw that this Variant had developed some sort of scales or bark on its skin. Before he could get a good look, the monster brought an elbow down on the camera.

"Bravo One, *goddamnit*, get the hell out of there!" Stanton shouted. He clenched his jaw and turned to the NCO. "Patch this channel over the speakers."

Mitchell shifted his gaze to Feed 4. The marine was running through the woods, brushing into trees and swatting his way through low limbs. He shot a look over his shoulder, and his cam picked up a Variant bounding across the dirt. Mitchell could almost hear the panicked breathing of the young marine.

The creature's swollen lips opened, exposing a black oblivion with needle teeth dripping strands of saliva. It lunged and knocked the marine down in a cloud of dirt that momentarily blocked the view. When it cleared, the Variant had clamped down on the man's stomach. Scaly, oily skin filled the screen. The beast lurched back with ropy cords hanging from its wormy lips. The marine squirmed frantically as the Variant reached down and pulled more steaming intestines from his gut.

"My God," Mitchell whispered. He swallowed the taste of the shitty coffee he'd had for breakfast and forced himself to watch the monitors. He didn't know any of these marines by name. He'd seen them only in passing, but he knew each had a mother and a father. Some of them had families of their own. Or they *did* have families of their own...

None of these men deserved to die out there in the dark forest at the hands of men turned into monsters.

Feeds 2 and 3 went dark a moment later, leaving only 1 and 6. Those two marines were still on the move. They darted around trees, swatting at limbs and underbrush. Mitchell felt his heart climbing toward his throat as they navigated the slick slopes and terrain. Sweat dripped from his hairline, but he didn't bother wiping it away. Instead, he took in a breath and did his best to remain calm.

On-screen, the remaining marines closed in on a frontage road visible through the fence of trees.

"Where's that lead?" Stanton asked.

"Access Point Fourteen," the NCO under the monitor said. "It's one of the back doors to the facility."

"Shit, they're leading the Variants right to it!" Stanton shouted. He squinted at the individual feeds, watching helplessly. After a pause he said, "Hanson, Ralph—do either of you copy? Over."

A garbled voice surged out of the speakers mounted over the displays. Labored breathing followed. Then came a raspy voice: "Hanson—Hanson here. That you, Lieutenant?"

"Yes, son. I need you to listen very carefully."

"They're everywhere!" Hanson stopped and turned to fire at four Variants leaping through the trees. The rounds took one of them down, but the other three scattered.

Hanson's cam bobbled as he continued to fire blindly into the forest. Long pine needles rained to the ground and bark exploded in all directions. Sap oozed from the bleeding trees.

"Hanson, move your ass!" Stanton shouted into his comm. The words came a beat too late. Hanson pivoted to the right and shouldered his rifle to fire at a pack of flanking Variants, but this time the muzzle didn't flash. The creatures tackled him to the ground.

Mitchell turned his attention to Feed 6, knowing Hanson was gone. The other marine, Ralph, was through the clearing and running down the frontage road. His camera was focused on a hill in the distance. As he got closer, the feed showed a pair of rusted doors built into the embankment.

A high-pitched, animalistic screech suddenly roared from the speakers. The tortured scream echoed through the room with a blare of static. At first, Mitchell thought it was coming from Ralph's comm, but when he looked back at Camera 1, he saw that a trio of the creatures had wrestled Hanson to the ground. The marine was still fighting. He had pulled his handgun and was firing over and over. A Variant skull exploded, covering the cam with brain matter. Beyond the red goo there was a flurry of motion—a talon, thick chest muscles, and a yellow reptilian eye. Hanson managed three more shots before the gun was knocked away. As the brain chunks slid away from the camera, the two remaining creatures slashed at Hanson's flesh. A second later, the video feed disappeared completely in a mist of blood and gore.

"No!" Hanson shouted. "Mama! Please, Ma—"

Mitchell cupped his hands over his ears as the monsters tore Hanson limb from limb. But no matter how hard he pushed, Mitchell could still hear the marine crying out for his mother. This time he made himself look away. His gaze darted to Feed 6—the final marine.

Ralph was almost to the door. He shot a glance over his shoulder. The camera showed a pack of Variants racing down the road. Powerful limbs pounded the dirt, stirring up a trail of exhaust.

"Ralph! Do not lead them back to the doors!" Stanton shouted. "That's an order!"

The marine either couldn't hear the lieutenant or was too frightened to answer. He arrived at the partially hidden entrance to the mountain a minute later and pounded the steel with both fists. A staffer activated the feed from a video camera over the door. It fed to the wall-mounted display to the right of the monitor connected to Ralph's helmet-mounted cam. Side by side, the screens showed Ralph's POV and the view from the camera above him.

Stanton turned to his marines positioned behind the command staff and shouted, "Sergeant, take every available man and get your ass to Access Point Fourteen!"

Mitchell alternated his gaze from monitor to monitor. Ralph was staring up at the camera, waving and screaming. His face looked far too young to know the horror of the Variants. He turned, and the display to the left captured the creatures just as they plowed into him. The camera feed went topsy-turvy, but Ralph quickly fought his way back to his feet.

"Jesus Christ," Stanton said in a voice barely audible over the chaos.

The knot in Mitchell's gut tightened as the monsters clamped their sucker lips onto Ralph's arms, legs, and back. They wrestled him to the ground. He squirmed and screamed, but it was no use. Four more creatures joined, clawing and biting their way to the feeding. Ralph reached up toward the camera with a bloody hand missing two fingers. Then he disappeared under the tidal wave of diseased, barklike flesh.

"Will those doors hold them?" someone asked.

"We need to get the POTUS and VPOTUS out of here now," another said.

Mitchell felt a hand tugging his shoulder, but he couldn't pull his eyes from the pack of Variants. There was something else different about them—something off compared to the others he'd seen in photos.

One of the monsters glanced up at the camera with its grotesque, slitted eyes, as if it could sense it was being watched. It staggered over, chewing on a chunk of Ralph's face. The naked creature's oily skin stretched as it moved, lean muscles flexing. The mounted video camera provided the perfect snapshot of humanity's ever-evolving enemy. In the span of a minute, the monster's skin slowly reverted back to the pale, veiny flesh Mitchell had seen before. The beast strode to the doors, feeding as it walked. When it got there, it cupped the piece of Ralph's flesh and leaned in to sniff the rusted metal. Then it placed an ear to the door.

"Sir! We need to move, *now*!" someone shouted.

Mitchell wanted to run, but he stood there frozen, staring with grim fascination as the Variant turned from the door and discarded the steak of human flesh. It crouched on the ground, pointed at the other Variants, and howled. If Mitchell didn't know any better, he would think it had issued a command to the pack.

A blink of an eye later, the other creatures abandoned Ralph's mutilated carcass and began ramming the back door to Cheyenne Mountain.

3

Beckham knelt next to the cross marking Lieutenant Colonel Jensen's grave. The ceremony had been short, and the men and women who came to honor Jensen had already dispersed. Beckham stayed to pay his final, silent respects. He bowed his head, said a prayer, and let his friend go—not because he wanted to, but because he had to. There was a war to fight, and Jensen wouldn't want anything to distract the survivors from victory. He had loved his country and loved being a soldier. Carrying on the fight was the best way Beckham could think of to honor his memory.

"I won't let you down, sir," Beckham whispered. "RIP, brother."

Standing, Beckham took a moment to scan the other white crosses jutting out of the soil. Although Jinx's grave wasn't marked, he knew exactly where it was.

A hand clapped Beckham on the shoulder. He turned to see Chow with Apollo. Lost in his thoughts, Beckham hadn't heard them approach.

"You ready, boss?" Chow asked.

Beckham nodded and reached down to pat Apollo on the head.

For the next hour, the two Delta operators patrolled

the shoreline in the fleeting moonlight. Apollo followed close behind, his fur glistening from a dip in the ocean. Regardless of the second bath, he still had a streak of blood on his beard from the night before that wouldn't go away.

Dense shadows rolled across the dark skyline. With every step Beckham took, a sinking feeling rose in his gut. He stopped on a ridgeline overlooking the water. The boat they had seen earlier was nowhere in sight, and for the first time in days the bay was void of any derelict ships. They had all either run aground or drifted farther out to sea. Crickets chirped from the bushes ahead, but beyond the sounds of nature, it was unnervingly quiet.

Beckham scanned the guard posts to the west. Tower 4 protruded from a bluff overlooking the beach. He could vaguely make out the muzzle of Fitz's MK11. With the marine covering his back, Beckham felt better about their lack of firepower.

Chow's radio crackled a moment later. "Ghost Two, Command. Over."

Beckham recognized Corporal Hook's sharp voice.

"Ghost Two," Chow said.

"Report back to Command ASAP."

Beckham scoped the bay one last time before he followed Chow back to the base. They made a pit stop at Tower 4.

"Fitz, you up there, brother?" Beckham said.

The marine looked out the window and waved. "Sure am. Got a long night ahead of me."

"You need anything?" Beckham asked.

"No, I'm good. Thanks, though."

Beckham looked down at Apollo. "How do you feel about keeping our friend here company?"

The dog's tail began to wag until it was thumping.

"I'm leaving Apollo here with you. Stay frosty, Fitz,"

Beckham said. "As you know, someone's been casing the island."

Fitz raised his MK11 into the air. "Oorah."

Beckham smiled at that and patted Apollo on the head. "Stay, boy. Look after Fitz."

Apollo tilted his head. The dog knew close to one hundred verbal commands and hand gestures. *Stay* wasn't one he seemed to like, even if it was to protect Fitz. Beckham could feel Apollo watching him as he continued with Chow through the underbrush. The dog was as loyal as any soldier and fought just as fiercely.

Back at the base, Major Smith and Horn waited on the landing of Building 5. The major looked anxious, but Beckham guessed it had to do with the lieutenant colonel's funeral.

"Secretary Ringgold would like to speak to you three. She's waiting inside," Smith said.

Beckham eyed Horn's bicep. A strawberry-sized stain had blossomed across the fresh white bandage wrapped around his muscular arm.

"Did she say what about, sir?" Chow asked.

Smith shook his head. "Nope, but Doctor Lovato and Doctor Ellis spoke with her this morning. She was asking about the VX-99 program. I'm guessing she's trying to get to the bottom of things."

Beckham scrutinized Smith more closely as he approached the stairs. Swollen bags rimmed the major's eyes. They weren't from lack of sleep either—they were from shedding tears. Beckham wasn't the only one on the island who'd been close with Lieutenant Colonel Jensen. His death had hit Smith hard. It had hit *everyone* hard, and they hadn't even had the time to mourn him. Hell, they hadn't had time to mourn anyone. Beckham was just glad they'd been able to lay Jensen to rest. He deserved more than they'd given him, but for now it was all they could do.

Smith led them down the hallway to the command center. He stopped outside and glanced through the window cresting the door. Secretary Ringgold sat at the war table, sifting through a pile of files in front of her.

An image of choppers descending on the island to arrest Team Ghost rose in Beckham's mind. He reached for the door handle, anxious to give her their side of the story.

"Be polite, Big Horn," Beckham said.

"Don't worry, boss. The blood loss won't affect my judgment, I promise."

Beckham hesitated. "I thought you said you were fine."

Horn grinned. "I am, man. Doc said I'm good to go."

Twisting the door handle, Beckham nodded. He strolled into the room and stopped a few feet inside to place his hands by his sides and straighten his spine, just the way he'd learned when he was a grunt.

"Madam Secretary," he said.

"Ah, Master Sergeant Beckham." She looked at the men in turn and said, "No reason to be formal. Come sit down with me."

"Ma'am," Beckham said, and reluctantly stepped forward to take a seat. Horn and Chow followed.

Smith remained at the door, his arms crossed.

Ringgold closed the file folder in front of her, pulled off her glasses, and set them neatly on the table. "I'm sorry about Lieutenant Colonel Jensen. I'm told he was a good man."

"One of the best," Beckham said. She had clearly done her homework, and he liked that about her. It meant she was objective and resourceful. She was looking for both sides of the story.

"You're probably wondering why I've asked you here," Ringgold continued. She raised a brow and glanced at Beckham. "Then again, you already know, don't you, Master Sergeant?"

Beckham had an idea and wanted to get right to it, but he thought he should play by the rules. He could see Horn and Chow getting impatient too, so he let Ringgold keep the floor and threw a cautionary eye at his men.

"I'd like to hear about Building Eight and your experiences with Colonel Gibson, Colonel Wood, and General Kennor," Ringgold said. "I've been in contact with President Mitchell's staff at Cheyenne Mountain. They know about the altercation that occurred here. I'm assuming General Johnson does too. Before I reach out to him, I'd like to hear the details from you."

Beckham's heart kicked harder than it would during a firefight with Variants. The future of everything he cared about depended on the next words that came from his mouth. Ringgold wasn't a crooked politician, as Chow had suggested, but despite the fact Beckham had saved her from Raven Rock, he could see in her eyes she didn't trust him.

Not yet.

Over the next fifteen minutes, Beckham walked Ringgold through the key events of the past five weeks, starting with Building 8 and concluding with the shot that ended Colonel Wood's life. Ringgold didn't so much as shift in her chair during the first half of the story. This was a woman who had been grilled on Capitol Hill—a woman accustomed to hearing the very worst of what the government had to offer. By the end, however, her dark cheeks were flushed and a bead of sweat dripped from her brow. She put her glasses back on, pushed them higher on her nose, and folded her hands on the table.

"Doctor Lovato told me much the same," Ringgold said, "although your story is a bit more detailed and graphic." She let out a sigh and looked to Horn and Chow, then back at Beckham.

"I'm in a very peculiar situation here. On the one hand,

I could reach out to President Mitchell personally and request his help. Vice President Black is acting secretary of defense and he could have some pull in the military, but with General Johnson at the helm, I'm not sure who we can trust. Johnson was Kennor's confidant long before the hemorrhage virus ever got out of Building Eight."

Beckham wanted to interject, but patiently waited for her to finish. In his peripheral vision, he saw Corporal Hook hurry away from the radio equipment to Smith. They spoke in hushed voices.

After a long pause, Ringgold locked eyes with Beckham and said, "I've lost everything—my family, my staff, every friend I ever knew. But what I do still have is my abilities to communicate and to read people. I've built a career on those two things."

Smith raised his voice, but Beckham held his gaze on Ringgold. He remembered the treaty she'd helped negotiate between Palestine and Israel a year before, when she'd first been elected secretary of state. No one had believed she could get it done, but she did, and it helped bring peace to a sliver of land in the Middle East that hadn't seen it for centuries.

"I saw something in you back at Raven Rock, Master Sergeant. Something that's rare in men. I'm going to trust my gut on this one and believe your story. But before I contact President Mitchell and lay our cards on the table, I need to know something."

Beckham waited, his heart thumping so hard it felt like it was going to break through his ribs and plop onto the table.

"I need to know if you can protect me here," Ringgold said.

Beckham considered looking over at Chow and Horn. Instead, he nodded confidently. "I will do everything in my power to ensure your safety, Madam Secretary."

"Good enough."

Before Beckham could reply, Smith interrupted.

"About that call to President Mitchell," he said.

Secretary Ringgold twisted in her chair. "Yes, Major?"

"Corporal Hook just got word from Cheyenne Mountain. They're evacuating. The Variants have found the complex."

Kate spent the majority of the day with Ellis in the lab that housed the bioreactors. Her only break had been Lieutenant Colonel Jensen's funeral. Since then, she'd struggled to focus on work. She tried to shake away the thoughts of his death, but every time she attempted to concentrate, she saw Wood shooting Jensen in the chest. Then the shock would come crashing back over her.

Kate walked through the labs to the north end of Building 1. The bioreactors were kept in a room sealed off from the other labs. When Kate had first seen the twelve one-thousand-liter reactors, she hadn't been sure what to think. It hadn't taken her long to figure out why they were there. Colonel Gibson hadn't bought the expensive equipment just in case; he'd procured them to create a cure for the hemorrhage virus that Dr. Medford had created—a cure that was never developed.

Shaking her head, Kate went to Bioreactor 1. She peered through the small window of the cylinder and then turned to the monitor. The machines didn't do anything but keep the cells in them alive and extract the media the cells lived in. The real machines were the hybridoma cells that produced the antibodies, and they were already churning them out at a remarkable rate. She couldn't see them growing, but the readouts from the computer showed something amazing.

"Is this right?" Kate asked.

Ellis typed several commands into the computer connected to Bioreactor 12. He turned in her direction wearing a glowing smile behind his visor. "Our modifications to the hybridoma cells seem to be working. The genes we added are successfully producing enzymes that increase antibody production by over three times the normal rate."

She hadn't expected the process to work so well. In fact, she was surprised to hear the antibody production had been expedited at this level. The cultures normally took about eight weeks to finish, but the cells inside these bioreactors had been genetically engineered using an experimental technique developed to speed up the production of antibodies. It would cut the time of production down significantly. They might meet their two-week timetable after all. Heck, at this rate, they could even beat it.

Kate put her gloved hands back on the reactor, leaning in for another look. The faster the antibodies propagated themselves, the more human lives they could save. She almost didn't even recognize the feeling rising inside her—hope. If the other three labs were yielding the same results, then maybe they could all push the time line up.

"This is good," Kate said. "Actually, this is excellent. Now we just need help connecting with other labs to expedite antibody production outside the country. Tomorrow morning, I'll see if Secretary Ringgold has made any progress."

Ellis nodded and followed her to the exit. They locked the room and walked through the empty labs until they got back to their quarters.

"Do you mind filing the report and documenting what we did today?" Ellis asked. "I have something to finish up."

"Sure thing." She looked at the clock. It was already

past eleven, and Beckham was probably back from his patrol. She hadn't gotten to say much to him after Jensen's burial, and she wanted to make sure he was okay.

Kate hurried through the report and double-checked her work before she finally shut off her computer. "All done; I'm heading home for the night."

Ellis kept his visor pressed against a microscope. "Sounds good."

She took a step toward the lab's exit, hesitated, and said, "Aren't you going to wrap things up here?"

"In a bit, but I'm going to study these blood samples a little longer."

"What are you looking for, exactly?"

Ellis pulled his visor away from the scope and swiveled his chair to face her. "Nothing specific. Just studying the samples we recovered from Colonel Wood's cache."

Kate thought of Beckham again. He was probably waiting for her in their room. She still hadn't told him about her pregnancy, and part of her wanted to rush out of the lab. But Ellis was keeping something from her, and she needed to know what.

"Doesn't sound like you," Kate said. "You always know what you're looking for."

"I'm worried, Kate." There was trepidation in Ellis's normally cheery voice, and his smile was gone.

"Worried about what? I thought you would be pleased about the results."

"I am, it's just…"

"What?"

"I'm worried that Kryptonite isn't going to work on the scale we think it will."

"What makes you think that?" Kate worked her way back to his station and pulled a stool over next to him. She had reservations too, but there wasn't much they could do about that until the rockets were launched. For now, all they could do was continue forward with the production of the antibodies.

Ellis gave her a sidelong glance. "Besides the fact we haven't run months of trials and tests?"

Kate felt her features shift into a frown. "Yes, besides that."

Ellis was silent for a moment. He stared down at his desk, then back at his scope. "I'm sorry, Kate."

"Sorry for what?"

Ellis gestured for her to come closer. "For not telling you about this earlier."

Kate paused, mentally preparing herself for the worst. She pressed her visor against the scope and blinked.

"This is a tissue sample from a Variant in the Florida Keys. A marine unit extracted it after their team came under attack about four days ago. Wood brought it with him yesterday."

"And you didn't tell me?"

"I haven't had time," Ellis said defensively. "I'm sorry."

"It's okay," Kate replied. "Now tell me everything."

"These Variants were different."

"Different how?"

Ellis raised a hand. "Before you yell at me, just know I wanted to study them so I could give you better info—"

"Ellis!"

He lowered his hand and let out a deep sigh. "These Variants had gills."

"Gills?"

"And that's not all. The marines claim the Variants set a trap. The Variants in Key West left an injured woman in a street for the marines to find."

"Setting a trap requires a level of intelligence far beyond that of any of the Variants we've studied, Ellis. The report has to be wrong."

"I don't think so. I read it over thoroughly, and everything it described indicates the Variants planted that woman there like a piece of bait to lure a fish."

Kate shook her head. "I don't—" She stopped herself short of saying she didn't believe the report. There was documentation from military units across the country regarding Variants that seemed to display higher levels of intelligence. Some even seemed to lead battles or hunting parties. But planting a trap?

"There's more," Ellis said. He leaned over to his computer and keyed in his password. When the monitor activated, he moused over to a file. "This was taken five days ago at a navy installation in Antarctica."

A video of a dark room appeared on the screen. Banks of lights flipped on, and the inside of a morgue came into focus. The camera panned from gurney to gurney, each with a white sheet draped over a corpse.

Ellis punched a key and fast-forwarded through the beginning. He stopped when the cameraman approached one of the bodies. A second soldier, wearing a parka and a white breathing mask, came into view and stepped up to the table. He slowly pulled back the white sheet to expose the slitted eyes of a dead Variant. But instead of a bald skull and veiny, pale cheeks, the creature had a head crested with fluffy white hair and a beard surrounding its bulging lips.

The soldier pulled the sheet down to the naked creature's waist. Its chest and torso were covered with a layer of the smooth white fur.

"What the hell?" Kate whispered.

Ellis fast-forwarded further. Each of the bodies was the same, all of them covered in shiny fur.

"Pretty remarkable evolution, isn't it?" Ellis said.

"That's not evolution. That's some kind of twisted metamorphosis. First the gills, now the fur. The Variants are adapting to their environments."

"I haven't even shown you the craziest part yet," Ellis said. "Check this out. This came in from a Special Forces team in Syria." He clicked Play on another video. A view of a desert came on the screen. Rolling sand dunes stretched across the horizon. The image bobbed for several seconds as the soldiers recording it drove a brown SUV up and down the mounds. The vehicle came to a stop on top of a dune overlooking a valley of rock formations. The driver jumped out onto the sand and angled his helmet-mounted cam into the canyon. To his right, a man dressed in tan clothes and a brown scarf raised a sniper rifle and pointed it downward.

"Does this have audio?" Kate asked.

Ellis raised the volume. Gusting wind and background noise made it difficult to hear much of the conversation between the two men. He fiddled with the controls until a voice finally crackled from the computer's speakers.

"There they are," the man with the rifle said.

"Holy shit," the cameraman replied. He centered the cam on the clusters of orange rocks below.

"I can't see any—" Kate began to say when the soldier recording the scene zoomed in on dozens of what looked like orange crabs clambering over the rocks.

The sniper fired into the valley, and the monsters scattered in all directions. They moved like other Variants, on jointed appendages, but their anatomy was slightly different, with fiery orange, scaly skin and humps on their backs. A round from the soldier's sniper rifle hit one of those humps. It exploded like a balloon, blood and fat bursting into the air.

"Astonishing, isn't it?" Ellis asked. He shut off the feed and swiveled his chair to face her.

Kate took a few moments to analyze what she had seen. The Variants were adapting all around the world in amazing ways, but unlike Ellis, she didn't feel anything remotely close to excitement. These new developments terrified her.

She folded her arms across her chest. "The gills, the fur, and the other changes we're seeing are just the beginning. There's no telling how the Variants are adapting in other climates. We have to get other labs on board before it's too late." She let out a breath of frustration that fogged the inside of her visor.

Ellis leaned back to his station and punched at the keyboard.

"God, there's more?" Kate asked.

"Yes. The physical changes are metamorphosis, and the behavioral changes are adaptation, but I'm about to show you something that's clearly evolution."

Kate steeled herself. The clock on the wall ticked toward midnight. Her thoughts drifted as she waited for Ellis to load another video. The day had gone by so quickly that she hadn't thought about what would happen when she got off work. She knew she had to talk to Beckham, but every time she tried, there was another distraction. Plus, they had just laid Jensen to rest. Now wasn't an ideal time to spring the news on him. Or at least that's what she kept telling herself. Maybe she was just too scared to tell him the truth. Maybe she didn't want to believe it herself. Even if they managed to survive for nine months, what kind of world would she be bringing a child into?

"Here we go," Ellis said. He clicked the Play button, and another video popped onto the screen, this one of a dimly lit tunnel.

"This is from a marine recon team that was inserted in Chicago," Ellis added. "According to the file, it was taken not far from Northwestern Memorial Hospital. As you remember, that was the epicenter of the hemorrhage virus outbreak."

Kate's stomach flipped as she thought of her brother, Javier. He hadn't been all that far from the hospital when he was infected.

"Give it a second," Ellis said. "Can't fast-forward this one."

The video rattled as the marine's helmet-mounted camera jolted up and down with his jogging steps for several minutes. The graffiti-covered walls of the underground tunnel blurred by. At the end of the passage, the marine crouched and raised his rifle. He then gestured toward a chamber with arching walls and a vaulted ceiling. In the center of the space, on the concrete floor, a sea of flesh shifted back and forth like dead grass blowing in the wind.

"What is that…" Kate began to say. The NVG camera focused, and Kate saw something that confirmed her worst fear: The Variants slithered over the ground in a solid wall of pallid, glistening flesh. Tucked back in a corner of the room, a female Variant with a swollen belly rested with its back to the damp concrete wall. The creature looked six months pregnant, but how was that possible?

The fence of flesh suddenly parted, and in the gap of bodies a colossal male Variant lumbered into view dragging a female, claw wrapped around bony arm. The marine followed them with his cam to a shadowy corner of the chamber. At first Kate watched with fascination, but as the Variants began mating, she had to look away.

"They're breeding, Kate," Ellis said. "The next step in the Variants' evolution is finally here."

4

Marine Staff Sergeant Jose Garcia looked out over Turner Field, trying to picture a stadium full of screaming Braves fans. The signs and scoreboards were all dark, and every seat was empty. Gone were the smells of peanuts and freshly cut grass, replaced by the perpetual reek of rot and trash that had claimed the city.

Four days had passed since Garcia had lost two of his men to the Variants in Key West. It was hardly enough time to heal from the mental and physical injuries, but more than enough time to scrutinize every mistake he'd made.

Morgan, Daniels, and some poor woman whose name he didn't even know were dead because he had broken the cardinal rule of Force Recon: Never, *ever* get compromised.

If Garcia had searched the water for Variants, they would all still be alive. On this mission, he wasn't going to make any mistakes. Marine Force Recon always got the job done right. He couldn't be perfect, but if anyone else fell, it wouldn't be because he fucked up.

Garcia crawled a few inches closer to the edge of the scoreboard. The fresh ink on the underside of his forearm burned. The tattoo gun he kept in his gear aboard the USS *George Washington* was old, but it worked. He had tattooed Morgan and Daniels's names on his arm earlier that morning. The cross that enclosed them was almost full now. There was only room for one more fallen brother.

Overhead, the ethereal glow of a full moon filled the sky. It illuminated the stadium, casting shadows behind the seats and into the dugouts. Garcia hadn't seen moonlight this intense since the last time he'd been on his acreage in North Carolina. The last time he saw his wife and daughter...

Closing his eyes, he said the Lord's Prayer. The words filled him with the strength to clear his head and focus on the objective. He opened his eyes, and in his peripheral vision, Steve-o moved just a hair. Neither of them made a sound; even their breathing was stifled.

Garcia wiggled another inch and brought the scope of his suppressed M4 to his eye. Thomas and Tank were across the stadium, somewhere in the top bleachers behind home plate. He couldn't see them, but he knew Tank would be chomping at the bit to move. He could never sit still too long, and weighing close to three hundred pounds didn't help. Thomas, on the other hand, could fall asleep in the middle of a gunfight if he had to. The man was an expert at meditation.

Zooming in, Garcia looked for them. There was still no sign of their position, but that was good. It meant no one else could see them either.

It was 2350 hours, and the Variant Hunters were finally in position. Garcia's body was already numb from lying on the roof for so long. A Black Hawk had dropped them off a few blocks away at dusk, and they had worked their way into the stadium without being spotted. The city was soundless, as if he was in a padded room, but experience told him that was about to change.

The Variants were most active around midnight, when they emerged from their lairs and hunted for prey.

Tonight, the monsters weren't the only ones hunting in Atlanta. Garcia's objective was to document enemy movements and any behavioral changes. Rumor had it the freaks were breeding. Garcia didn't like the idea of being the cameraman for a Variant porno, but orders were orders.

He clicked on the camera mounted to his helmet. For fifteen minutes, he remained in the same prone position. When he couldn't stand it anymore, he wiggled his boot and balled his hands in and out to keep the blood flowing. Steve-o, however, didn't seem to move at all. He remained completely still a few feet to Garcia's left, his SAW angled at the field. Garcia could see the man's features in profile. The other marines teased Steve-o for his big ears, lack of facial hair, and perpetual grin. They were all rough men with scars and bad skin from bad habits. Steve-o had the type of honest face that made them all jealous. But he blew at poker; the man couldn't tell a lie.

Garcia almost smiled. Instead, he ran his tongue over his teeth and swallowed the bitter taste of coffee and canned fruit. He moved his shoulder a fraction of an inch and pressed his eye back against the scope to check a flicker of movement coming from the third row of bleachers behind home plate. In the first gate opening to the concourse, a contorted figure emerged. It stood in the moonlight and scanned the stadium before clambering over the first two rows of seats. The beast perched on the final row, tilting its head toward the sky and sniffing the night air.

After a few minutes, the Variant leaped onto the field and dropped to all fours. Garcia could hear its joints popping from his position. It moved, with its back hunched, to the pitcher's mound, where it stopped and sat on its hind legs like a dog. Sniffing at the air again, the creature slowly turned and focused on the top row of bleachers behind home plate.

A lump formed in Garcia's throat when he followed its gaze to the approximate location of Tank and Thomas. He centered his cross hairs on the monster, waiting to see if it had made their position. If it had, he wouldn't hesitate to blow its diseased face off.

Moving slowly, Garcia twisted the scope and zoomed in. This Variant was unusually large. Instead of the usual lean form, this beast was built like a lineman, with wide shoulders laced with bulging muscle. Scars that looked like whip marks crisscrossed its body. There were fresh lacerations on its legs and arms. Crusted blood and scabs surrounded the gashes.

The monster abruptly stopped sniffing, but continued to stare in Tank and Thomas's direction. The Variants had an amazing sense of smell, but from this far?

Two beats passed—it felt like an eternity. Garcia flicked the M4's selector to single shot and moved his finger to the trigger. A shriek followed that echoed through the entire stadium. Garcia's heart hammered. Had they seen him?

All at once, Variants exploded out of the gateways onto every concourse in Turner Field. A discord of wails morphed into a horrifying, high-pitched chorus. Flickering movement filled the sky as thousands of black birds soared away from the trees surrounding the ballpark.

Over the otherworldly screeches, Garcia heard another noise—a human scream. Female or male, he wasn't sure. The Variants streamed from the concourses and emptied into the bleachers behind home plate. In the chaos, he saw that the monsters were dragging human prisoners down the stairs toward the field. There were smaller figures tucked into the mass of pale flesh, but Garcia didn't dare move his rifle again for a better look.

Steve-o fidgeted in Garcia's peripheral vision. The scene had the man spooked, and Garcia didn't blame him. The stadium had transformed into a nightmare, but this was what they were here for: to observe and document. The Variant Hunters were not to engage unless there was no choice.

Garcia gritted his teeth in an effort to block out the raucous screeches. He reconsidered reaching up to reposition his NVGs. He wanted to capture every second of this scene, but any fast movement could set the entire Variant army on them. This time, there was no way his squad would survive a mistake. They were trapped in their positions.

Sitting. Fucking. Ducks.

A cloud rolled overhead, the carpet of light shifting into shadows across the field. Garcia could hardly see anything now. He cursed himself for not keeping his NVGs in position. As he waited for the cloud cover to pass, hundreds of Variants stopped in the first two rows behind home plate. The clatter of plastic chairs and claws scratching over concrete joined the symphony of tortured screams.

At the pitcher's mound, the muscular beast that had entered first dropped to all fours. Every single creature went silent, like the speakers of a TV being shut off. Garcia watched the Alpha of this group of Variants with morbid fascination. These beasts were rare; he had seen only a few of them in the past five weeks.

Overhead, a single bird flapped away from the stadium, squawking as it tried to catch up with the thousands that had fled moments earlier. With the animalistic noises gone, Garcia narrowed in on the sounds of the screaming humans. There were two of them, both on the move. Several Variants dragged the prisoners down the aisles and onto the field. Smaller shadows moved behind them, their bodies seeming to distort awkwardly in the darkness.

When the edge of the cloud passed overhead, the moonlight spilled back over the field. Garcia held in a breath, his eyes feeding his mind something he couldn't seem to comprehend.

What in holy hell?

Below, in the wild grass between the Alpha and home plate, were six tiny Variants, all circling an unconscious female prisoner in rags and a male prisoner wearing blue jeans and a blood-soaked T-shirt that read GO YANKEES! There were four female Variants surrounding the group, all with sagging belly fat hanging like a macabre skirt made of flesh.

Garcia slowly reached up and clicked his NVGs back into position, then shifted his gun toward the prisoners. This is why the Variant Hunters were here. Garcia had to capture this for Command.

Garcia zoomed in on the man's face, covered in filth and blood that made it impossible to determine his age. The man crawled across the grass, screaming, "Please, somebody help me!" He sobbed and dug his fingernails into the soil.

Garcia resisted the urge to put a bullet in his head and end his suffering, knowing that what came next would be worse than torture. In his scope, the tiny Variants continued to skitter around the man. They were all young, maybe the size of human two-year-olds, but they were fast as hell. He had never seen any Variants this young before.

Two of the creatures collided clumsily. They fell to their backs, then jumped onto two feet, hissing. Long, snakelike tongues shot out of their sucker lips, and the small beasts clawed at one another.

The Alpha Variant shrieked and separated the two creatures before Garcia could get a good look. They scampered away, still hissing like oversized lizards. The female Variants crowded around, and the offspring arched their backs as the male human prisoner crawled toward first base. He turned every few feet, tears streaking down his face.

"Please don't do this! Don't kill me! I'm begging you!"

The Alpha ambled after the juveniles and roared at them. Then it pointed a thin talon at the man dragging his injured body across the grass. When the prisoner saw what was happening, he pushed himself to his feet and staggered toward the pitcher's mound.

A high-pitched shriek came from the Alpha's mouth. This time the young Variants took off on all fours, scampering after the man with their backs still arched. One of them crossed in front of Garcia's scope. As it moved, he saw there was something different about it—something he'd never seen. Its skull curved into a cone, and its ears were pointed like a cat's. He carefully lowered his helmet cam toward the scene, documenting every second as one of the small beasts lunged and clamped its sucker lips onto the prisoner's ankle.

"NO!" the man screamed. He dragged the beast attached to his leg into the outfield, where the other five finally caught up and brought him to the ground. They all latched down on him, tearing strands of flayed flesh away with their jagged teeth. One of the beasts, the smallest, was knocked away from the feeding. It hissed and slashed its way back to the man. Again, it was swatted away.

In the bleachers behind home plate, the other hundred Variants watched as if it was some sick fucking game. Garcia said a mental prayer, asking God to end the man's suffering. But it was not to be. The screams continued, the young Variants ripping through muscle and tendons.

As the moonlight spilled over them, Garcia finally got a good look at their misshapen bodies through his scope.

Jesus H. Christ.

Scaly plating covered their appendages and wrapped around their chests and backs like a vest. The armor continued up their necks and curved skulls, where it crested into a bony Mohawk. The smallest beast shot a glance in his direction, chewing on a hunk of meat it had managed to scavenge. Wide and oval, the child's eyes were different from the reptilian eyes he was accustomed to seeing. It threw back its cone-shaped head and swallowed the chunk of flesh whole.

They look like alien armadillos.

Garcia shifted his M4's muzzle back to the female Variants standing in front of home plate. He wasn't a doctor or a scientist, but even he could figure out they were the mothers of these Variant offspring. But how was that possible? The outbreak had started only five weeks ago, yet these creatures looked at least two years old. Garcia moved his scope back to the smallest of the beasts, the runt of the litter. It scampered back to the feeding, swiping and hissing at its larger siblings.

Steve-o tapped Garcia's arm.

"Sarge," he whispered. "I think we need to move."

Garcia swept his cross hairs back to the muscular Variant and saw what the corporal meant. The beast was no longer observing the feeding. It was watching them.

It was just before midnight, but Riley couldn't sleep. His legs and his back ached. He was so fucking sick of sitting in his damn chair. Lying in a bed didn't help—especially the beds in the barracks—but this was where he wanted to be, with his fellow soldiers.

"Chow—you awake, brother?" Riley asked, craning his neck.

The Asian American man lay in the bunk to his right, jet-black hair covering the left side of his face. If it weren't for Chow's instant response, Riley would have thought he was sleeping.

"Yeah, Kid. You hurtin' tonight?"

Riley gripped the sides of his bed and sat up. "Yeah, my back is killing me."

"You've been sitting in that chair for almost, what, a whole month?"

"Something like that," Riley said. "You can't sleep either?"

"Haven't slept much since Jinx died," Chow said. He brushed the hair from his face and sat up. "I need a smoke."

"Since when do you smoke?"

Chow didn't reply. He swung his legs over his bed and looked at Riley's wheelchair.

"I'll come," Riley said. "Help me up."

Chow hoisted him into the chair and pushed him through the aisle between bunks. They passed a few snoring marines on the way out, but the rest of the room was empty. Everyone else was on duty. It reminded Riley how much everything had changed.

A few good things had happened since the apocalypse. Riley focused on them as Chow maneuvered him through the room. Even though Riley felt isolated from Team Ghost, he was happy Beckham had finally found someone, and Horn reuniting with his daughters was a miracle worth celebrating. Then there was Meg, the superhero of a woman Beckham had rescued from New York. Riley found a smile on his face every time he thought of the firefighter.

Chow pushed the doors open to a brilliant moon. The

glow covered the entire island. Riley sat there, listening to the chirp of crickets and feeling the breeze on his face. For a moment it reminded him a of summer night in Iowa, but he knew the quiet wouldn't last. The silence never seemed to stick around. It was always shattered by the crack of gunfire or the high-pitched shriek of a monster. If science couldn't stop the Variants, then no one would be left to enjoy moments like these.

Riley reached down for the knife tucked in his belt and stared at his casts. He bit his bottom lip, clenched his jaw, and gripped the handle of the knife. The casts seemed to tighten around his legs. He felt more trapped than ever before. He needed to walk again. Needed to *run* again. If Kate failed and the Variants won, he wanted to go out on his own terms.

Chow glanced over. "What the hell are you doing, Kid?" He flicked his cigarette away and rushed to the chair.

Riley slipped the tip of the blade under the cast on his right leg. "I'm not going to sit here any longer." He was breathing harder now, his chest heaving.

"Kid, you can't remove those yet. You still have—"

"Three weeks," Riley quickly replied. "Plus rehab."

"That's not long, man. Three weeks is—"

Riley looked up and caught Chow's gaze. "The world may not last that long." He dug the tip of the blade inside of the cast and said, "You going to help me, brother, or what?"

The stink of wet dog hair hung in the air of Kate's small bedroom. Beckham sat on the bed, holding Lieutenant Colonel Jensen's Colt .45 in his hands. Apollo was camped out at his feet, sleeping peacefully with his muzzle resting on the cold floor. The sight made Beckham jealous. He was exhausted, but every time he closed his eyes, he saw Lieutenant Colonel Jensen choking on his own blood. Even if he could sleep, he wouldn't be able to for long. The base looked nearly deserted through the window, and without other soldiers to count on, Beckham couldn't afford to rest, especially not after the boat they'd seen earlier.

He thought of Wood's men, still locked up in Building 4. He simply didn't trust them, no matter how many times they claimed they would follow Major Smith's orders.

Beckham placed the revolver on the bedside table and looked at the clock. It was after midnight, and Kate still wasn't back from the lab. He was half tempted to grab his M4 and take Apollo out for a quick patrol, but he didn't want to miss her when she did return. They hadn't talked much since Jensen's death, and he needed to know she was okay.

Reaching down, Beckham ran a hand across Apollo's thick coat. After a few minutes of feeling the dog's fur against his palm, Beckham's racing heart began to calm. He unlaced his boots and sat on the floor next to Apollo. As much as he wanted to lie down in the bed, he couldn't bring himself to do it. Guilt ate at him—guilt that he was alive when so many others had died, men and women he couldn't save.

Apollo glanced up, then rested his muzzle on Beckham's lap. He patted the dog's head and looked back at the window. Time seemed to warp as Beckham sat there, staring into the glow of the full moon. He was lost in his thoughts when the door creaked open.

"Reed?" Kate whispered. "Are you sleeping?"

He shook his head. "No, I was waiting for you to come back from the lab. Wanted to make sure you were okay."

"That's sweet, but you shouldn't have. You need rest."

"So do you."

Kate placed a small backpack on the floor and walked over to the window. She pulled her hair tie away and let her brown hair fall over her shoulders. In the moonlight, he could see her shivering.

Pushing himself to his feet, he stood next to her. "Kate..."

She kept looking out the window, her gaze locked on the tree branches shifting in the breeze. Raising her hand to her mouth, she cupped it over her lips and sobbed.

"Kate," Beckham said again. He wrapped his arms around her and pulled her to his chest. "It's okay. Everything's okay."

"No," she said, pulling away. "It's *not* okay, Reed. The Variants are adapting around the world. They're evolving. They're...faster...and..."

Beckham gently turned her toward him and searched her eyes. He could tell she was hiding something that went beyond the evolution of the monsters. For several days he'd sensed it, but he hadn't wanted to pry it out of her. He wanted it to come naturally. She was supposed to trust him.

"I'm just a soldier, Kate, but haven't they been evolving all along?"

"Something's changed."

"What?"

Beckham imagined the creature's talons growing and their meaty bodies morphing into something even worse. After a deep breath and a pause, Kate whispered as if she wanted to keep her words a secret.

"They're breeding."

Beckham wasn't sure what to say at first. The thought had crossed his mind. It was disgusting, but so what? If her weapon worked, it wouldn't matter. The idea of killing kids made his heart ache, but he reminded himself these weren't human kids. He had gunned down very young Variants in Niantic and New York. He would do it again if he had to. It struck him, then, that maybe Kate did care. Maybe she couldn't bear the thought of being the one tasked with killing millions again, even if those millions were monsters.

"This new world we live in, it's not a place for kids. Variant or human," Beckham reminded her. "Don't let this affect your judgment or your work. You have to stay strong. We have to kill the Variants, young and old alike."

Kate nodded and sat on the bed. He slid down next to her and put his arm around her shoulder. A single tear streaked down her face in the moonlight. After a few minutes of silence, she turned toward him, as if she wanted to tell him something important, but all she said was, "You're right, Reed. It's no place for kids."

5

"Lieutenant, those things were communicating!" President Mitchell's lungs burned as if he'd swallowed a breath of frozen air. His early-morning runs on Capitol Hill seemed like ages ago, and it showed. He could hardly keep up with the well-trained marines leading him and his staff down the narrow corridor.

Lieutenant Stanton either hadn't heard Mitchell or was ignoring him. He waved the group, twenty strong, into a tunnel that emptied into a massive chamber deep inside Cheyenne Mountain. There were multiple buildings here, some of them three stories high, all of them built on springs that would allow them to shift if a nuke hit the mountain.

Each structure had its own purpose, from living quarters to a movie theater. The underground mini-city was buried under two thousand feet of rock and designed to protect approximately three hundred people for several months. More than one hundred thousand bolts had been drilled into the mountain to ensure structural strength and security. Eight diesel engines powered the facility, and air filtration systems protected them from chemical, biological, and radiological agents. The engineering was incredible, but the springs, bolts, and advanced filtering system couldn't protect them from the Variants if they got inside.

"Evacuating POTUS and VPOTUS through Portal A!" Stanton shouted into his radio. He glanced over his shoulder and jerked his chin for the others to follow.

Mitchell kept his eyes on the open blast door at the north end of the chamber. Part of him wondered if they were making the right decision. Especially after what he'd seen on those monitors.

Lieutenant Stanton assured him the creatures couldn't get past the twenty-five-ton blast doors. But they had managed to get into other secure locations. What would stop them now?

In his mind's eye, Mitchell saw his wife as the hemorrhage virus tore through her. It started as a trickle of blood dripping from her eyes and nose. Then her body contorted. The snapping of her joints sounded in his head. He winced, remembering his narrow escape from the PEOC. It was supposed to be as secure as Cheyenne Mountain.

I will not die at the hands of those monsters in this hell hole, he vowed.

Stanton balled his hand into a fist and stopped at the blast door. "Everyone, quiet." He brought his radio to his lips and whispered, "Charlie One, Cheyenne One. Is Access Point Fourteen secure? Over."

The squad of marines formed a perimeter around the president and his staff as they waited. Only a handful of Mitchell's original team remained now. Most had perished in the early days of the outbreak. Those still with him had hardened into shells of their former selves. They weren't the same men and women he remembered working with on Capitol Hill.

Over the alarms, a faint reply came from Stanton's radio.

"Cheyenne One, Charlie One. Access Point Fourteen is secure. I repeat, Access Point Fourteen is secure. The Variants have retreated."

"Are they sure?" Mitchell said. "Those things were camouflaged before. Maybe they're blending in with the terrain and waiting for us to come outside."

Stanton pulled a sleeve across his shiny forehead. His eyes flitted to the president as he brought his radio back to his lips. "Command, Cheyenne One. Can you confirm Charlie's last?"

With the alarms still ringing in the background, Mitchell had a hard time hearing the reply. But he caught most of it. "...Cheyenne One...drone...any heat signatures...vicinity."

"Copy that, Command. Cheyenne One proceeding to inner roadway with POTUS and VPOTUS." Stanton glanced back at the group. "We're all clear. Three squads of marines are waiting on the inner roadway to evacuate us to the tarmac in an armored convoy."

Mitchell wanted to say something presidential, something that made him seem strong, but the only thing that came out was, "Okay."

He followed Stanton through the open blast door into a narrow tunnel. Framed on both sides by the red glare of emergency lights, it was like a portal to hell. Here in the tunnel, the sirens screamed from wall-mounted public-address speakers as if they were warning the group to stay back. Overhead, ductwork and pipes snaked across the ceiling.

Mitchell pictured a camouflaged Variant squeezing through one of the gaps like a mouse and dropping to the ground. Could all of these soldiers really protect him from the evolution of these monsters?

More marines moved up ahead at the end of the passage, their boots pounding the concrete. They disappeared into another tunnel. Mitchell hesitated, squinting to see ahead. The alarms were like a dinner bell for the Variants. He still didn't trust Stanton when he said there was no way they could hear them through the millions of ton of rock.

God, Mitchell hated this place.

"Come on," Stanton said. The lieutenant led them through the final maze of passages for ten minutes at a pace Mitchell barely kept up with. Each breath was a struggle and carried the scent of cold moisture. They made their way through the splashes of red light. Olson worked his way to Mitchell's side with the atomic football clutched against his suit. A large backpack bobbed up and down on his shoulders.

"Hold," Stanton said. He balled his hand into a fist outside the tunnel intersecting with the inner roadway. The door was closed ahead, and two marines stood guard.

"Sir, the convoy is ready to move," one of the men said.

Stanton nodded and plucked the radio from his vest. "Command, Cheyenne One. Proceeding to inner roadway." He faced the group clustering in the passage and gave Mitchell a critical look, as if he was sizing him up.

The president had given up caring what others thought of him. He avoided Stanton's gaze and waited; the promise of fresh air made the glares of those around him tolerable. His chest was tightening, and he reached up to loosen his collar.

"Cheyenne One, Command. You have a green light to proceed to the tarmac. Good luck. Over."

Stanton's scowl twisted into what could have been a smile. He nodded at the two marines holding sentry duty, and one of them unlocked the door. Artificial light washed into the passage, and the hum of diesel engines sounded in the distance.

"Let's move," Stanton said.

Mitchell squinted and ran after the lieutenant. Five Humvees waited in the tunnel, the turret of each manned by marines. Some bore viscerally terrifying M240 machine guns. Others had what looked like mounted M260 rocket launchers.

Stanton opened the door to the third truck and motioned for Mitchell to get inside. The president did as ordered and slid into one of the seats. Olson got in on the other side and rested the case on the center console. Black continued to the second Humvee, while the rest of the staff piled into the vehicles behind them.

"Got a green light to move out!" Stanton shouted. He let out a low whistle, patted the top of the truck, climbed into the driver's seat, and said, "Buckle up, Mr. President. We're going to be moving pretty fast once we get outside."

Mitchell nodded and clicked his belt into place. The lead vehicle lurched forward, the tires squealing as the overzealous driver stomped the pedal. One by one, the other trucks followed, leaving the remaining survivors behind to defend Cheyenne Mountain.

Meg sat on the couch of her new room in Building 1, reading the April edition of *People* magazine. It was after midnight, and she was wide awake. She eyed the knife Riley had given her. The sheathed blade rested on the table within arm's reach. She still would have preferred her old fireman's axe, but the nimble knife would do for now. At some point, she was going to have Riley teach her to shoot. If she was going to have any hope of surviving, she had to learn how to fire a gun, no matter how much she hated them.

After flipping through the magazine a third time, Meg plopped it back onto the table and secured her long brown hair into a ponytail. Then she grabbed her knife and tucked the sheath into her belt. She had always been an independent woman, but she was lonely now. She missed her husband, her friends, and her fellow fire-fighters. If it weren't for her friendship with Riley, she would've gone stir-crazy already. He was a good man, and so were the other members of Team Ghost.

Time had become fluid since she arrived at Plum Island. She wasn't even sure how many days she'd been here, but her legs were healing, and her energy came back more each day. Dr. Hill said she might even be able to walk on her own again in a week or two.

She needed some fresh air. Using her crutches to stand, she hopped from the couch to the door. The hallway outside was quiet. Everyone else in the building seemed to be sleeping except her. She walked by Kate's room, then Horn's, and finally Riley's old room. He had given it to Red and his family after Beckham rescued them from Niantic. Meg heard a panicked voice as she passed the door. It was Bo, she realized, and she stopped to listen.

"Mama, I'm scared."

"It's okay, Bo. Go back to sleep. Nothing can get you here."

"Promise?"

"Yes, baby. We won't let anything happen to you."

Listening to the hushed conversation broke Meg's heart. Red, Donna, and their son had been through hell out there. They were protected by some of the best soldiers left in the world now, but the boy was still terrified.

Meg didn't blame him. Team Ghost may have restored her faith in a military that had all but failed the country, but no matter how impressive they were on the battlefield, they couldn't stop an army of Variants. If the wolves came, there was only so much Ghost could do.

The door to the building opened as she continued

down the hallway. Horn squeezed through and quietly shut it behind him. He whispered, "How you doing?" His breath reeked of cigarette smoke.

"Fine. How's your arm?"

He regarded his right bicep and shrugged limply. "Nothing to fuss over. I've been hit worse."

Meg smiled. "Your girls doing okay?"

Horn brought a finger to his lips and jerked his head toward the door to Meg's left. "They're sleeping."

Meg patted him on his good arm. "Good night, Big Horn."

"Night, Little Meg."

She smiled again and crutched through the door Horn had opened. On the landing outside Building 1, a lonely marine stood guard. Two others patrolled among the other facilities, and two more manned the machine gun behind sandbags in the center of the lawn. It was a far cry from what Meg had seen when she was first brought here. The door clicked shut behind her as she hopped into the cool night.

"Ma'am," the marine said.

"Evening," Meg replied, then corrected herself. "I mean, good morning."

He grinned and strolled to the other side of the landing to scope the tree line. Across the lawn, past the machine-gun nest, several figures stood outside the barracks, while another sat in a wheelchair. Tendrils of cigarette smoke trickled into the air.

Alex Riley, you little shit.

She had started hopping down the steps when the door opened behind her. A woman wearing a dress shirt and slacks stepped outside. She smiled at Meg, then closed her eyes and took in a deep breath. Exhaling, she said, "Never thought I would be so happy to breathe fresh air again."

The marine lowered his rifle and held up a gloved hand. "Secretary Ringgold, ma'am, I would encourage you to return to your quarters, where it's safe."

The woman regarded the marine with another smile. "I'm sure a few minutes to enjoy the peaceful night won't get me killed. You'll keep watch, right?"

"Yes, ma'am."

Meg paused at the stairs. It wasn't every day she had an opportunity to speak to the secretary of state. Riley's lecture could wait.

"I'm Meg Pratt," she said, cupping a crutch under her armpit and offering her hand. "Excuse me for asking, but have you been out there?"

Ringgold took her hand and shook it with a powerful grip. Her smile twisted as if she was in pain. "I was at Raven Rock Mountain Complex since the outbreak started in April. Seems like I was in that tomb for years."

She loosened her grip and regarded Meg's crutches. "How about you?"

"I was trapped in New York. Master Sergeant Beckham and his men pulled me from a tunnel."

"Beckham is quite the hero."

Meg nodded. "Every member of Team Ghost is."

Ringgold didn't respond, but her kind eyes told Meg she agreed.

"So, Beckham found you hiding in a tunnel?"

"Not by choice." Meg looked skyward to study the dazzling stars and Milky Way. The beauty was a respite from her memories.

"You don't need to tell me," Ringgold said.

Meg shook her head. "No, it's okay. I don't mind talking about it. I feel damn lucky to be alive. The Variants dragged me down there. That's where they nest. Where they feed."

The marine glanced over at Meg with an arched brow, then strolled to the other side of the landing.

"I'm sorry," Ringgold said. "I hope Doctor Lovato and her colleague know what they're doing. From what I understand, it sounds like we have less than a month to take back the world before it's too late."

"I hope they know too, but I believe in Doctor Lovato, just as I believe in Team Ghost."

Across the lawn, the cigarette smoke had ceased and one of the soldiers was leaning over next to Riley's chair. Meg squinted and crutched a pace forward. If she didn't know better, she would think the man was helping Riley remove one of his casts. But that couldn't be right—he still had weeks left in them. Plus, they were on the freaking barracks steps, not in the medical ward.

"Madam Secretary, if you'll excuse me," Meg said.

"Certainly."

Meg crutched over to the steps and carefully worked her way down each one. When she got to the grass she hopped as if there was a Variant chasing her. As she moved closer, she saw it was Chow next to the chair.

"Alex *T.* Riley," she said, in a voice just shy of a shout. "What do you think you're doing?"

Both Delta operators looked up in surprise. Riley grimaced.

"What are you doing out here, Meg?"

She stopped at the bottom of the stairs. Riley had cut into the cast covering his right leg. She took another step closer, nearly tripping from the shock. "What the hell am *I* doing out here? What the hell are *you* doing?"

Riley looked up at Chow for support.

"Don't look to him for an answer. You're a *grown man*. Tell me what the hell you're thinking, trying to remove your casts three weeks early. Do you realize how much permanent damage you could cause by taking them off before your bones have knit?"

Riley's blue eyes shifted back to Meg. There was sadness there—sadness and guilt. The same thing she saw when she looked in the mirror.

"I want to help my brothers. I want to fight again," Riley said.

"You're not going to be any good to anyone if you can't walk. Do you even know what happens if you take those off early?"

Chow still hadn't said a word. He backed away when Meg shot him a glare. Then she crutched her way up the stairs and stopped a foot in front of Riley, her gaze locked with his. She leaned down, using his chair to steady herself. With every inch she moved closer, his blue eyes brightened. And with every inch closer, she felt something she kept suppressing. No matter how hard she tried to convince herself, she couldn't keep burying her feelings for him.

But shame washed them away, and she stopped herself from kissing him on the lips. Instead, she pecked his cheek.

"I need you to be smart, Alex. If you promise to do that, then I promise to help you."

Riley slowly nodded, and his breath came out in a tiny puff.

She hovered over his chair, ignoring the burn of her legs and the fluttering in her stomach. "You have to promise something else too."

Riley kept nodding.

"Promise me you'll teach me how to shoot that." She lowered her gaze to the pistol tucked into his waistband.

"Okay," Riley replied. "I promise."

Meg pushed herself off the chair and put her weight on both of her feet. She tried to hide the pain but couldn't hold back the tears that streaked down her face.

"We're going to make it through this together," Meg said confidently. "We're going to survive."

6

A cool breeze drifted through the open windows of Tower 4. Fitz removed his helmet and ran a hand through his shaggy auburn hair. It hadn't been this long since he was in high school. He took a seat on the stool nestled against the wall and rested his aching back against the wooden support.

You can relax, just for a few minutes.

Fitz covered his mouth to suppress a deep yawn. He was exhausted, but he couldn't let the thought of sleep slip into his mind. It wouldn't take much to drift off.

"I need a pack of Red Bull and a deep-tissue massage," Fitz muttered. He rubbed at his eyes, then put his helmet back on. His entire body hurt. His neck and back were tight with tension, and the knot in his right thigh was getting worse. Using his thumb, he dug at the ball.

He glanced at his watch. Three more hours left in his shift. Then he could finally sleep. Fitz twisted to stare out over the water. A helicopter patrolled the bay, its searchlight dancing over the dark water.

The wind rustled through his uniform as he sat there. He closed his eyes and rubbed his lids again. It felt good— so good he convinced himself to keep them closed for a few minutes.

Just a few . . .

Sleep came before Fitz could fend it off—a sleep so deep he didn't even realize he was dreaming.

Sand. There was so much fucking sand. It glided toward the eastern edge of Fallujah in a solid wall of tan grit. Fitz was camped out in a prone position on the roof of a four-story building with his spotter, Private First Class Don Garland, lying to his left.

"Better clench your ass. We're about to get nailed," Garland whispered.

Fitz grinned and tightened his goggles. Then he moved the bipod on his MK11 so the muzzle was angled at a rooftop six structures away. He thought he'd seen a flicker of movement, but when he narrowed in with the cross hairs of his scope, it was just a flapping tarp.

The storm rolled into the city a few beats later, and sand blasted Fitz's fatigues. Garland wasn't kidding when he told him to tighten his ass. The sand got into everything: boots, ears, even ass cracks.

A quarter mile to the south, First and Second Platoons worked their way through the city, clearing buildings one by one. The men were almost to what Fitz called "Shitter's Corner." Most of Fallujah smelled like raw sewage, but it was worse there.

Fitz couldn't even see the street now. The storm had kicked up a cloud that filled the entire city. He pressed his eye against the scope of his MK11, cursing the blasted heat and the sting of grit on his sweaty skin.

Despite the sandstorm, today was calmer than normal. No marines had died, and it was already four in the afternoon. A PFC had been shot in the leg a few hours earlier, but he'd survive.

The roar of the storm grew, and Fitz braced himself, squeezing every muscle he could. Sand gusted over the roof, pecking at his uniform and rifle. He kept his eye pressed against the scope, scanning for targets. The tarp he had seen earlier tore off the roof and sailed away in the wind.

Fitz batted sweat away from his eye when he heard the cough of diesel engines. The mechanized unit had finally reached the street below. Above the growl of the storm and the hum of idle engines came the unmistakable crack of an AK-47. Fitz's senses snapped to full alert as his earpiece hissed to life with the voice of the platoon sergeant.

"Medic! We got sniper fire!"

"Anyone see the shooter?" This voice was cool and calm. Fitz knew right away it was the lieutenant.

"Negative, we can't see shit down here!"

Fitz focused on his breathing. He couldn't let his heart rate escalate. It would mess up any potential shot.

In and out. In and out. You got this, Fitz.

He searched the rooftops frantically as another crack sounded in the distance.

"You got anything, Garland?" Fitz whispered.

"I can't even see five feet in front of me."

A voice rang in Fitz's earpiece, and he winced at the report of another casualty. Two marines down.

The lieutenant's voice, weakened by static and the piercing whistle of the wind, came back online. "Anyone have a target?"

"Saw a shot come from the second floor of Al Shifa Hospital," said the platoon daddy.

"Light that fucking building up," the lieutenant replied.

"Roger."

Fitz trained his MK11 in the general direction of the hospital. Through the curtain of sand, he glimpsed the third floor and four oval windows below it.

Another crack sounded, and sure enough, the flash of a muzzle came from the fourth window on the second floor. "Medic!" shouted a voice in Fitz's earpiece. He held in a breath, zoomed in, adjusted for distance and wind, then waited for a clear shot.

"Somebody take out that fucking sniper!" the platoon sergeant growled.

"I don't see jack shit," Garland whispered.

Fitz ignored his spotter and the frantic chatter over the comms. He counted to ten in his head. It always helped calm him, but three marines were already dying or dead, and this time, the numbers did little to relieve the spike of adrenaline rushing through him.

Just one clear shot. Just one clear—

As if in answer, movement in the middle window filled his scope. Past the grit and sand, in a moment of clarity, he saw the insurgent sniper holding an AK-47. The scarf fell from the shooter's face, and instead of the bearded man he'd expected, Fitz saw the youthful face of an Iraqi woman. She could have been an innocent teenager.

The wind settled then, and the gusting sand with it, like divine intervention. "Forgive me, Lord," Fitz said. He squeezed the trigger. The bullet hit her in the forehead, blood exploding from the exit wound and painting the hospital room crimson as she tumbled backward. The wind picked up again and sand shifted to block out the view. He lost sight of the window a second later.

"Hostile down," Fitz said over the comms.

Garland brought his binos back to his eye. "Shit, man, you got him? I didn't even—"

"Her," Fitz replied, hoping the hiss of wind would hide the regret in his voice. He wasn't used to killing women, but she was the enemy. As much as he tried to tell himself that, he still couldn't quite come to terms with the fact he had just killed a woman. She had been someone's daughter, possibly a wife or a mother.

She would have killed you if she had the chance.

The storm blew out of Fallujah, and the mechanized unit lurched forward. Fitz drew in a breath that tasted like sand. Before he could exhale, a flurry of small-arms fire rang out down the street. The heavy crack of a Dragunov followed.

Fitz knew by the echo of the shot that the sniper was too far for him to hit. He did a quick scan of the rooftops just to make sure, then said, "We need to move. Get back to the street and work our way ahead of the platoon."

"We got another sniper," the platoon sergeant said over the comm.

There were other responses, something about an ambush and a potential suicide bomber. Each transmission made Fitz's heart rate spike.

He pushed himself to his knees and backed away from the ledge on all fours. Garland picked up his rifle and followed suit. They entered the dusty building the way they had come out and loped down the stairway. When they hit the street, Fitz ran from vehicle to vehicle, stopping when he got to the command Humvee. The platoon sergeant crouched behind the bumper.

"Fitz, what the hell are you doing? You're supposed to be in position," the man snarled. The bulky marine spat a chunk of chewing tobacco on the street.

"I couldn't see shit up there. Garland and I need to get ahead of the platoon."

A second crack sounded, and the comms flared with the report of another marine down.

Small-arms fire broke out again over the cough of the diesel engines. The platoon sergeant dragged a sleeve across his face and stared for a moment as if he didn't know what to do.

"Sergeant, we got to move," Fitz insisted. "I have to get back out there and cover the marines in the street."

The platoon sergeant said something into his headset.

He scrambled to the side of the bumper and motioned at two marines hiding in the entrance of a building. "Walters, Duffy—I want you to escort Fitz and Garland to a new position."

Walters and Duffy were both privates. Fitz hardly knew them, but Duffy had a reputation for shooting anything and everything that moved. Fitz didn't like that. The marine was a liability, but he didn't have time to protest. They darted across the street in combat intervals, taking an alleyway that opened into a ghetto. Fitz called this place "the Orphan Zone."

The shelled-out buildings here were far from abandoned. Clothes and towels hung from balconies. Fitz glimpsed several kids looking through the iron bars. They melted back into their homes when they saw the marines.

"Eyes up," Fitz said.

They ran into a second alleyway that curved between the structures until they came to another street. Fitz stopped at the sidewalk to search for contacts. The pop of insurgent gunfire echoed through the city.

Another transmission crackled over the comms; another brother had been lost. Heart pounding, Fitz resisted the urge to run out into the middle of the road. He had to do something, and he needed to do it soon. Halfway down the street stood a five-story hotel. It was the tallest structure in the area and would have a view of the street where the armored convoy was pinned down.

"There," Fitz said when the other marines caught up. "Cover me."

Garland mumbled a protest that Fitz ignored. He took off across the street as if he was running in a sprint relay, nearly stumbling from the momentum. He made it across without a single shot being fired. The insurgents were too busy tearing the rest of the platoon apart.

Across the road, Fitz slammed his back against a wall

and motioned for the others to follow. Garland came first, then Walters and Duffy. They crouched in the entrance to the hotel.

"I'll take point," Duffy said.

"No," Fitz replied forcefully. "Garland has point. You take rear guard. Walters, stay close to me. Let's move."

Fitz waited for Garland to proceed. He slung his rifle over his shoulder and drew his Beretta M9. Then he put a hand on the back of Garland's armor and followed him into the empty lobby. Bullet casings, trash, and splattered fruit littered the floor. Dusty tables and chairs decorated the small space. They cleared the room with a quick sweep and advanced to a narrow set of stairs.

The suffocating heat grew worse as they made their way to the second level. Garland and Walters took turns checking rooms while Fitz and Duffy held security in the hall. By the time they cleared the second and third floors, another marine had been shot outside and the lieutenant wasn't any closer to identifying where the shots were coming from. A battle was raging in the streets, and Fitz hadn't yet made it to the top of the decaying hotel.

"Duffy, Walters, clear the fourth floor. Garland, you're with me," Fitz said. He knew it wasn't the best idea to split up, especially if there were insurgents hiding out in the building, but there was little choice.

At the fifth floor, sunlight streamed through a partially boarded-up window on the right wall of the hallway. Fitz flashed an advance signal. Garland slowly walked across the creaky floor. There were two doors on each side, and Garland stopped at the first one on the left.

Fitz took up position on the other side and nodded at Garland. The freckled marine nodded back, grabbed the doorknob, twisted it, and swung the door open.

A draft of rot assaulted Fitz's nostrils. He choked back bile as he swept his pistol left to right, confirming nobody was hiding in the corners. Besides a soiled mattress lying on its side, the room was empty. The door across the hall led to an identical scene. When they reached the second door on the left, Fitz had them hold up. He thought he heard coughing. They waited several seconds before the sound came again.

Fitz pointed at the door, then to Garland, and they followed the same process as before. Sweat crept down Fitz's face, and he wiped it away the moment before Garland grabbed the knob and flung it open. Fitz tightened his grip on his side arm and followed his spotter inside.

"On the ground!" Garland shouted.

Fitz arced his weapon over the room, shifting from the face of a boy about five years old to a girl no older than eight, and finally to a man who might have been their grandfather. His hands were up, and he was screaming something in Arabic that Fitz didn't understand. The man took two steps forward, reaching out toward Garland. His face was hidden in the shadows of the scarf he wore.

"*Ogaf bmkanek la tetharek!*" Fitz shouted. He had no idea if they were the right Arabic words, but they were supposed to mean *Stop where you are.*

"*Ogaf bmkanek la tetharek!*" Fitz repeated.

The children ran to the man, hiding behind him and peering out from the folds of his brown robe.

"On the ground!" Garland shouted. He kept motioning for the family to get down, but they simply stared at him. The elderly man finally lowered his voice and dropped his hands to his sides. He raised them again when footfalls echoed from the hallway.

"It's okay," Fitz said. He turned and shouted, "All clear here," hoping that Walters and Duffy heard him before entering the room. The two marines stopped in the entrance, weapons lowered toward the floor.

"Pat this guy down, Walters. Duffy, you hold security here. Garland, let's set up shop across the hall."

Fitz eyed the elderly man one last time. His brown eyes were visible now. There was no anger there, only fear. The kids knelt by his side, both of them shaking and sobbing.

"Don't do anything stupid," Fitz said to Duffy on the way out.

The crack of heavy gunfire continued outside, reverberating through the guts of the building. Fitz hurried over to the final room with Garland. Opening a door in hostile territory was always nerve-racking—the moments beforehand came in slow motion—but this time it was different. Fitz didn't fear what was on the other side; he feared every second that he wasted. More marines were dying as they waited.

"Execute," Fitz said.

Garland put a boot into the wood, and the door swung open with a crack. Sunlight poured into the hallway as Fitz swept the room and moved inside, taking up position on the right. A pair of wooden chairs lined the wall, and a filthy rug was partially rolled up in the center of the room. The bathroom smelled of cigarettes, and the toilet was covered in blood.

"Clear," Fitz said. He pulled his scarf back over his nose and hurried to the window.

Below, two Humvees were pinned down in the middle of a street. The Bradleys were stuck behind them, their 25-millimeter chain guns roving for targets. Marines fired from prone positions at a pair of buildings at the north end of the street. Automatic gunfire rained down on the platoon from all directions.

"Holy fuck," Garland whispered.

Fitz holstered his side arm and got his rifle ready while Garland called in to the platoon sergeant. "Golf Four-One, Golf Four-Four. We are in position."

"Golf Four-Four, get that damn sniper," came the reply. "He's already hit three marines." The comm went dead, and Fitz cursed. He checked that he had a round chambered and ground his back teeth. Reaching up, he pulled the curtain halfway across the open window. Then he shouldered his rifle and stood in the shadows for cover.

"Find me this asshole, Garland," Fitz whispered.

The spotter hurried over to the other window facing the street. He rested his rifle against the wall and centered his binos on the battle. There was no curtain to pull across, and Garland kept to the side.

The Bradleys opened up a moment later. Rounds lanced into the buildings at the north end of the street. Pockmarks the size of pumpkins spread across the walls. An insurgent fell from a window on the fourth floor, splattering on the pavement below. The crack was louder than the gunfire as his bones shattered on the asphalt.

Fitz raked his muzzle back and forth, searching the rooftops and windows of adjacent buildings for any sign of the second sniper. Truth was, it would likely take another shot   and another dead marine—before Fitz spotted him.

Or her.

The flash came a moment later from a building three down, but this time there was no transmission stating another marine had died. There was no transmission at all, only a muffled screech from the window beside him.

Fitz lowered his rifle and glanced to his right just as Garland crashed to the rolled-up carpet. The right side of his face fell off, a ruptured eyeball sliding across the ground like the yoke of an egg.

"No!" Fitz screamed. He pivoted away from the window. Garland's body was twitching, but the muscle spasms were involuntary. There was a grumbling sound, and his body drained of fluids, the stench of death filling the room.

"Medic!" Fitz yelled. He raised his rifle, knowing

Garland was gone. He was just a kid, a fucking kid with as many pimples as he had freckles. Fitz stood completely still in the shadows and zoomed in on the six-story building two streets over. He centered his cross hairs on the window the shot had come from, his trigger finger itching for revenge. He held in a breath that smelled like shit. Before he could pull the trigger, a torrent of flashes fired in his direction. The rounds bit into the frame of his window, piercing the curtain and grazing the side of his helmet.

Walters rushed into the room and dropped to the deck as another volley of shots peppered the exterior of their building.

"Stay down!" Fitz yelled.

Fitz crawled back to the wall. He glanced over at Garland's ruined body. It lay twisted on the floor at an odd angle, like a pretzel. Walters looked away and met Fitz's gaze.

"Listen carefully, Walters. I want you to stay low and fire out the other window. I'll take the sniper out."

"You're crazy, man!"

"More marines are going to die unless we stop that bastard."

Walters looked over at Garland's corpse again. "They blew his fucking face off."

"Snap out of it, Private! You're a goddamn marine!" Fitz shouted.

Trembling, Walters managed a nod, then crawled over to the wall.

Fitz looked back to the hallway. The old man was sitting on the floor across the way, the boy and girl curled up against him. Duffy had his rifle angled down at them.

"What the hell's going on?" Duffy shouted when he saw Fitz looking.

"Stay put!" Fitz yelled back.

Goddamnit. Stay frosty, Fitz. Stay. Fucking. Frosty.

Duffy's rifle was shaking in his hands. With Garland dead, the platoon under fire, and a sniper on the loose, Fitz wasn't sure what the marine would do. He turned back to Walters, who was clutching his rifle against his chest as if it was a baby blanket.

"On three," Fitz said.

Walters swallowed. Another flurry of shots plastered the wall a beat later, sending both men back to their stomachs. Fitz pushed himself back up and said, "One... Two... Three!"

There was screaming now from the other room, but Fitz didn't have time to see what the hell had happened. He was only going to get one shot at this. It was by luck, and luck alone, that the sniper hadn't killed him the first time.

As soon as Walters opened fire, Fitz held in a breath, stood, squared his shoulders, and aimed at the window two streets away. He pulled the trigger once, then twice, and finally a third time. The 7.62-millimeter shells discharged from his gun in slow motion, and he watched the sniper's body slump out the window and plummet to the ground.

Fitz pivoted away from the window and sat with his back to the wall. Chest heaving, he looked across the hallway. The old man was lying on the ground across the floor, blood pooling around his body. But he wasn't the only one. Both kids and Duffy were on the floor too.

"Fuck!" Fitz shouted. "Walters, on me!" Ears ringing, he pushed at the ground, but his equilibrium was off, and he stumbled. He braced himself when he got to the doorway and staggered across the hall into the other room.

Duffy was gasping for air and writhing on the ground. Blood gushed from his right arm and left leg, but he didn't appear to have sustained any mortal wounds.

"Help Duffy," Fitz said as Walters burst into the room. Fitz rushed over to the old man. He stared at the ceiling, his eyes vacant. The boy was gone too; a bullet had hit him square in the chest. Fitz reached for the girl. She was still alive, somehow, although Fitz wasn't sure for how long. Blood blossomed around two holes in her shirt. He put his hands over the wounds and applied pressure. She let out a low gasp, her lips opening and closing like a fish struggling for air.

"It's okay," Fitz whispered, wishing he knew how to say it in Arabic. Shit, why hadn't he paid more attention to the translator? He flicked his headset radio to open with a finger covered in blood. "Golf Four-One, Golf Four-Four. Sniper is down. I have one man down, another dead, and a civilian who needs immediate medical support."

"How bad is your man?" asked the lieutenant's voice.

"He'll live," Fitz said.

"Good. We can't spare any medics right now. I'll send a squad your way when I can. Send us your coordinates and hunker down. Over."

Fitz glared at Duffy, his blood boiling. "What the *hell* happened?"

Duffy was breathing steadily now. He sat up with one hand clutched over his leg while Walters wrapped his arm.

"I shot them," Duffy whimpered. "I didn't mean to."

Fitz's hands were slimy and warm with blood. He looked back down at the girl. Her brown eyes were wide and panicky, her lips still trembling as she struggled to speak.

"I got hit, and I—" Duffy said. He lowered his head, grimacing in pain.

"What?" Fitz said. "You what?"

"I shot them," Duffy said. "I shot all of them. I didn't know who shot me, man."

The girl's eyes rolled up into her head and she died, Fitz's hands still pushing down on her small belly. His earpiece crackled again, and a new voice hissed into his ear.

"Tower Four, Command. Please report. Over."

Fitz jerked awake. He opened his eyes to a view of Plum Island, not Fallujah. Instead of feeling relief at waking from the nightmare, he felt a stab of panic. It wasn't just a dream. It was a memory, one he always woke from at the last minute. Right before he beat Duffy's face to a pulp.

"Shit," Fitz muttered. He rose to his feet and raised his MK11 to scan the beach. It was the first time he had ever fallen asleep on duty. Anger from the dream and at himself for falling asleep raced through him. He just wanted to be a good marine.

The best marine.

"You idiot, Fitz, you fucking idiot," he mumbled. Flicking his comm to his lips, he said, "Command, Tower Four. All clear out here. Over."

In the distance, past the domed buildings and the water, arms of smoke reached into the sky over New York. Somewhere out there, the Variants were hunting and killing human survivors—the young, the old, it didn't matter.

He shook the nightmare of Fallujah away. He would rather be back there, in all that fucking sand, than fighting monsters in this new world.

7

President Mitchell sat in the back seat of the Humvee, staring at the back of Lieutenant Stanton's helmet. Command had sealed the blast doors a few seconds before the convoy was supposed to leave the mountain. A drone had discovered unusual heat-signature readings outside. After several hours trapped in the dimly lit tunnel, Mitchell was starting to get claustrophobic.

"Got an update, Lieutenant?" he asked.

Stanton looked up in the rearview mirror. "We're just taking extra precautions, sir. Air assets are finishing a second sweep of the area for heat signatures. We should be clear in a few minutes."

Mitchell twisted to Olson. "Any news on Central Command?"

"Not yet, sir. I just put the request in a few hours ago."

"You got your satellite phone?"

"Yes, sir."

"Find out the status and tell them we're on our way to the *GW* strike group."

Olson reached into his backpack and pulled out a long black phone. He punched in a number and cradled the phone between his shoulder and ear.

"Lieutenant Colonel Kramer, this is President Mitchell's chief of staff, Brian Olson."

"Got a green light, sir," Stanton said. He looked to the marine in the passenger seat. "Reno, keep your eyes peeled once we get outside."

"Yes, sir," Reno said.

Mitchell rested his head on the back of the seat as the convoy rolled down the roadway toward the final blast door. It was already opening, and the first natural light Mitchell had seen in weeks flooded into the tunnel. The glow from the moon was mesmerizing and terrifying. Fear stabbed at his gut, his bowels complaining and his heart rate amplifying as the Humvees sped through the opening. Beams from the trucks cut through the night, penetrating the thin fog crawling across the road. Barbed-wire fences lined both sides, but the industrial light poles above them were off. Stanton had kept the entrance to the mountain as discreet as possible.

"Yes, sir," Olson said, still on his phone. "We're on our way. What's the status of Central Command?"

The convoy passed the first guard station and raced onto the main road. Mitchell twisted in his seat for one last view of Cheyenne Mountain Complex. The blast door was almost closed.

Mitchell did what he always did when nervous: He thought of the hundreds of quotes he'd memorized during his decades in politics. This time the words of John F. Kennedy came to mind: *We have the power to make this the best generation of mankind in the history of the world—or to make it the last.*

The president looked out the Humvee's rear window just as the blast door to Cheyenne Mountain sealed shut. Those twenty-five tons were supposed to hold back the blast from a nuclear warhead. Americans had prepared for the apocalypse since the creation of the United

States, but in the end, even places like Cheyenne Mountain couldn't save them. The best generation of mankind was most certainly behind them now, and he feared this *would* be the last. His own stamp on history would be short—and quickly forgotten.

The screech of tires pulled Mitchell from his thoughts. Headlights from the convoy illuminated the ponderosa pines lining the rocky hills. A low and dense fog drifted through the forest on both sides of the road.

"Excellent," Olson said into his phone. "We're about to board Marine One and will see you in a few hours."

Mitchell pulled his gaze from the window, anxious for a report.

"Good news, sir. That was Lieutenant Colonel Kramer. Our request to move Central Command to the *GW* strike group was approved. They are currently sailing north from the Keys."

A rush of what felt like relief flooded Mitchell's chest. Olson leaned forward and patted the back of Stanton's seat.

"Lieutenant, what are you hearing over the radio?" Olson asked.

"Road's clear so far, sir, and Command reports no sign of Variants."

Olson gazed out the side window. "I hope they're right."

Mitchell inched closer to his window. Moonlight streamed through the roof of the forest. Shadows danced in the fog, sending a prickle of fear through the president.

The radio barked to life in the front of the Humvee. "Cheyenne One, Command. Over."

Reno plucked the radio off the dash. "Command, Cheyenne One. Go ahead."

"Cheyenne One, be advised, we have detected several faint heat signatures north of your position. Stand by."

Stand by? What the hell do they mean, "stand by"?

Mitchell shifted in his seat for a better look out the

windshield. Fog bled over the road, surrounding the Humvee with a carpet of gray mist. His heart rate spiked so high he felt light-headed. He leaned closer to the window, frantically searching the landscape.

Stanton eased off the gas. "Goddamnit," he muttered. "Better be some deer. You see anything, Reno?"

"Nothing, sir." Reno glanced over at Stanton, then looked up into the turret. "Got anything up there, Cunningham?"

"Negative, sir," came the reply.

"Command, Cheyenne One. We don't see any hostiles. Do you have coordinates?" Reno placed the radio back on the dash and shouldered his rifle.

The radio hissed. "Cheyenne One, we are now picking up faint heat signatures south of your position."

"Faint? What does that mean?" Olson asked.

"Means it could be nothing," Stanton said.

"Or it could be Variants," Olson replied. "How do they not know?"

Stanton twisted the steering wheel and said, "The fog could be masking heat signatures. That's why we did several sweeps with the drone earlier. If the Variants were still out here, the drone should have seen them."

"That doesn't exactly inspire confidence," Olson said.

"Keep sharp," Stanton told Reno. The marine nodded back.

The road curved again, providing Mitchell a view of the valley. At the bottom of the hill were several long buildings. And there, in the middle of the heliport, he saw the shapes of the choppers that made up Marine One. They were almost there.

Olson leaned back and caught the president's gaze. Mitchell saw his chief of staff, one of the former Lions of Capitol Hill, had a look of regret in his squinted eyes. But for once, Mitchell didn't share his confidant's sentiments.

"Perhaps—" Olson said. "Perhaps we should turn back."

"No!" Mitchell didn't care that his voice cracked, or if Olson didn't agree. They had to keep moving. He had to get away from this place. This *tomb*.

Stanton shook his head. "Too late to turn back now. We're closer to the heliport than the blast doors anyway. We have to keep moving." He pushed down on the gas.

The road curved again, and Mitchell lost sight of their salvation. The brake lights of the first Humvees suddenly flared red ahead. Both of the trucks screeched as the drivers slammed the brakes.

"Hold on!" Stanton shouted.

"Cheyenne One, Command. Variants in the vicinity. Repeat, heat signatures are confirmed to be—"

Mitchell's world cascaded into chaos, his heart skipping and every muscle tensing. The crunch of metal sounded, drowning out the radio operator's voice. Mitchell braced himself with a hand against the front seat.

The lead Humvee had smashed into a fallen tree draped across the road. Vice President Black's Humvee had swerved to the side of the road to avoid the wreckage. Tendrils of smoke rose from the first truck. The marine in the turret was slumped over his machine gun, surrounded by swirling smoke and fog.

"Are you okay, sir?" Olson asked.

Mitchell gasped for air, his hand on his chest. The radio crackled before he could reply. "Cheyenne One, Command. Variants closing in from your north and south—"

"There!" Olson yelled, pointing to the left side of the road.

Hand still on his chest, Mitchell followed Olson's fingers to the trees. Pale limbs and bald skulls shifted in and out of the mist. All at once, a trio of Variants exploded from the wall of fog and landed on the lead vehicle. Four more leaped off the ridgeline and skittered across the road. Another pack galloped from the trees to the right. They swarmed over Vice President Black's truck before any of the marines fired a single shot.

"Shoot them!" Mitchell screamed.

"We can't risk hitting the VP!" Stanton protested.

"He's already dead!" Mitchell yelled back. "Get us the hell out of here!"

Stanton put the truck into reverse and glanced up at the mirror. Mitchell saw something in the marine's gaze that made him feel even more terrified: desperation.

"We're boxed in!" Stanton shouted.

Mitchell spun to the back window. Humvee 5 had retreated, but the fourth truck was stalled. The gunner was gone, and a pack of Variants had already overwhelmed the truck. On the ridgeline to the right, a thick ponderosa leaned over the side of the road. The pine needles shook violently as it lowered, the branches bobbing up and down with dozens of Variants. At the bottom of the tree, a Goliath of a naked monster with ropy, thick muscles pushed at the base, ripping the roots from the ground. Three other beasts joined in, but the leader dwarfed them in size and strength. Fog swirled around the creatures like a ghoulish curtain.

"Move this fucking truck!" Mitchell shouted when he finally realized what was happening.

"Now, Lieutenant!" Olson added.

"Working on it!" Stanton yelled back. He put the truck in reverse and raced toward Humvee 4. "Cunningham, clear us a path! Don't let that thing bring the tree down!"

Mitchell flinched as the marine opened fire from the turret. The bark of the heavy machine gun reverberated inside of the truck, and the president cupped his hands over his ears. Rounds kicked up dirt toward the leaning tree. A dozen Variants climbed the branches while the beasts at the base continued pushing. Cunningham centered his fire on the shaking branches, sending the monsters spinning away into the night.

"Stop the one at the bottom!" Stanton yelled.

The green tracer rounds flew lower, and the gun's .50-cal. projectiles lanced into the ground, kicking up a geyser of dirt and pine needles. A round clipped the colossal Variant pushing the trunk, taking off its right arm in a blast of red. It glared at Mitchell's Humvee, and a sucker mouth the size of a dinner plate opened to release a guttural roar.

Determined, the monster slammed its left shoulder into the tree. Cunningham raked the gun to the right, taking out the other three creatures with precise bursts. Chunks of gore bloomed out of the mist, but the injured beast kept pushing, relentless.

"Take it out, goddamnit!" Stanton shouted again.

The heavy machine gun finally turned the monster into confetti, rounds punching through flesh and slamming into bark. Cunningham roved the gun away, but he inadvertently hit the exposed roots, finishing what the Variants had started. They snapped, and the ponderosa crashed onto Humvee 4.

"Go right, go right!" Olson shouted.

Stanton slammed the brakes, put the truck back in drive, punched the gas, and maneuvered the vehicle onto the shoulder of the road. Rocks crunched under the tires as the truck jerked up and down.

The beams hit a Variant pulling a kicking man from Humvee 2. It wasn't hard to spot the vice president's shiny, bald head in the bright lights.

"They got the VP!" Reno yelled.

"Cunningham, fire on Humvees One and Two," Stanton said, making an effort to try and remain calm.

But Mitchell knew the truth: The lieutenant wasn't in control. They had never been in control.

The turret swiveled overhead and the gun coughed back to life. Rounds spat down the road, splitting through metal and shattering glass. The monsters abandoned the vice president's vehicle and scampered up the ridgelines on both sides of the truck, providing Stanton a window for escape. He gunned the truck past Humvee 2, smashing into a soldier crawling across the road. Mitchell's gaze flitted to the man as he skidded over the pavement. When he came to a stop, he moved an arm, then a hand. It happened so fast that Mitchell hardly had time to recognize the man as Black. The vice president reached up at Mitchell's Humvee as Stanton sped past.

Mitchell opened his mouth, but all that came out was a groan. He had been the only one to see Black still alive. They couldn't go back for him—they had to keep moving. They couldn't do anything for him. At least that's what Mitchell kept telling himself.

So this is what it feels like to lead in the apocalypse, he thought.

"Through there!" Olson yelled. He pointed to the right of the fallen tree Humvee 1 had crashed into. There was a narrow gap between the roots of the tree and the hill it had tumbled from.

A Variant yanked a civilian from the twisted metal of the wreckage of Humvee 1 by his arms, both of which were broken at the elbow, bones protruding from flesh. He let out a scream that Mitchell could hear over the bark of the machine gun.

Stanton steered the Humvee onto the right shoulder. The driver's side clipped the roots of the fallen ponderosa, and the passenger's side scraped the ridgeline to the right. In a screech of metal, their Humvee shot through the gap.

Stanton pulled back onto the road just as a Variant lunged from the hill. It landed on the roof with a thud. Cunningham let out a muffled scream. His boots rose up into the turret as the beast pulled on him. Olson grabbed one of the marine's boots and shouted, "Help me!"

Mitchell hesitated before he reached forward and grabbed the marine's other boot. Both men pulled, but the Variant lifted the man out of the truck with ease. Mitchell jerked back in his seat, still feeling the sting of the marine's bootlaces on his palms. Gasping for air, he wrapped his arms across his chest.

"Cunningham!" Reno screamed. He unbuckled his seat belt and climbed into the turret just as Cunningham came crashing onto the windshield. The impact splintered the glass, blood filling the cracks. The Variant jumped onto the hood and tossed the marine's body away.

"Get it off!" Stanton yelled.

The truck swayed from side to side, Stanton trying to see around the beast. The turret roared to life again, and the monster disappeared in an explosion of blood that coated the entire windshield with slimy gore.

"Brace yourself!" Stanton shouted.

Mitchell reached up for a handhold as the truck spun out of control. The bumper clipped something he couldn't see, and then they were spinning with such force that Mitchell crashed into the side of the door.

For a second, Mitchell locked eyes with his chief of staff, sharing a moment of terror. The Lions of Capitol Hill had reached the end of the line.

Mitchell's fingers wrapped around the handhold just as the truck flipped. His neck lurched, pain shooting down his spine and up his skull. The atomic football sailed through the air in slow motion. The vehicle landed on its side, shattering every window before it rolled onto the roof. Mitchell's seat belt dug into his waist and he gripped the handhold harder. Sparks trailed the truck, upside down now, as it screeched over the pavement.

A few agonizing seconds later, the Humvee ground to a stop. Smoke and fog spilled inside, filling Mitchell's straining lungs. He coughed and swatted at the smoke. Olson hung from the ceiling, his neck twisted in a way that left no question.

"No," Mitchell said. "Olson—no…" He unbuckled his belt and crashed to the floor with a thud that echoed through the vehicle.

Stanton coughed from the front seat. "Mr. President, are you okay?"

"I think so," Mitchell replied, glancing over at his chief of staff again. "But Olson's dead."

The radio crackled, cutting him off. "Cheyenne One, you have hostiles surrounding your position. Get POTUS out of there now!"

Stanton swiped for the radio, but his hand came up short. He let out a groan and coughed. Mitchell scrambled into the front of the truck, where the lieutenant hung from the ceiling. He reached down to Mitchell with a hand covered in blood.

"Let me help you," Mitchell said.

"No, sir, I can't feel my legs. I'm done…You have to get out of here," Stanton said.

Mitchell grabbed the radio as a high-pitched shriek rang out. Stanton let out a cough, but quickly covered his mouth with a sleeve to suppress the sound. Then he pulled a pistol from a holster on his vest and handed it down.

"Sir, take this."

"But I—I don't know how to shoot," Mitchell stuttered.

The noise of snapping branches came from the rear of the vehicle. Mitchell whirled as jointed appendages whizzed by the shattered back passenger window. The scrape of talons sounded over the concrete, as if one of the beasts was dragging a pickaxe across the ground.

Mitchell froze out of fear, his body paralyzed but his eyes darting from window to window. A pair of naked feet staggered by the passenger's side of the truck. The creature stopped and pounded on the back gate. Another joined from the front passenger's door, and together they rocked the Humvee from side to side.

Stanton pushed the gun down to Mitchell.

"Take it, Mr. President." The lieutenant whispered in a formal voice even as they were being surrounded, but Mitchell couldn't seem to find the courage to be presidential.

"You have to protect me," he said, his voice cracking. "I'm not a marine."

A thud sounded on the undercarriage of the vehicle. The creatures were on top of it now. Others circled outside. Wet, naked feet slapped over the asphalt as two emaciated Variants raced in front of the windshield, their backs arched and yellow eyes roving, scanning for prey. Stanton handed the gun down and Mitchell finally grabbed the pistol, his heart rising into his throat.

"Aim for the head," Stanton said, firmly.

Mitchell swallowed hard and nodded. When he glanced back to the passenger's-side window, a female Variant on all fours tilted her head just outside the vehicle, blinking thick eyelids. Wispy blond hair dangled over a scarred face. The creature's tongue shot out of its swollen lips and made a circle, leaving a trail of saliva. It cocked its head at an unnatural angle, focusing on Mitchell. Then it was moving forward on oddly jointed arms and legs.

"Shoot it!" Stanton shouted.

Raising the pistol, Mitchell let out a whimper. He pulled the trigger, but nothing happened. The monster's wet, veiny lips twisted into what looked a lot like a smile.

"The safety lever!" Stanton shouted. "Back of the slide."

Mitchell struggled with the gun as the creature clawed into the truck. Its talons whooshed by his head, and he heard another pair slash through the broken windshield to his side. He flicked the safety up and squeezed the trigger at the screeching female Variant. A bullet punched through her neck, hot blood splattering onto Mitchell's face.

Before he could turn, something stung his left arm and yanked him through the windshield.

"Mr. President!" Stanton shouted.

Mitchell pointed the gun at the Variant dragging him onto the pavement. He fired twice at the creature's withered stomach. Howling, the beast loosened its grip on his arm and reached down at the gushing holes in its belly.

Mitchell tried to push himself to his feet, but his left arm gave out in a rush of pain. Stanton was struggling upside down in his seat. The marine raised a hand and pointed.

"Behind you!"

The president turned and squeezed off two more shots at a male Variant. Both bullets hit the beast in the left side of the chest. It retreated back into the rising curtain of fog, crying in agony.

Mitchell crawled toward the Humvee, pulling his body with his right arm, the pistol in his hand scraping across the concrete. He risked a glance behind him. Dozens of Variants watched him from the ridgeline. Some perched, while others prowled. There were three more on the road, the fog shifting around their barklike flesh.

"No!" Mitchell yelled. He continued crawling toward the truck. When he got to the windshield, he dropped the pistol and pulled himself inside.

There, just in front of him, was the nuclear football. Suddenly the idea of ending all of this with nuclear fire didn't seem like such a terrible idea. How could humans fight such monsters and win?

Mitchell screamed as a Variant clamped down on his left calf. His eyes widened as needle-sharp teeth mowed through his muscles. The hot pain was so intense it took away his breath. He gripped the frame of the windshield with his right hand, hardly noticing the broken glass slicing into his fingers. Stanton watched helplessly, his eyes locked on Mitchell as another beast clamped onto his right leg.

"Help," Mitchell whimpered, tears blurring his vision. He tried to hold on, he tried to fight, but no matter how much he wanted to live, there was nothing he could do to stop the monsters.

A third Variant clamped down on his left thigh, and together the creatures yanked his grip away. They dropped him on the ground a few feet from the truck and tore into him a second later, twisting and stretching him so hard his tendons snapped.

He let out a guttural, tormented scream and closed his eyes. As the Variants fought over him, he didn't think of his glory days on Capitol Hill, or even his wife, June. All he could think about was how history would remember him, or if it would even remember him at all.

8

Ellis put his hands on his hips. "You still haven't told Beckham yet?"

Kate sighed, shook her head. She thought of a response but figured it would be more of an excuse. Instead, she downed the rest of her morning coffee and prepared to enter the lab.

When they'd finished suiting up, Kate joined Ellis at the entrance. They stood there for a few seconds staring at the stations beyond the BSL4 labs, neither of them discussing the empty spaces. Specters of the men and women Kate had worked with emerged in her mind. There was geeky Rod from Toxicology, and her lab assistant, Cindy, with her cocky smile. Sergeant Lombardi was there in his riot gear.

All of them were dead now. Murdered by the monsters they were trying to stop.

"Another day in paradise," Ellis said. His tone was apathetic, a far cry from the normal, animated delivery Kate usually heard.

"Let's check the status of the reactors first," she said. "You take One to Six, I'll go over the results from Seven to Twelve."

Ellis raised his key card as the wall intercom behind them blared.

"Hold on, Doctors," said a voice over the speakers.

Behind the secure door to the changing room, Secretary Ringgold peered through the glass window. Kate strode over to the intercom and punched the button with a gloved finger.

"Madam Secretary," Kate said. "I wasn't expecting to see you here this morning."

Ringgold smiled. "I wasn't expecting to be here either, but apparently my curiosity won me over." She took a step closer to the glass. "Where are all the other doctors?"

When Kate didn't reply, Ringgold's smile vanished. "So it's just the two of you now?"

"Pretty much," Ellis replied.

"I see," Ringgold said, her gaze shifting to the empty labs behind Kate. "Would you mind if I join you and watch you work?"

Ellis glanced over at Kate, but she wasn't about to turn down one of the most powerful women in the world.

"We'd love for you to join us," Kate said. "We'll help you get suited up."

A process that typically took ten minutes ended up taking thirty, but when they had finished, Secretary Ringgold looked just like any scientist inside her CBRN suit.

"So, what's on your agenda?" Ringgold asked.

"First, we're going to check the bioreactors to see how the cultures are populating. Then we were going to focus on contacting labs in other countries," Kate said. She paused in the center of the first lab. "Actually, we were hoping you could help with that."

"I still haven't spoken to President Mitchell, but I do have a call with General Johnson in a few hours. I was hoping to speak to the president first, but it sounds like I have no other choice."

Kate frowned. "You'll ask him about facilitating the

production of Kryptonite with other labs across the world?"

Ringgold took a moment, breath fogging up her visor. "I'll see what I can do."

"Thank you," Kate and Ellis said at the same time.

The trio shared a chuckle, then proceeded to the lab housing the bioreactors. Antibody production levels seemed on schedule across the board. Kate breathed a sigh of relief that the experimental gene modification strategy was actually working. All the reports indicated there were no foreign contaminants or microbes negatively affecting the cell proliferation within the massive tanks. The hybridomas were dividing and producing antibodies at a rate sufficient to coat all the chemotherapeutic drugs they'd secured. If they were lucky, the accelerated rate would continue to hold steady.

"There's something I still don't understand," Ringgold said. "How did people turn into those things, the Variants, so quickly?"

"Funny you ask," Ellis replied. "I was about to go over a new theory with Kate this morning about their evolution. Especially now that they're breeding."

Ringgold fidgeted in her bulky suit. "Those things can breed?"

"Yes," Kate said. "And the gestation period appears to be weeks, instead of months."

Ringgold's features compressed behind her visor, her fifty-plus years showing in the wrinkles on her forehead. "By all means, please share your theory, Doctor."

Ellis looked to Kate for approval, and she offered a nod.

"They aren't just breeding; they are continuing to adapt, even going through metamorphosis. A marine reconnaissance team discovered Variants that had developed gills. We've seen examples of other Variants in climates across the world that are morphing in order to adapt to their environments."

"Fur in Antarctica, gills, fatty humps. We've also seen them camouflage," Kate added.

"That's where my theory comes into play," Ellis said. "I'm not sure what you know about VX-99 or the hemorrhage virus, but in short, upon infection, the VX-99 nanostructures activated genes in the subject. Depending on geography, climate, and a host of other factors, I believe the Variants began adapting from day one. The gills are just one example of thousands worldwide that we don't even know about yet."

Kate watched Ringgold's features for a reaction. She listened attentively, nodding to show them she understood the science.

Ellis continued speaking with his hands, both of them forming wide arcs. "I believe we haven't seen all of the stages yet. My theory is the adaptations and metamorphoses take place in the first stages. Stage one changes are physical, like the sucker lips, talons, increased olfactory receptors, breeding, et cetera. Stage two is the higher level of intelligence we see in their behavior, like their ability to set traps."

"And stage three?" Ringgold asked.

Ellis lowered his hands, his face draining of any excitement. "As the brain recovers from the Ebola infection, in some cases, it will lead to cognitive changes and new abilities, thus bringing us to the third and final stage."

Kate squinted. "What are you saying?"

"Stage three is communication," Ellis said. "I believe that we're going to see more examples of Alpha Variants that dominate individual lairs, kind of like a queen bee. These creatures will be able to communicate with and control the less intelligent minions."

"What do you mean by 'communicate'? Like, *talk*?" Ringgold asked.

"Yes. In short, they will be able to use basic language and commands. Depending on how severe the Ebola infection was and how much trauma there was to the brain, some may be capable of complex actions. These Variants will likely become the Alphas of their lairs. This, however, will be very rare—I estimate one in a thousand Variants will become Alphas, which is why we haven't seen many of them. These Variants were most likely infected with the hemorrhage virus shortly before VX9H9 was deployed. The Ebola infection wouldn't have had enough time to cause severe damage to their brains."

Ellis paused for a moment before continuing. "We've also seen lots of evidence that packs are territorial and fight for resources. They will likely begin warring against one another when their resources are strained."

Ringgold glared at Ellis like he was crazy, but deep down Kate had a feeling he was right. It explained the actions of some of the Variants in the past. They weren't just getting smarter; they were working together and displaying traits of highly intelligent predators that hunted in groups, like wolves. And with Alpha leaders, the Variants were becoming more dangerous than ever before.

"So, this Kryptonite drug is going to kill them all, right?" Ringgold asked.

Ellis and Kate exchanged another glance. This time neither of them responded right away.

"Right?" Ringgold entreated.

"We're not sure," Kate said. "It should work on the adults, but we have no idea if it will work on the juveniles."

"And why exactly would it not?"

"Do you want the long or the short answer?" Ellis asked.

"I just want to understand."

Ellis cracked a smile. "Each infant Variant born will experience genetic mutations. As you may remember,

VX-99 turned on genes and caused genetic variation during cell division. Theoretically, there could be enough mutations and errors in the division process that each generation of Variant will be slightly different from the last."

"Which means Kryptonite might not work," Kate interjected. "The weapon targets the Superman protein, but it's possible that the protein will have changed in the newborn Variants. Thus, the cells might express slightly different proteins on their surfaces that the Kryptonite antibodies can't bind to."

"That means the chemotherapeutics won't be able to get into those cells to kill them," Ellis finished.

Ringgold rubbed at her visor. "And you think the young are growing rapidly?"

"Judging by what we've seen, rapid is an understatement," Ellis said.

"And there are half a billion adults? How many juveniles?"

"We're not sure," Kate said.

Ringgold glanced up at Kate, her fingers still on her visor. "How can we possibly win a war against these things?"

Before Kate could respond, the intercom crackled. Major Smith stood behind the observation window. "Secretary Ringgold, we have General Johnson on the line in the command center. He said it's urgent."

"I'll be right there," she replied.

Kate and Ellis hurried after Ringgold and helped her change out of her suit.

"Come with me. I want you to sit in on this call," Ringgold said.

They met Major Smith in the war room a few minutes later. The main video display was already on. When Johnson's bald head came into view, Kate felt the same emotions as when she'd spoken to Colonel Gibson, General Kennor, and Colonel Wood—distrust and disgust. Johnson looked just like the others. He wore the same uniform and, even more important, he had the same hardened look in his eyes.

Kate pulled up a chair and sat between Ellis and Ringgold.

"General Johnson, it's good to finally speak to you," Ringgold said. "This is Doctor Kate Lovato and Doctor Pat Ellis."

Johnson held up a hand. "I'm sorry, Madam Secretary, but we don't have time for formalities. There's been an incident at Cheyenne Mountain. President Mitchell and Vice President Black were killed while trying to evacuate to the *George Washington* strike group. I'm sure you know what this means."

Kate slowly twisted in her seat and watched Ringgold's stern features soften.

Johnson cleared his voice and said, "You're the acting president of the United States now, Secretary Ringgold."

Crack!

An empty bottle of Jameson shattered in front of the sandbags piled behind Building 5. Riley squinted in the afternoon sunlight, squared his shoulders, and squeezed the trigger of his Beretta M9 three more times. One of the three remaining bottles flew apart.

"Nice shooting!" Meg yelled.

Riley frowned. "I can't freaking shoot from this goddamn chair!"

"Calm down, Alex. Sheesh. No wonder your squadmates call you 'Kid.'"

Riley felt the burn of embarrassment rising in his cheeks. He was acting like a baby, and if it weren't for

Meg, he'd be limping around without his casts, unable to shoot shit. He flicked the safety on and extended the weapon to her.

"Sorry. How about you give it a try?"

Meg eyed the pistol as if it was a weapon of mass destruction. That made Riley smile. She was tough as nails, a true firecracker, but when it came to guns she was shy.

"What are you looking at?"

"I just didn't peg you as one of those liberal anti-gun types."

Meg rolled her eyes. "I'm not, but I am from New York, remember? I used to see a lot of gunshot wounds. And by a lot, I mean at least one a week. Always seemed so pointless. Until..."

"Until the Variants."

Meg nodded and took the gun.

"Remember, the muzzle goes downrange," Riley said, tapping his head as if to remind Meg about the range safety rules they'd gone over earlier that day. When Meg had the weapon pointed at the targets they'd set up, Riley went through the rest of the steps. "You flick the safety lever up first. Then, after you line up the sights, you just squeeze the trigger. Pretty simple."

Meg balanced her crutches under her armpits and grimaced when she put weight on both feet. She scrunched up her freckled nose, and her lips twisted to the side in a scowl that showed off her teeth. Even with the pained look on her face, Riley found her absolutely stunning.

"Stop looking at me," she growled.

Riley apologized for a second time and shifted his gaze to the empty bottles of Jameson. This time he was the one to grimace. The bottles were a reminder that the soldiers on Plum Island had gone through the entire cache. There wasn't anything left to drink but Fanta and Smirnoff.

He glanced over at Meg. "When you have a target—"

Pop! Pop! Pop!

Both of the remaining bottles exploded into hundreds of tiny shards.

"Damn, you're a natural," Riley said. When he looked at Meg again he expected to see a smile, but she was staring at the sky.

Meg lowered the pistol and pointed with her other hand. "Those aren't our choppers, are they?"

Riley heard something louder than any chopper. A squadron of F-18 Super Hornets shot over the island. He watched them fly toward Connecticut, where they vanished in the clouds.

"What the hell?" Meg shouted.

On the horizon to the east, an armada of helicopters raced across the sky. There were two Chinooks, a trio of Black Hawks, and a single Osprey—the most aircraft he had seen since the outbreak started.

"Come here," Riley said, gesturing for her.

Meg hesitated, still watching the sky with awe.

"Now!" Riley said. He reached for his pistol and snatched it from Meg's hands.

"Are those reinforcements?" When he didn't respond, she added, "Alex, what the hell is going on?"

Riley flipped magazines, chambered a round, and flicked the safety on. Then he tucked the weapon in his waistband and gripped the wheels of his chair. "Follow me!"

He wheeled like a madman back to the path wrapping around Building 5. Meg crutched after him. Riley blinked at the afternoon sun, his heart thumping in time with the helicopter rotors overhead.

Riley pushed the wheels harder and faster, the rubber screeching across the pavement. These soldiers weren't coming to help. They were coming to avenge Colonel Wood. He could feel it in his gut. Beckham had told him to stand down if this moment came, but that was one order Riley couldn't follow. He refused to let them haul Beckham away.

Meg and Riley rounded Building 5 to the sight of the choppers landing on the tarmac. Horn came rushing across the lawn with Chow on his six. They shouldered their rifles and aimed them at the birds.

"Kid, get yer ass over here!" Horn shouted. The words came out garbled from the cigarette wobbling between his lips. He grabbed it and flicked it onto the grass. "Those are General Johnson's men!"

"Where's Beckham?" Riley shouted back. He had to reach him before Johnson's men did. Beckham would take full responsibility for Wood's death. He'd slip the noose around his own neck if it meant saving Team Ghost. Riley wasn't going to let that fucking happen.

Horn shook his head and tightened his grip on his M249 SAW, his tattooed forearms flexing. "I don't know where Beckham is, man. Last time I saw him, he was with Kate."

The jets performed another flyover, screaming through the low-lying clouds. A wall of wind gusted across the lawn, nearly knocking Meg to the grass.

"What the hell is going on?" she screamed.

Riley pulled his M9 and spat. The F-18s disappeared back into the clouds. When the rumble faded, Riley said, "Get to Building One, Meg."

"No way." She grabbed her knife and unsheathed it. "I'm staying with you guys."

Riley felt himself smile. Despite the fact that they were vastly outgunned and they were probably all going to die, all he could think about was how cute Meg was when she was pissed. Going down in a hail of gunfire next to her sure as hell beat getting torn apart by the Variants.

Beckham stood in the radiant afternoon sun knowing damn well what was about to happen, although somehow, standing on the landing of Building 1 and watching the aircraft descend upon Plum Island, he couldn't quite grasp it. Part of him wanted to order his men to fight—part of him wanted to draw the Colt .45 that Lieutenant Colonel Jensen had given him and use it on those coming to arrest him—but he knew there was only one option. Not because he was a coward but because he couldn't let anyone else die because of him.

In an effort to save his men, his friends, he would tell General Johnson that Team Ghost had only been following orders, the exact same thing he had cursed Wood's men for.

The range of feelings rushing through him shifted from anger to fear. He wasn't scared of being taken away and locked in the brig of some navy destroyer or of rotting in the darkness. The thing that terrified him most was not being able to protect the people he loved.

At least he wasn't alone. Secretary Ringgold, Major Smith, Kate, and Ellis stood behind him. All of them shielded their eyes from the sun as the choppers landed on the tarmac. The lawn between the buildings quickly filled with civilian spectators. Red and Donna were there with their son, Bo. The boy peered out from between them and pointed at the helicopters.

"Beckham! Where the hell's your rifle?" a voice shouted.

It was Horn. He was jogging down the walkway with Chow by his side. Riley wheeled his chair as fast as he could with his head tucked down, shaggy blond hair blowing in the wind. Meg hopped after him with a crazed look in her eyes. Fitz came around the corner of Building 1, MK11 slung over his back, panting as if he had just run a half marathon. Apollo darted after the marine, his ears perked.

Every member of Team Ghost could sense the danger. One by one, they surrounded Beckham. Horn and Chow hoisted Riley up the stairs, the kid cursing each step. Fitz grabbed Meg's crutches, and Horn turned to help her. Apollo loped up the steps and sat on his hind legs next to Beckham.

"Beckham, you got a plan?" Major Smith asked. He was twisting his wedding ring around his finger. Lieutenant Colonel Jensen's death had broken him, and Beckham wasn't even sure he could count on Smith if he did decide to stand his ground.

Kate brushed up against Beckham and grasped his hand in her own. Everyone was there now. They had all been through so much since the outbreak started. He wasn't going to put them through anything else. If General Johnson had come to arrest him, then so be it.

"When they come for us, you all stand down," Beckham said. "You were all following *my* orders."

"Hell no!" Riley protested.

Beckham glared at him. "That's an order, Kid."

"Boss, we ain't letting them take you," Horn added. He whispered something to Kate about his daughters and pulled the magazine from his gun to check the rounds.

Chow stepped forward, chewing fiercely on a toothpick. "After all we've been through, you're just going to let them take you? Fuck that!"

"I'm with everyone else," Fitz said from the side of the landing. He shouldered his MK11 and started picking out targets.

"What are you going to do?" Beckham asked, whirling and pointing at the choppers. A platoon of soldiers decked out in tactical armor spilled out of the Black Hawks and Chinook. "Are we going to fight that army? Team Ghost is not what we used to be!"

Chow stopped chewing on his toothpick, and Riley

looked toward the ground. Horn was the only one to stand strong. He held Beckham's gaze, his eyes smoldering with pain.

"I'm sorry, brother," Beckham said. He reached for the muzzle of Horn's SAW and slowly lowered it toward the ground. Then Beckham scanned his other friends. Kate's eyes remained resilient, and Secretary Ringgold folded her arms across her chest. Meg had her fingers wrapped around the handle of a knife tucked into her pants, and Riley's face was ripe with anger. Even Ellis had a look of defiance. All of them were still ready to stand for the man who had saved them. He almost choked on a flood of emotions.

"Let me through," Secretary Ringgold said. She worked her way to Beckham's left.

When he finally turned back to the tarmac, three dozen soldiers were marching toward Building 1 with their rifles shouldered.

"Put your weapons on the ground!" one of them yelled.

The marines and Rangers who had been patrolling Plum Island slowly lowered their rifles.

Regardless of what was about to happen, the sheer amount of force present was oddly beautiful. For a moment, the show of military muscle provided some small hope that they still had a chance to defeat the Variants if they could just work together.

"I'll handle this," Ringgold said. She glanced over at Beckham and smiled. "Hell, I'm about to be sworn in as the president of the United States. That better count for something."

9

All it takes is all you got.

Garcia tried his best not to blink. He lay in the mud of a construction site, soaked from head to toe, rain beating down on him and washing away thoughts of the past. Water pooled in his ears and in his boots, but he didn't dare move. He and Steve-o had been on the run for...shit, Garcia wasn't even sure how long. They had barely escaped with their lives from Turner Field the night before. Tank and Thomas were MIA, and there was a pack of Variants stalking the Variant Hunters through Atlanta. The stakes had been raised now that Garcia carried actual video evidence of the grotesque child Variants, something he wasn't aware of any other team discovering. He had to keep the package secure and get it back to the *GW* strike group safely.

The distant howl of a Variant reminded him that wasn't going to be easy. Goose bumps prickled up and down Garcia's arms, his fresh tattoo tingling. He tried not to think the worst, but he suspected if he made it out of here he was going to have to ink another cross on his other arm to fit the names of his fallen brothers.

Tank, you son of a bitch. You and Thomas better be out there.

Garcia blinked and slowly rotated his head for a view of

the skeletal ten-story building at the south end of the muddy field. A beast clambered across the steel beams on the fifth floor. It stopped and squatted on the metal. Sheets of rain hammered its withered body, washing away the grime on its glistening flesh. This Variant was starving; Garcia could see the ribs protruding from its chest. He avoided its slitted eyes and looked down, his heart pounding.

Although he was covered in mud, Garcia felt naked. He was in the open. Plunging into this swamp had been a last resort. They would never have made it across the construction zone, though. He flinched at the hiss of static from his earpiece.

"Hotel One, Foxtrot One. Over."

The transmission was the first good sign he'd heard all morning. It meant Command hadn't given up on them. They'd been forced to go silent for hours and had missed two radio checks. A flicker of hope rose where Garcia used to have a heart. He slowly lifted his helmet and watched the Variant until it finally climbed up the metal beams and disappeared into the guts of the structure.

Think, Garcia. You have to use your fucking head.

He took two seconds to manage his breathing and look for an escape. They were east of the stadium and north of Georgia Avenue. Martin Street SE ran perpendicular a few blocks away, Garcia knew, and beyond that was a neighborhood of luxury apartments. If they could get there, they might have a chance to ride it out. Then again, he wasn't sure what they would find inside those buildings.

He tilted his head to the west, where a storm drain beckoned him. He didn't like the idea of going underground, but the tunnel would reduce the likelihood of an ambush from multiple directions. It would also reduce the chances of finding Tank and Thomas. They could still be alive, although their radio silence meant they were either pinned down, as he was, or they were dead.

First Daniels and Morgan in the Keys, now Tank and Thomas. Garcia resisted the urge to punch the mud. His men. His friends. The Variant Hunters were slowly being eradicated.

And if Garcia didn't want to join them, he had to make a move. He tilted his helmet toward the drain. He didn't need to look to see Steve-o nod. The corporal was waiting for his orders.

Pushing at the slop, Garcia rose to his knees, letting his M4 dangle across his chest. He scooped up a handful of mud and smeared it across his face. Steve-o was doing the same thing. When they finished, they ran in a hunch toward the storm drain's opening, their boots slurping through the muck.

With every stride, Garcia expected to hear the high-pitched roar of a Variant or the popping of jointed append-ages, but the only thing he heard was the distant rumble of thunder. Steve-o didn't hesitate when he got to the lip of the tunnel. He ducked inside with his SAW in front. Garcia followed close behind, sweeping his M4 over the narrow space. A steady stream of water rushed past their boots and spilled out into the swampy construction site.

Steve-o flashed an advance signal, and they continued into the drain until they were far enough in that only a sliver of light penetrated the darkness. Trickling water echoed off the concrete walls. Garcia sniffed the air like one of the monsters to check for the scent of rotting fruit, but he only picked up the sour stink of his own sweat.

Garcia waited several minutes before he felt comfort-able breaking radio silence.

"Hotel Three and Four, Hotel One. Over."

The frustrating hiss of white noise filled his earpiece.

"Foxtrot One, Hotel One. Over."

Steve-o scratched at his beard of mud. "Out of range?"

Garcia looked down the tunnel back toward the construction zone. The walls were blocking the signal, but he couldn't go back out there and risk the Variants spotting him. There was only one option—to continue into the bowels of Atlanta.

"Let's keep moving," Garcia whispered. "On me." He raised his rifle and motioned for Steve-o to follow.

Thunder clapped in the distance, the sound reverberating in the tunnel like a gong. As they worked their way deeper, the natural light dwindled until Garcia couldn't see five feet in front of him. He stopped and clicked his NVGs into position. The green-hued darkness emerged across his field of vision, enveloping him from all sides.

Garcia marched forward, his senses on full alert. Every hundred feet he stopped to listen for Variants, but there was only the trickle of water and intermittent growls of thunder. A few minutes later, the walls curved into a junction. Light streamed through a manhole and spread across the pooling water cascading from the street.

He stopped and balled his hand into a fist. The missing manhole cover meant one thing—the Variants used this tunnel to move under the city. What would have terrified Garcia weeks ago didn't even faze him. He knew the monsters used the passages and could be dwelling inside this one. Every move he made was a risk.

Garcia pointed to his eyes, then to Steve-o, then to the open manhole. They quietly worked their way through the ankle-deep water until they were under the opening.

Steve-o cleared the right side of the corridor, and Garcia took the left. Both tunnels continued into a black oblivion. He flipped off his NVGs and angled his suppressed M4 toward the street above. Clouds rolled overhead, drops of rain splattering on his face. He blinked away the water and grabbed the bottom rung of the skeletal ladder.

"I'm going to see if I can raise Tank and Thomas," Garcia said. "Hold here."

Steve-o winked and raised his SAW. Garcia checked both ends of the tunnel and then continued climbing up the ladder. He stopped just shy of poking his helmet into the street. Overhead, a web of lightning sizzled through the clouds. The electric blue light lingered, and thunder clapped like a grenade exploding. Dull echoes followed, booming and fading. Garcia waited for the cacophony to pass, then inched his helmet through the opening to scan the street with naked eyes. An abandoned pickup truck blocked his view to the west, and a squad car obstructed the east. To the north there was a sign that read REED STREET SE.

He flicked his mini-mic into position.

"Hotel Three and Four, this is Hotel One. Over."

Another network of lightning tore through the clouds, masking a faint reply. Garcia cupped his right hand over his earpiece.

"Hotel Three—"

Tank's voice cut Garcia off. "Hotel One, Hotel Three. Over."

Garcia held back a grin. The Variant Hunters were still in business. "What's your location, Three?"

"A church on Martin Street Southeast. Over."

"Roger, Three. We're at Reed Street Southeast."

"Roger. There's a park two blocks to your east. Good for extraction, One?"

"Copy that, we'll—"

A flash of motion below stopped Garcia midsentence. Steve-o roved his SAW back and forth as if he was searching for something. Then he took a step out of view.

"Yo, Steve-o," Garcia whispered. "I said hold—"

"Contact!"

Garcia squeezed the rung of the ladder before sliding down. The second his boots hit the water, Steve-o opened fire. Even with the AAC silencer reducing the muzzle flash, it still lit up the shapes of a half dozen

Variants advancing down the tunnel. The larger creatures galloped through the water, while the smaller ones took to the walls and ceiling. Long, stalky appendages moved in the staccato light of muzzle flashes. Swollen lips opened, releasing tortured screeches. The abominations raced forward, bringing with them a putrid scent.

"Fall back!" Garcia yelled. His earpiece crackled, but he couldn't make out Tank's transmission. He pulled on the back of Steve-o's flak jacket and guided him to the ladder.

"Come on, you freaks!" Steve-o yelled. He fired short, steady bursts. The 5.56-millimeter rounds pierced flesh and shattered bone, splattering the passage with crimson gore. He picked the monsters off one by one, his muzzle raking back and forth in methodical sweeps. Outside of combat, Steve-o was the quietest man Garcia had ever met, but in battle, the youngest member of the Variant Hunters was a fucking beast.

"Ten...eleven...twelve," Steve-o shouted, keeping track of his kills. The flashes from his SAW illuminated his features, which had transformed from those of a passive good ol' Southern boy into those of a raging sociopath.

"Move it, marine!" Garcia shouted. He jerked Steve-o away from the fight and turned to the ladder as the popping of joints sounded behind them. Without his NVGs in position, he couldn't see the Variants, but he could hear the snapping in the brief pauses between Steve-o's suppressed gunfire and the tormented shrieks of the dying creatures.

They'd never make it up the ladder if they didn't clear these monsters first. Garcia gritted his teeth, aimed his M4, and fired into the darkness. A hellish noise followed as the rounds punched through meat. He came back-to-back with Steve-o, bullet casings splashing into the water at their boots.

"Changing!" Garcia yelled.

Steve-o was screaming like a madman now, going cyclic on the Variants as they charged down the tunnel. Garcia slapped a magazine into his gun and was firing at the silhouetted creatures a beat later. He counted five, but they were just the recon party. Others quickly flooded the passage behind them. The battle would draw others from the city. It was only a matter of time before Garcia and Steve-o were overrun.

Once again, he had broken the cardinal rule. The Variant Hunters were fucking compromised.

In the chaos, an image of Ashley emerged in Garcia's mind. She was holding their daughter, Leslie, her big blue eyes staring down at their beautiful gift from God. The flashback ended as soon as it begun, and in its place came the gaping maw of a Variant that had made it through the shots without losing more than an ear.

Garcia shot it in the kneecap and finished the last three rounds of his magazine, each tearing away a chunk of the beast until it crashed to the ground. Behind it, a solid mass of distorted figures approached. His earpiece crackled again as he flipped magazines and fired two quick bursts at the approaching monsters. Several of the Variants darted into the spray.

What the hell?

In the past, the creatures had shown lack of discipline, especially the starving ones, but this was different. As he fired again, two more of the Variants broke off from the mass into his fire. They crashed to the water, thrashing and screeching.

In the gap between bloody limbs and emaciated bodies, the misshapen skull of the biggest Variant Garcia had ever seen came into focus. The beast was as big as a lineman, with huge chest muscles and thick abs rimming its wide torso. He ambled forward, protected by the wave of frail monsters surrounding him. One by one they broke off from the pack, using their diseased bodies as shields to protect the beast.

This was an Alpha, like the one he'd seen at Turner Field, but he dwarfed the other leaders Garcia had encountered. He had never seen one this fucking big before.

"Steve-o, we got to move!"

"Almost clear, Sarge!"

Garcia held in a breath, lined up the cross hairs, and waited for a shot.

Come on—just one.

The beast's head moved into his scope and he pulled the trigger. The shot clipped its neck, a geyser of blood squirting over the monsters on its right. The Alpha roared and reached up, clamping its right palm over the wound.

The other Variants came together in a phalanx to protect their leader, and the entire pack halted. Garcia didn't waste the opportunity to escape.

"Let's go!" he shouted, grabbing the ladder. Steve-o fired off another shot, then followed him.

Garcia climbed the wet rungs as fast as he could, his gaze locked on the churning storm clouds above. His earpiece crackled again.

"Sarge, what the hell is happening?"

"We're—" Garcia choked on his words. He froze at the sight of a Variant that had clambered right up to the edge of the open manhole not four feet above. Before it had a chance to react, Garcia pulled his side arm and shot it between its yellow eyes. A chunk of skull and spongy, wet brain matter rained down on Garcia's face, blinding him with gore.

He never saw the monster tumble, but he felt every pound as it crashed into him, knocking his grip loose from the slippery rungs. He didn't even have a chance to scream as he fell backward and smashed into Steve-o.

The plunge felt like a time warp. He blinked the

blood from his eyes. At the rim of the manhole opening, a trio of Variants appeared. They stared down at him, lips smacking as he fell. A second later, he crashed to the ground, Steve-o taking the brunt of the fall.

The impact knocked the air out of Garcia's lungs. He rolled off Steve-o and tried to push himself to his feet, but the pain was too intense. His body was in shock. Swirling red and the skeletal figures of Variants rushed across his vision.

Garcia fumbled for his side arm, but his hand came up empty.

"Steve-o," he groaned.

The only reply was the squawking and cackling of the Variants surrounding them. The packs closed in from both sides, and the Alpha Garcia had shot in the neck broke from the wall of monsters. Blood gushed down the side of its glistening chest, but the wound didn't seem to slow the beast. It staggered forward, stopped, and rotated to slash at the creatures behind it. When it turned, Garcia saw what it took to rise to the top of the Variant hierarchy. The beast's back was covered in lacerations and long scars.

Garcia grabbed his knife and pulled the blade from its sheath. He fought the pain lancing down his legs, desperate to survive, to fight. He had thought he was ready to die and join his family, but lying in the water, surrounded by the monsters, he felt the undeniable grip of fear that came before death. He had seen it in the eyes of marines in countless situations, and now, if he could see his own eyes, he knew they would have the same look.

This time he didn't say a prayer or repeat any motto. Words wouldn't save him—only steel. He gripped the handle of his knife as the beast whirled back toward him and dropped to all fours. Clambering forward, it moved to Steve-o first, sniffing his still body. Then it moved to Garcia, climbing over the top of him and holding itself up with muscular, jointed arms tattooed with scars. The membrane over its reptilian eyes blinked rapidly.

Behind it, the group of shrieking Variants surged forward, their bulging lips wide open, starving and desperate. The Alpha hovering over Garcia turned its head, and Garcia seized the moment. He drove the knife toward the monster's glistening jugular vein, but hit the beast in the palm as it swiped at the blade. Steel sliced through skin and gristle. The creature leaned back to let out a roar and then brought its forehead down on Garcia.

The blow hit him in the nose, shattering cartilage and clouding his vision with stars. His helmet snapped off and clanked over the concrete.

Wails came from all directions as the creatures closed in. Somewhere, over all of the noise, there was a hissing. But there was no way he could hear his headset. This was something else.

"Steve-o," Garcia mumbled. He reached for the marine, then for his helmet. He couldn't lose the picture of his family . . .

A pair of claws gripped Garcia's ankles, piercing his flesh and prompting a wave of adrenaline that cleared his vision. Two Variants dragged him through the water. The Alpha walked alongside, its slitted eyes locked on its prey.

Garcia reached for his other knife, a switchblade he kept on his belt. The motion earned him a kick to the ribs. Talons tore across his flak jacket as the beast kicked him again. He coughed, and his lungs struggled for air. The stars came back, then the encroaching red, and just before he lost consciousness, he saw the things emerge from the small army of emaciated Variants.

There were six of the hissing, armored offspring, all of them sitting on their hind legs, their coned heads tilting and their almond-shaped eyes studying, scrutinizing . . .

Learning.

10

Kate massaged the side of Beckham's hand with her thumb. Team Ghost may have been instructed to stand down, but she still had a plan. If General Johnson attempted to arrest Beckham, she was going to refuse to work on Operation Extinction. And considering she was the architect behind the science, she figured that would tip the scales back in their favor. Plus, Team Ghost had the future president of the United States on their side.

In less than ten minutes, Plum Island had transformed into what Kate imagined a real combat base looked like. General Johnson's men, dressed in blue navy fatigues, were busy disarming the marines and Rangers stationed throughout the island. They swarmed onto the lawn, fanning out and shouting, "Lower your weapons!"

Four of the men hustled over to the steps of Building 1, where they stopped and waited for a middle-aged man with a handsome face, chiseled jawline, and buzzed gray hair. He approached with the muzzle of his rifle angled toward the ground, but the others aimed theirs at the landing. Kate's heart flipped when two of the men slowly approached the steps. Beckham gripped her hand tighter.

"It's okay," he whispered. Apollo brushed up between them, his teeth bared.

The man with gray hair held up both of his hands and continued walking toward the landing. "Secretary Ringgold, I'm Lieutenant Brock Rowe of the United States Navy, and we're here to escort you back to the *George Washington* strike group. The rest of you, please hand over your rifles to my men." His gaze shifted from face to face, stopping on Beckham's. "Master Sergeant Beckham, I presume."

Beckham loosened his grip on Kate's hand. "Yes, sir."

Horn and Chow moved in Kate's peripheral vision. Riley's hand went for his pistol, but Ringgold stood still and replied, "Lieutenant, with all due respect, I'm not going anywhere until I speak with General Johnson."

"That's fine, ma'am," Rowe replied. "But I need Master Sergeant Beckham and the members of Team Ghost to come with me." There was measured restraint in his voice.

"Master Sergeant Beckham is not going anywhere," Ringgold said. "You may disarm him and Team Ghost, but they are staying with me."

Rowe lowered his hands and motioned for his men to proceed. They advanced up the steps, one of them bumping into Kate. She turned as a soldier reached for Horn's SAW. The operator spat on the ground and glared at Beckham, who nodded back. Grunting, Horn pushed his weapon into the soldier's chest.

"All clear, sir," one of the men said.

Rowe flicked his mini-mic to his lips. "General Johnson, Plum Island is secure. I'm with Secretary Ringgold at Building 1. Master Sergeant Beckham and Team Ghost are here as well."

When Kate looked back at the tarmac, a small group was piling out of the Osprey. No one said a word as the entourage approached. Kate felt every second tick by, knowing their situation was more fragile than a house of cards. A single wrong move could spark a chain of events that would ruin everything they had built here and destroy their chance of defeating the Variants.

The formation of soldiers marched across the tarmac and then the lawn. Through the fort of weapons and body armor, Kate glimpsed General Johnson. He walked with the posture of an old man, slow and slightly hunched.

Ringgold raised her hand to shield her eyes from the sun as the men approached. Kate continued massaging the side of Beckham's hand. They stood there in near silence, the only sounds Horn's labored breathing and Apollo's low growl.

By the time Johnson reached the stairs, Kate thought her heart was going to implode. He waved his men away and strolled forward, leisurely and nonthreatening. At the bottom step, he took off his helmet and used a handkerchief to wipe the sweat off his wrinkled forehead. Then he continued up the stairs and extended a hand, offering a smile that showed a gap between his top two front teeth.

"Pleasure to meet you, Secretary Ringgold. I'm General George Johnson."

She shook his hand. "With all due respect, General, I don't appreciate the tone of this 'extraction,' and I would very much appreciate it if your men lowered their weapons. Need I remind you that humans aren't the enemy?"

Johnson's gaze flicked to Team Ghost briefly before returning to Ringgold. "I'm sorry, Madam Secretary, truly, but after the incident that occurred here several nights ago, I was forced to take appropriate action. Security isn't something I take lightly, and I have to do everything to ensure the safety of those still fighting." He paused. "Unfortunately, we're going to need to take

Master Sergeant Reed Beckham and Team Ghost back to the *GW* strike group."

"I know," Ringgold said.

Kate inched forward, but Beckham squeezed her hand.

Ringgold turned to Beckham and nodded. "He goes where I go. If you have a few minutes, I'm sure I can explain in detail the 'incident' you speak of. It implicates a long list of service members, primarily officers with whom you are associated, including General Kennor, Colonel Gibson, and Colonel Wood, whom Team Ghost killed in self-defense."

"That's damn right," Riley blurted out. Kate caught Beckham's hissed warning at Riley, but kept her eyes on the general and his men, waiting to see how they'd respond. Before the general could speak, Secretary Ringgold continued.

"From what I understand, *all* of those men were connected with the development of the hemorrhage virus, dating back to a platoon of marines in Vietnam."

Johnson put his helmet back on his head and pursed his lips, but Ringgold kept talking. "So before I'm sworn in as the next president, I guess my question is: What kind of country am I swearing to defend? One that continues to kill its own citizens? Or one that will do everything in its power to defeat the Variants?"

"Madam Secretary, at this point I don't suppose anything I can say will convince you I'm one of the good guys. In fact, if I were you, I wouldn't trust me."

"I sure as hell don't," Riley snorted.

The general sent a glare between Ringgold and Kate, aimed at Riley. Horn elbowed the kid in the shoulder, and Beckham shook his head. That was okay with Kate. She was simply relieved she didn't have to witness another gun battle.

Johnson turned to Rowe. "Lieutenant, fall back and wait for me on the lawn."

Rowe stared at him.

"*Now*, Lieutenant."

"Yes, sir." Rowe waved at the other four soldiers. They obeyed, filing down the steps and marching onto the grass.

Johnson took in another breath, released it, and then said, "I'm going to be frank with you all. I knew nothing of Colonel Wood's connection to Colonel Gibson, and if General Kennor knew, he sure as hell didn't tell me."

"You weren't confidants?" Ringgold asked. "Why do you expect me to believe you?"

Johnson pulled at the cuffs of his sleeves, his impatience starting to show. "Madam Secretary, there's a fair amount I have yet to get to the bottom of, but I'm afraid you don't have any choice but to trust me."

"And why's that, General?"

"Because the *GW* strike group is the last safe place in the world. Almost every single military base across the country has fallen, and judging by the defenses I saw on a flyover, Plum Island isn't safe either. If you come with us, you will live on a nuclear-powered aircraft carrier protected by two Ticonderoga-class guided-missile cruisers, two Arleigh Burke–class guided-missile destroyers, and a submarine armed with nuclear weapons. We also have a Clark-class dry-cargo ship and a Pathfinder-class oceanographic survey ship."

Ringgold glanced over at Beckham, who offered a small nod of approval.

"I'm trying to defeat an enemy that wants nothing more than to eradicate our species. I hate to say this about my old friend, but maybe General Kennor's death—and President Mitchell's—was a good thing. Kennor was bullheaded and set in his ways. He didn't give science a chance until it was almost too late. And Mitchell was never fit to be a president. But you..." Johnson wagged a finger. "You are *strong*. It's the reason you're still alive. I believe you and I can work together to defeat the Variants—with Doctor Lovato's help, of course."

Kate's heart rate had just returned to normal when the general's words sent it spiking back out of control. What the hell did he want with her?

"I didn't come just to escort you to Central Command. I also came for Doctor Lovato," Johnson said. "If we're going to win this war, I need her. At least for the short term."

Kate tried to keep her voice from reflecting what she really thought. "General, I can't leave. We just started production of antibodies here. I need to supervise—"

"I can take care of it," Ellis interrupted.

"Excellent," Johnson replied. "With your permission, then, Madam Secretary, my men will escort you, Master Sergeant Beckham, and Doctor Lovato to the *GW* strike group."

Ringgold pivoted toward Beckham. "What do you think?"

Beckham let Kate's hand fall to her side. "May I make a request, sir?"

Johnson nodded.

"We have civilian families here that need protection. Request permission for immediate evac to the strike group."

"I'm sorry, but we're all maxed out right now. Not a single bunk left. But I'll tell you what: How about I leave thirty men to help secure and defend the island?"

Lieutenant Rowe took several steps forward on the lawn. "Sir, we can't afford—"

"We will also loan the island two gunships and an

additional Black Hawk," Johnson said, cutting off his lieutenant without even turning.

"Whose command will these men and vehicles be left under? Major Smith has been in charge since Lieutenant Colonel Jensen was killed by Colonel Wood," Beckham replied. "We also have a dozen of Wood's men locked up in Building Four who need to be dealt with."

Major Smith stiffened, and Johnson gave him a critical look. "Smith will stay in charge of operations here. And we will bring Wood's men back to the *GW*."

"Thank you, sir," Beckham said. "I'd also like to bring members of Team Ghost with me."

"Granted," Johnson quickly replied. "So, what do you say, Madam Secretary?"

Ringgold put her hands on her hips and sighed. "I think we have a lot of work to do."

Johnson smiled. "We'll get you sworn in as soon as we arrive at the *GW*." He clapped his hands together. "Now, which one of you killed Colonel Wood?"

Fitz slowly raised a hand from the side of the landing. "I did, sir."

Johnson walked over to him. "What's your name, son?"

"Fitzpatrick, sir. Fitz for short."

Johnson gave him the elevator eyes look, up and down. "Well, Fitz. Murder of a superior officer. They still call it *fragging*?"

It seemed all the easy talk before was just a ruse. Now the general would show his true colors. Fitz stayed upright and calm, but Kate knew he was worried. Beckham, Horn, and Riley had their eyes glued to the general. Kate opened her mouth to say something, but she couldn't find the words to make it all go away.

"The Uniform Code of Military Justice says I'm supposed to arrest you, son," he said to Fitz. "But I think I should give you a goddamn medal. I never liked that son of a bitch anyway."

Fitz grabbed his MK11 from one of Johnson's men and watched half of the soldiers march back to the tarmac. The others were already being debriefed and assigned patrols by Major Smith.

Rifle in hand, Fitz strode across the lawn outside Building 1 toward a group of civilians, his heart still hammering. Meg and Riley were busy arguing about something, and Tasha and Jenny Horn held Kate's hands while she discussed science shit with Ellis.

"You're sure you can handle this on your own?" Kate asked Ellis. "I could be gone a couple of weeks."

Ellis ran a hand through his thick black hair and flashed a smile. "I can handle it. By the time you get back, I'll have our batch of Kryptonite ready to go."

"I know." She smiled back at him and turned just as Beckham, Horn, and Chow came jogging from the barracks, rucksacks and rifles slung over their shoulders. Apollo ran alongside, his ears perked and head roving as he studied the new soldiers.

The Delta Force operators were headed back out there, and once again Fitz was being left behind. This time he wasn't as disappointed as before. He felt a purpose here, and Tower 4 was starting to feel like home. Besides, Team Ghost wasn't going back to war—they were going to one of the safest places left in the world. Standing up in the tower for hours on end with nothing but the scent of salt water and the breeze wasn't so bad. And if the Variants came back, he would give them hell.

"Daddy," Tasha said, "why do you have to go?" Her freckled features mashed together as she tried to understand.

"Can't we come with you?" Jenny asked.

Horn stopped in front of them and picked them up, one in each arm. "I have to go alone this time, but you'll be safe here. I won't be gone that long, I promise."

Beckham put his rucksack on the ground and dug inside, talking to Fitz as he rummaged through the contents. "You keep an eye on Johnson's men. Don't trust anyone."

"What about me?" Riley fumed.

"Of course he can trust you, Kid," Beckham said, still digging. "I said *Johnson's* men."

"You watch over my girls. Don't let anything happen to 'em. Got that, Fitz?" Horn put Tasha and Jenny on the ground, and both of them latched onto his legs.

"Roger that," Fitz replied.

"You can count on me and Meg," Riley said.

Horn patted Riley on the shoulder. "I know I can, Kid. And thanks, Meg. I know you two will take good care of them."

Meg smiled. "No problem. Try not to worry."

Fitz's eyes darted back and forth. "Any other requests?"

"If the Variants come back, I expect you to do what you did last time," Chow said.

The group chuckled at that, and Beckham pulled a small green pouch from his bag. He opened it and said, "Team Ghost, gather around." He waited for the men to circle. "The shit I said earlier, outside Building One, wasn't right. I was wrong about Team Ghost not being what it used to be. In some ways, we're better. Better because we've got Chow, Fitz, and Apollo with us now."

The MK11 felt heavier than it ever had before. Fitz

slung it over his shoulder as Beckham handed him a patch sporting an image of a skull surrounded by smoke.

"Wear it, and wear it proud," Beckham said.

"*Semper fi*," Fitz replied. He grabbed the patch and nodded, beaming with pride.

Beckham distributed the other patches to Riley, Horn, and Chow. "You guys can thank Chow for these. Apparently he'd had them stowed in his pack since Fort Bragg."

"I pulled patches for all the Delta teams after shit hit the fan. Just in case anyone made it," Chow said.

Riley stared at the symbol as if he hadn't seen it for the longest time. He wiped his eyes quickly with his sleeve. Beckham pulled his blade and punched a hole in a fifth patch. Then he bent down and looped it through Apollo's collar. The dog sniffed at his hand and licked his fingers.

"Welcome to Team Ghost, boy," Beckham said.

There were more short-lived chuckles, followed by silence. It lingered, broken only by the door to Building 1 opening and shutting. Secretary Ringgold and General Johnson stepped outside. The secretary waved at Beckham and motioned for him to follow.

"All right, let's move out," Beckham said. "You ready, Doctor Lovato?"

Kate nodded at Ellis and bent down in front of Tasha and Jenny.

"Be good girls," Kate said. They hugged her, then returned to Horn.

"I'll be back soon," he said, kissing them each on the forehead.

Fitz stood next to Riley as the group departed. Tasha and Jenny sobbed while Meg tried to console them. Riley remained still, his eyes locked on his brothers and Apollo. Fitz felt the kid's pain, but at the same time, Fitz knew in his heart they were where they were supposed to be. Every marine had a duty. This was Fitz's island to protect.

Garcia jerked awake to an awful smell, a mix between puke and the Dumpster behind a Chinese restaurant during the height of summer. He opened his eyes to inky darkness.

He tried to move his head. That earned him a shot of pain that ran up his nose and bled through his skull like the worst brain freeze he could remember. Realization hit him with the force of a sucker punch in the gut as he remembered the Alpha Variant that had broken his nose.

"Steve-o," Garcia mumbled. He tried to turn to his left, but he was stuck in some sort of... He didn't know what the hell it was. His body was pinned, but he was standing up with his back to a wall. Everything was blurry in front of him. At first he thought his vision was clouded, but it wasn't a problem with his eyes. Something was blocking his sight like a thick piece of murky glass. The suffocating darkness didn't make things any easier. Somewhere on the other side of the obstruction, there was motion.

Dazed but aware, Garcia finally accepted where he was. For weeks he had been tracking and killing Variants. He had seen their lairs—and the humans they kept there. Now he was one of those prisoners.

A rush of fear and adrenaline shot through the marine. He speared his head into a sticky film, his short-cropped hair getting caught in the glue.

"Damn. Fucking piece of shit," Garcia grumbled. As he ripped his hair from the sticky substance, he cursed again. Not from the pain, but because he remembered his missing helmet. Losing it meant he hadn't just lost the picture of his family—he'd lost documented evidence of the juvenile Variants.

Stay calm, Marine. All it takes is all you got. All it takes is . . .

He closed his eyes. He was still alive, and he still had the images of the child freaks locked away in his memory. As long as he was breathing, he would do everything possible to get the information back to Central Command. But first, he had to find his way out of here. Wherever the hell *here* was.

How long had he been out? Had Tank and Thomas left without him? Where was Steve-o?

Garcia focused on his breathing and did an inventory of his body, checking to see what hurt and didn't. Besides his nose, the only pain came from his back. For a moment he listened to the trickle of water and the sporadic screams that echoed as if he was inside a cave with no end.

He tried to move his torso, wiggling from side to side. Then he attempted to move his head again. Each ear brushed up against the same sticky surface in turn, tugging on his skin. He took in a breath filled with the scent of rotting flesh and stomach acid. That made him gag, and this time he dry-heaved so hard he lurched forward and tore his right arm free of the cocoon.

Distorted shapes darted by, and Garcia froze. When he was sure they were gone, he slowly moved his right hand, scraping his gloved fingers against the film. He dug the glue away from his stomach for fifteen minutes. If he could just get to his switchblade, then he might be able to free himself without being noticed. That was a big *if*, and he had no idea what he would do after. But a small plan was better than having no plan at all.

The high-pitched cry of a Variant broke out somewhere in the distance. The noise echoed, making it nearly impossible to determine how far away the creatures lurked. Thirty seconds later, a tormented human scream followed.

Garcia clenched his jaw and continued peeling back the sticky sludge around his waist. There were more human screams in the minutes that followed, but his focus was only on his switchblade.

You still have air in your lungs, and you still have fight in you.

He had been given a second chance and wasn't going to waste it. His instinct and training had helped him survive after his wife and daughter were killed. Each mission, no matter how big or small, kept him moving. He was a marine, and it was his nature to keep fighting.

The screaming faded away, replaced by the snapping of bones. At first he thought it was the oddly jointed Variants, but the popping seemed to be coming from just one place. Garcia had heard it before. It was the noise the creatures made when they fed—the sound of gristle and ligaments being torn from their prey.

Garcia held in a breath of the putrid scent of his sticky prison cell, wondering if he would be next. He waited there, unmoving, for several minutes. The screeches came and went, each time seemingly closer. He didn't dare move. If the Variants were this close, they would certainly see him digging for his switchblade.

Fuck. Think, Garcia. Think.

He had to do something. He wasn't just going to sit here and wait to die. With exaggerated care, he used his right index finger to pick at the glue.

Another tortured voice rang out. This one seemed familiar.

"You motherfu—"

Steve-o?

Garcia peeled away strip after strip of the glue until

he felt a pocket. He plucked it open and fingered for the knife. As he grabbed the handle, two blurred figures stopped in front of him. His fingers were wrapped around the handle of the switchblade, but he didn't pull the knife. Not yet.

His gut tightened as a hand outside his cocoon reached forward. For a second, he thought he even heard the thing speak. But that couldn't be right.

Garcia tilted his head back to the cold wall as a talon sliced through the outside of the cocoon. He closed one eye, waiting for his opportunity to stab the freak in the jugular. This time he wouldn't miss.

The monster cut a square through the film in front of his face and tore it away. Garcia blinked rapidly in the glow of natural light. Between blinks, he glimpsed the creature that had come to eat him.

Only it wasn't a Variant at all. It was a man, his face filthy with grime and his forehead covered in scabs and open cuts. His right eye was wider than the left, almost bulging from his head. He wore a tattered army uniform that was soiled with dark splotches of crimson and brown.

"That's him, Frankie," the man said.

The second figure leaned in front of Garcia, who now saw that he had his arm around a third man, a soldier in fatigues. It took Garcia a moment to recognize the battered, slumped figure as Steve-o. Garcia tried to say something, but all that came out was a groan. He loosened his grip around the switchblade, studying his rescuers. Frankie, bearded and dressed in a mud-soaked army uniform, hoisted Steve-o farther up.

"Hurry up and get him loose," Frankie said.

The soldier with the face covered in scabs flashed a grin with two missing front teeth. Behind them, the shadows shifted, and a blur of emaciated flesh raced by.

Garcia's heart flipped at the sight of Variants lurking in the shadows. "Quiet," he whispered. "Those things will hear you."

Scabs let out a lunatic laugh. "Wait till you see him."

"See who?"

"The White King."

Garcia wrapped his fingers around the switchblade again, still dazed but finally comprehending. He glanced over at Steve-o, who looked up and caught his eye. Realization set in for both marines—Frankie and Scabs weren't soldiers who had come to rescue them. They weren't there to save them at all. They were taking them to the Variants' leader.

11

Beckham lost track of how many days had passed since the outbreak began, but he certainly hadn't forgotten the Osprey ride that started it all. He could picture Dr. Ellis's nervous yet excited face and the herd of horses running free through a field in North Carolina. It seemed like a long time ago—much longer than the month or so that had gone by.

Now he was on another Osprey, on another mission with limited intel. Working with men he didn't trust was part of being a Delta Force operator. For years he'd operated in Iraq, Afghanistan, and in Africa with foreign soldiers. He never imagined his own military would be responsible for the end of the world.

Kate smiled at him from her seat in the other aisle before turning back to her hushed conversation with Ringgold. Beckham reached down to stroke Apollo's coat.

"When you said 'members of Team Ghost,' I didn't realize that would include a bomb-sniffing dog," General Johnson said from a few seats to Beckham's left.

"Apollo here has become my shadow, sir. He wouldn't have let me go without a fight."

Johnson chuckled. "Is that so? Well, he'll fit right in on the *GW*. We have a whole squad of bomb-sniffing dogs. Some Variant sniffers too."

"Variant sniffers?"

"Dogs trained to locate Variants long before they locate us. From what Captain Humphrey told me, it's partly why the *GW* is still in the water. Before they realized those things could swim, the strike group lost several sailors at the dockyards of Virginia. Now we patrol the decks with dogs. The Variants have excellent olfactory senses, but nothing like a German shepherd's."

Beckham stroked Apollo's coat again. "Sounds like Captain Humphrey succeeded where plenty have failed. Surviving out there this long must have been difficult."

"Resilience, strength, and a bit of luck had something to do with it, I would say," Johnson said. "I'll tell you one thing—the view sure as hell beats what we had at Offutt."

Johnson rested his head on the seat back, and Beckham attempted to relax in his own. He wanted to trust it was over. He wanted to believe in the military he'd sworn his allegiance and life to, but Johnson's connection to Gibson, Kennor, and Wood made that nearly impossible. Johnson seemed like a nice Southern gentleman, but Beckham had known Southern politicians. They were good actors.

As long as the human race still walked the earth, there would be evil men and women in positions of power. But Beckham knew the woman sitting next to Kate wasn't one of them. The future president listened quietly for most of the flight, only chatting with Kate from time to time. Ringgold was skeptical, just like Beckham, and that was good. It was what he liked about her—that and the fact she didn't seem to want to be president. He had always thought anyone who ran for president had to be a little crazy.

The blare of the comm system echoed in the troop hold a few minutes later. "Home plate ETA fifteen minutes," one of the pilots said.

"We should be passing the coast of Georgia," Johnson

said. He twisted to look at Lieutenant Rowe a few seats to his left. "Are the Variant Hunters still in the field?"

"Yes, sir," Rowe answered. "But they haven't checked in for four hours."

Chow and Horn, sitting in the row in front of Beckham, both tilted their heads to listen. Johnson cursed under his breath.

"Not going to lie to you, Master Sergeant," Johnson said. "Your reputation precedes you. I'd heard of Team Ghost long before Fitz put Colonel Wood down. I was hoping you and the Variant Hunters would meet—share some of your secrets, even—but I'm afraid they might have used up their nine lives."

"Variant Hunters?" Beckham asked.

"A Marine Force Recon team. According to Captain Humphrey, they've provided valuable intel on the Variants since day one. Racked up quite the number of kills too. They were on a mission in Atlanta to collect intel on reports of breeding."

"Don't give up on them yet. We've been stuck in the field too," Beckham said. He tried to sound sincere, but deep down he knew they were probably dead. Now he wondered what was running through Chow and Horn's minds. He guessed they were thinking the same thing. Maybe Johnson hadn't agreed to let Team Ghost come with Ringgold just because she'd asked. Perhaps the general had plans for Team Ghost—plans to send them back into the field.

Beckham balled his hand into a fist, released it, and patted Apollo on the head. When he glanced over at Kate, her blue eyes were dull. She must have been thinking the same thing as everyone else. But it felt as if she was still hiding something from him. He just hoped they'd have a chance to talk in private before Johnson gave Team Ghost its orders.

"Prepare for landing," one of the pilots said over the comm.

Lights flicked on above to alert them of their imminent arrival. Beckham broke Kate's gaze and turned to look down the left aisle, past Johnson and Rowe. On the horizon was one of the most beautiful sights he'd seen in a long time: Navy destroyers, cruisers, and even an aircraft carrier coasted over the sapphire water in the glow of the moonlight. The sailors and soldiers down there knew how to fight a war. Beckham wanted to believe they were on his side.

Garcia stepped over the ragged, bloody stump of a human neck. The missing skull was a few feet away. Both eyeballs were gone, and the cheeks, forehead, ears, even the scalp had been ripped clean off the bone. The only thing left was a piece of upper lip.

The ex-soldiers, Frankie and Scabs, were leading Garcia and Steve-o down a tunnel littered with bones, stripped of all but ligaments and gristle. Garcia couldn't believe his eyes. He didn't *want* to believe them. He had never been this deep into one of the Variants' lairs before.

An electrical line snaked overhead, to where a single flickering bulb emitted just enough light to see the slaughterhouse. Garcia had no idea where the electricity was coming from, nor did he care. It looked as if the monsters had moved on from this passage, and so far Garcia only heard their distant echoing shrieks.

He continued through the carnage with Steve-o leaning on him as a crutch. The marine's knees had been injured in the fall, and he couldn't walk on his own. They followed a curve in the tunnel into a darker corridor, leaving the weak glow of light behind.

Garcia caught a drift of the rotting human prisoners

before he saw them. The potent, acidic aroma of their gluelike cocoons filled the air. There was also the rancid stench of decay and infected wounds. Steve-o stumbled, and Garcia tightened his grip on the marine.

"Slow down," Garcia whispered.

Scabs stopped twenty feet ahead and waved his hands at a lightbulb. It clicked on, casting dull light on the shadowy shapes of human prisoners stuck to the walls. The bulbs were motion sensitive, running off battery power, Garcia realized. Most were dead, like the prisoners.

In the darkness beyond, a figure clambered across the ceiling and looked down at a human hand protruding from one of the cocoons.

"Hel-p," mumbled a weak female voice. Scabs bent down and watched the Variant turn to the human prisoner.

Garcia reached for his switchblade. He could easily kill Frankie and Scabs, but what about the Variants? And how would he get Steve-o out? The man could hardly move. Garcia had to wait for the right opportunity to escape. The *perfect* opportunity, when no Variants were around.

The creature hung upside down by its hands and feet. Then it dropped to the ground and ambled up to the female prisoner plastered to the wall.

"No!" the woman pleaded. "Please. Please!"

"We got to do something," Steve-o said.

Scabs turned, a screwdriver in his hand. "Shut the fuck up," he growled.

A guttural, choking sound erupted from the Variant's mouth. It reared back, gagging on something in its throat. Then it lurched forward, a stream of goo projecting from its mouth and covering the woman's loose arm.

The powerful scent of stomach acid and sour fruit filled the tunnel as the creature spewed the white glue. The prisoner's pleas dwindled until they were stifled and faint.

"You bastards," Steve-o said. "Why don't you help—"

Garcia shushed the marine, but it was already too late. The beast angled its head at an unnatural angle that would have broken the neck of a human. Yellow irises homed in on Frankie.

The Variant sniffed the air, let out a low squawk, and lunged to the wall above the woman. It scaled the concrete and leaped to the ceiling, where it hung for several seconds. Frankie and Scabs bowed their heads to the ground as if in shame, but Garcia couldn't look away.

In a swift motion, the Variant dropped to the floor and burst into a gallop toward Frankie. He cowered, raising his hands to shield his face as the monster charged. It slid through the muck and came to a stop inches from the man, splattering his already soiled pants.

Garcia took a step backward, ready to pull Steve-o away, but the creature didn't attack. Instead, it rose on two feet, towered over Frankie, and leaned in until its sucker lips were mere inches from his nose. The beast snorted into the man's face, then smacked its wormy lips together and let out an appalling roar that sent the man backpedaling until he fell on his ass. The Variant retreated, its howls reverberating away as it vanished in the darkness.

Frankie got back to his feet as if nothing had happened. He staggered under the light, his boots slopping through a soup of blood and sewage.

"Come on, and keep your mouths shut," Scabs said, gesturing with his middle finger. "We're almost there."

Garcia wanted to ask the ex-soldiers questions. There was one that was especially itching to get out of his mind. Instead, he hoisted Steve-o up with his right arm and continued forward.

"You doin' okay, Steve-o?"

"I'm okay, Sarge."

"That's right, marine," Garcia whispered. "We're going to get out of here."

Steve-o nodded and let his head sag to his chest. That was good, Garcia thought. That way he didn't have to see the woman prisoner. They passed her a moment later. Her body was covered in the drying glue. She didn't make a sound as Scabs hurried by her. Garcia slowed, but was powerless to help. There was nothing he could do, and that ate at him.

As they worked their way down the corridor, they passed dozens of human prisoners. Dread rose inside of Garcia with every step. He was a marine. He was supposed to help these people. But even if he could fight off his captors and the Variants, he wasn't sure any of these people could be saved. Some were missing limbs. Moving them would be nearly impossible.

Scabs stopped and squatted at the end of the passage next to Frankie, who was perched in the filth like a Variant.

"You two are lucky sons of bitches," Scabs whispered. "Lucky sons of bitches."

Garcia kept silent. Despite his aching head, his senses were on full alert. He used the time to search the shadows for the Variants and for a potential escape route.

Scabs rubbed at his twitching eye and said, "The White King lets us live if we bring him more."

"More meat," Frankie cut in.

"He likes soldiers," Scabs said, pointing to Garcia and then Steve-o. "People who can show him where other survivors are. People who *know* stuff."

Garcia wanted to throw up—and stab Scabs in the neck with his switchblade. The ex-soldier made him sick, but killing him wouldn't do any good. Not yet. Garcia needed to keep his sanity. For now, all that mattered was escaping with Steve-o and getting topside. That was the mission, but judging by Steve-o's slurred words, the marine was injured even worse than Garcia had originally thought.

Garcia brought his left sleeve to his face and wiped the crusted blood off his mustache. He kept it there on the second pass in an attempt to block out the rancid smells.

"The White King lives close. Do not look at him. Do not talk. Maybe he will let you live," Frankie said. "Maybe he will let you serve him as we do."

Garcia kept his mouth shut, giving away nothing. God, how he wanted to ask why Scabs and Frankie had betrayed their uniforms and their country. How long had they been collaborators?

He was reminded of a quote from Luke 6:37. *Judge not, and you will not be judged. Condemn not, and you will not be condemned. Forgive, and you will be forgiven.*

Yeah, right, Garcia thought. He didn't have it in him not to judge or to forgive these men. They should have done what they were trained to do—fight, even if it ended their miserable lives.

"You listenin' to me?" Scabs asked.

"Yeah, you sick fuck," Steve-o moaned, spitting at the man.

Scabs scratched at an open cut on his forehead. He snorted, a cross between a laugh and a whimper. Then he clambered over on all fours, stopping to sit cross-legged in front of Steve-o's face.

"You don't get it, man. You don't get it at *all*. We're not on the top of the food chain anymore. If you don't help, you end up like them." Scabs slowly tilted his head, his wide eyes bulging even farther from his skull as he scanned the human meat locker.

"We'll help you find others," Garcia said. "I know where they are."

"Sarge," Steve-o protested.

"Shut the fuck up and follow orders," Garcia said. He hoped the marine understood what he was doing. But the fall had rattled Steve-o pretty bad. He wasn't sure the man was completely coherent.

Scabs's eyes flitted to Garcia. He scratched at his head again, then picked at a scab on his chin. "What do you think, Frankie?"

Frankie seemed even more mentally fucked than Scabs. He stared ahead vacantly, his rail-thin figure making him look like a skeleton in the dim light.

Scabs poked Steve-o in the ribs with his screwdriver. The marine swiped back with his fingers. That made Scabs chuckle harder, a deep, wet laugh. He pushed himself to his feet.

"You guys have no idea," he repeated, glancing over his shoulder. "They got no idea, Frankie."

"No idea about what?" Garcia asked in a subdued growl.

"Those things aren't what you think they are," Scabs said. "They are *so much* more. The White King tells me things."

This time Garcia couldn't hold back a question. "It talks?"

The grin on the man's scab-covered face vanished, his features transforming in a single heartbeat. Stern and serious, he nodded, first slowly and then more rapidly.

Garcia looked down the tunnel, trying to see into the next passage, but the darkness was impossible to penetrate. His stomach flipped, but he knew he had no other choice. He needed to see if Scabs was lying. The mission had just changed: If those things could really communicate, then that was intel Command needed. A talking Variant was just as important as the Variant offspring. His new objective was identifying this White King and confirming if he could really speak.

"Well, what are you waiting for?" Garcia asked. "Take us to your leader, assholes."

The Osprey landed on the USS *George Washington*, a Nimitz-class aircraft carrier with a runway full of F-18 Super Hornets. Team Ghost stood on the deck, staring out over the waves. It was easy to get lost in the beautiful display of American military muscle, but Beckham wasn't about to let his guard down.

On the port side, two Ticonderoga-class guided-missile cruisers, the USS *Cowpens* and USS *Antietam*, split through the water. The USS *Lassen* and USS *Mustin*, both Arleigh Burke–class guided-missile destroyers, cruised along the starboard side. The USS *Florida*, an Ohio-class cruise-missile submarine, hid somewhere beneath the water. There were two other vessels following the strike group: the USNS *Charles Drew*, a Clark-class dry-cargo ship, and a Pathfinder-class oceanographic survey ship called the USNS *Bowditch*.

General Johnson gave them a moment to relax after the flight, but as soon as the other helicopters had touched down, he wasted no time. An entourage of officers and civilians spilled out onto the deck. Team Ghost and Kate cleared out of the way, watching the events from the sidelines.

Captain Rick Humphrey, a tall man with gleaming white hair and skin weathered by sun and sea, walked quickly over to Secretary of State Ringgold. General Johnson introduced them, then waved at a sharp-looking navy officer with a Bible tucked under his arm.

A few minutes later, under the moonlight, the salty breeze rustling through her hair, Secretary Ringgold stepped up to put her hand on the Bible. The presiding judge told her to repeat after him.

"I do solemnly swear that I will faithfully execute the office of president of the United States, and will to the best of my ability preserve, protect, and defend the Constitution of the United States," Ringgold said.

The first female president of the United States of America didn't smile. She simply lowered her hand from the Bible and shook Johnson's hand.

"You're the forty-sixth president of the United States of America now," he said. "Congratulations. Only one thing left to do to make this official, President Ringgold."

Ringgold folded her arms across her chest, her typical pose.

"Pick a vice president? I've been thinking about that," she replied, "and about what you said back at Plum Island about working together. How would you feel about being vice president as well as head of Central Command? You will continue to lead the war effort, and I'll take over the science side of Operation Extinction, working with Doctor Lovato and coordinating the development of Kryptonite with other labs around the world."

Johnson seemed to be taken aback by the suggestion. He didn't immediately reply. Beckham wasn't sure what to think either. Hell, he wasn't even sure what the protocol for this sort of thing was anymore. Truth was, Beckham hated politics almost as much as he hated the Variants, but he couldn't think of a person more fit to lead than Ringgold. He trusted her, and if she had picked Johnson, she had a damn good reason.

"I suppose I have no choice but to accept," Johnson finally said. He reached out and shook President Ringgold's hand a second time. "I look forward to working with you, Madam President."

The words raised goose bumps on Beckham's skin. He watched history unfold with cautious optimism. Another short ceremony followed, Johnson placing his hand on the Bible and swearing his loyalty to the country. A few minutes later, he was Vice President George Johnson.

There was no inauguration ball or parade that followed, no cheering crowds. After they had finished the short ceremony, Ringgold put her hands on her hips and tilted her head toward the star-filled sky. Beckham had a feeling she was suddenly realizing the overwhelming burden that came with her new position. She was the leader of the free world, or what was left of it.

He thought of Lieutenant Colonel Jensen, wishing he were here to see this. The small beacon of hope the partnership between Ringgold and Johnson represented was exactly what he had given his life for. It was fragile, but it was a start.

As soon as they were in their quarters, Kate hugged Beckham. The gray bulkheads and sparsely furnished space felt safer than any place she'd been since the outbreak started. Best of all, she was with him. For the first time in as long as she could remember, her mind wasn't on science, or bioweapons, or even the Variants. "I thought I was going to lose you again."

"To be honest, I thought I was going to end up in the brig."

Beckham took a seat on the bunk and unlaced his boots. Apollo was already camped out in the corner of the room, his head tucked between his paws and eyes staring upward.

"Thank God for President Ringgold," Kate said.

"She's quite the woman. I have a good feeling about her. My gut says she's just what we need to win this war."

"I just hope it's over," Kate said, letting out a sigh.

"General Johnson does seem kind and intelligent—different from his predecessors. Don't you think?"

Beckham shrugged. "He's a hard man to read." He pulled out Jensen's Colt .45 from his holster and placed it on the table. "Only time will tell who we can trust, but at least we have Chow and Horn here to watch our backs."

Kate sighed again and took a seat next to Beckham. After he had gotten comfortable, she said, "There's something I need to tell you, Reed. Something I've been wanting to tell you for a while."

Beckham turned toward her. He patted the bed between them, motioning her closer. "You know you can trust me, Kate. Whatever it is, we'll deal with it together."

Kate nodded. It wasn't that she didn't trust Beckham. There just hadn't been the right opportunity.

Until now.

Without further thought, she said, "I'm pregnant."

Kate searched Beckham's brown eyes for a reaction. They seemed to brighten, but quickly dulled.

"Say something, Reed."

"I—I don't know what to say," Beckham said. "I mean, I love you, Kate, but holy shit."

"I know," Kate said. "I've been thinking the same thing. What type of world will our child grow up in?"

"Actually, that's not what I'm thinking at all," Beckham said. He scooted closer to Kate. "Please don't misunderstand. This is the greatest gift I could ever have hoped for. I never thought I would be a father or have someone as wonderful as you to share my life with—but that's just it, isn't it?".

Kate's heart sank. She reached out and put her hand on Beckham's. "What? What is it?"

Beckham looked down at the bed. "I'm not sure either of us will survive long enough to see this baby born."

12

The switchblade in Garcia's pocket suddenly seemed like a toothpick. As soon as he heard the hellish discord that only hundreds of snapping joints could make, he began second-guessing his decision to follow Scabs. Maybe he should have tried to escape with Steve-o. Then again, *maybe* was a word that didn't belong in a marine's vocabulary. He swallowed the regret and owned up to his decision. Their mission was clear: Find the White King and get the intel back to Command.

Garcia searched his memory for inspiration as they drew closer to the lair of the White King. He was doing his best to stay frosty, but the decay, the rot, and the sight of the human traitors had overwhelmed him with anger.

Deliver me, my God, from the hand of the wicked, from the grasp of those who are evil and cruel.

Garcia had never believed God intervened or picked one side over another in war. Not until the monsters came. Trudging through these horrific tunnels reinforced his sense that the Variants were the work of the devil. God was with the marines, and knowing that gave Garcia the strength he needed to continue.

"You doin' okay, Steve-o?" Garcia whispered.

His compatriot managed a weak nod.

"Good. Keep your mouth shut when we get there, and don't look any of the freaks in the eye."

Another nod.

A draft of the overwhelming scent of rotting fruit, stomach acid, and decaying flesh filled Garcia's nostrils. It burned its way up into his broken nose, lingering in his sinuses. He had to stop and cover his face with a sleeve.

Scabs and Frankie paused a few feet ahead. They stood at the edge of a tunnel that emptied into a long and vaulted chamber. Water spilled over the side, cascading into a pool twenty feet below. Scabs threw a glance over his shoulder every few seconds, as if he was expecting Garcia to push him into the abyss. But Garcia was too busy staring at the abomination below. A wave of misshapen bodies that had once been men and women rippled over the concrete next to the water.

At first, Garcia thought they were breeding, but in the rays of moonlight streaming through storm drains somewhere far above, he saw they were just slowly slithering against one another—so slowly it was hard to see what they were doing. His eyes gradually adjusted to the dim lighting in the cold chamber, and he saw the creatures were actually sleeping, keeping close to share body heat.

"Down there," Frankie whispered.

Garcia followed his finger to a raised concrete platform in the center of the vaulted room. There, sitting with legs dangled over the side, was a Variant paler than any Garcia had ever seen. His flesh seemed to glow in the ghostly light. At the foot of the platform rested dozens of tiny armored lumps with curved skulls. Unlike the other Variants, the juveniles slept alone, their scaly flesh insulating them from the cold.

"That's him. That's the White King," Scabs whispered excitedly. "Follow me."

They took a right into another tunnel that wound

down to the bottom of the chamber. Carefully and quietly, the two men led Garcia and Steve-o around the ocean of sleeping creatures until they were a hundred feet from the platform. Normally, the sight would have driven fear deep into Garcia, but this mission and his own curiosity pushed him on. Frankie and Scabs knelt then, bowing their heads to the ground as if they were about to worship at Sunday mass.

The pallid beast slowly rose to his feet, skin stretching like a wrinkled white blanket. His jointed arms folded oddly at his sides, snapping as he tried to straighten. The creature was lean, with bony appendages and square chest muscles. At first, the White King didn't look all that different from the other Variants, but the darkness was deceiving.

As soon as the beast stepped into a ray of light, Garcia saw a wizened torso laced with bloated veins under transparent skin. This Alpha had white eyeballs with milky irises. Garcia tried to look away, remembering Scabs's warning, but he realized it didn't matter. The Variant was blind. Maybe Scabs was completely mad after all.

But the closer Garcia moved, the more he felt the sense he was being watched. A chill spiked up his aching back as the beast's creamy eyes followed his movements. He lowered his gaze to the wet ground, breathing faster, his heart kicking. Perhaps Scabs wasn't lying after all, and the Variant *could* see them. After all the adaptations Garcia had seen in the other creatures, he shouldn't have ruled anything out.

He helped Steve-o forward, stopping a few feet behind Scabs. Garcia slowly glanced up again just as the monster's jaw dropped open, unleashing a tormented shriek that hurt Garcia's ears. He dropped to his knees, and Steve-o crashed into him.

Scabs cupped his hands over his ears and glared back as if to say, *What did you do?*

Garcia looked down at his belt, resisting the urge to reach for his switchblade. Joints cracked in the distance, and a pair of feet thunked on the wet ground. He lowered his head, panting and petrified. Steve-o collapsed belly first on the concrete.

The juvenile Variants and the army behind them woke from their slumber, and in a matter of seconds the entire chamber came to life in a chorus of dreadful shrieking that ebbed and flowed into a noise louder than an air-raid siren.

Garcia closed his eyes, trying to pull up a memory of his wife and daughter, but no matter how hard he tried to picture their faces, all he saw were the grotesque images of his girls transformed into monsters. His eyelids jolted open. Pale calves and feet were standing between Scabs and himself. Garcia forced his eyes from the beast's gaze. He waited to be torn limb from limb, but seconds later a raspy, guttural voice boomed.

"*Si lence!*"

The word, if he could call it that, was nearly indecipherable. It echoed through the chamber, repeating over and over, until Garcia and every Variant in the room understood. Beast and human alike fell quiet.

The White King roared again, this time nothing more than a raucous howl. He squatted to sniff Garcia, then Steve-o, and then Garcia again. Specks of saliva burst from his mouth, peppering Garcia's forehead and dripping into his eye.

Besides the creature that broke his nose, this was the closest Garcia had ever been to a Variant. He involuntarily blinked the burning spit from his eye.

A coarse crackling noise rose from the White King's throat, as if he was trying to speak through atrophied vocal cords. The beast choked on his second attempt, a sheet of slobber hitting Garcia's forehead. He coughed and cleared his throat. A strangled word broke from his mouth.

"*You.*"

Garcia remained silent, trying not to move.

"*You,*" the White King repeated, rasping again. He leaned to Garcia's right side, his face next to the marine's cheek. The grotesque smacking of his lips sounded next to Garcia's ear.

He flinched as the creature hissed in a strained whisper. "Ssserve and live. Runnnn…" His voice trailed off as he slithered away, and then suddenly the White King stood and shrieked. "*Run, and die!*"

With deliberate care, Garcia slowly raised his gaze to see the beast grab Steve-o's flak jacket with a horned claw and drag him away.

"No!" Garcia shouted, unable to contain his rage.

"Sarge!" Steve-o thrashed at the beast, swatting it with sluggish blows.

Frankie and Scabs kept their heads bowed. One of them was laughing. Shaking with anger, Garcia balled his hands and rose, watching in horror as the White King hoisted Steve-o onto the platform. The juvenile Variants were hissing now. Circling the raised concrete, their armored heads tilted to watch Steve-o crawl away from the White King. The beast ambled alongside him, naked flesh glowing in the moonlight streaming from above.

"Don't kill him," Garcia said, trying to keep his voice low. "I'll do as you say. I'll find others."

The White King stopped midstroll, twisting halfway around to glare back at Garcia with his milky eyes. He avoided the creature's gaze by lowering his head. Just as he was about to beg for Steve-o's life, there was an excruciating tearing sound and a scream of agony. Garcia's eyes flitted upward as a limb sailed through the air and landed with a thud in front of the juveniles. They hissed with delight, their miniature clawed hands reaching up into the geyser of blood gushing from the riven hole where Steve-o's right arm had been. The marine squirmed on the concrete, howling at the top of his lungs, his left hand flailing to stop the spray coming from the frayed flesh.

Garcia was moving then, running toward the platform. Something barreled into him from the side before he made it ten feet. He crashed to the floor, his eyes still on Steve-o as two female Variants pinned him down. The White King crouched next to the marine, studying the squirting stump. A wet cough broke from his lips, and a lump rose through his neck until he gagged and puked out a stream of white goo on Steve-o's arm. Steve-o was still writhing on the ground, but his cries dwindled into a whimper.

In a matter of seconds, the liquid solidified over the open wound. Now Garcia knew how the other human prisoners had survived for so long with missing limbs. The cocoons, or whatever the hell they were, looked to be made of the same material. It cauterized Steve-o's injury, prolonging his life so his flesh remained fresh. It was the Variants' version of refrigeration.

The White King rose to his feet and pointed at Scabs and Frankie. "*Take him!*" he growled, in a voice that almost sounded human.

Both collaborators backed away, heads still bowed. They worked their way over to Garcia, and the weight of the female Variants fell off him. He felt Frankie and Scabs lift him to his feet and pull him away.

"Bring more." A cough. "Else we eat him," the creature hissed, extending a claw toward Steve-o.

The other Variants formed a phalanx around the three men. Scabs and Frankie pushed Garcia forward, and slowly the beasts scattered to make an opening. Garcia tuned out the sounds of the shrieking monsters and ignored the swipe of talons that came within a foot of striking him.

Halfway out of the chamber, a pair of creatures crashed to the floor in front of Frankie and Scabs. The beasts skidded and tumbled from the force of whatever had shoved them from the line. The brawny frame of a Variant staggered into the opening to block the way out. Crusted blood caked the outside of a wound Garcia recognized. This was the same Alpha that had broken his nose. And judging by his snarling maw, he wanted revenge.

Frankie and Scabs froze. The creature cracked his neck from side to side and dropped to all fours. His jointed arms and legs snapped as he arched his back and prepared to strike.

The two collaborators staggered backward, pulling Garcia with them. But where there should have been fear in his heart, he felt nothing but hatred.

The room erupted with a chorus of excited shrieks, the other monsters watching as if it were a game. Scabs and Frankie loosened their grips under Garcia's armpits and backed away, perhaps realizing the monster wasn't there for them. But Garcia held his ground, his eyes locked on the Variant. When the beast charged, Garcia didn't so much as flinch.

The beast galloped toward him, long limbs pounding the ground. In a matter of seconds, he narrowed the gap between them, and still Garcia did not retreat. Instead, he reached for his switchblade. Joints cracked as the Alpha lunged toward him, horned claws extended for his throat. Just as Garcia was about to draw his knife, a blur of white flashed so close to him that he felt the rush of air. A beat later a sickening thud echoed through the space, and a screech of anguish followed. The White King stood on two feet, claws wrapped around the bleeding neck of the Alpha that had charged Garcia. What the White King lacked in size, he made up for in speed.

Behind them, a trio of muscular Variants emerged from the line. The White King twisted, shrieking at the three other beasts. They clambered forward, snarling.

The White King tightened his claws around the injured Variant's neck, digging a talon into the bullet hole. The monster howled, fresh crimson blooming around the wound. In a swift motion, the White King brought his other hand up and snapped the monster's neck. The body slumped to the ground, and silence immediately washed over the room. All three of the snarling beasts slowly backed away, vanishing into the army of diseased flesh, their pack leader limp and dead.

The White King let out a commanding roar, and the wall of monsters opened once again. Frankie and Scabs wasted no time. They grabbed Garcia under the armpits and dragged him forward.

As Garcia left the chamber, his mind kept coming back to that first word he'd heard the monster Variant speak. This White King had controlled every other monster in the chamber by verbal communication. Even more striking was the fact he was using Steve-o as collateral to ensure Garcia brought back more food. Somehow, this beast had retained a level of intellect that surpassed that of all Variants Garcia had seen. The freaks were getting smarter, and that terrified him more than the thought of being torn apart or even losing another man. Because, in the end, the evolution he witnessed meant more marines were going to die.

"The White King shows you mercy," Scabs said.

Garcia ignored the man, his thoughts having shifted back to the mission. Nothing else had ever been this important. He needed to get this intel back to Command and then return to save Steve-o. But first, Garcia had unfinished business to take care of. He reached for his switchblade and let his body go limp as Scabs and Frankie dragged him out of the chamber.

Two of the men General Johnson had left behind at Plum Island were assigned Tower 4 that night. Fitz would have been lying if he said he was disappointed. He hadn't slept more than three hours straight for days. The comfort of a bed and pillow sounded heavenly. Sometimes it was the simple moments, like a warm shower after a cold patrol or a taste of his favorite food, that made everything worthwhile. Tonight, it was the fleeting moment of safety that General Johnson's men provided the island.

Fitz grinned when he thought about what Chow said. *Maybe whoever is in charge will send some pogues to arrest us.*

These guys weren't pogues. Not by a long shot.

They were everywhere. Patrols combed the shoreline and woods. The towers were full, and two choppers with searchlights circled overhead.

Not five minutes after removing his blades and crashing onto his bunk, Fitz felt the veil of fatigue sweep over him. But the peaceful slumber he hoped for never came. Instead, he was propelled into a dream he knew all too well.

Fitz rode in a Humvee with his squad. Ralphie, Tang, and Jerrod were discussing their sexual experiences, each trying to top the other with their stories. It was a common conversation that Fitz never took part in. The other guys didn't seem to notice his silence. He watched the tan shanties and dilapidated buildings outside race by in silence. From all around him, Fitz breathed in the overwhelming scent of body odor. And he couldn't lift his hand to swat at a buzzing fly. He wanted to shoo it out the window, but his hand wouldn't move.

A group of Iraqi children carrying books under their arms ran down the side of a dusty road as Ralphie followed the convoy of five military vehicles onto the highway. Once they were out on the open road, with sand dunes blurring by, Fitz started to relax. He pushed his sunglasses back into position and followed the paths of two Apache helicopters racing across the sky.

The other guys were quiet for a few minutes before they started arguing about who got to play *Call of Duty* when they got back. Fitz heard their voices and saw their faces perfectly. His waking memories were never this clear. It was calming for a moment even though Fitz knew what came next.

When the fly landed on Fitz's cheek, the panic of the nightmare swept back over him. He willed it to stop, begging his mind to release him.

Tang looked in the rearview mirror just as the blast hit the truck. An explosion rocked the vehicle, the concussion barreling into them from the right side. They were rolling across the road. The roadside bomb was packed with nails and hunks of jagged metal that punched through the truck's light armor. A shard sliced right through Fitz's right leg, severing it just above the knee. He never saw what hit his left leg.

Upside down, the stumps squirted blood that smelled like battery acid. The steaming liquid drenched his uniform in seconds, and his entire body went numb. The last thing he saw was Tang's face stuck to the back seat.

The mask of flesh had been charcoaled by the heat of the blast.

Fitz awoke gasping for air in the barracks at Plum Island. A Ranger sleeping across the way stirred in his bed, glanced over at Fitz, then rolled on his side. Finally released from the nightmare, he looked down at his missing legs. For a second, phantom pain hit his body.

He calmed his breathing, repeating the words that got him through these episodes.

You're fine, Marine. You can still fight. Nothing can take that away from you.

The dreams were always so vivid, but when he was awake, he couldn't picture the faces of the brothers he'd lost, couldn't hear their voices. The doctors had told him that PTSD could do that sometimes, the memories cauterized like wounds in his mind.

Filled with anxiety, Fitz swung his stumps over the side of the bed and reached down for his blades. He had crashed onto his bed with the hope of a good night's rest, but instead had been propelled back to one of the worst days of his life.

He abandoned the idea of sleep, knowing it wouldn't come anytime soon now. He grabbed his MK11 even though he didn't have a tower assignment. He was sure that he could still put the gun to good use somewhere on the island. After securing his blades, Fitz walked to the door, sighed, and stumbled out into the night with his rifle in hand.

Meg was worried about Riley. Over the past few days she'd seen his anger sparking out of control, during target practice and again in mouthing off to General Johnson. Now that the rest of Team Ghost had departed, she was concerned he was going to pick a fight. He certainly seemed to be itching for one. And after his attempt to remove his casts, she feared he was also losing his sanity.

Meg had grown to care deeply for him. He was her best friend on Plum Island, one of her only friends left in the world. There was no denying the way he looked at her, or the way she felt when she was with him. She considered letting those feelings develop, but she was still grieving over the loss of her husband. Friends they were, and just friends they would remain for now, no matter how cute his shit-eating grin and blue eyes were.

It was almost midnight, and Meg studied the stars from the sidewalk outside Building 5. Riley slowly pushed his chair down the path while she crutched beside him. Her arms were tired and her legs hurt, but she wanted to make sure he was okay. He hadn't said much since the rest of his team had left.

When she was about to say good night, the click of metal sounded from nearby. The sound was a familiar one. She didn't need to turn to see Fitz walking toward them.

"I thought you were going to bed," Riley said, his voice a bit more chipper.

"Couldn't sleep," Fitz replied. "What are you two doing up?" He strode through the glow cast by a spotlight, his face pale and haggard.

"Enjoying the night," she replied.

"Wishing I was out there," Riley said.

Fitz tucked his fingers between the sling of his rifle and his chest. He looked skyward and then away. The beauty of the stars didn't affect him. Meg had seen the look before: He was searching for something. Both soldiers beside her were dealing with the guilt and trauma of surviving the apocalypse, and Meg realized she was too.

"I'm going to call it a night," she said.

Riley glanced up. "You sure?"

"Yeah. I'm tired." She hesitated for a moment. "You going to be okay out here?"

"Yeah, Mom. I'm good. Do you want me to 'walk' you back to your room?"

Meg smiled at that. "I'll be fine."

"Good night," Riley said.

"Night," Fitz said, tipping his head slightly.

She left them there to chat about whatever it was soldiers talked about at this hour. The sidewalk back to Building 1 was empty, and she enjoyed the brief moment of solitude. It lasted a full minute before a patrol of marines she hadn't seen before came bursting from a path that led from the beach.

"Out of the way, ma'am!" one of the men shouted.

She crutched to her left just as the men bolted past her.

"What's going on?" Riley shouted.

One of the marines said something to him that Meg couldn't hear. Fitz unslung his MK11 and followed the group, blades clicking against the concrete.

The panic in Meg's gut returned. She hopped after Riley, who was already wheeling after Fitz and the patrol. It took a few minutes to catch up with him, but when she did, he said, "Get back to your building."

"Why? What's going on now?"

"Tower Ten spotted a boat."

"What kind of a boat?"

"I don't know," Riley snapped.

Meg stopped midstride, and Riley slowed to throw a glance over his shoulder.

"I'm sorry," he said. Then he jerked his head. "Come on."

A few minutes later they were at the edge of a ridgeline. Fitz was scoping the water, and the marines were setting up a perimeter behind the electric fences.

"You see anything, Fitz?" Riley asked.

The growl of an engine sounded in the distance. An outline of a cigar-shaped speedboat shot over the waves. It was fast, but no match for the Black Hawk on patrol. The chopper raced after it, and the spotlight hit the side of the vessel a moment later.

"Survivors?" Meg asked.

Fitz lowered his rifle and nodded. "Same guys I saw before."

"Will Major Smith take them in?" Meg asked.

Riley snorted. "I wouldn't. They're probably bandits looking for a place to claim as their own." The chatter of voices came from the beach. The marines who ran past her earlier were trekking over the sand. They climbed the ridgeline and passed Fitz.

"You know what's going on?" he asked one of them.

All but one of the men continued walking. The last marine, a man no older than twenty, stopped and nudged his helmet farther up onto his head. He turned to watch the Black Hawk circle. Pushing his finger against his earpiece, he said, "Sounds like whoever it was, they didn't want to stop. Command ordered Echo Four back to base."

"Let's move, Dillon!" another marine yelled out.

The young man nodded at Fitz and took off after his squad, leaving Meg alone with Fitz and Riley once again. This time Fitz stared at the thousands of lambent stars, searching for whatever it was he had lost. And Meg, swept up in the moment, did the exact same thing.

13

The sporadic drip of water pecked at the blood and grime smattered across Garcia's face. He stumbled after Scabs and Frankie into the dark curving tunnels, his sleeve covering his nostrils. Somewhere behind them in the pitch black, a pack of Variants followed.

Insurance, Garcia thought. And more evidence the White King had retained or developed an unprecedented level of intelligence. First they started breeding, and now this?

Scabs seemed to ignore the click-clack of joints and scratch of talons over the concrete. Perhaps he was used to it by now, or perhaps he was more focused on Garcia. He continued asking questions, his tone becoming more irritated each time Garcia didn't answer.

"Where's your base?" Scabs grumbled. "Where are the rest of your buddies?"

Garcia kicked at a human rib cage, the echoing rattle of bones interrupting Scabs. Garcia continued on, pretending he hadn't heard Scabs over the clatter. The distraction didn't work.

"I asked ya a question," Scabs said. He stopped a few feet ahead. "Where are your buddies? Wasn't just the two of you out there, was it?"

And I will execute great vengeance upon them with furious rebukes; and they shall know that I am the Lord, when I shall lay my vengeance upon them.

Garcia clenched his fist, hoping the bastard didn't see it in the dim light. "Dead," he finally said. "But there are survivors not far from here. We passed them on the way in."

Scabs picked at his chin. "Any soldiers?"

Shaking his head, Garcia said, "Not that I saw. Our mission was recon, not rescue."

"Good," Scabs said, peeling away a ripe scab. Pus leaked from the wound, dripping down his chin and dropping to the muck at their feet. He pulled his screwdriver from his waistband and poked at Garcia's chest. "Don't get any ideas topside. Got it?"

Garcia scrutinized the tip of the screwdriver, imagining driving it through Scabs's neck.

"Got it?" Scabs asked a second time, poking Garcia harder.

Garcia simply nodded and staggered after Frankie. They worked their way through the passages until the reek of the Variants and human prisoners had faded to a tolerable stench. Ten minutes later they reached the spot where Garcia and Steve-o had been ambushed. Garcia's helmet was still there, resting in a puddle of rancid water. He scooped it up as he passed, relieved to find the picture of his family and praying the headset still worked.

"The fuck you doin'?" Scabs asked. He grabbed at the helmet, but Garcia yanked it from his reach.

"Got a picture of my wife and baby in here," Garcia said, turning the helmet upside down for Scabs to see. "I'm bringing it with."

The anger in his voice seemed to deter Scabs. A flicker of what might have been empathy sparked in Scabs's twitching eyes. It vanished in a blink. He spat in the water and then said, "Fine."

Garcia slipped the helmet on, buckling the strap. The earpiece hung loosely, but he didn't dare reposition the mini-mic to his lips. He wasn't sure how much time had passed since his capture. It wasn't likely, but Tank and Thomas could still be out there.

Frankie stopped under a ladder. He grabbed at a rung and climbed without uttering a word. Scabs motioned for Garcia to go next. The Variants were still lurking in the darkness behind them, waiting and watching. It felt odd not to be running from the monsters.

Overhead, Frankie pushed the manhole cover onto the street and pulled himself up. The sky grew darker as he leaned down and extended a hand to Garcia. The motion took the marine off guard. He would never accept help from these shitbags.

Anxious to get out of the putrid tunnel, Garcia ignored Frankie's hand and quickly climbed up the final rungs of the ladder. A gust of wind bit into his dank fatigues as soon as he was above ground. He shivered in the cool night and drew in a sharp breath, filling his lungs with clean, sweet air.

"Let's go," Scabs said.

The screeches of the monsters prowling Atlanta rose and fell. Garcia hustled down the residential street, his mind multitasking as he looked for the Variants and a street sign. He was moving so fast he quickly put fifty feet between him and the other men. They were on Martin Street SE, the same road as the church Tank and Thomas had holed up in the day before. That meant he was close to Phoenix II Park.

"Hey, wait," Scabs said.

Garcia increased his pace and hustled up a sloped lawn of wet grass. He rounded a house, memorizing the number as he passed. Momentarily out of sight, he reached up and pushed his earpiece in, then flicked his mini-mic to his lips.

"Hotel Three, do you copy? It's Garcia."

Static hissed in his ear.

"I said, wait up," Scabs said.

"Okay," Garcia replied. Lowering his voice he said, "Hotel Three, do you copy?"

More white noise crackled out of the earpiece. Then a voice.

"Sarge, holy shit. Where the fuck are you guys?"

Garcia could hardly believe his ears. Tank and Thomas were still out there.

"Just passed Eight-Eleven Martin Street. Being pursued by Variants," Garcia replied. "Repeat, hostiles in pursuit." He turned off the mic and pushed it out of view just as Scabs came running around the house. The man hunched over, hands on his knees, panting.

"I said *wait*!"

"Sorry," Garcia said. "I didn't realize you were so slow."

Scabs narrowed his bulging eyes, his nostrils flaring. He sucked in several deep breaths. "Stay—" A gasp. "Stay in sight."

Garcia turned back the way he had come.

"Where the hell are you going now?" Scabs asked.

"Thought I was taking a shortcut, but didn't realize there was a fence back there," Garcia replied, still walking. He heard boots hitting the concrete driveway, Scabs and Frankie hurrying to keep up this time.

The Variants that had followed them through the tunnels were emerging from the manhole now. They scattered under the moonlight. Some clambered across the street, their jointed arms and legs sounding like the snapping of twigs. Garcia counted more than a dozen of the beasts. More were still slithering out of the hole as he turned back to the south.

"Hold up," Scabs said. He jogged to catch up and

grabbed Garcia's wrist. He had his screwdriver drawn again. "You fucking with me, man?"

Garcia shook his head. "Trying to get my bearings." He looked to the east, pretending to search the rooftops. "Yeah, now I remember. The survivors are holed up in a church not far from here. Come on, maybe we can reach them before those things give in to their hunger and have us for a snack."

Scabs drove his fingernails into Garcia's flesh. "Get moving."

Garcia pushed on at a slow pace, keeping his strides short now. His eyes roved back and forth, searching for any sign of his men, although he knew he wouldn't be able to see them. If they were close, they were watching him. Tank would be analyzing and forming a plan. He wondered what would go through Tank's head when he saw the Variants following Garcia, Scabs, and Frankie without attacking.

The farther Garcia walked, the more nervous he became. He stopped at an abandoned car and peered through the window.

"What you doin'?" Scabs asked.

"I need water, man."

"Fuck that. Keep moving," Scabs said. He let out a chuckle and said something under his breath that Garcia only caught the tail end of, but it sounded like *little pussy*. God, it was going to feel good driving his knife into the man's throat.

The popping of jointed appendages snapped him from the fantasy. The Variants were moving in the shadows of the houses behind them. Some climbed onto roofs, watching his every action like gargoyles. In the sky to the east, low storm clouds rolled over Atlanta, blocking the glow of the moon. Darkness stretched across the landscape.

A howl sounded in the distance, halting Scabs and Frankie midstride. They both scanned the street, the sudden noise prompting fear in both men.

"What is it?" Garcia whispered.

Another shriek answered the first.

Frankie's eyes widened with panic. "Others," he whispered.

"Beasts," Scabs said. "A rival group. Hunting. Usually they don't come this far."

A cloud of fatigue clamped down on Garcia, and it took him a bit longer than it should have to understand. Exposed and in the open, he hunched next to the closest car and gestured for the men to do the same.

"They've never come this far," Scabs whispered. "They fear the White King."

He continued talking to himself, but Garcia was hardly paying attention. In the brief pause between shrieks, there was another sound. Faint but sharp, the whistle sent a wave of adrenaline through Garcia. He scrambled on all fours to the bumper of the car and looked south just as the head of a Variant exploded on a rooftop. The body slumped over the side of the chimney and slid down the roof, leaving a wake of gore.

Unheard and unseen, the Variant Hunters were doing what they did best. He wondered how many Variants had made no sound at all as the 5.56-millimeter rounds ended their miserable lives.

"Is that fucking gunfire?" Scabs whispered.

Still on his knees, Garcia reached for his switchblade and pulled it from his pocket, using his body to shield the motion from Scabs. He clicked the button and the blade popped out just as a dreadful howl filled the night. His heart was thumping, filled with adrenaline.

Another torrent of suppressed shots streaked down the street.

Scabs looked over the hood of the car. "What the hell is that sound?"

Clenching his hand around the knife, Garcia gritted his teeth and said, "Death."

When he spun to stick the man, Scabs was already holding his neck, his face hidden in Frankie's shadow. Garbled, choking sounds broke from Scabs's lips.

"Die, you fuck," Frankie whispered, his wild eyes flitting from Scabs to the bloody screwdriver he held in his hands.

Crimson streamed between Scabs's fingers, running down his wrists and soiling his chest. He fell to his back, legs kicking, as he choked on his own blood.

The whistle of suppressed gunfire continued. Frankie dropped the screwdriver to the ground. It clanked on the concrete next to Scabs's body. He glared at Garcia and said, "Those your men?"

Shocked but comprehending, Garcia nodded.

Frankie had suddenly transformed back into a soldier. Had he been playing along all this time? Waiting for an opportunity to strike and escape, just like Garcia?

"Get out of here," Frankie said.

"I can't leave without Steve-o."

Frankie grunted. "The marine we left down there? He's already dead. From the moment we left the lair."

"No," Garcia whispered. "But—"

"But what? You think those fucking things have any sense of honor? Fuck, man, the White King is no more trustworthy than this piece of shit." Frankie looked back at Scabs before turning to the Variants advancing toward the car. "I'm sorry, but your friend is dead. And you will be too, if you don't run. Come on," he said, shooing Garcia away with a hand. "Get out of here while you still can."

Scabs writhed on the ground, still fighting for life.

Garcia wasn't even slightly bothered by the satisfaction he felt at the sight.

"What about you?" Garcia asked.

"I'll distract the others." Frankie paused, his eyes unfocusing into a vacant stare. "I don't deserve to leave this city." There was regret in his voice, and Garcia suspected it wasn't because of what he was about to do but because of what he had already done.

Five more shots whizzed over the street, and five more Variants crashed to the ground.

Garcia held Frankie's gaze for a single moment, then looked at Scabs one last time. His breaths were shallow and short. He wouldn't live much longer. Garcia prayed the Variants got to him before he took his last gasp.

"I said, *go!*" Frankie shouted.

Garcia didn't hesitate a second more. He jumped to his feet and ran toward the sound of gunfire. He was finally leaving Atlanta, but he was leaving without Steve-o. The cross on his arm would now be complete. The Variant Hunters had lost another member, but Steve-o's death hadn't been for nothing. The intel Garcia carried in his camera and his brain was about to change everything Central Command thought they knew about the monsters.

The pounding on the hatch came at 0400, but Beckham wasn't sleeping. He wasn't sure he'd slept at all since Kate told him he was going to be a father. The hammering on steel echoed his already racing heart.

"Who's that?" Kate mumbled groggily. "I don't know who it is, but they better have a damn good reason for waking you up. Go back to sleep, sweetheart."

Apollo sat up, growling at the hatch.

"It's okay, boy," Beckham said. He patted the dog's coat on his way across the small quarters.

"Beckham, open up," Chow said from the passage outside.

Beckham walked over to the hatch and pushed it open.

"Hey," Chow said. He crossed his arms and squinted at the darkness. Horn was standing with his back to the bulkhead, still half asleep.

"What's wrong?" Beckham asked.

"Lieutenant Davis wants us to report to Command, ASAP," Chow said.

"What for?" Beckham hadn't met Davis yet and wondered why she would wake them at this hour.

"Didn't say."

Beckham pivoted back into the room and walked to the bed. "Got to go, Kate. I'll be back in a bit." He leaned down and kissed her on the cheek.

She sat up and reached for him. "What's wrong? Where are you going?"

"To the bridge."

"Should I come?" She looked into the passage.

"No, you need to get your rest." He kissed her on the lips, then joined his men outside.

Horn and Chow waved at Kate. Beckham went to close the hatch behind him, but Apollo tried to sneak out. "You've got to stay too, boy. Keep an eye on the lady."

Letting out a low whine, Apollo sat on his hind legs, and Beckham shut the hatch.

The Delta operators walked through the carrier in silence. Beckham desperately wanted to tell Horn and Chow the news, but this wasn't the place or the time. Five minutes later, they entered the carrier's command center, formally called the bridge. Despite the hour, the space was a beehive of activity, and the officers on duty watched their screens like hawks stalking prey. A lean woman with short, cropped hair, cool blue eyes, and a sharp jawline met them at the entrance.

"I'm Lieutenant Rachel Davis," she said. "We're about to get started."

Beckham followed her into a small room with a table covered with maps. It was a standing-room-only crowd. At the head of the table was Vice President Johnson. To his right were Lieutenant Rowe and Captain Humphrey.

Unaware of Team Ghost's presence, Johnson continued studying a map as Humphrey pointed at several locations. Beckham used the moment to scan the crowded room. Most present were officers and subordinate commanders, but there were four bearded Navy SEALs and three marines, who, like Team Ghost, looked out of place. The marines had on fresh fatigues, but the grime and hard looks they wore indicated they had just gotten back from the field.

One of the men stood out more than the others. The marine sported a thick mustache, sharp brown eyes, and a freshly broken nose. He was flanked by a buff, dark-skinned man on his right and a marine with olive skin and a mustache on his left. Typically, enlisted personnel weren't invited to an ad hoc mission briefing, but normal protocol had gone out the door long before they'd lost Operation Liberty. The odd assembly of men at that hour could mean only one thing: There had been a major development on the battlefield, and the soldiers in this room would be dealing with the aftermath.

Lieutenant Davis shut the hatch, sealing the room. The murmurings among the soldiers dwindled, and every back in the room straightened. Beckham pushed thoughts of Kate and everything else out of his mind, preparing himself for whatever had prompted the early-morning meeting.

Johnson spoke abruptly. "Listen up, everyone: This briefing is top secret. Nothing leaves this space. Got it?"

He didn't wait for a response. Instead, he regarded the marine with the broken nose. "At 0100 hours, Staff Sergeant Garcia and his recon team returned from a two-day stint in Atlanta. Long story short, they discovered something significant."

The weight of the words was amplified by Johnson's urgent tone. His friendly demeanor from Plum Island was completely gone. Vice President Johnson was all soldier now.

"As many of you know, there have been reports trickling in from around the world about the development of the Variants, from breeding ability to"—Johnson paused to search for the right word—"communication."

Beckham fidgeted as he flashed back to the Variants Team Ghost had encountered in battle over the past five weeks. There was the beast at Fort Bragg that had seemed to be leading the ambush, and there were the monsters in New York that had displayed higher intelligence. He wanted to ask why Kate hadn't been invited to the meeting, given the subject. The military was well represented in the room, but where were the scientists?

"In this case, video speaks louder than any words, but first I'll let Sergeant Garcia brief you all," Johnson said. He offered a short nod to the marine with the broken nose.

Garcia grimaced as he leaned slightly and shifted his weight. Apparently his broken nose wasn't the only injury he had sustained in Atlanta.

"As Vice President Johnson mentioned, my team returned from Atlanta at 0100. We were there to recon breeding habits of the Variants. Following intel, we set up position at Turner Field. This is what we saw."

Davis shut off the lights, and every face in the room shifted to the bulkhead with the wall-mounted screen. An aerial video of Turner Field emerged. On-screen, there was a blur of motion behind home plate. Hundreds of Variants streamed out of the concourses. A few minutes later, a human survivor crawled across the overgrown grass toward the pitcher's mound. Several smaller Variants circled the man. There was nothing overly disturbing about the video—nothing Beckham hadn't seen already.

"What are we looking at, Sergeant?" Johnson asked.

Garcia ran a finger over his mustache, back and forth. In a matter-of-fact tone voice, he said, "The next phase of the Variants' evolution, sir."

This time Beckham raised a brow. He squinted, trying to get a better view of the video, but Garcia's camera had been too far out to see much.

"Those little ones aren't what they look like," Garcia said. "They aren't human kids turned into monsters. They are monsters *born* from monsters."

Beckham's heart flipped in his chest. Kate had mentioned the creatures were breeding, but this was the first time he had seen one of the juveniles.

"The offspring are born with scaly skin, which seems to develop into some sort of armor. I'm not sure how strong it is. We didn't get a chance to shoot any of 'em."

There was a single grim chuckle in the room. Garcia continued without giving the man a second of his attention. "As you can see, the Variant on the pitcher's mound seemed to be teaching the things how to hunt."

"Which means they're going to be just as dangerous, if not more dangerous, than the adults," Johnson cut in. "Another reason to deploy Kryptonite as quickly as possible."

"There's something else, sir."

Johnson nodded, signaling for Garcia to continue the briefing.

"After escaping the stadium, Corporal Steve Holmes and I took refuge in a sewer. Our position was compromised, and we were captured and brought to a lair by two human collaborators.

"There we encountered a Variant the collaborators referred to as the White King. It appeared to be blind, but that wasn't the case. What I'm about to tell you is going to sound crazy." Garcia paused again. "I honestly wondered if it was real at the time. But it happened."

There was a moment of silence that lingered long enough to be uncomfortable.

"The White King spoke to me. It wanted"—he corrected himself—"it *ordered* me to show the two collaborators where other survivors were."

"Bullshit," said a Navy SEAL in the back of the room. "Those things can't speak. I've been out there. I know."

"It's not a lie," Garcia snapped. "That thing ripped off Steve-o's arm and fed it to its fucking kids. Then it told me if I didn't find survivors, it would kill him."

The SEAL snorted. "Nah, man. You were hearing shit. Those things aren't that smart."

Johnson held up his hands. "We're all revolted and shocked, but keep your questions and comments until later."

The words silenced the SEAL, but Garcia continued glaring at him. "That thing used Steve-o as bait, then killed him. The White King wasn't some mad, mindless beast like the others. It couldn't communicate like you and me, but when it did speak, it was very clear in what it wanted."

"Yeah, it wants food," the SEAL said. "I believe that."

"Not just food," Garcia said, his eyes hardening. "It wants the same thing that we want—for its species to survive."

Vice President Johnson wrapped the meeting up as abruptly as it started. As the room emptied, Lieutenant Davis motioned for the Delta operators and the Variant Hunters to join her at the table with Captain Humphrey, Lieutenant Rowe, and Vice President Johnson. Garcia watched Team Ghost with a curious eye. He was still fuming at the Navy SEAL who had given him shit. For the Delta team's sake, Garcia hoped they weren't going to act like dicks. He wasn't in the mood to argue.

"Sergeant Garcia, Corporal Talon, and Sergeant Thomas, there're some gentlemen I'd like you to meet. I don't think you've been officially introduced," Johnson said. "This is Master Sergeant Beckham, Staff Sergeant Horn, and Staff Sergeant Chow of Delta Force Team Ghost."

Garcia thought the legendary Team Ghost didn't look like much. After hearing about Beckham's role in bringing down Colonel Wood, he wouldn't deny Beckham was a hero, but the dull look in his eyes indicated a warrior broken by the horrors of war. For a fleeting moment, Garcia saw the faces of the Variant Hunters in front of him. They were all there, staring back. Both teams had weathered the same horrors, and both had lost brothers to the monsters.

"Good to have you on board," Garcia said. He pointed at his men and gave them informal introductions. "Tank and Thomas."

"Horn and Chow," Beckham said, jerking his chin toward the men in turn.

With formal and informal introductions out of the way, Captain Humphrey took over. The real reason for the early-hour briefing finally became apparent.

"We're in the beginning stages of putting together a

joint strike team. You have all been out there and survived multiple encounters with the Variants. You've succeeded where countless others have failed."

Garcia wondered if Beckham was thinking the same thing—that they had hardly succeeded. Scraping through with your life was surviving, not succeeding.

"The intel Garcia brought back has given us a glimpse into the evolution of these creatures, but we are still in the dark about their offspring. We need to know if Kryptonite will kill them," Humphrey said.

Johnson scratched at the five o'clock shadow on his chin. "In a few hours I'm going to share this information with President Ringgold and Doctor Lovato, but first I want a game plan."

"A game plan, sir?" Beckham asked.

"I'll lead a mission, sir," Garcia said. He had a feeling he knew where this was going.

"No," Johnson quickly replied. "You're in no shape to go back out there right now. You need to rest. Lieutenant Davis has been assigned the task of picking members for strike teams. They will be inserted in multiple cities across the United States to give us the best chance of capturing a live specimen."

"Sir, with all due respect, my team is the best shot you've got." Garcia glanced at Beckham. "*We're* the best you've got."

A knot twisted in Garcia's stomach. He knew exactly what was being planned, and no matter how Johnson sold it, this was a fucking suicide mission. There was a reason the juvenile Variants had only recently been discovered: They dwelled in the lairs, where they were protected by their parents. Garcia's surviving his journey underground had been mostly luck, but the experience he had gained was invaluable. It made the Variant Hunters the perfect team for the job.

"That's why you're being assigned to prepare the teams that will go out there, Garcia. You will brief them, train them, provide intel, and supervise the mission. But you will remain here on the *GW*," Davis said.

Garcia looked at the floor, holding his tongue. Now wasn't the time to protest. Especially in front of the vice president of the United States.

"Any questions?" Johnson asked.

None of the men said a word, but Garcia could tell he wasn't the only one holding back questions. Beckham looked as if he wanted to speak too.

"Good. Rest up for a few hours. The science briefing is at 0900 on the *Cowpens*. And clean yourselves up," Johnson said, looking at Garcia. "The new president of the United States will be there."

14

Kate left Apollo with a sailor assigned to the other bomb-sniffing dogs and boarded the Black Hawk at dawn. Outside, lumpy clouds rolled across a gray sky, and curtains of rain fell across the horizon like a waterfall. She took a seat next to President Ringgold, admiring the woman's neatly pressed suit and the small American-flag lapel pin on her collar.

"Good morning," Ringgold said.

"Good morning, Secretary—I mean, President Ringgold," Kate said.

Ringgold smiled and placed a headset over her ears.

A squad of marines guarded the aircraft as they waited. Two minutes later, a female navy officer with cool blue eyes ducked under the rotors and climbed inside the chopper. A four-man squad of marines bearing the look of battle-hardened warriors piled in behind her. Kate avoided their gazes and looked at the woman across the troop hold.

"President Ringgold, Doctor Lovato, I'm Lieutenant Davis. Captain Humphrey has asked me to escort you to the meeting on the *Cowpens*." Davis took a seat and put on her headset. "Good to go," she said to the pilots.

The rotors fired, thumping overhead on their first

passes. Kate turned to look out the open door as the bird climbed into the air. Below, a small armada of Zodiacs ferried a group of soldiers across the waves to the navy cruiser.

Kate still hadn't seen the labs on the *Cowpens*, and she was anxious to begin her work. She wasn't, however, excited about the idea of working with a new staff. Since the outbreak had started, she had become accustomed to working with Ellis. He was her friend and a trusted colleague—the only one she had left.

The marines piled out of the chopper the moment it landed. Davis offered her hand to help President Ringgold out of the craft, but Kate jumped out onto the deck unaided.

"Watch your head, Madam President," Davis shouted. She helped Ringgold cross the deck in a hurry. Boots stomped behind Kate, their marine escort following close behind. The entourage entered the ship in a hurry.

Inside, the cruiser seemed darker than the aircraft carrier. The passages were dull but spotless. Everything reeked of bleach. Sailors went to and fro with their heads down. Kate got the feeling they didn't like visitors. It reminded her a bit of her first impressions of Plum Island.

"This way," Davis said.

They passed the berthing areas and the galley at the same hurried pace, as if Davis was worried she was going to be late. The farther they got into the ship, the more Kate wondered if this was the woman's normal walking pace.

Davis picked up speed when they got to the brig. Steel plates covered the porthole windows on the hatches lining both sides of the passage. Over the heavy scent of bleach was another smell that hung in the air—rotting lemons and sour fruit. Kate warily glanced at the steel shutters. Had they kept Variants here? Were they *still* keeping Variants here?

"Hurry, please, Doctor," Davis said. She waved at Kate.

At the end of the passage, two marines stood guard. They straightened their backs as Davis approached and offered a salute. The lieutenant hardly acknowledged the men and increased her fast walk to a jog, as if anxious to leave the brig. Kate wanted to ask about the shutters, but Davis stopped in the next passage, outside a hatch that read AUTHORIZED PERSONNEL ONLY. Hazmat and radiation symbols marked the bulkhead.

"This is your new lab, Doctor Lovato. I'll show you inside later." Davis jerked her square chin. "We're almost there."

She continued to a hatch guarded by two marines in the next passage. They avoided eye contact, threw up meticulous salutes, then opened the hatch. Inside, Kate's eyes instantly gravitated to Beckham. He was in the back of the room with Chow and Horn, behind a table full of officers and scientists.

"Good morning," Vice President Johnson said. He stood and gestured toward a chair. "Have a seat, President Ringgold and Doctor Lovato."

Kate took the chair next to Ringgold and crossed her legs.

"I'd like to introduce you to Doctor Kevin Yokoyama and Doctor Jon Carmen. They have been with the *GW* strike group since the beginning," Johnson said. "Doctor Yokoyama is the lead of our science team here on the *Cowpens* and supervises a staff of twenty."

Yokoyama bowed his head slightly, exposing graying roots in a head full of wavy brown hair. He wore a pair of rectangular black glasses. If Carmen nodded, Kate didn't see it. The bearded man's face was accentuated by crow's-feet and deep creases. Both men were old enough to be her father.

"Doctors, this is President Ringgold and Doctor Kate Lovato. They will be an integral part of the science team from here on out. President Ringgold will oversee the science division, and Doctor Lovato will be working with her to coordinate the deployment of Kryptonite on a *worldwide* scale," Johnson said.

Kate appreciated his emphasis on the word, but it was going to take more than that for her to trust him.

The vice president took a seat. "All right. You all know each other, so I'm going to jump right into new developments. Earlier this morning, one of our Force Recon teams returned from Atlanta, where they discovered juvenile Variants and a Variant leader they are calling the White King. This creature possessed communication skills unlike any other Variant documented in the world."

Kate's stomach dropped as Johnson explained what Sergeant Garcia and his men had encountered. The icy rock in her gut seemed to expand with every word.

When he finished, he paused to let the information sink in. Kate resisted the urge to look at Beckham, questions swimming through her mind. She should have seen this coming, but once again, the evolution of the Variants shocked her.

"That's what we know for now," Johnson continued. "Before Phase Two of Operation Extinction can commence, I need to know more about these Variant offspring. How fast do they grow? How tough is that armor? How many of them are there? And, most importantly"—Johnson narrowed his eyes at Kate— "will Kryptonite kill them?"

Kate had anticipated the question, but she didn't have a solid answer. "Mr. Vice President, I would need a—"

"We're working on getting you a specimen," Johnson

interrupted. "Over the next couple of days, we will be training strike teams and sending them into coastal cities to gather a juvenile Variant. We're calling the mission Operation Condor."

This time Kate couldn't help but look at Beckham, her heart beating so hard she could hear the drumming in her ears.

"The Variant Hunters and Team Ghost have been tasked with training these teams," Johnson said.

Kate let out a breath she hadn't realized she was holding in and raised her hand.

"Go ahead, Doctor."

"If you can get a live specimen, I can tell you if Kryptonite will work on them, sir. But time is of the essence. Each Variant is born with genetic mutations, and this means the proteins could change slightly from the last generation. Kryptonite targets the Superman protein. If the antibodies can't bind to that protein, the drugs can't get into those cells and kill the Variants."

Johnson shifted subtly in his chair. "I see."

"We need to deploy Kryptonite as soon as it's ready," Kate said. "The faster we get it in the air, the more chance we have that it will work on the offspring."

Johnson nodded. "Make no mistake, Doctor—when Kryptonite is ready, we will deploy it. But if what you say is true, and the antibodies don't bind to proteins in the new generations of Variants, then I will need something else that will."

"There can't be that many offspring," Ringgold said. "Surely the military can defeat those that remain if Kryptonite kills the adults."

Johnson's gaze flitted to Ringgold. He laced his fingers together on the table. "Forgive me, President Ringgold, but are you aware of how many humans are left out there?"

Ringgold shook her head. "No, I'm not."

Johnson looked at Davis, who stepped forward and said, "As of yesterday, projections put the human population at approximately five million. In two weeks, that number will be less than one million. In a month, we will number in the hundreds of thousands. A month later, that number drops dramatically, and continues to drop. In six months—"

"Extinction," Kate interjected. "Which is all the more reason it's imperative we not only deploy Kryptonite here as quickly as possible, but that we also help other countries start production so they can too."

Kate's words seemed to echo in the room. No one replied. Ringgold's jaw was clamped shut as she processed the information. She had been locked away in the Raven Rock complex. The numbers were enough to shake anyone, and this information was all new to her. And now she was the leader of the country. Kate couldn't blame her for not responding right away.

"So there are five million people left worldwide?" Ringgold finally said. "And there are half a billion Variants?"

"One hundred Variants for every human survivor," Davis said. She paused, and then said, "Not counting the offspring."

Ringgold stared at the table. "Vice President Johnson, where are we in regard to connecting with other labs?"

The vice president gestured to Dr. Yokoyama. The scientist pulled off his glasses and held them in his hand. "So far, we have only been able to reach a few countries."

"How about Italy—have you been able to contact Italy?" Kate blurted.

"I'm afraid not," Johnson said. He must have sensed his response bothered her. "That doesn't mean there aren't survivors in other countries—far from it. And we won't give up on contacting them."

Kate nodded and tried not to think about her parents as Yokoyama continued briefing them on other labs they had reached. She was listening, but her thoughts strayed back to the White King. There was more to worry about than Kryptonite working on the juvenile Variants, or finding labs in other countries. If the Alpha Variants were using human collaborators, then they had a way of infiltrating strongholds of survivors. Nowhere on the planet was safe. Not even the *GW* strike group.

After Yokoyama finished, Kate said, "Vice President Johnson, can you tell me more about this White King? If there is one, that means there are others," Kate said.

"Yes," Johnson said. "There are."

Kate sat up straighter in her chair. "You have documented cases of other Variants like the White King?"

Johnson nodded. "Yes, Doctor. In fact, we have one on this ship."

"You have one of those things on board?" The icy knot in Kate's gut melted, her insides suddenly on fire as she recalled the hatches back in the brig. Was it really possible they had passed Variants earlier?

Johnson nodded proudly. "We've been calling him Patient Zero, but you may know him by a different name."

Davis stood and gestured to the door. "Who wants to visit Lieutenant Brett?"

According to documents, Lieutenant Trevor Brett was seventy-five years old, but at first glance he looked as if he was closing in on a century. Kate cupped her hand over her mouth as she stepped up to examine his filthy quarters. His emaciated body was stretched into an *x* by chains inside the cell. Skin sagged off his bones, gravity tugging at what was left of the poor bastard. His head, slumped against his chest, was covered in varicose veins. There wasn't a single hair on his naked body. Most disturbing were the scars; his arms, legs, torso, and even his groin were covered in them.

One by one, the group took turns looking through the thick glass window. Horn, Chow, Garcia, and even President Ringgold peeked inside. The sight seemed to revolt her the most. She stepped away, shaking her head.

"How?" Kate whispered.

"Why?" Beckham asked at the same time.

Johnson clasped his hands behind his back. "I'm not sure why Colonel Wood kept Brett alive over the years. All of this happened before my time. I didn't even know until I was evacuated from Offutt Air Force Base. If it were up to me, we would have put Brett out of his misery decades ago."

"He's a tough son of a bitch," Davis said. She leaned in next to Kate, peering through the window.

Dr. Yokoyama took his turn at the hatch. "I've been studying him for weeks now. That dose of VX-99 in 1968 killed the man he was, but ironically, it gave him the closest thing to immortality. As you can see, Brett doesn't have all of the adaptations of the other Variants, but his healing abilities are truly remarkable. Over the years, Colonel Gibson and Colonel Wood tweaked the chemical formula of the drug to make it even more potent."

Kate studied the scars. Some looked fresh.

"Have you been experimenting on him?" she asked.

Ringgold shot Yokoyama a glare. From the corner of her eye, Kate saw Beckham tense his right hand into a fist.

"We have been studying him," Yokoyama replied, hesitation in his voice. "I was under strict orders from Colonel Wood."

"And now you're under strict orders from me," Kate said. "No more tests. No more torturing him."

Yokoyama looked to Johnson for support, and Kate was relieved to see the vice president nod in her direction. He earned a little more of her trust in that moment, and she hoped it wouldn't come back to haunt her.

Kate stepped back to the hatch. "Can he still speak?"

Davis motioned for one of the guards. A marine with a key stepped up behind Kate without hesitation.

"Please move, Doctor," the man said.

Kate did as instructed, but Beckham grabbed at the man's wrist, stopping him midstride.

"What the hell are you doing?" Beckham asked.

"It's okay," Johnson said. "We're not opening the door, just the window. Besides, chains like that have held him for over fifty years. They're not going to break now."

Beckham's jaw moved, but no words came out. He looked at Kate, but curiosity prompted her to nod. She needed to see this—she *wanted* to see this.

The marine unlocked the window and slid back the glass. Lieutenant Davis moved up to the hatch and cleared her throat.

"Lieutenant Brett, can you hear me?"

The chain holding Brett's right arm rattled, but he didn't look up.

"Lieutenant," Davis said, her voice raised.

Brett struggled to raise his head. He slowly looked up, blinking as if he couldn't focus. A groan escaped his mouth, and his head slumped back against his scarred chest.

Davis shook her head. "He's probably coming off the tranquilizers."

Johnson joined her at the window. "Lieutenant!" he shouted.

This time Brett's head shot up, but instead of the crazed, bloodshot eyes Kate remembered from the video Ellis had uncovered, there was only the sad basset-hound face of what had once been a man.

And then Kate knew.

Brett wasn't just different from the Variants physically. Somewhere over the years, all that rage and blood-lust had drained out of him. Now he looked sad and almost afraid.

"Lieutenant," Johnson continued. "How are you feeling today?"

Brett cocked his head to the side, groggy but comprehending. He pulled weakly at his chains.

Turning to Davis, Johnson said, "When's the last time he spoke?"

"A few—"

A tormented howl cut her off. Everyone took a guarded step backward as Brett let out a second roar and stiffened in his chains. His eyes widened as they explored the dark room. He pulled at his restraints, every lean muscle in his body flexing. The veins in his neck bulged like the thick roots of a tree in dry soil.

"*Ka*," Brett said, coughing. He pulled harder at his chains, staring at his observers now. The wild look Kate had seen in the video was returning. She froze, thinking for one horrified moment that the monster was trying to say her name.

"*Ka-i-ll*," Brett choked. He twisted his wrists, the chains whipping back and forth.

Kate felt Beckham's hand brush up against hers.

"*Kill me!*" Brett shouted.

Ringgold glared at Johnson, her jaw set with rage. "I don't know what the hell you've been doing here, Johnson, but unless Doctor Lovato can give me a good reason to keep this man alive, I want him put out of his misery. *Now.*"

Yokoyama raised his hands. "With all due respect, Brett has provided us with valuable insight into the Variants. We need him."

"No," Kate said. "No, we don't. He can't tell us anything we don't already know. What we need is a juvenile Variant."

Ringgold was already walking away. She paused to glare at Johnson. "You heard Doctor Lovato. I want Brett put down and given a proper military burial. After all, this man was the creation of the government, was he not?"

Johnson opened his mouth to argue, but Ringgold stopped him with a look. "That's an order, Mr. Vice President."

Beckham skipped lunch after seeing the atrocity that was Lieutenant Brett, but by dinnertime he finally had his appetite back. He carried a fully loaded tray to an open table in the mess and took a seat next to Horn. The man was wolfing down a pile of orange slop that was supposed to be carrots. Chow slid his tray onto the table a few minutes later and sat down facing Beckham and Horn.

"Looks like shit," Chow said. "I figured they would have better food than we did at Plum Island."

"Me too," Beckham said. He finished chewing a piece of rubbery chicken and scooped up a spoonful of mashed potatoes. The cold mush went down easier than the meat.

"What you think, boss?" Horn asked. "About this White King?"

Beckham shrugged. "Doesn't surprise me."

Horn shoveled the last of his carrots into his mouth and looked over his shoulder. Satisfied no one was listening, he said, "And what do you think of Johnson?"

"Still trying to get a read," Beckham replied. "So far, I'm cautiously optimistic."

"Yeah, me too," Horn said. "I'm more worried about the Variant offspring. Those things can really fuck?"

Chow laughed. "Apparently."

"Kate's right; it changes everything," Beckham said. "Means the enemy can increase in number. And the rate they're growing at is even more fucked up."

Horn held a spoon in front of his mouth. "Maybe I shouldn't have left my girls on the island after all."

Beckham patted Horn on the shoulder. "They're safe with Meg and Riley. Fitz will keep an eye on them too. Try not to worry. There's more firepower on that island now than ever."

"That doesn't make me feel better, man," Horn said. "We can't trust anyone."

Beckham sucked in a long breath, let it out, and said, "We'll be back to the island in no time, brother."

Chow took a swig of juice and wiped his mouth. "Got something else on your mind," he said to Beckham. "I can tell. And I don't think it has to do with the war."

Beckham thought he'd done a better job of hiding his emotions, but Chow was an expert at picking up on the little details. Before he had time to think about it, Beckham came out and said it.

"Kate's pregnant."

Horn dropped his spoon onto his tray, and Chow's black brows arched.

"Holy shit," Horn said. He patted Beckham on the shoulder. "Congratulations, brother."

Beckham snorted. "Pretty shitty timing."

"Hell, man, it could be worse. I mean, at least she's on the carrier. Think about if this happened out there. She's going to have the best medical care left in the world."

"He's right. It'll be okay, boss," Chow added. He reached across the table. "You're going to make a good father."

Beckham shook Chow's hand and cracked a half grin. "Thanks, guys. I appreciate it."

"Those seats taken?" asked a coarse voice.

Beckham shot a glance over his shoulder. Garcia stood there, his tan skin bruised and battered.

"Be my guest," Beckham said, scooting over.

"You guys know Tank and Thomas," Garcia said. The two marines took seats on both sides of Chow.

Tank was bald, with a rough face and a bit of a beer gut, but his arms were bigger than Horn's, and that was saying something. Thomas, on the other hand, was built a lot like Garcia: trim and lean, the type of body that took hundreds of push-ups and sit-ups a day to maintain. They both had thick brown mustaches and olive skin. If it weren't for Garcia's longer hair, they could have passed for siblings.

Horn regarded them with a half nod and sized Tank up with a quick glance. He rolled up his sleeves to expose the tribal tattoos on his forearms, then went back to mowing through his green beans.

The operator wasn't the only one with ink. Garcia had a cross on the underside of his right arm that Beckham had noticed when they first shook hands. With a closer look, he saw Tank and Thomas had the same tattoo. There were names etched there that Beckham couldn't make out.

"I figured we should break bread before we start training whoever Lieutenant Davis throws at us," Garcia said.

Beckham exchanged a glance with Horn and Chow. Neither of them trusted the marines. Hell, Beckham didn't even trust the cook who had slopped food on his tray. The Variant Hunters, and everyone else assigned to the strike group, were under Johnson's umbrella.

Garcia seemed to be waiting for a response, but Beckham was just fine letting the marine run the conversation from here.

"So you guys have been out there?" Thomas asked. He picked at the right side of his mustache.

Chow grinned. "Really, man?"

"Yeah," Horn growled. "We've been out there."

"How many Variants you killed?" Tank asked. He swallowed a hunk of chicken without even chewing.

Beckham bit back a retort. What the fuck kind of question was that? Sure, he remembered every human hostile he'd ever killed, but it wasn't something he bragged about. He had never liked or understood men who did.

Horn and Chow remained silent, and Beckham continued to scrutinize the Variant Hunters. Every soldier had a mannerism that Beckham looked for; it could tell him a lot about the man. Some were harder to spot than others. Most were physical, but some were mental. Thomas's was the nervous tic, and Tank's was the same as Horn's—they both wanted to be the biggest badass on the block. Sometimes there wasn't room for two.

"Last time I checked, this wasn't a contest," Beckham finally said. "But we've done our fair share of killing. That's not really what you want to discuss, though, is it?" He directed the question at Garcia. The marine still hadn't touched his food.

"Nah, it's not. But before I dive in, I wanted to let you in on something," Garcia said. He lowered his voice and leaned over the table.

Beckham didn't like that. The marine was too close, and Beckham smelled the coffee on his breath.

"You're heroes in our eyes," Garcia said, to Beckham's surprise. "You all deserve a fucking medal, if you ask me. From what I hear, Colonel Wood was a piece of shit, and you helped rid the world of one more asshole."

Beckham used his tongue to pick at something stuck in his teeth, unsure what to say, yet still scrutinizing Garcia. Was this a ploy? He hadn't discovered what made this man tick.

"Anyway," Garcia said, softly slapping the table with his right hand, "those things have gotten smarter, and they will continue to get smarter. This White King…" Garcia trailed off, grimacing. He stabbed at the plastic-looking fillet on his plate with a fork. "And those collaborating pieces of shit. You ever come across anything like that?"

"No," Horn said. "But if I did, I'd snap their fucking necks."

Garcia nodded. "I'm with you. If it weren't for Frankie." His eyes glazed over for a moment, a memory surfacing.

"The dynamics have changed out there. As food gets harder to find, the Variants are going to be looking for new resources. And they're going to use whatever they can to survive," Beckham said.

"Steve-o's still down there," Tank said. "What if they try and turn him?"

"I told you, he's dead," Garcia whispered, almost as if he didn't really believe it.

"I'm sorry," Beckham said, but he couldn't help but think of the marine phrase *No man left behind*. Yet the words didn't apply here as it had on battlefields of the past. Jinx's was the only body Team Ghost had recovered.

Beckham gritted his teeth, fending off the rage rising inside of him. "Look," he said, "we've all seen what's out there. We know how bad it is. And we all know that this is basically a suicide mission, no matter how well we prepare the soldiers LT Davis assigns us. They're going to have to survive hell to capture one of those things."

"That's why we should be the ones to do it," Garcia said.

Beckham held his gaze. Now he understood what made Garcia tick: He wanted to go back out there and get his man. Beckham could relate, and deep down he knew the marine was right. They were the most qualified for this mission. Even deeper, past the grit and conflicting emotions, Beckham wanted to go back out there too. He struggled, torn between his commitments to his country and to Kate. In the past, he had never let a man do a job he could do himself. But in the past, it had been just him and Team Ghost. He had a bigger family now, and he would be damned if he would put those he loved in jeopardy.

15

Summer was closing in. The scorching sun warmed Riley's right arm, which was hanging out of the passenger's-side window of a Humvee. As spring turned to summer, the bodies rotting in the cities would enter the final stages of decay. The stench would be intolerable, the concrete jungles transformed into cesspools.

Riley hadn't looked at a calendar for days, but it had to be June by now. That was right, wasn't it? Being cooped up on the island for so long had messed with his internal clock. All he knew for sure was that it had been four days since Kate and his brothers left for the *GW* strike group. Riley had spent that time training Meg to shoot and watching the new troops stationed at the island. It was boring as hell, but that was all about to change.

I have a mission for you, Staff Sergeant Riley, Major Smith had said earlier that morning. Now Smith was driving them to the docks on the south side of Plum Island. Gravel crunched under the truck's off-road tires as the major drove away from the post.

"You got any idea what I'll be doing?" Riley asked.

Smith turned down a frontage road. "Not sure. I've only been told Lieutenant Rowe is back. He docked an hour ago and asked to speak to you."

Riley pulled his arm back into the vehicle and scratched a mosquito bite on his elbow. He didn't bother asking more questions. Smith would have told him if he knew anything more.

They endured the rest of the trip in silence, passing through groves of trees and thick underbrush. Through a clearing, he saw two rows of electric fencing, and beyond that a dock stretching across the glistening water. Two Mark V Special Operation Crafts were docked there. A dozen marines were already unloading gear from the crafts. A third Mark V SOC hammered across the water a quarter mile out.

The charcoal gunboats weren't the navy cruisers Riley had hoped for, but they were better than the alternative, which had been nothing. Built with a V shaped hull, the angular ships were designed to travel in rough waters with efficient handling and maneuverability. Team Ghost had trained on them before, and Riley still remembered how comfortable the seats were.

These ships were outfitted with five weapon mounts, but they had removed the Stinger Man-Portable Air-Defense System. There was no need for anti-aircraft capability anymore. Instead, the craft was decked out with two 7.62-millimeter Gatling guns and three .50-cal. machine guns. It was an extra layer of security Plum Island hadn't previously had, but hardly enough to fend off a major invasion.

Smith coasted to a stop outside the gate leading to the dock. A marine approached and checked his ID.

"Good to go, sir," the guard said.

The gate opened, and Smith drove them down to the beach. He parked the truck next to another Humvee. It took five minutes for Smith to help Riley into his wheelchair, but none of the marines on the dock seemed to pay them any attention. Normally, Riley would have been self-conscious, but the thrill of a potential assignment kept him focused.

As soon as he was in his chair, Riley wheeled toward the dock. Major Smith had to jog to keep up with him.

"Lieutenant Rowe," Major Smith said.

The lieutenant was supervising three marines unloading extra ammunition. He turned from the crates and came over to salute Smith, but he kept his chiseled jaw locked in place, like an alligator.

"This is Staff Sergeant Riley. Corporal Fitzpatrick is finishing up guard duty and should be here shortly," Smith said.

"Yes, sir," Rowe said, training his gaze on Riley. "I remember you from the landing the other day, Staff Sergeant. You said something about not trusting *Vice President* Johnson."

Riley felt his cheeks burning. "Yes, sir. At the time we had reason to believe he was connected with Colonel Wood and Colonel Gibson. But I was wrong, sir."

Rowe gave him a once-over and said, "Understandable, considering the situation." He pointed at the boats. "In two days, we're launching a covert mission called Operation Condor. Thirty-four strike teams will be inserted into coastal cities with a single objective: to capture and extract a live juvenile Variant."

Riley swallowed. A child? He'd heard rumors of the breeders, but shit, he'd had no idea they were real.

"That's where you and Fitzpatrick will come in. Master Sergeant Beckham said you're the best the island has. You've both been out there. You've fought the Variants. Now I want you to train the strike teams from Plum Island to do what you did. Most of these men haven't seen any real action against the Variants. I'm hoping your experience will help keep them alive." He strode back to the dock and picked up a crate marked EXPLOSIVES.

The words left Riley with a chill. They had their work cut out for them, especially if they were to have any hope of saving any of these young men. He waited for Rowe to finish, but the lieutenant continued unloading boxes as they waited for Fitz.

This wasn't exactly the mission Riley had hoped for, but it beat shooting at bottles. Even if shooting bottles meant he got to see Meg.

All three men turned at the sound of an approaching engine. Another Humvee crunched through the gravel and ground to a stop outside the gates. Fitz jumped out onto the rock. He reached inside the truck, pulled out his rifle, then slung it over his back.

"Corporal Fitzpatrick reporting for duty. Sorry I'm late, sir," Fitz said.

Rowe simply nodded. He turned toward the dock and whistled at the dozen marines still unloading crates. They hurried over and fell into line.

"Men, this is Delta Force operator Staff Sergeant Riley and Marine Corporal Fitzpatrick. They'll be training you over the next two days for your mission to New York."

Fitz joined Riley in front of the group of staring marines. A minute of awkward silence passed. Riley had been so focused on the mission that he'd forgotten his chair, and he'd known Fitz for so long he didn't even look twice at the man's blades. But these marines weren't used to them. Riley knew what they were likely thinking: How could these guys train them? Would they end up looking like Fitz and Riley if they went out there?

"Take a good look," Riley said. "Go ahead." He gave the marines a few seconds. Most of them probably had buddies with war injuries, but Riley doubted any of those buddies had ever ended up training them.

"You good?" Riley asked. "You obviously don't need to look at us to know what the Variants are capable of.

But Fitz and me"—Riley reached over to pat Fitz on the arm—"we've survived out there. And if you want to come back in one piece, you're going to listen to everything we say."

Rowe grinned. Perhaps it was respect, or something else. Riley wasn't sure. But it felt damn good to have it again.

"You heard the man," Rowe said, clapping his hands. "At 1900 hours you're to meet at the mess hall for your first briefing. Now get back to work."

The dozen marines hurried back to the dock and continued unloading the boats. Fitz leaned down to Riley and whispered, "They probably think I lost my legs to the Variants."

Riley cracked a shit-eating grin. "That was the point, brother."

"Europe seems to be mostly dark," Dr. Yokoyama said. "We did manage to contact a lab in the U.K. and one each in Switzerland and France, but besides those, there isn't much out there. Italy, Greece, Russia—the governments have all fallen."

He continued listing the labs they had contacted in the Middle East, Asia, and South America, but Kate wasn't paying attention. Her heart sank in her chest as her body slumped in her chair. She avoided President Ringgold's gaze from across the table. The last thing she wanted was pity. All she wanted was time to grieve, but that wasn't going to happen anytime soon.

"That's all that's left?" Ringgold said after Yokoyama had finished.

He nodded, gravely. "I'm afraid VX9H9 wasn't deployed quickly enough in other countries. The hem-

orrhage virus was able to infect a much larger percent-
age of the population. When the weapon was finally
deployed, it eradicated ninety percent of the infected, but
those that had turned into Variants seem to have already
killed most of the surviving population. Since then, military bases and critical facilities have fallen, just as they
have here," Yokoyama said. "I'm not saying there aren't
survivors in other countries, but their governments and
infrastructures have crumbled."

Kate bowed her head. She understood perfectly what
Yokoyama meant, and knew then her parents were
among the dead. Kryptonite couldn't save them. It would
be too late. She had thought she'd feel something in this
moment—anger, sadness. But she only felt hollow, as if
she'd lost another piece of herself.

There was a knock on the door, and Vice President
Johnson entered the room with Lieutenant Davis.

"Sorry we're late," Johnson said. He took a seat next
to Ringgold. "There was a report of Variants swimming
off the coast."

Ringgold arched a brow. "And?"

"Nothing a few Apaches couldn't handle," Johnson
replied. "So where are we? Have you connected with any
other labs?"

Yokoyama repeated the sitrep, but his words didn't
have the same effect on Johnson. Any trace of emotion
disappeared from the vice president's face.

"With the help of those labs, we should be able to produce enough Kryptonite to deploy around the world, but
they're already behind schedule. Even if they start today,
they won't have finished batches for another two weeks,"
Dr. Carmen said, scratching at his beard.

"Where exactly are these facilities? And how do we
know they won't be overrun with Variants when we go
to launch Kryptonite?" Ringgold asked.

It was a good question, one Kate had thought of a few times. She tried not to think about her parents and to focus on the task at hand. There were still humans out there, people she *could* save.

"Lieutenant Davis, show us the locations of Project Earthfall," Johnson said.

The lieutenant walked over to the computer in the corner of the room and tapped at the keyboard.

"I can't promise these locations are secure, but I can promise we will send enough soldiers to take the facilities back from the Variants if they have been compromised. At least for the silos that will launch Kryptonite over the United States," Johnson said. He folded his hands on the table.

"What about the others?" Kate asked. "The worldwide sites?"

"My staff has been in communication with the British and French militaries. There are other small contingents in Spain and Finland. We might be able to count on their soldiers to secure the Earthfall facilities in Europe. We're still working on making contact with militaries in Asia and elsewhere, but rest assured, it's only a matter of time."

The overlay of a map spread over the wall behind President Ringgold and Vice President Johnson. They twisted for a better look.

Davis stood to the side of the image and used a pen to point at the red dots. "There are sixteen locations for Earthfall, each placed strategically to manipulate the weather on a global scale. There's one facility on each continent, and the others are spread out across the five oceans."

"In order to coat the United States with Kryptonite, we will need to launch from these locations," Davis said. She pointed to the dots in the Atlantic and Pacific Oceans, and one in the center of the United States.

"Is that in Colorado?" Ringgold asked.

"Yes, President Ringgold. It's located in Rocky Mountain National Park, just above Estes Park, Colorado. The silo was constructed on one of the highest peaks," Davis said.

Ringgold addressed Kate. "So we will definitely have enough Kryptonite to use over the United States?"

"Yes. I have a call with my partner, Doctor Ellis, after this meeting. He should have a better idea when the batch at Plum Island will be ready, but I would guess it'll be a little over a week."

"Excellent," Johnson said. "In the meantime, we will work on capturing a juvenile Variant. The first of the teams will deploy tomorrow."

"And if Kryptonite doesn't work on them?" Ringgold asked

"We'll find another way to kill them. Which is all the more reason to figure out how fast they're growing, what their strengths and weaknesses are, and how many are out there," Johnson said. "Assuming they aren't breeding at alarming rates, even if Kryptonite doesn't work, I'm confident our troops will be able to clear them from the cities."

"You're confident," Ringgold said, almost in a whisper. She rose from her chair before Johnson could reply. "We're strained for resources here, folks, and I want to make sure we're placing our chips in the right pot."

Johnson stood and pulled at his cuffs. "I believe we are, President Ringgold. Leave the military side to me, as we agreed. I'll have my staff set up a satellite call with our friends across the pond and continue working on contacting other countries."

"I just hope there are enough soldiers to get the job done when the time comes," Ringgold said. She exhaled and looked to Kate. "There's still hope, Doctor Lovato. There's always hope."

"The Variants will smell you before you ever see them, I fucking guarantee you," Horn said. He folded his tattooed arms across his chest. "And they will see you in the dark, so there's no sense hiding. If you run, they will catch you."

"That's why we're here to train you before you go out there," Beckham said. He stood between Chow and Horn on the deck of the *George Washington*. Apollo sat in front of Beckham's boots, watching a sailor patrol the starboard side of the vessel with another German shepherd. Garcia, Tank, and Thomas stood to their right. The two teams shared more experience fighting the Variants than all the other soldiers in the strike group combined. At least that's what Garcia kept telling Beckham.

It was dusk, but darkness was already closing in. The blinking red lights of the *GW* fleet sparkled on the horizon. The two dozen marines standing before Team Ghost and the Variant Hunters listened attentively. They were divided into six four-man strike teams bound for the coastal cities.

"What we've told you about the Variants will help once you're in enemy territory, but rely on your training and never, ever drop your guard," Beckham continued. He nodded at Garcia, and the marine stepped forward.

"Many of you know who I am. You've heard of my team, the Variant Hunters. Truth is, we've become the hunted. I've seen about every type of those freaks, from the bony, thin ones to the massive, muscular beasts that look like Kimbo fucking Slice. I've seen them run up the surface of buildings and leap ten feet into the air. Hell,

I've even seen them puke goo that can cauterize a wound or plaster a human prisoner to the wall.

"The Variants are monsters, and make no mistake," Garcia continued, "they aren't easy to kill. They shouldn't be underestimated. Many of you have heard they're mindless beasts, but they aren't. They are evolving, and they can communicate. They can even set traps."

Garcia regarded Team Ghost. "Our Delta Force friends have seen the same things. Using our experiences, we have put together a strong plan that should give you the best chance of completing Operation Condor." He looked at the deck and then out over the water, his stare distant as though he was lost in thought.

Beckham took over. "Working together, we're going to teach you to survive when you go out there. But before we get into details and assignments, are there any questions?"

He scanned the faces. Most were young, but there were several older marines in the group. None of these men looked like they had any combat experience. The marines Beckham had fought with at Fort Bragg or Plum Island were a rare commodity, and the Timbos and Rodriguezes of the world were mostly dead. Fitz was one of the last surviving marines with the experience to spearhead a mission like this, and that was exactly why Beckham had requested Lieutenant Rowe let the marine train the troops at Plum Island.

A pale marine with the saggy face of a bulldog raised his hand. "How many of those things will be protecting the juveniles?"

"Garcia, you want to answer that?" Beckham asked.

"Hundreds. Maybe more."

The whistle of the ocean breeze was the only sound that followed.

Another marine raised a hand a few moments later.

218 **NICHOLAS SANSBURY SMITH**

"When you say they communicate, do you mean they talk?"

"Some can, yes. It's likely that the Variants protecting the young will display a higher intelligence," Garcia said.

A man who could have passed for a teenager blurted out, "And how are we supposed to get past them? Do you expect us to just run into the lairs, snag a kid, and call in for evac?"

"No," Beckham said. "Each team will enter their city at 1100 hours tomorrow. The Variants are least active during this time period. Squad leaders will be assigned a direct route to known lairs.

"As I already said, the Variants are capable of setting traps, but so are we. And that's exactly what the plan is. We're going to use air support to lure them out of their lairs. Intel indicates the juveniles rarely come out, but the adults do. Before teams sneak through the sewers, we will launch a decoy to draw out those adults. Then the flyboys are going to hit them with everything they got left. When that happens, each team will proceed to the lairs, put on gas masks, and deploy smoke grenades inside. Your primary weapon will be equipped with UV lights to distract the Variants. Between the smoke and the light, you should have the cover you need to sneak inside and tranquilize one of the offspring."

"That's the *strong* plan?" the young man said. "You want us to lob some smoke grenades in there and kidnap one of their kids?"

"You got a better one, Marine?" Garcia asked.

Chow spat his toothpick on the deck and brushed a strand of black hair from his face. He wasn't a man of many words and hadn't said a single one during the briefing, but Beckham could see he had something to say now. Beckham nodded his approval, and Chow crossed his arms, something he always did before he spoke.

"We've all survived what many would consider impossible odds," Chow said. "But we came back. Not without scars, and not without nightmares. But we came back. You will too, if you stick to the plan."

The young marine with all the questions looked at his boots. He wasn't the only one who didn't look convinced. Most of these men shared the same frightened, uncertain gaze. They knew what they were up against, and it was Beckham's job to reassure them this wasn't a suicide mission. Rarely did soldiers run into the fray without confidence inspired by their leaders.

"Chow's right," Beckham said. "This is a solid plan. And you all have the advantage of knowing how the Variants hunt—something we never had when we were out there."

The clank of boots directed Beckham's attention to a ladder wrapping down to the deck. Lieutenant Davis strode down the steps and joined them.

"Master Sergeant," she said. "Lieutenant Brett is going to be executed in a couple of hours. Vice President Johnson told me to inform you. It's up to you if you'd like to observe."

"With all due respect, Lieutenant, thanks, but no thanks. I have work to do. These men aren't ready," Beckham replied in a low voice.

"Understood," Davis said. She took a step back and waited for the training to continue with an interested eye.

When Beckham turned, the young marine was staring at him again, his jaw partially open, as if he couldn't believe he was being thrown into the meat grinder.

"Any further questions?" Beckham asked.

The moon was out now, the rays bathing the *GW* in soft light. In the pale glow, the marines looked like ghosts. This time tomorrow, Beckham doubted many of them, if any, would still be alive.

16

Kate sat next to President Ringgold at the small lab station she shared with Dr. Carmen. They were in one of the three outer, nonsecure sections where research was conducted. Dr. Yokoyama and Dr. Carmen were inside the secure zone, waiting on test results from a recent Variant blood sample.

The room was chilly even with the heavy navy sweatshirt Kate wore. She turned on her monitor and keyed in her credentials, anxious to talk to Ellis. It had been several days since they'd spoken, and she still hadn't told him about Lieutenant Brett.

The dark monitor warmed, and a face Kate hardly recognized swam onto the screen. While the display was half the size of her monitor at Plum Island, she could still see Ellis's features clearly—and he looked awful. His black hair was tangled and matted in several places. His blue shirt was rumpled, and he'd grown a thin mustache above his five o'clock shadow. The cheery brown eyes she'd grown accustomed to were dull and voided.

"Good evening, President Ringgold and Doctor Lovato," Ellis said.

"Ellis—how are things there?" Kate asked.

"Okay."

"Don't lie to me. You look like you haven't slept for days."

"I haven't, but I'm fine. Have you managed to contact other labs?"

President Ringgold exchanged a worried glance with Kate.

"We've connected with a few, but there aren't many out there," Kate said. "Europe was hit hard, and so were the Middle East and Asia. South America, Australia, New Zealand—it's all the same."

"Jesus," Ellis said. "Worse than I thought. And Italy? What about...?"

A lump formed in Kate's throat. She swallowed it and changed the subject. "So, why do you look like you haven't slept? Is something wrong with the bioreactors?"

Ellis raked his hands through his hair. "All twelve batches are fine. We're on schedule to finish in a little over a week, but I'm going to need help encapsulating the chemotherapeutics and conjugating them with the antibodies. When do you think you'll be back?"

"I'm not sure." Kate regarded Ringgold with a rueful glance. "I think Vice President Johnson wants me to stay here to study the juvenile Variant that they're capturing."

Ringgold reached up and ran her finger over the American-flag lapel pin on her collar. It was the second time Kate had seen her do it since they landed on the *GW*.

"I'm sure Doctor Yokoyama and his staff can handle that," Ringgold said after a moment of silence. "If Doctor Ellis needs you, then I'll authorize your trip back to Plum Island."

Kate hadn't told Ringgold about her relationship with Beckham, and she certainly hadn't told her about the child she was carrying, but she had a feeling Ringgold already knew. Selfishly, she wanted to stay on the carrier with him, but finishing Kryptonite was more important. He would understand, as long as she was safe.

"Okay," Kate said. She glanced back at the monitor. "How are Tasha and Jenny? Are Meg and Riley taking good care of them?"

"The girls are fine. Meg's been looking after them, since Riley's training troops here with Fitz."

"And the soldiers there are treating you well?" Ringgold asked.

"No complaints."

Kate scrunched her brows together. "Why aren't you sleeping?"

"I'm just worried, Kate."

"I can see that, but about what specifically?"

Ellis bowed his head slightly. "If Kryptonite doesn't work on the offspring, then what the hell are we going to do?"

"Vice President Johnson said we'll find another way," Ringgold said.

"With all due respect, President Ringgold, we've heard that from every general since day one," Ellis said.

Kate was taken back by the outburst. She hadn't ever seen her partner like this. There was no trace of the scientist she knew on-screen, no smile or enthusiastic commentary. The lump in Kate's throat climbed higher.

"Anything else?" Ellis asked.

Shaking her head, Kate said, "No. That's all. I'll see you in a couple of days." She went to shut off the feed, but remembered Brett. "Wait, Ellis."

He looked back at the camera.

"There's something I haven't told you. Lieutenant Brett—he's *here*."

Ellis managed a weak smile. "Bullshit. That's a good one, though. I needed that. Thanks for the chuckle."

"Doctor Lovato isn't lying," Ringgold said. "We saw him. But he's going to be put down in a few hours."

Kate liked Ringgold's choice of words. They sounded a lot better than *executed*. No matter what they called it, they were doing the right thing. Brett was no longer a man—he was an animal. But Kate did have a sliver of empathy for him. He had suffered unimaginable pain for over fifty years, all because of Colonel Gibson's dream of a supersoldier. It was more than anyone should ever have to suffer. She had to remind herself he was a liability. Every day he still had breath in his lungs, he was a threat to humanity.

Ellis inched closer to the camera, staring incredulously. "You have got to me kidding me. How is that even possible? He would be over seventy years old."

"Seventy-five, to be exact," Kate said. "Colonel Wood kept him alive all of these years."

Ellis ran a thumb across his mustache. "Guess nothing surprises me anymore. Anyway, I'll see ya in a few days, Kate. Good night."

"Good night," Kate said.

She shut off the feed and leaned back in her chair. Ringgold grabbed her coffee mug and took a sip.

"I'll be sad to see you go back to the island, but that's where you're needed," Ringgold said. "I suppose I was selfish in hoping you'd be able to stay here."

"I'm sorry I have to go," Kate said solemnly.

Ringgold put the mug down, the ceramic clinking on the metal surface of the desk. A thud followed, making the clink sound like a pin drop. The ship groaned, and an echo bounced off the bulkheads inside the room. Both women jumped at the sound.

"What the hell was that?" Kate asked. She stood and followed Ringgold to the glass window looking out over the center of the lab. Yokoyama and Carmen stood with their visors angled toward the exit hatch that led back into the ship.

Kate flinched at a flurry of popping sounds.

"Was that gunfire?" Ringgold gasped.

The hatch to the central lab suddenly swung open, disgorging a naked, skeletal figure that darted into the room. The frail man dropped to all fours and vanished in the maze of lab stations.

"My God," Kate said. On reflex, she grabbed the president's wrist. "We need to get out of here."

Ringgold stepped closer to the window.

"A Variant!" Kate said, panic cracking in her voice.

Carmen and Yokoyama stumbled away from their desk, their screams drowned out by an emergency alarm blaring from the wall-mounted speakers. The overhead LEDs flicked off a moment later, and red light splashed over the lab, bathing it in crimson.

Monitors and equipment toppled over as the doctors ran across the room. The bony Variant followed, its veiny skull bobbing up and down. Claws scraped over the metal surface of lab stations, but this creature wasn't howling like the others. It moved awkwardly, its stalk-like appendages distorted and slow.

Yokoyama and Carmen were circling the room, dragging their oxygen cords behind them. The Variant leaped onto a metal table to cut them off, swiping at Carmen's cord. Its horned claws cut through it like a fish snapping a line. Oxygen hissed out of the whipping cord, and the creature perched on its bony legs to watch the doctors run toward the observation window Kate and Ringgold stood behind.

"We have to help them," Ringgold said. She turned to Kate. "We have to open that door!"

The lump in Kate's throat hardened. She turned away from the window as Yokoyama pounded on the glass.

"Open the hatch!" he shouted.

"*Please*," Carmen said. "*Please* let us in."

Kate looked at the wheel handle of the hatch leading into the central lab. She couldn't open it even if she wanted to. It was sealed off to prevent contaminants.

Yokoyama continued pounding on the glass, but Carmen twisted, his shoulders shaking as his body responded to the lack of oxygen. The creature continued to observe from the lab station, interested but holding back. It cracked its head from side to side, then stretched its wrinkled neck like a turtle extending its head from its shell.

In the glow of the circling lights, Kate finally glimpsed the monster. It moved its head toward her. She gasped as the droopy, bloodshot eyes of Lieutenant Brett locked onto the window, as if he was staring directly at her.

After nearly fifty years of captivity, the lieutenant had finally broken free. And he had come for his revenge on the scientists who experimented on him.

He leaped off the table and tore across the room, plucking something off one of the stations as he moved. Wild and deranged, Brett was still shockingly agile.

Kate's heart hammered at the sight. She pulled Ringgold toward the exit door of the small office.

"Help me open the door," Ringgold repeated, resisting Kate's grip.

"We can't—" Kate began to say. Her words were lost under a tormented howl. Brett leaped onto Carmen and wrapped his thin legs around the scientist's waist. He plunged a shiny object into Carmen's side, and blood squirted onto the window glass. Hot, raspy breaths fogged the scientist's visor as he shrieked in agony.

Carmen flailed, then palmed the glass. He fell to his knees, Brett still wrapped around him and sticking him in the guts with a lab instrument the entire way to the floor.

Yokoyama ran for the exit, but his oxygen cord yanked him backward. He crashed to the ground and quickly scrambled to his feet. Brett looked up as the doctor fled.

"President Ringgold, we need to leave. *Now!*" Kate yelled.

Ringgold had her hand cupped over her mouth but managed a weak nod. They crossed the small room, and Kate grabbed the handle of the exit hatch. The locking mechanism clicked and she pushed the hatch open, leaving Carmen and Yokoyama behind.

Meg strolled across the lawn with Tasha and Jenny on each side. She wanted so badly to hold their tiny hands, but instead, she gripped the rubber of her crutches tighter. In a few days, if Dr. Hill agreed, she was going to toss the metal pegs into the ocean. Depending on her mood, maybe she would do it even if he didn't agree.

"When's my daddy coming home?" Tasha asked.

"I'm not sure, sweetie."

"Is he fighting the monsters again?" Jenny asked.

Meg stopped a couple hundred feet from where Riley and Fitz were briefing a group of soldiers.

"No, he isn't fighting them, but he's teaching others to fight," Meg explained.

"Like those guys?" Tasha asked. She pointed to the soldiers.

"Yes, like those men. Do you want to watch?" Meg didn't want them overhearing anything scary, but they were bored. And besides, she missed Riley. He had been so busy with the troops, she'd hardly seen him recently.

Both girls nodded, and Meg crutched over to the landing outside Building 3. Riley was talking about a mission to New York and explaining how the creatures moved and attacked—something about pack behavior, and other crap that Meg didn't care to know. She carefully took a seat on the concrete steps and put her arms around the girls. When she married her husband, they'd agreed not to have children, but spending time with Horn's girls had shown her how much she enjoyed kids.

She gripped the girls tighter, her mind wandering like the Black Hawk patrolling the sky over the island. The briefing, or training, or whatever it was, continued for another fifteen minutes. Lieutenant Rowe and Major Smith were answering questions now. She had tuned out for most of it, but her ears perked up when she heard a marine ask who would be leading the mission.

Rowe turned to Riley and Fitz. For a moment her heart skipped a beat. There was no way Riley could go back out there. Not like this.

"Corporal Fitzpatrick will be leading the teams into New York. Don't let his appearance deceive you. I'm sure Fitz can outrun most of you, and he sure as hell is a better shot." Rowe flashed the first grin—the first sign of *any* emotion—Meg had seen since she'd met him.

Fitz dug his right blade into the grass like a batter stepping up to the plate. He managed a grin and said, "I know you're all scared. Heck, I'd be lying if I told you I wasn't. But the Variants can be killed. I've killed more of those monsters than I killed insurgents in Iraq. And I'm not proud of it, but I killed quite a few insurgents." He bowed his head slightly, his auburn hair blowing in the breeze, a memory surfacing on his mind.

He looked up again, the smile gone. "Be smart out there, stay frosty, and tomorrow we will return with a juvenile Variant. And, God willing, in less than two weeks we will win this war."

The words resonated with a few of the marines.

"Oorah!" someone yelled.

"Oorah," Fitz said in a deep voice.

Within a few seconds, all of the men had joined in. Rowe stroked his jawline, then held up a hand. "Thank you, Corporal," he said. "That's all for tonight, so get some rest. Tomorrow's going to be a big day."

The marines dispersed, but Riley didn't move his chair. He glanced over at Meg, his features lacking enthusiasm. There was a frown on his face, and she knew why: He wanted more than anything to go out there with the other soldiers. Fitz patted him on the back, acknowledged Meg with a short nod of his head, then followed the other men across the lawn.

Both girls were nestled next to Meg on the top step, pointing out the shapes of clouds to each other. She didn't disturb them, but in that moment she wanted nothing more than to hug Riley.

"What do you mean, Fitz is leading a strike team to New York?" Beckham said. There was no holding back the shock in his voice. He had suggested Fitz *train* a team, not lead it. He didn't bother asking Lieutenant Davis why she hadn't informed him of the decision earlier. He was too mad for that.

"Lieutenant Rowe thought he was the most qualified man on Plum Island," she replied.

"Shit—we're the most qualified teams left in the world, but we're not being sent out there."

"We should be," Garcia added.

The Variant Hunters and Team Ghost were still on the deck of the *GW*. Behind them, marines talked quietly during a short break. The gusting wind couldn't hide the trepidation in their hushed voices.

"I specifically ordered Fitz to guard the island," Beckham said. "We need him in Tower Four. He's a sharp-shooter the island can't afford to lose."

Davis blinked her crystal-blue eyes as if she was considering a harsh response. After a pause, she said, "Corporal Fitzpatrick is no longer under your command, Master Sergeant. He reports to Major Smith. I'm sorry, but he is leading the men from Plum Island to New York."

"And Smith authorized this?" Horn asked. He flared his nostrils. It was the same thing he always did before he blew a gasket. He was clearly agitated and worried about Fitz and his girls. Beckham didn't blame him. There were so few of them left that losing Fitz and the girls would be unbearable.

No. They aren't going to die.

Beckham took a knee in front of Apollo, scratching his ears. The dog's nose sniffed at the air, and he leaned in to give Beckham a wet kiss on the cheek.

"Yes, Major Smith approved the orders," Davis said after a short pause. She blinked again and crinkled her nose, one eye on Horn. Beckham shot his friend a glare that said, *Back off*.

"If Fitz is going out there, then I want Apollo to go with him." Beckham rose to his feet. The dog wasn't doing anyone any good cooped up on the carrier, and he would protect Fitz with his life.

Davis twisted her lips to the side. "I suppose I can arrange that. We have a Black Hawk leaving for Plum Island in . . ." She looked at her watch. "An hour."

Beckham stroked Apollo's fur and bowed his head to his companion's until they were touching. The dog's wet snout brushed against his forehead. He didn't want to let Apollo go, but doing so made him feel as if he was helping his friend.

"You take care of Fitz, boy," Beckham said. "Don't let anything happen to him." He reached into his pocket and pulled out a notepad he had used to take notes for Operation Condor.

"You got a pen?" Beckham asked Davis.

She pulled one from her pocket and handed it to him. Beckham tore out a piece of paper and scribbled a message to Fitz, then tucked the note into Apollo's satchel. The dog wagged his tail as he licked Beckham's cheek a second time. Rising to his feet, Beckham handed Davis her pen. "Thank—"

A shout from a ladder leading to the carrier's command center cut him off. "Lieutenant!"

Captain Humphrey stood on a platform above them, "vulture's row," his hair blowing wildly in the wind. "There's a situation on the *Cowpens*."

Beckham's rising fear of losing Apollo and Fitz shifted to full-blown panic. Kate was on the *Cowpens*, and so was President Ringgold. He reached for the Colt .45 on his hip, unstrapping the buckle.

"Lieutenant Brett has escaped," Humphrey said. "Get over there ASAP and kill that son of a bitch. Eagle Five is warming up right now."

"Yes, sir!" Davis shouted back.

Beckham whistled at the sailor patrolling the flight deck with a German shepherd. "I need you to watch Apollo!"

The man ran over and grabbed Apollo by the collar.

"If Master Sergeant Beckham isn't back, make sure the dog is on Eagle Three in an hour," Davis said.

The sailor nodded, holding Apollo tightly. The dog could sense something was wrong; he growled and fought in the man's grip.

"You have to stay—I'm sorry, boy. Protect Fitz," Beckham said. He patted Apollo's head and hesitated for a single second, looking at the dog one last time before yelling, "Let's move, Ghost!"

Chow spat his second toothpick of the night onto the deck and ran after Beckham and Horn. Apollo howled after them. Then came a pounding of boots, and when Beckham glanced over his shoulder, Garcia, Tank, and Thomas were following them.

"We need weapons," Horn said.

Beckham pulled out his Colt .45 and raced after Davis, who was already halfway to the flight deck.

On the horizon, a red light flashed from the satellite tower of the *Cowpens* like the beacon of a lighthouse warning ships away from danger. Most men would have run the other way, but as he had so many times before, Beckham led his men toward the threat.

The Black Hawk was airborne five minutes later. Team Ghost and the Variant Hunters sat on the gunship in silence, all of them sorting through pre-combat thoughts. None of them asked the obvious question of how Lieutenant Brett had escaped. All that mattered was killing him before he killed anyone else.

Before he hurt Kate or President Ringgold.

Beckham shut down the thought before it could do any more damage. He was going into battle. He needed his confidence, not his fear, driving him forward. He watched Apollo on the flight deck, still fighting his handler. The dog's barking faded beneath the *chop* of the rotors. Beckham forced himself to look away and turned back to the *Cowpens*.

He opened the Colt's cylinder, checked the six .45 rounds, and then snapped it back into place. The bird descended over the stern and touched down on the *Cowpens*'s helipad. Davis jumped onto the deck and ducked under the rotors. Beckham and crew followed close behind. A squad of sailors in tactical gear met them on the deck, M16s in hand. They distributed weapons to Team Ghost and the Variant Hunters.

"This way, Lieutenant," one of the men said.

They passed RIM-66 surface-to-air missile launchers and ran for a ladder that led to the next level. Two soldiers draped in shadow were waiting at a hatch.

Davis paused there. "What's the situation, Sergeant?"

Beckham slung the M16 over his back and then pulled back the hammer on his Colt .45, one eye on the dark-skinned sergeant at the hatch.

"Lieutenant Brett killed both technicians preparing him for execution about thirty minutes ago. He then proceeded to kill the guards stationed at the brig. The blood trail leads to the lab next, where he killed Doctor Carmen. From there, we're not sure where he went. We have two teams searching for him. Fortunately, Doctor Yokoyama escaped."

Davis cupped her hand over her earpiece. "Yes, Mr. Vice President, I've just landed…I'm not sure, sir. Stand by."

"Where's President Ringgold?" Davis asked the sergeant.

"And Doctor Lovato?" Beckham added. He could hardly hold himself back; his muscles ached to move.

The sergeant shook his helmet. "I'm afraid we don't know."

17

"We can't stay in here," President Ringgold whispered.

Kate continued searching the storage room for a weapon in the faint light. The room was lined with shelves, but there was nowhere to hide, and Kate saw no weapons. "If we go back out there, we risk running into Lieutenant Brett," she whispered. "We need to stay here and wait for the soldiers."

She quietly rummaged through a box of supplies. They'd locked themselves in the storage room after escaping the lab. What Brett had done defied everything Kate knew about the Variants. The creatures didn't use weapons, but he'd killed Dr. Carmen with a knife. Then again, Brett wasn't really a Variant: His platoon had been infected with VX-99 in 1968, not with Dr. Medford's hybrid version from 2014. That meant he was even more dangerous. If he could use a knife, he could open doors, and Kate suspected he'd used one of the dead guard's key cards to get into the secured lab.

Kate grabbed a broom and jammed it through the wheel handle of the hatch.

Where the hell are all the soldiers?

As if in answer, the pop of gunfire echoed from the passage outside. A flurry of rounds pinged off the bulk heads. Kate put her ear up to the hatch to listen. A muffled scream followed, but it wasn't Brett's hoarse voice. This was a sailor.

Two more shots rang out, silencing the scream.

Kate found President Ringgold's haunted eyes in the dim light. Another screech reverberated through the passage outside. Kate backed away from the door and retreated several steps to stand by the president, her hands cupped over her mouth.

A torrent of gunshots ricocheted off the overhead outside the storage room.

"No, please...*No!*" someone shouted.

There was another shot and the wet crack of a bullet breaking through a skull.

Then only silence.

Not a lucky shot—an execution.

Kate staggered backward, her fears realized. Brett could use a gun.

Over the blare of emergency alarms came the scratching of a blade on metal. Kate took another step away from the hatch, inadvertently ramming a shelf and knocking several boxes onto the ground. The clanking reverberated through the room.

Heart lodged in her throat, Kate froze, her hands pressed tightly over her mouth. The scratching grew louder and closer, until it stopped just outside the hatch to the storage room.

"Kate," Ringgold whispered.

Kate held up a finger as the hatch rattled. The thin broom handle shook violently, clanging against the steel.

Voices called out somewhere in the bowels of the ship, muffled and distant. Reinforcements were finally coming. Kate hurried to the corner of the room with Ringgold. Together, they tipped over one of the shelves and crouched behind it. The president gripped Kate's hand tightly in her own and began to mouth a prayer.

Kate knew Beckham was out there somewhere, searching for her. It was only a matter of time before they found Brett, but how long before Brett—

The broom handle snapped in half, the splintered pieces dropping to the floor.

The wheel twisted and the hatch clicked open. Light streamed into the room, spreading a blanket of red that crept toward Kate and Ringgold.

In the doorway stood the emaciated frame of Lieutenant Brett. Shoulders hunched and torso withered, his awkward posture unnerved Kate.

He explored the room with deranged eyes, as if everything he saw was completely new to him. The circling red lights illuminated his droopy skin, sagging muscles, and the pistol he gripped with brown horned fingernails.

Ringgold grabbed Kate's arm as he turned toward the shelving unit. Brett swept it aside almost casually. He slowly aimed the barrel of his gun at the president. Kate held up her hands and shifted her body in front of Ringgold.

"Please, you don't have to do this, Lieutenant Brett!" she cried.

He tilted an ear ever so slightly, as if he didn't quite remember his own name. Gun trembling in his hand, he croaked, "Th-ey ..."

The pounding of footsteps echoed down the hall, but Brett didn't turn.

"They," he coughed. He rotated slightly to look into the passage, veins stretching across his pale skin. In a rapid movement, he turned back to Kate and Ringgold, eyes wide and wild. "Hurt me ... destroyed me!"

Kate held her hands in the air. "I'm so sorry for what they did to you, but the killing has to end. You can stop it, Lieutenant."

"Medic!" someone shouted down the passage. The soldiers had found the sailors Brett had already killed.

Kate winced as he pushed the gun at her.

"You don't have to do this," Kate whimpered. "Please. You don't have to kill anyone else. I'm—I'm pregnant."

Brett's eyes centered on her stomach. His wrinkled face twisted in a grimace, and he tilted his head slightly as if he was trying to understand.

Kate dropped one hand to shield her stomach. "Don't do this, Lieutenant. I know there is a good man locked inside you. They didn't destroy all of you. Lieutenant Trevor Brett would not kill an innocent child."

A croak escaped Brett's mouth as he attempted a reply. His next strained words were lost in the crack of a gunshot. Kate closed her eyes on reflex, her muscles tightening to prepare for the bullet that would end her life, shot by the same man who was there when VX-99 was first used in Vietnam over sixty years ago.

There was a second shot, then a third.

Ringgold cried out. Kate's eyes snapped back open to a sight she didn't understand. Brett slumped to his knees in front of her. The top left side of his skull was blown away, and there was a gaping hole in his chest where his heart should have been. What was left of his insides slopped through his exposed rib cage and onto the ground with a wet plop. The pistol fell from his hand and clanked next to Kate. A soldier kicked it away from Brett's reach and rushed to Kate's side. Her heart kicked so hard she couldn't catch her breath.

"Kate!" the man said. "Kate, are you okay?"

The voice was familiar, but her vision was blurry, as though she was looking through thick glasses. She blinked away the stars and the room came into focus. Beckham was staring down at her, his lips still moving.

"I'm okay," Kate said.

Horn, Chow, and Lieutenant Davis ran into the space. Sailors and marines waited in the passage, radio chatter echoing around them. Kate's hand rested on her stomach. Beckham joined the other soldiers surrounding the president.

"She's been hit," someone said.

"Get a medic!" yelled Lieutenant Davis.

Brett's mangled corpse was sprawled a few feet away, pooling blood surrounding his withered body. His eyes were locked on her, and he blinked one final time before they rolled up into his ruined skull—finally at peace after a lifetime in hell.

Kate looked to President Ringgold. Her white blouse was covered in blood. Horn pressed his hands over the lapel pin on her collar. Beckham was on her other side, holding one of her hands.

"Where's the medic?" he shouted.

"On the way," Davis said.

Beckham glanced over at Kate. "Are you sure you're okay?"

She managed a nod and reached out to grab Ringgold's other hand. It was limp. There was so much blood, but she couldn't tell if it was from Brett's exploded rib cage or the hole he'd blown in Ringgold.

"Stay with me, President Ringgold," Beckham said. "Fight."

Red light churned around the small room, panicked voices and crackling radios filling the tiny space. Ringgold's eyelids fluttered. She caught Kate's gaze for a single heartbeat before they closed.

Clouds the color of aging bruises drifted across the horizon. It was midmorning, but Plum Island was already humid. The temperatures would easily rise into the upper nineties today. Fitz didn't mind the heat; he just hated the high humidity. He was sitting on the tarmac gluing rubber pads on the bottoms of his blades when Lieutenant Rowe strode toward the four strike teams heading to New York City.

Everyone, including Fitz, stood to attention. Most of the men looked well rested, despite the fact they had trained into the late evening hours the night before. Riley sat in his chair a few feet away, maps draped over his knees, going over the plan with several other soldiers. The kid was meticulous, never overlooking a single detail.

"All right, listen up!" Lieutenant Rowe shouted. "Check and double-check your gear. Everyone should have three smoke grenades and two suppressed weapons. Try on your gas mask to make sure it works. Check your buddy's gas mask to make sure it does too. I don't want any surprises when we get out there."

The three men in Fitz's strike team circled around. They were all marines, but none of them had any combat experience with Variants. Lance Corporal Andre Cooper, a thirty-year-old with thin lips and a crooked nose, had served in Afghanistan, but PFCs Benjamin Knapp and Erik Craig hadn't fired their weapons outside of training. He didn't trust them for shit. Hell, he hardly knew anything about them. But this was what it had come to—heading into battle against an overwhelming force with inexperienced men.

Fitz finished applying the rubber pads. He jogged in place for a few seconds, and to his surprise, he felt little to no impact.

"Looking good," Cooper said. His lips stretched into a long grin that reminded Fitz of a gator.

Knapp and Craig continued prepping their gear without saying a word. When they pulled on their gas masks, Fitz checked to make sure they worked. Then he screwed the suppressor onto his MK11. It added only five and a half inches of length to the barrel, but he had a feeling it could become unwieldy when maneuvering through tunnels.

"Staff Sergeant Riley is going to explain the final details of the mission," Rowe said when all of the soldiers had finished their gear checks.

Riley looked up from his map. "The air force has identified Grand Central Station in Manhattan as the primary target to lure the Variants above ground. We know there's a huge hive there. How many of them survived the firebombing of Operation Liberty is anyone's guess."

"I heard there were more than a hundred thousand," Knapp said.

Riley shrugged limply. "That's why we have two bombing runs, to burn any of the fucks that crawl out of their nests. You know the rest: Once you're inside the lair, you will turn on your UV lights, deploy your smoke grenades, kill any adult Variants, and use your tranq guns on the juveniles. Remember to watch your zone of fire. The last thing we need is a casualty from friendly fire." He paused to straighten the kinks out of the map. "This entire area is a war zone. Prepare for bodies and debris. Any questions?"

"Lieutenant! A word, please," called a voice. Major Smith hurried across the asphalt. He stopped and whispered something to Rowe. The lieutenant cursed.

Fitz slung his rifle over his back and strode over to the officers while the other soldiers asked Riley questions.

"Something wrong, sir?" Fitz asked.

Rowe continued chewing on a piece of something, his square jaw moving, but he didn't reply.

"President Ringgold has been shot," Major Smith said.

Riley folded the map and exchanged a worried glance with Fitz, both of them likely wondering the same thing.

Had Vice President Johnson betrayed her? Were Beckham and Team Ghost okay?

"Apparently, Lieutenant Brett was being held prisoner aboard one of the ships," Smith said. "He was supposed to be executed, but he escaped and killed a scientist and several sailors last night, shooting the president in the process."

Riley wheeled over. "Who the fuck is—wait." He blinked, realization setting in. "The lieutenant from Vietnam?"

"Yeah," Smith said. He narrowed his eyes at Rowe.

"Shit, don't blame me for what the lab jockeys do in their chop shops," Rowe said.

"Is President Ringgold going to be okay?" Fitz asked. He didn't give a shit about how it happened or why they'd had Brett on the ship, but he did care about the president. She had been kind to him, and she was an intelligent, honorable woman. The country needed her. The human race needed her.

"I'm not sure. She's still in surgery," Smith said.

"I hope she pulls through," Rowe replied. There was sincerity in his voice that Fitz appreciated. He was about to go back out there with this man and was glad to know he was one of the good guys.

The other soldiers slowly circled around, and Rowe waved them off. "Get back to your goddamn gear checks. We leave in three hours."

"Fitz—one other thing," Smith said.

"Yeah?"

"Beckham wants you to take Apollo with you to NYC. The dog should be here in a few hours."

Fitz nodded. "Better find a gas mask that fits a dog, then."

"I'm told Apollo will have a satchel pack with everything he needs."

Fitz cracked his neck. He loved Apollo, but the thought of taking him out there and trying to protect him...Maybe Beckham was hoping Apollo would help protect Fitz.

No, Fitz realized. *He wants us to protect each other.*

Fitz felt the familiar rise of pre-combat anxiety. He turned and looked out over the island. Tree limbs shifted in the breeze, chirping birds filling the morning with their soft melodies. The peace he'd finally started to enjoy here was about to end. In a few short hours, he would be returning to hell, and somewhere deep in the marrow of his bones, he felt as if he deserved it.

Beckham wanted to scream, but instead he wrapped his arm around Kate. She nestled her head against his shoulder. The stitches in his arm still stung, but the stab of pain was nothing compared to what he was feeling inside. The small waiting room outside the sick bay was dark, and it wasn't hard to let the despair creep in.

He was supposed to keep President Ringgold safe, but he'd failed, just as he had with so many others—Tenor, Edwards, Panda, Timbo, Jinx, and Jensen. Now Fitz and Apollo were going back out there without him.

Thinking about the chain of events that had led him here was maddening. A soldier could go insane obsessing over the details and decisions. If Beckham had turned a moment earlier on that rooftop, maybe Riley would still be walking. If he hadn't let Jinx go topside in New York, maybe he would still be alive.

That was war.

But this was different.

None of it should have happened. Lieutenant Brett should never have been kept alive, and the hemorrhage virus should never have been developed. The incompetence of those above him continued to enrage him.

"It's not your fault," Kate whispered as if she could read his mind. "You can't be everywhere. Vice President Johnson wanted you to train the strike teams here."

"But I promised President Ringgold I would keep her safe. If she dies—"

"She isn't going to die."

"Brett fired his gun on reflex, didn't he?" Beckham asked.

Kate raised her head off his shoulder. "Don't go there. You saved our lives. If you hadn't shot him..."

"He would have shot you both?"

Her slight hesitation told him he was right; it was his two shots that had caused Brett to fire on Ringgold. It was another detail that would drive him mad. He'd heard Kate trying to talk Brett down at the last minute, and the lieutenant hadn't fired until Beckham did.

"I have to go back to Plum Island," Kate whispered.

Beckham straightened his back. "What? When?"

"As soon as I can," she said. "Ellis needs help finishing the batch of Kryptonite."

"When were you going to tell me?"

Kate massaged his hand with a thumb. "I'm sorry. I just found out a few hours ago."

"I thought Ellis said he could handle it."

"He needs help encapsulating the chemotherapeutics with the antibodies," Kate said. "President Ringgold authorized it right before—"

Beckham's guts hardened into a knot.

"Guess now's just as good a time to tell you as any," Beckham said.

"Tell me what?"

"Fitz is leading one of the strike teams into New York, and I sent Apollo to go with him."

"What?" Kate bit her lip. "I didn't even get to say goodbye."

Her tone made the knot in Beckham's stomach tighten. "I said goodbye to Apollo for both of us. But Kate, it's not goodbye anyway. We'll see them again. Command has put together a strong plan to capture a juvenile Variant. Apollo will protect Fitz."

"And he'll protect Apollo."

Beckham nodded. "They'll be okay, Kate."

Kate looked down. Her face was flushed and her lips pale. The grief and guilt was overwhelming her. Beckham reached over and kissed her on the cheek.

"It's okay," he repeated. But he wasn't sure he believed his own words. The mission wasn't going to be easy, and he hadn't even had a chance to talk to Fitz. He was lucky to have slipped a note for the marine into Apollo's satchel.

Kate and Beckham looked up as the hatch to the room opened. Captain Humphrey followed Vice President Johnson inside. The captain removed his hat and tucked it under his arm.

"How is she?" Johnson asked.

"Still waiting," Kate replied.

The men sat in the chairs behind them.

"Thank God you got there when you did, Beckham," Humphrey said.

Beckham wanted to tear into Humphrey and Johnson for keeping Brett alive. At the very least, they should have had him heavily guarded. The men had underestimated Lieutenant Brett. The military simply never learned the lessons of the past.

Instead of replying, Beckham shifted in his chair for a better view of the glass doors to the sick bay. There was movement on the other side, but he couldn't see what was happening.

The hum of white noised filled the room as they waited in silence. Fifteen minutes later, the door opened and a middle-aged man with kind green eyes stepped into the waiting room. Everyone stood, anxious for news.

"Doctor Klinger," Johnson said. "How is she?"

Klinger pulled off a surgical mask and said, "She's going to be okay, sir. The bullet only nicked her collarbone and missed all major arteries. We managed to stop the bleeding early."

Kate squeezed Beckham's hand, and he clasped it back, relief flooding over him.

"Good news," Johnson said. "When can I see her?"

"She's still under right now, but maybe in a couple of hours, sir."

"Thank you, Captain," Johnson said.

There was genuine sincerity in his voice, but it didn't take away from the fact that he'd allowed Brett to live. There was a small sliver of Beckham that thought maybe Johnson had allowed this to happen. He suppressed the paranoia. If Johnson wanted the presidency, he could have taken it.

"I need to get back to the bridge, sir," Humphrey said. "We're prepping for Operation Condor in Atlanta."

"I'll be up there shortly," Johnson replied.

Humphrey nodded and left at the same time as the surgeon. The glass doors to the sick bay and the hatch leading back into the carrier clicked shut simultaneously.

Johnson regarded Kate and Beckham in turn. "I hope you're ready, because in a few hours we're embarking on the next stage of Operation Extinction."

Beckham squeezed Kate's hand even tighter. They were ready, both of them, even if they weren't going to be together for what came next.

Fitz hung his blades out the open door of the Black Hawk as it ascended into the sky.

Riley sat in his chair on the tarmac below, Meg by his side. Tasha and Jenny, just tiny dots now, waved at the chopper. Fitz raised his right hand. He couldn't deny the fear swirling through him, but seeing what he was fighting for helped keep things in perspective.

The other three Black Hawks were already in the air. They raced across the cloudy sky toward New York City. Fitz turned from the view and pulled his blades into the troop hold. He patted Apollo's coat as he scrutinized his team. Lance Corporal Cooper nodded back, a sign he was ready to go. PFCs Knapp and Craig, however, had their heads bowed as if they were praying. Craig, it turned out, actually was praying: He pulled a rosary from his pocket, made the sign of the cross, and lowered his head again.

A few minutes into the flight, Knapp gripped his stomach and gagged.

"Puke out the fucking door, man," Cooper chuckled into the comm.

Fitz shot him a glare, then checked on Knapp. He was hunched over in his seat, face as white as a ghost, but he didn't throw up.

"Keep your head above your heart," Fitz said over the comm channel. "Take some deep breaths. You'll be fine."

Fitz reached down and stroked Apollo's coat again. It helped keep the anxiety at bay. Plus, the dog had more experience fighting than Cooper, Craig, and Knapp combined. Looking back at the three amigos he'd been saddled with, Fitz was glad to have Apollo along.

Reaching into his vest pocket, Fitz pulled out the note he'd found tucked into the satchel on Apollo's back. He'd discovered it when going through the dog's gear.

Fitz—

    Stay frosty out there, and bring my dog home in one piece.

                       Godspeed, brother,
                       Beckham

Fitz smiled and slipped the message back in his pocket. Any fear he'd felt was gone now, replaced with confidence. He had a mission to complete, and the last thing he was going to do was fail Beckham. He still struggled with what he'd done in Iraq. Killing the female sniper, shooting a teenager, and not being able to save innocent civilians—that was on him. He owned those deaths. Same with Wood's men. But even if he did deserve to be punished, he couldn't die just yet. Not before he made up for some of his sins.

"Listen up," Fitz said. "I'm Shepherd One on the comms. Cooper, you're Two, Knapp is Three, and Craig is Four. When we land, I'm on point. Cooper, you've got rear guard. The subway entrance is only a few minutes from our insertion point. We hold tight until the flyboys swoop in for the first drop."

By the time Fitz had finished going over their plan, the skyscrapers of Manhattan were in view.

"Holy shit," Craig said. "Sarge Riley was right. City's a fucking war zone."

"ETA two minutes," one of the pilots said over the comm.

Knapp looked up, his face still as pale as a Variant's. When he saw the city, he threw up on the floor.

"Jesus," Cooper said.

Fitz crouch-walked over to Knapp. "Get a grip, man."

The PFC wiped his mouth with a sleeve and nodded.

The potent scent of stomach acid filled the troop hold, but it was easy to ignore. Fitz had smelled plenty of bad shit over the past month, and it was only going to get worse from here.

Cooper chuckled, but didn't say anything. Fitz just shook his head. There wasn't anything he could do for Knapp but keep an eye on him. If they were compromised, they'd need all the firepower they could get. Fitz only hoped it wasn't Knapp's actions that got them compromised in the first place.

The chopper turned, providing a rolling view of Manhattan. One World Trade was still standing, but the lower third of the building was missing every window, and the streets were covered in ash. Scorched vehicles pockmarked the concrete arteries connecting the boroughs. Smoke rose from darkened buildings across the city. Heavy rainfall had put out most of the fires, but several structures continued to smolder.

Fitz saw no sign of the Variants from the air. He knew better: Like any enemy, they were probably watching him right now. The other Black Hawks vanished behind the skyscrapers, each one disgorging its team into the grinder.

Fitz scanned his team in turn one final time. Knapp's face had regained some color, but Cooper had an odd grin. Craig slipped his rosary back in his pocket. Apollo was sitting up, ears perked and wet snout ready to go to work.

Fitz ran a gloved finger over the Team Ghost patch on his arm, then reached for a magazine.

He was ready to rock and roll.

18

"Phase One of Operation Condor is complete. All teams are on the ground at assigned targets," Lieutenant Davis said from the front of the bridge. Team Ghost and the Variant Hunters were crowded behind the radar equipment, with the commissioned men and women positioned at the front of the room behind Vice President Johnson and Captain Humphrey. Outside the porthole windows, the clouds were starting to disperse, the sunlight bleeding through.

Thirty-two strike teams had been assembled and deployed across the country. It sounded like a lot, but with just four men on each team, they were each facing an enemy that vastly outnumbered them. Stealth was key if any hoped to complete their objective.

Beckham wiped sweat from his forehead and tried to get a look at the four monitors set up on the wall in front of Davis. The live video feeds were only from the strike teams that had taken off from the *GW* to Atlanta. On the left, two navy officers sat at a wall of radio equipment, listening for information from the other strike teams.

The room was crowded, and the scent of perspiration drifted in the air. Every hatch was closed, and the ventilation units didn't seem to be working. The only respite was the view of the ocean outside the porthole windows.

Watching from the safety of the *GW* felt like betraying Fitz, Apollo, and all the men going back out there. Beckham had faith in Fitz, but no matter how good of a shot he was, the sheer number of Variants he would face made success unlikely.

Beckham wasn't the only nervous soldier in the room. Garcia was fiddling with his broken nose a few feet away, anxious and distraught. He looked a lot like a raccoon with the bruises around his eyes. If it weren't for the situation, Beckham might have given him shit about it.

The first officer at the radio equipment turned to Davis. "All strike teams have radioed in, ma'am. They're in position and report no hostiles."

"Let's go to Phase Two. Air assets are clear to drop."

Horn and Chow huddled next to Beckham and Garcia. Tank and Thomas hung back, their arms folded across their uniforms, tattooed crosses showing. Beckham saw there was still a space for another name. Now he knew why Garcia was anxious to see the feeds. The marine still held on to hope that his man, Steve-o, was alive out there.

"I can't see shit," Horn said.

"Good," Chow whispered back. "This is going to be a fucking slaughter."

Beckham twisted to the side, his brows coming together. "Keep positive or keep your mouth shut."

Chow brushed a strand of black hair that had fallen across his forehead. "You got it, boss."

There was bitterness in his tone, but Beckham ignored it. He didn't have time to discipline right now.

The second radio operator said, "A squadron of F-16s just took off from Robins AFB. They're on their way to Atlanta, ma'am."

There was more riding on this operation than promotions and respect. They likely wouldn't get the opportunity to capture a juvenile Variant twice, and it showed in Davis's strained features. Beckham understood her nerves. If the mission failed, it was on her.

He reminded himself of his own advice to stay positive. One of the teams would surely succeed. Fitz and Apollo *would* succeed. This wasn't Operation Liberty, a mission planned by a lunatic where failure seemed to be a sure bet.

A few minutes later the F-18 Super Hornets on the flight deck of the *GW* launched for New York. Beckham couldn't see them, but he heard each one take off. It felt good knowing they were on their way to support Fitz and Apollo.

Through the wall of sweaty bodies, Beckham finally glimpsed the monitors at the front of the room. The strike teams were all holed up in buildings surrounding Turner Field. It didn't take long for the F-16s to reach the city. Ten minutes later, the feeds shook, and static hissed from the speakers. On monitor one, a marine centered his camera on the stadium. Four blips emerged on the horizon. The jets roared over the city, dropping their payloads just above Turner Field.

An orange mushroom blossomed above the stadium, and a deafening explosion blared from the wall-mounted speakers on the bridge. The brilliant flash of light filled the monitors, and when it faded, Turner Field was nothing but a smoking crater. Smoldering debris rimmed the hole, small fires raging across the blast zone.

If that didn't get the Variants' attention, Beckham wasn't sure what would.

Fitz held on to his helmet as fragments rained from the ceiling of the New York Public Library. Thud after thud rocked the structure, but it wasn't the library that was being hit. He looked out the second-floor window just as the final F-18 Super Hornet swooped over Grand Central Station.

A boom that rattled Fitz's bones shook the library, and the train station vanished in a cloud of smoke in the distance. Fiery orange tendrils reached out and licked the surrounding buildings.

"Radio discipline from here on out. Let's move," Fitz said into his headset. He wasn't going to wait around to see if the decoy drew the monsters from their lairs. If it worked, he would hear them coming anyway.

Apollo ran ahead, his nose sniffing the stairs. The entire building reeked of death and smoke, but a thin layer of dust and ash on the floor told Fitz the Variants hadn't been here for some time. His blades crunched over shattered glass. The doors to the main entrance were wide open, charred and burned from the firebombs that had been dropped during Operation Liberty. Chunks from the building's massive stone pillars littered the steps where high-caliber rounds had chipped away at the historic structure.

It smelled even worse outside. Fitz took in a whiff of a mixture of barbecue, rot, and sour fruit. Hundreds of decaying Variant corpses were sprawled across Bryant Park. They reminded him of the images he'd seen of Pompeii, bodies burned and twisted. Horned claws reached in every direction like tree branches. Fitz considered putting on his gas mask but opted for pulling his scarf up over his mouth and nose instead. He guided his team across the charred lawn, running between shattered trees and bodies piled on top of one another. First Platoon had put up one hell of a fight, but the masses of Variants had overwhelmed them.

A blast rocked the remains of Grand Central Station. Fitz motioned his team into the street without hesitation. He shouldered his suppressed MK11 and took point. The rubber padding he had glued onto the bottom of his blades cut down on any noise, as long as he wasn't moving over glass, and the grips clung to the ash covering the concrete.

He picked up his pace, his weapon's muzzle sweeping the road for contacts. Flakes of ash rained across his path like black snow. Above, the sun struggled to peek through the rolling cloud cover.

Apollo was a few feet ahead, sniffing for the scent of Variants. Having the dog was a blessing, but Fitz feared he couldn't protect him if shit hit the fan. He gritted his teeth and ran for an ambulance at the intersection of Fifth Avenue and Forty-Second Street. Knapp, Craig, and Cooper caught up a moment later. They hunched behind the vehicle and waited for Apollo to give them the all clear.

Several seconds passed. Then a minute. The dog was staring down Forty-Second, unmoving. He was so still he could have passed for a statue.

Besides the intermittent explosions from Grand Central Station, the derelict city was silent: no shrieking monsters, no screams of frightened civilians. There wasn't even a breeze. Sitting in the quiet of the massive city was surreal, as if Fitz was alone in the vacuum of outer space.

Apollo came running back to the ambulance with his tail down. Something had him spooked. Adrenaline rushed into Fitz's system for the first time since they landed. He got on his belly and crawled for a better view of Forty-Second, doing his best not to drag his blades.

Another blast rocked Grand Central Station, and a ball of fire ballooned into the air. A tormented howl that could have been from a dying animal sounded in the distance.

The hair on Fitz's neck prickled when he saw the pallid, skeletal figures squeezing from the sewer openings. The Variants darted into the streets on all fours, jointed appendages clicking as they raced across the concrete like an army of spiders. In seconds, hundreds of the monsters were exploring the streets.

The decoy had worked.

Fitz slowly crawled back to the other men. The snapping of joints echoed through the street, and he could see in the looks of the three marines they knew what was coming. Pushing himself up, Fitz slowly made his way around the other side of the ambulance. The subway station entrance was halfway down West Forty-Second. Several abandoned vehicles littered the road along the way. They could use the cars and trucks for cover.

Fitz signaled for his team to move. Knapp shook his head, wide and panicked eyes pleading for Fitz to reconsider. Craig's face was a mask of sheer terror.

For a moment Fitz wasn't sure what to do. He couldn't drag them down the street, and he couldn't sit here either. There wasn't time to give them a pep talk. Instead, he pointed at the ground and then slowly dragged a finger across his neck. Next, he pointed at both men in turn, as if to say, *Stay and you die*.

Cooper grinned at that. A few beats later, all three of the marines were following Fitz and Apollo toward the Bryant Park subway station, an army of monsters prowling the streets behind them.

"Only a few minutes, Doctor Lovato," Dr. Klinger said. "She needs her rest." He finished washing his hands off with a towel and left the room.

Ringgold struggled to open her eyes as Kate approached her bedside. She cracked a smile when she focused on Kate.

"Hi," Ringgold said, her voice hardly a whisper. "I didn't think we were going to make it there for a second."

Kate smiled back and took a seat in the chair next to her bed. "I didn't either. If it weren't for Beckham, we wouldn't have."

"He saved me again," Ringgold said. Her voice was stronger now, and her eyes were fully open. Despite her white hospital gown, she retained her professional poise.

"I suppose I should assign Beckham to my security detail full-time," Ringgold said with a chuckle.

Kate faked a smile as she remembered what Beckham had said about Brett firing as a result of his first shot. They would never know if his theory was right.

"If it weren't for Beckham, Brett would have shot me in the head," Ringgold continued. She looked down at the patch covering her collarbone. "One thing's certain— he had some reasoning ability left before he pulled the trigger, because he shifted his aim from you to me."

Kate shook her head. She had closed her eyes right before the gunshots. Had she talked Brett out of shooting her, only to have him shoot Ringgold?

"Congratulations, Doctor," Ringgold said.

Kate caught her gaze, heart flipping in her chest.

"I didn't know you were pregnant," Ringgold clarified. "I think that's why Brett didn't fire before Beckham came to our rescue."

Kate sucked in a long breath. "I'm sorry I didn't tell you earlier."

Waving her good hand, Ringgold said, "I understand. Trust me, I respect your privacy."

"Thank you," Kate replied.

"Speaking of Beckham, where is he? I'd like to thank him. Again."

"On the bridge. Operation Condor is under way. The strike teams should be on the ground."

Ringgold's smile vanished, and she sighed. "So it's begun? Part of me is glad I'm not up there to see what happens," she said. There was an uncharacteristic hint of timidity in the words.

Kate understood. She understood better than anyone. She had seen military failure after military failure since the outbreak. It was hard to imagine one of the teams would bring back a live specimen. She leaned back in her chair and looked at Ringgold, recalling the words the president had spoken just yesterday.

"There's always hope," Kate said.

Ringgold smiled and nodded. "Damn straight, Doctor."

Team Ghost and the Variant Hunters stood behind five other men and women on the bridge. Four screens hung from the bulkheads. Each display was divided into four boxes showing the feed from one of the soldiers. They were working their way through the sewers now, closing in on the lair of the White King that Garcia had identified during the briefing the night before. Beckham shivered. It wasn't long ago that he'd been running through the tunnels beneath New York City. Chow and Horn watched attentively, flashbacks likely playing in their mind. Tank and Garcia stood with their arms crossed, and Thomas was massaging the sides of his mustache.

Beckham felt their pain. Steve-o was likely dead, but soldiers always held on to hope. It was what made the grittiest part of war easier to stomach, believing that maybe a brother was still alive, or that a battle could be won.

He turned back to the screens. As an observer, it was difficult to distinguish between shadows in the dark passages. Every time the light shifted, Beckham thought it was a Variant.

"Echo, Romeo, Kilo, and Sierra are all approaching targets," Davis said from the front of the room.

Beckham kept an eye on the first monitor. On-screen, Echo 1 trudged through ankle-deep water. At the end of the passage, on the walls and ceiling, were the mangled bodies of human prisoners. All four members of Echo team stopped in the middle of the tunnel. They flipped on the UV lights attached to the ends of their weapons. The beams cut through the darkness and illuminated the cocoons.

The chatter from the command staff silenced. No one in the room said a word. Everyone stared at the monitors. Most of them hadn't seen the human prisoners before, but for Team Ghost and the Variant Hunters, this was nothing new.

"Proceed to target, Echo One," Davis said into her headset.

Echo 1 went forward, his rifle out in front. His team followed him, marching through the first passage of prisoners, muzzles up.

A distorted face stared back at Echo 1, flayed flesh hanging from cheekbones and eyes frozen in shock. Limbs hung from the ceiling, hands curled from rigor mortis. Most of the cocoons were torn, exposing the skeletal remains of the prisoners. The Variants had already fed on these corpses. Most were chewed to the bone.

The team pushed into the next tunnel, beams dancing from corpse to corpse. Beckham didn't need a high-resolution image to see some of these poor souls were still alive.

"Jesus," Vice President Johnson said. He looked at Garcia. "How much farther to the lair?"

In the second it took to ask the question, there was a flash of movement on all four screens. The light from Echo 1 captured a Variant hanging upside down from the ceiling. It tore a string of flesh from the prisoner it was feeding on and rotated in their direction, pulling away tendons and muscle. Before it had a chance to escape, Echo 1 fired a torrent of well-aimed shots.

The beast dropped from the ceiling, bringing the human prisoner down with it. The gluey residue of the cocoon stretched into a web as the two bodies fell. The Variant crashed to the ground, but the strings of glue held halfway down, suspending the prisoner in midair like an insect caught in a spiderweb.

All four soldiers approached slowly, their guns sweeping for more contacts. After a few steps, they stopped, but Beckham didn't see any other hostiles. Echo 1 lowered his cam on the corpse hanging from the ceiling.

The body suddenly twitched, and the prisoner fought to look up. Somehow, he was still alive. His lips trembled, and his eyes widened in the glow of the beams. He said something that looked a lot like *Help me.*

Beckham flinched as Echo 1 took a step back and shot the man in the forehead with his suppressed M4. It was then Beckham realized the man had said *Kill me.*

The troops continued through the final passages without stopping until they came to a tunnel overlooking a massive chamber.

Garcia nudged his way through the crowd for a better view.

"That's where the White King lives," he said.

Fitz pulled his shemagh scarf just below his eyes as he snuck into the stairwell of the Bryant Park subway station. The stench here was unbearable, and he almost tossed up his breakfast, as Knapp had in the chopper. Fitz paused on the second step with Apollo by his side, then motioned his team forward. They couldn't halt here, not with the Variants prowling the streets above.

He gagged as he carefully made his way down the steps. They were littered with corpses and flies. The insects were everywhere. Fitz batted them away as he moved. Thousands of them buzzed around the four marines. Some were the size of .38 rounds, bloated from feeding.

At first it didn't make any sense. These bodies should have decomposed weeks ago. The flies would have had their fill then, but now . . . As soon as Fitz clicked on his UV light he saw he was surrounded by the withered bodies of Variants.

Fitz had led his team to the site of a battle.

No. A massacre.

The walls, ceiling, and floor were covered in a thick layer of sticky blood. The frail frames of starving Variants dotted the ground at the bottom of the stairs. Some were torn to pieces, jointed appendages scattered in every direction.

What the hell happened here?

Fitz had heard of rival packs attacking one another. But this? This was beyond barbaric. Whatever creatures had done this were the result of more than freak mutations—this was the work of pure evil.

Fitz was transported back to Iraq. His squad had discovered a building of dead Sunnis in the town of Samarra just days after the Al-Askari Mosque bombing in 2006. Women, children, the elderly: The Iraqi extremists had spared no one. It had been a slaughterhouse, but even that paled in comparison to what Fitz was seeing now.

He paused halfway down the steps to the train tracks. The platform was riddled with more corpses. He continued staring, still lost in the memory of Iraq.

"Corp'ral Fitz," Cooper whispered. "Yo, Fitz."

It wasn't Cooper's words that pulled Fitz from his trance; it was the rumble coming from the street above, as if there was a sudden stampede of hundreds of bulls running through the city.

He looked back toward the exterior stairs just as what must have been an army of Variants raced by. The beasts blocked out the sun, covering the team in shadow. Fitz loped down the final stairs, the pads on his blades sticking to the coagulated blood.

The other marines were already on the move. They ran through the maze of bodies, down the stairs, and toward the edge of the platform. Apollo was already there, silent and unmoving. If it weren't for a slight twitch of his tail, Fitz wouldn't have even seen the dog. Apollo suddenly bared his teeth and turned toward the stairwell just as a voice hissed in Fitz's earpiece.

"Shepherd One, Command. Are you in position?"

"Negative, Command, we are not in position. Moving to—" The high-pitched wail of a Variant cut him off.

Distorted shadows flickered across the top of the stairwell. Fitz motioned for his team to take cover behind several pillars. Cooper pointed to Fitz, held up four fingers, and looked at his gun.

No, Fitz lipped.

Cooper stared back defiantly. He wanted to light the Variants up; Fitz could see it in his wild eyes. Knapp was shaking his head from his location two pillars down, his gun trembling in his hands.

They sent me out here with a sociopath and a coward.

Apollo nudged up next to Fitz's leg, growling.

And the best dog in the world, Fitz mentally amended.

"Shepherd One, air assets are incoming for second pass, confirm your pos—"

Fitz shut off the hissing frequency before the Variants could hear it. The marines had to get the fuck out of here if they didn't want to end up barbecued. He glanced around the pillar. A pack of Variants four strong sniffed from the top of the staircase, but none of them were advancing. It was as if they were afraid of what lurked in the shadows.

Not afraid enough.

The leader, a bulky creature with a Mohawk of scars, crept down the first three stairs. It stopped and raised a nose that was split down the middle. The second it let out a shriek, Fitz shouldered his rifle and stepped out from behind the pillar. He squeezed the trigger four times in a series of quick movements.

Three skulls detonated, and the fourth Variant took one in the neck, nearly decapitating it. The corpses thumped down the staircase.

Fitz shot an advance signal to the left of the tracks. He swung his blades over the side of the platform and jumped to the ground. Then he turned and hoisted Apollo down. Knapp and Craig came next. Cooper did a final sweep of the stairwell before leaping to the tracks.

Switching on his comm, Fitz said, "Command, Shepherd One is heading to objective. Over."

"Move it, Shepherd One, birds are coming in hot."

Cooper jogged up next to Fitz. "Nice shooting, but those were my kills."

Fitz stopped midstride. Knapp and Craig froze and watched the area with haunted looks. Cooper paused with that same stupid grin on his face from before. Fitz had a problem, and it was time to fix it.

"Lance Corporal, this is the one and only time I'm saying this: We're not on a fucking trophy hunt. Check your fucking attitude or go out on your own and rack up your kills. If we see your body on the way out, I'll bring it back for a burial at sea. But I wouldn't bet on that if I were you."

The challenge shut Cooper up, and the team raced into the darkness, the sliver of light at the end of the tunnel dwindling with every step. But now Fitz had another problem. Knapp was falling out. His labored breaths surged over the comm. Fitz wasn't about to slow down for him, but he couldn't leave the man behind.

A mechanical roar swept through the tunnel as the jets shot over the city for a second run. The next round of bombs fell over Manhattan. The impacts rattled the entire tunnel, dust and fragments sprinkling from the ceiling.

Fitz glanced over his shoulder to see a fireball explode across the platform they'd just left. The blast scorched the wall and ballooned in their direction.

"Run!" Fitz shouted. He lowered his rifle and sprinted with his helmet down. The wave of heat licked his back, singeing the hairs on his neck. He had glanced back to check on Knapp again when Apollo howled a warning.

"Watch out!" Cooper shouted, seeing the monsters at the same moment as the German shepherd.

Four Variants came barreling out of a side passage onto the tracks to avoid the explosions. The first two clipped Fitz as they darted into the tunnel, apparently just as surprised as the marines. He spun, tripped, and crashed to the ground.

Fitz scrambled to get up, but one of the creatures leaped onto his back. It dug its talons into his body armor. Swinging his helmet back, he smashed the beast in the nose, knocking it off.

The fireball surged forward, stopping a hundred feet short of their position. Fitz shielded his face from the heat with one hand and reached for his M9 with his other.

There was suppressed firing, and the ricochets of wild shots. Fitz blinked, his eyes stinging from the smoke, but he didn't have time to put on his gas mask. The blurred shape of the Variant staggered toward him. He raised his M9 as the creature slashed at him, knocking his pistol away and cutting his arm.

Fitz rolled away and dropped to the ground to find his weapon.

"Apollo!" Fitz shouted. He took in a gasp of air, coughing on the smoke.

More suppressed gunshots rang out, and a Variant wailed in agony. Then Fitz heard what sounded like a human scream. A body was catapulted through the air, crashing against a wall with a sickening thud.

Fitz felt for the M9 and picked it up. The monster tackled him to the tracks before he could fire off a shot. He landed on his back and grabbed its thin, wrinkled neck with his left hand, trying to raise his pistol with his right, but the beast's knee had that arm pinned down.

Snarling, it shook itself from his grip and lunged for his jugular. Fitz pulled his arm free and pistol-whipped it in the face, shattering jagged teeth. The beast howled in anger and yanked his gun away. Hot, rancid breaths puffed from its mouth, more awful than the decay and the smoke. Saliva dripped onto Fitz's nose as the monster leaned back in. He grabbed its neck with both hands and squeezed, but the monster was much stronger than it looked.

Fitz jerked his head to the right to avoid the needle teeth as the creature snapped at him again. He fought the urge to cough, tightened his grip, and pushed. Behind the lump of pale flesh on top of him, Fitz saw Knapp firing at the two remaining Variants as they prowled through the smoke. Craig was slumped against the wall, unmoving. The creatures made a run for Cooper, who'd been reloading his weapon when Fitz lost sight of them.

The gaping maw of the Variant on top of Fitz closed in, chomping behind swollen, veiny sucker lips. He pushed harder, but the beast inched closer.

"Help!" Fitz shouted.

Something slammed into the beast, and Fitz used every ounce of strength left to push it off him. He rolled out from under the monster as Apollo tore at the Variant's neck. The dog ripped a hunk of flesh away and then went back in for another bite. Warm blood slopped onto Fitz as Apollo chewed through arteries.

The Variant's body went limp, bleeding out in a matter of seconds. Relentless, Apollo continued tearing away flesh. Fitz pushed himself up, anxious to help his team. He stumbled, overcome by a sudden wave of dizziness. Through muddied vision, he saw Knapp had killed one of the other Variants, but the final one had pinned Cooper against a wall.

Knapp was sobbing uncontrollably. Before Fitz could tell him to stop, he raised his rifle and fired. Bullets slammed into both Variant and man, syrupy blood plastering the wall.

"No!" Fitz shouted. He ran for Knapp's position. "Hold your fire, goddamnit!"

Knapp continued shooting until his magazine was dry. Fitz stopped midstride and stared in horror at the mess the PFC had created. Cooper let out a whimper as he dropped to his knees. Blood gushed from his ruined body. The monster slumped to the ground by his side, twitching.

"Stand down, Knapp," Fitz said, his voice bordering

on a scream. He checked the passage to make sure there weren't any other Variants, then staggered over to Cooper and squatted down next to him.

Blood gurgled from the marine's lips. It only took a beat to see he wasn't going to make it. Cooper had taken rounds to the neck and chest. Geysers of crimson gushed from the bullet holes in his flak jacket. His arms and legs were shot to shit. There wasn't anything Fitz could do for him but grab his hand. He didn't like the man, but that didn't mean he deserved to be left to die alone.

"It's okay, Cooper, you're going to be okay," Fitz lied, trying to comfort him in his final seconds.

Cooper's throat made a wet, sucking noise as he struggled to speak. His eyes glazed over, but then suddenly locked on Fitz in a moment of awareness.

He cracked a bloodied grin as if he couldn't believe what was happening, then choked violently. "He..."

"It's okay, man," Fitz said.

Cooper coughed again. "He...He fucking shot me." His eyes rolled up into his head, and his hand fell away from his neck, a wicked grin still on his face. Fitz glared up at Knapp as Cooper died in his arms.

19

Steve-o was still alive.

Garcia could feel it in his bones. He raised his arm and discreetly pulled back his sleeve. The tattooed cross still had another spot for a fallen brother. When Tank and Thomas asked why he hadn't filled it in yet, Garcia didn't reply.

The more he contemplated Frankie's final words in Atlanta, the less he trusted them. He was a fucking human collaborator, for God's sake. Garcia was convinced he shouldn't have left Steve-o on the word of such a scum-sucking bastard. He'd made the wrong call again.

"Echo One, Romeo One, Kilo One, and Sierra One, you are clear for next phase," Lieutenant Davis said.

The words pulled Garcia back to the present. The bridge was hot as hell, and he dragged his arm over his forehead. His broken nose stung from the slight touch. He blinked away a bead of sweat and focused on the monitors.

This was it.

On-screen, the strike teams crept to the edges of the tunnels emptying into the massive chamber. Below, the shapes of dozens of sleeping Variants came into focus.

The decoy had worked. Most of the monsters were scouting for prey topside. Hopefully the bombs had toasted the majority of them.

So far, so good.

Garcia exchanged a glance with Beckham. The Delta Force operator nodded sternly, and Garcia nodded back. Whatever happened next would determine both their fates. If the strike teams failed, then chances were good they were heading back out there.

On-screen, Echo 1 angled his camera toward the raised platform in the center of the room. Garcia continued searching for any sign of Steve-o. There was movement on the floor, a single Variant walking through the maze of armored lumps. He instantly recognized the gait and anemic skin of the hunched, emaciated monster.

"That's him," Garcia said, pointing. "That's the White King."

Again, there was no reply. Everyone continued to stare at the screens, fingers on chins, arms crossed. The palpable tension couldn't have been shattered with anything short of a sledgehammer.

One by one, the men on-screen slipped on gas masks. Then came the smoke grenades. The canisters sailed from the four tunnel entrances. In seconds, the chamber was filled with smoke. Sabers of UV light shot from their weapons, penetrating the cloud below as the marines prepared to move. The White King blended in with the gray swirling cloud. Flurried movements broke out in the heart of the smoke as the other Variants woke from their slumber.

Echo 1 wasted no time. The soldier slid down a ladder to the ground. As soon as his boots hit the concrete, he moved forward with the butt of a suppressed M4 cupped under his armpit and the tranq pistol in his other hand.

The strike teams formed a perimeter around the

White King's throne and advanced toward the juvenile Variants. It was hard to follow what happened next. All hell broke loose in a single heartbeat, and adrenaline dumped into Garcia's veins as if he were there himself.

Rounds lanced into the smoke, slamming into disoriented Variants galloping from the fray. Riddled with bullet holes, the monsters crashed to the floor, coughing and clawing at the air. Echo 1 nailed kill shot after kill shot. He was a skilled shooter, and for a second Garcia couldn't believe it was the kid from the flight deck with all those questions. The lance corporal was hardly inexperienced. He marched through the smoke firing short bursts into the desperate monsters, mindful of his zone of fire.

Garcia couldn't hear the battle, but in his head, he imagined the tormented howls of the creatures. The chaos and death was nothing new to his eyes, nor those of the Delta operators next to him. The same couldn't be said for the command staff. Most of them had never seen a Variant up close.

Smoke shifted across the screens. Through the shroud of gray, several Variants stood their ground. They thrashed wildly at the approaching marines, but the men cut them down easily from a distance.

This wasn't a battle. It was a slaughter.

Halfway to the platform, only two of the sixteen feeds were idle, indicating fallen marines. Garcia felt a dangerous emotion rising inside of him.

Hope.

Ooh-fucking-rah.

"Hell yeah," Horn said.

Tank made a fist with his right hand.

The Variants darted away from the advancing teams. Swirling smoke covered their retreat. Echo 1 moved faster now. There was a sudden blur of motion across his screen.

He whirled toward the flash of pallid flesh as it slashed the neck of Echo 3. The marine fell to his knees, hands wrapped around his neck as he bled out. Echo 1 continued past the dying man, his weapon sweeping for the Variant.

Garcia checked the other screens. Echo 4 and Echo 2 were slowly making their way through the screen of gray. A cape of skin flew past their cams. Both men whirled, but the beast was already gone. In the second it took for Garcia to shift his gaze to Echo 1, a pair of claws reached out and grabbed Echo 4, pulling the marine into the smoke.

"Shit," Tank said. "What the hell was that?"

Sierra 1 and Romeo 3 were whisked away in the span of two minutes. Garcia still hadn't seen what killed them. Their feeds showed nothing but smoke and pooling blood on the concrete.

The other marines worked their way forward, but one seemed to drop every minute. The tide was quickly changing.

"What the hell is happening?" Vice President Johnson asked. There was fear in his voice. He ran a nervous hand over his shiny scalp. Davis was pacing now, shifting from screen to screen.

Echo 1 continued into the smoke, muzzle searching for the Variants killing his brothers. An emaciated beast rolled across his feed. The flash of motion continued to the screen of Echo 2. The marine fired off a shot as two clawed hands swiped at his face. Echo 2 avoided the talons and jumped away, his camera catching a snapshot of the back of the creature that had attempted to kill him. It moved like the wind, disappearing into the smoke.

"How can they see?" Johnson asked. There was no response, and the vice president hissed in frustration. "Somebody tell me what the hell is happening!"

"I don't know, sir," Davis replied. "Intel indicated that—"

"That intel was bullshit," Johnson said.

A fragmented memory of Garcia's time in the lair emerged in his mind. He was walking toward the White King. The creature's cloudy eyes had locked onto him. Then another image replaced it: the White King barreling into the Alpha that had broken Garcia's nose.

The realization hit him then. How could he have been so stupid? This wasn't a desperate attempt by several Variants trying to save their offspring. It was the last stand of the White King. The fucker *was* blind after all, but he had adapted to see without eyes. Whether it was by sonar or something else, it didn't matter. They had to stop the monster before he killed every marine in the chamber.

Garcia pushed his way to the front of the room. "Lieutenant, tell all strike teams to regroup and kill that one! It's the White King!"

Davis glared at him with her crystal-blue eyes, then looked at Johnson for approval.

"Do it," the vice president said.

"Echo, Romeo, and Sierra, regroup and advance in pairs. Target is the White King."

Ten minutes had passed since the teams had entered the chamber, and half the men were already dead.

Echo 1 and 2 came together side by side on-screen. Sierra 2 and 3 managed to find each other, but Romeo's screens were all idle now, smoke rolling past their still feeds. The only team left intact was Kilo. They advanced toward the raised platform where the juvenile Variants were.

Garcia searched the walls in the background, still holding on to a sliver of hope that Steve-o was alive. Distorted shapes like eggs emerged on Kilo 3's screen. The marine turned away before Garcia could see if any of the human prisoners were alive.

The hunt for the White King continued on the monitors. Sierra and Echo gunned down the injured Variants crawling across the ground.

"There," Davis said. "Those are the targets." She pointed to Kilo's monitors. There was movement in the swirling gray. Dozens of scaly juvenile Variants clambered across the ground, cone-shaped heads watching the approaching soldiers. They reached out with long, armored limbs. These monsters were larger than those Garcia remembered seeing at Turner Field. They looked as if they had grown several inches in a matter of days.

Kilo 1 and 2 were hit just as they raised their tranq pistols. The White King slashed their necks before either of the men could deflect the blows. Kilo 3 and 4 opened fire, but the beast disappeared back into the smoke. They backpedaled away from the targets, their weapons arcing wildly.

Johnson put his hand on his forehead and sighed. "Tell those men to stand their ground."

Sierra 3 went down next, one of the injured mother Variants pouncing on him. A second creature, missing a hand, lunged toward the camera. Sierra 2 killed both of the monsters, but the White King found him as he reached to change his magazine. This time the beast snapped the marine's neck. He fell face first to the concrete, the feed cutting out from a shattered cam.

Sierra and Romeo were gone.

Garcia took in a breath to manage his nerves. God, he wanted to be out there fighting with these men.

Echo 1 and 2 walked slowly through the smoke, their rifles steady. They came across the limp bodies of Sierra 2 and 3.

The White King attacked Kilo 3 and Kilo 4 next. This time, one of the marines wounded the beast, shooting it in the chest before it melted back into the gray.

Both men ran after the retreating monster, only to run smack into the cluster of juvenile Variants. The marines stopped, raised their tranq guns, and fired.

The smoke was dissipating now, and it wasn't hard to see the darts bounce off the armor. Garcia had trained the soldiers to aim for the soft spot on the neck, but the little bastards were so fucking fast. They circled the marines, slashing angrily. Long, snakelike tongues shot out of their mouths.

At the front of the room, an NCO rushed up to Davis and whispered in her ear. The lieutenant's face contorted with fear. She turned to Vice President Johnson and said, "Drone reports show the surviving Variants from the bombings are retreating back into the sewers, sir."

"How many?"

Davis swallowed. "Hundreds."

Johnson cursed and looked at the deck, then back to Davis. "How much time?"

"Ten minutes, maybe less."

Kilo 3 and 4 were firing on the juvenile Variants with their M4s now, unable to take them down with their tranq guns. Even those rounds pinged off their thick skin. Several of the creatures scampered away on all fours, but the others suddenly charged.

Echo 1 raised his rifle at the monsters from a hundred feet away, then trained his gun on a Variant standing on top of the raised platform—the White King. Blood flowed from multiple gunshots across his withered body. Despite the injuries, the Alpha was still alive, and his jaw was moving.

"The White King is controlling them, giving them orders!" Garcia said, pointing to the screen. "Tell Echo One to kill him."

A wave of scaly flesh washed over Kilo 3 and 4 before

Davis could reply. Their video feeds blurred as the hungry creatures fed on the men.

Echo 1 and 2 were all that was left now. Both men walked toward the White King, firing as they moved. The creature jerked as the rounds tore into him, but the monster's lips continued to move, howling in a voice Garcia couldn't hear. Echo 1 fired a shot that hit the beast in the right eye. The White King flew backward onto the platform, vanishing from view.

The final wisps of smoke lifted, and the chamber came fully into focus for the first time. The two surviving marines did a quick sweep of the room. Bodies were sprawled in all directions, but it was clear of adult Variants. The six remaining offspring continued to feed on Kilo 3 and 4. They tore away flesh and tilted their heads up as Echo 1 and 2 approached cautiously. Without the White King giving them orders, they didn't seem to know what to do.

"Tell them to kill all but one of the juveniles," Johnson said. "And tell them to hurry."

Davis said something into the comm, but Garcia wasn't paying attention. On the wall behind the platform were dozens of cocoons. He took a step toward the monitors, searching the wet, curved shapes for Steve-o.

"Our drones have lost sight of the Variants topside, sir," Davis said.

On-screen, Echo 1 and 2 fired at the juvenile Variants. The creatures abandoned their prey and scattered. They circled the room, then came together as a group, like a phalanx, and charged in formation. Three of them dropped from Echo 1's well-aimed head shots. Echo 2 killed a fourth, but the final two crashed into the marines.

Echo 2 pulled a knife and jammed it into the creature's neck. The one on Echo 1 slashed at him, claws swooshing in front of the camera. The beast suddenly went limp, and the marine pushed its body off.

Both men quickly jumped to their feet. Garcia followed their cams, still looking for Steve-o. The human prisoners were draped like curtains across the walls in every direction.

Working together, the two surviving marines reached down and picked up the Variant offspring Echo 1 had tranquilized. Echo 2 helped him swing the creature over his back. Then they were running, the scaled flesh of the monster's skin in clear view of Echo 1's cam.

The two men bolted for the ladder leading back to the tunnels above. They made it to the bottom, where they suddenly stopped. Both men slowly rotated, their cameras showing all four of the tunnel entrances above. Hundreds of figures clambered up to the edges. The creatures stared down at the men, yellow eyes blinking rapidly, apparently trying to make sense of what they were seeing in their demented minds.

Garcia could only imagine the terror the two marines must have felt in that moment. The army slithered down the wet walls. He clenched his jaw, forcing himself to watch. Echo 1 and 2 came together, back-to-back, and opened fire. They fought valiantly, taking down a dozen of the creatures before they were overwhelmed.

Echo 1 was the last to go down. He fell to his back, two of the monsters dragging him across the concrete. Other skeletal Variants galloped by, slowing to shriek at the marine.

The bridge fell into complete silence, everyone watching in horror as Echo 1 was taken to his final resting place. The monsters slung him up on the wall next to the other soldiers who had just been killed. His head slumped to the right, and the helmet camera captured the image of another soldier a few feet away. This body was already partially cocooned. Judging by the man's torn flesh and missing guts, he had been there for some time. Garcia wanted to look away when he saw the face. There was no mistaking those huge Dumbo ears.

A phantom burn prickled across Garcia's tattooed skin. He forced his gaze away from the screen. He would be adding his brother's name to the cross after all.

The *George Washington* split across the waves at full speed away from the Georgia coastline. With the mission to capture a juvenile Variant in Atlanta a failure, Captain Humphrey had ordered the fleet north to Virginia.

Kate stood on the flight deck, waiting to board the chopper that would take her back to Plum Island. The sun hid behind a solid mass of dark, bulbous clouds. Rough waters beat against the ship, whitecaps speckling the horizon.

She had mixed feelings about leaving, even if Ellis did need her help. President Ringgold was a strong woman, but she had been wounded badly, and Kate felt guilty leaving her behind.

A voice pulled her back to reality.

"Kate."

Beckham jogged across the flight deck with Horn and Chow in tow. Their features gave no indication of the horror they'd witnessed on the bridge. She could only imagine what the marines in Atlanta had found in the White King's lair. They'd told her that the mission was a failure, but she'd been spared the details.

The crew chief from the Black Hawk jumped onto the deck behind her. "Doctor Lovato, we're leaving in ten minutes."

Kate gave him a thumbs-up, then walked over to

meet Team Ghost. Beckham didn't slow his hurried pace until he reached her. Wrapping his arms around her, he squeezed tightly as though they hadn't seen each other for weeks. They embraced for several seconds, interrupted by Horn clearing his throat.

Beckham whispered into her ear. "I love you."

"I love you too," she whispered back.

He released his grip and pulled away, running a sleeve across his face.

"Atlanta was a complete loss?" Kate asked.

Beckham nodded. "No one made it out."

"I'm sorry, Reed. You did your best training them."

Beckham put his hands in his pockets but didn't reply.

"Have you heard about New York yet? Anything about Fitz and Apollo?"

There was a moment of hesitation before Beckham shook his head. "Nothing yet."

Chow let out a soft whistle as footsteps sounded in the distance. A dozen men jogged toward the choppers, all armed to the teeth.

"Vice President Johnson has authorized more troops to protect Plum Island in case the strike teams don't make it back from New York," Beckham said.

"I'm surprised he hasn't ordered us to go back out there yet," Chow said.

Every muscle in Kate's body seemed to tighten at once. "You guys aren't going back out there, right?"

Beckham shook his head without hesitation this time. "There are no plans to send us into the fray. Don't worry."

"What if the other teams fail?" Kate thought of Fitz and Apollo. They were coming back—they had to come back.

But what if they didn't?

"Fitz will get the job done," Beckham said. "He

always does." He sounded confident, but Horn and Chow both looked skeptical.

"Tell my girls I love them," Horn said. "And tell Riley he better be behaving himself. I don't want to hear about any sexual harassment suits. God only knows what he's been saying to Meg."

Chow chuckled, and a smile touched the sides of Beckham's lips.

"I will, Big Horn. I'll give them your love," Kate said.

The rotors on the trio of Black Hawks made their first rotations as the pilots warmed up the birds for Kate and the troops.

"I have to go," Kate said. She hugged Beckham again. "Take care of President Ringgold—and if you are asked to go back out there, remember what you have to lose. It's not just us anymore." She finished her thought with a kiss to Beckham's cheek, then ran to the chopper.

20

Fitz would have left Knapp behind back in the tunnel if it weren't for his conscience. The kid kind of reminded Fitz of himself when he first got to Walter Reed after the IED took his legs—weak, scared, and desperate for an out. The difference was Fitz had powered through those dark days. Knapp had emptied his magazine into Cooper to save his own skin. Knapp was just like Duffy, the marine who had killed two kids and their grandfather in Fallujah. Fitz thought about beating Knapp's face in, as he had Duffy's, but that would bring Fitz down to their level.

No. I'm nothing like them.

Fitz slowly turned his head. He could hardly see the marine's silhouette in the darkness. Knapp was still huddled back there against a wall. Apollo sat a few feet behind Knapp, guarding their rear.

They were at the edge of an abandoned junction of three rail routes. The maps showed other tunnels that went even farther underground. At its deepest point, the system had seven levels. A team of Navy SEALs had identified an old station stop as the Variant lair. The other strike teams had already radioed that they were in position, but Fitz was still a quarter mile from the stop.

A voice crackled over the comm channel. "Shepherd One, Whiskey One. Where the fuck are you?"

It was Lieutenant Rowe, and Fitz could tell by the anger in his voice they were waiting on him. Fitz didn't know what to say at first. Should he tell the lieutenant about what happened to Cooper?

Fuck. We have bigger problems than Knapp.

"Whiskey One, Shepherd One is Oscar Mike. Down two squad members. Encountered hostiles. ETA five minutes."

There was a short pause, then, "Roger, Shepherd. We can't wait for you."

Fitz gritted his teeth, then muttered, "On our way." He shut off the comm channel and ran to Knapp, towering over him with his UV light shining in Knapp's face. "Let's go, Marine."

"But…"

Fitz smacked him on the helmet. "You're a marine; there are no buts. Move yours, or I'm leaving you here." He gestured for Apollo and started jogging down the tunnel away from Knapp.

The soft sound of footsteps followed. Fitz wasn't sure if he should feel relieved. He decided not to feel anything at all and focus on the mission. He had a promise to fulfill.

Fitz draped his MK11 across his chest as he ran. The weapon and Apollo were the only true reassurances he needed, although he would have given anything for a shot of whiskey.

He ran faster in his track lane, with the dog racing inside the lane to his right. Knapp kept up pace behind. The tunnel curved ahead, and Fitz reached to dim his weapon-mounted UV beam. Water trickled from the ceiling, hitting his face as he adjusted the light.

The passage opened into a larger tunnel. Fitz halted

and signaled for Knapp to hold up. He slowly raked his light back and forth, illuminating graffiti-covered walls and trash littering the ground. Not too long ago, this had been a camp for dozens of homeless people, but the sour scent of rotting fruit told him the Variants had claimed it as their own.

He was close now.

Fitz flashed an advance signal and continued. Knapp hurried after him, the muzzle of his rifle aimed at the ground. That was good. Fitz hated having the man at his back with a loaded rifle.

Halfway down the tunnel, their lights danced across the first of the human prisoners. Masses of webbed glue hung from the skeletal remains. These people had been dead for weeks.

"Shit," Knapp said. "Are those—"

The shrieks started all at once, cutting the marine off mid-sentence. A macabre chorus swelled in the tunnel. Fitz froze alongside Knapp, and Apollo's tail dropped.

"What is that?" Knapp whispered. He backed away from the corpse of a woman stuck to the wall on their left. One eye hung from the socket, and strips of dried flesh that looked like beef jerky hung from her skull.

"Shut up," Fitz whispered back.

The enclosed space made it difficult to determine where the sounds were coming from, but Fitz figured the other teams were engaging the enemy. He jerked his chin and bolted into the darkness, his rifle out in front now.

The three sets of tracks curved again, and the boxy shape of a train came into focus. It was still docked at the main platform that had once served a busy concourse. Metal gleamed in the glow of his light. He stopped at the entrance to the station, threw his back against the wall, and peeked around the corner.

Smoke drifted across the platform, spilling over the

back of the train. A chunk of rock suddenly exploded from the wall, peppering Fitz's uniform with shrapnel. He took cover as rounds bit into the ground around him. Back on Plum Island, each team had been assigned a zone of fire. They'd gone over the station layouts, and every man understood where the other teams would be.

Somebody had forgotten that. Or maybe it was just the chaos of fighting on an unknown battlefield with an enemy that could come from any direction.

Another flurry of rounds struck the ground nearby, and Fitz backed away from the platform a step. As soon as the stray gunfire stopped, he looked at Knapp and said, "Get your mask on. Then we move." He paused and caught Knapp's gaze. "And don't fucking shoot me or anyone else. Keep your cool and shoot the Variants. Your brothers *need* you in this fight."

Knapp managed a short and unconvincing nod.

"Apollo, you stay here," Fitz said. He hated leaving the German shepherd, but with the stray rounds, he was worried the dog would get hit in the smoke, even with the small gas mask he'd brought for him.

Apollo whimpered but obeyed. Fitz slipped on his mask, shouldered his MK11, and burst around the corner. He didn't wait to see if Knapp was following.

The view of the concourse was partially obscured by the train. Smoke churned across the clear side to his left. He jumped over the tracks and made for the platform. A Variant suddenly exploded from the wall of smoke and landed on all fours in the first of the three tracks. Fitz shot the beast in the back as it galloped for the safety of the train.

The howls of dying monsters swelled into a din so loud it hurt Fitz's ears. More of the creatures poured from the smoke as he approached. His light captured their scarlet-streaked bodies, most of them riddled with bullet holes and gasping for air. Three of them climbed on top of the train at the same time. He mowed them down with head shots that speckled the dusty metal with a coat of red paint.

Two more sprinted toward Knapp. Fitz shifted his aim, but Knapp took them out with short bursts before Fitz could squeeze the trigger. He didn't have time to celebrate the small victory.

During a lull in the high-pitched wails of the Variants, a human scream sounded. At first Fitz thought it had come from the comm channel, but he'd turned it off before entering the chamber.

He ran faster, leaping into the second set of tracks. The strike teams were in trouble, but he was almost to the platform. He prepared to pull his tranq gun when a marine somersaulted out of the smoke and landed between the tracks with a thud. He skidded to a stop, his body twisted and broken.

Fitz flinched as a second man came flying out a second later. The marine smashed into the side of the train with a crack. Fitz squared his shoulders and planted his blades. He raked his gun back and forth, waiting for a target, heart rising in his throat.

Two more marines flew out of the smoke as he strained to see through the polycarbonate visor of his mask. One of the men landed just in front of Fitz. The injured marine tore off his mask and tossed it away. Then he crawled forward, glancing up with wild eyes that locked onto Fitz.

"Lieutenant," Fitz said. He crouched next to Lieutenant Rowe.

Rowe coughed. "Kill it," he croaked.

Knapp stopped a few feet away, his rifle aimed at the churning vortex of gray. Something was moving in there—something big.

Fitz reached down to help Rowe up, but the lieutenant shook his hand away.

"No! Leave me. You have to kill that thing."

The lieutenant's right leg was snapped, the bone sticking out of his thigh. His eyes bulged. "Fitz. There's a Variant in there unlike the others. An Alpha—"

Knapp fired into the cloud at something Fitz couldn't see.

"It's protecting the little ones," Rowe said. He dragged himself closer, coughing as he moved.

Fitz looked up at Knapp. "Help him and get the hell out of here. I'll complete the mission." He was running toward the smoke before Rowe had a chance to protest. He could only hope that Knapp would stay and help the lieutenant before fleeing the concourse.

The whistle of suppressed rounds caught Fitz's ear. There were still marines in the fight. He climbed onto the platform. With his MK11 out in front, he carefully worked his way through the dissipating screen of smoke. He could see bodies, but nothing was moving. At least he didn't have to worry about the marines maintaining their zones of fire.

The high-pitched shrieks had quieted now. There was only the rattle of dying monsters and shouts of marines. Fitz pivoted to the right as a meaty hunk of flesh darted by. The curtain of smoke continued to lift the deeper he moved. His blades bumped into one of the grenade canisters. It clanked noisily across the ground. He cursed and took in deep breaths of filtered air that tasted like rubber.

Focus, Fitz. Focus. You can do this. You have to do this.

The screech of nails over concrete came from above. Fitz raised his rifle toward the ceiling just as another flash of movement raced toward him. The Variant above scampered away, but the one in front smashed into Fitz. A second of shock overwhelmed him as he hit the ground.

"Help! You have to help!" someone shouted.

Fitz struggled to get up, reaching for his bayonet and preparing for hand-to-hand combat with a Variant. Instead, he stared into the visor of a marine covered in blood.

"We have to get out of here!" the man shouted.

Another second of shock jolted Fitz as the man was yanked backward. Fitz scrambled for his MK11 and scooped it off the ground. By the time he had it, the man was gone. A scream rang out in the distance, the awful, guttural wail of someone who knew he was going to die.

Fitz ran toward the outline of a concrete pillar. He stopped there to catch his breath. After a few gasps, he cautiously peered around the side.

There were two sets of stairs leading to another level to the north and east. That was where the other strike teams had entered. A ring of bodies, both human and Variant, lay on the platform at the bottom of the stairs. Through the thin smoke, he glimpsed a pair of marines firing on a pack of armored juveniles. The beasts were circling the men, swatting at the rounds as if they were nothing but pebbles. He had just raised his tranq gun when he heard Knapp's high-pitched scream.

Behind Fitz, a monster of a Variant was dragging Rowe and Knapp across the ground. Four other creatures hung from the ceiling. Farther back, two men, filthy and bearded, stood on the platform. Fitz recognized them: They were the same men he had seen scoping out Plum Island from the boats days before.

Son of a bitch!

The meaty beast dropped both Knapp and Rowe. He raised his hulking arms as he released a tortured howl. Fitz resisted the urge to cup his hands over his ears, focusing instead on the cord hanging from the creature's neck and the plates of human bone covering his flesh. He blinked to make sure it wasn't an illusion, but his eyes weren't playing tricks on him. Ears, noses, and hunks of unidentifiable flesh hung from the grisly necklace.

All but the beast's head was covered in armor made of human bones. He twisted to look at the collaborators, exposing a dehydrated cloak of flesh hanging from his back. The bones making up his armor were all held together using the same skin.

Fitz knew right away this was the monster responsible for the massacre back at their insertion point at Bryant Park. He was the Alpha—the king of this lair. And Fitz's marine squadmates had made him very, very angry.

In his peripheral vision, Fitz saw the other marines still firing on the Variant offspring. The beast towering over Knapp and Rowe extended a clawed hand and pointed with a single horned nail at the two men. The roar that burst from his mouth echoed through the entire concourse, repeating over and over like a skipping record.

The four Variants on the ceiling raced over the concrete, and the beast barreled for Fitz. He already had the monster's colossal head in his sights. The reptilian irises came into focus, and Fitz squeezed off a shot that missed by a fraction of an inch.

He pulled the trigger twice more; both of the rounds shattered femur and sternum bones making up part of the plate covering the creature's swollen chest muscles. The Alpha shouted in agony and jerked to the side as Fitz shot him a third time in the gap between bones covering his right shoulder. This time the round punched through flesh, splattering the human hip bone he wore as a shoulder pad with crimson.

Before he could fire a fourth time, the beast bowed his veiny skull and plowed into Fitz, spearing him in the chest. The impact sent him flying backward. He landed hard, skidding across the concrete and flipping ass over end. His chin strap snapped open and his helmet tumbled away.

Gasping for air, Fitz grabbed his tranq pistol and rolled to his back. He pulled the trigger three times as the beast of a Variant lumbered toward him. One of the darts penetrated the nose hanging from his necklace. The other two sank into the muscular collar of flesh just above his plates of bony armor.

The darts only enraged the creature more. He grabbed Fitz by his right blade and tossed him into the air. He landed on the ground a few feet from Rowe. The man's neck was twisted like a pretzel. He was dead, killed by the hands of the human collaborators.

The two men towered over Knapp to the right. They were babbling about someone called the Bone Collector. Fitz knew exactly who they were talking about.

First the White King, now the fucking Bone Collector. I'm stuck in a nightmare.

Fitz sucked in a breath, pushed himself up, and pulled out his knife. He spun back to the gargantuan beast, but the Bone Collector was staggering now. Blood streamed down the femur and fibula bones making up the breastplate of his armor. Reaching up with a needle-sharp nail, he plucked the darts from his neck and tossed them away. Then he twisted to check on his precious offspring.

Across the concourse the remaining two marines fought for their lives. They had killed one of the Variants, but the other three beasts had the men pinned to the ground, slashing, ripping, and tearing at them relentlessly. The juvenile Variants circled the slaughter, swiping at one another and hissing, each wanting to be the first to feed.

Fitz hunched his back, raised his knife, and prepared for hand-to-hand combat. The Alpha turned and moved awkwardly in his direction. His bulging lips opened, and a strangled voice came from the blackness of his gaping maw.

"K-ill." He angled a horned claw toward Fitz as he dropped to both knees, joints clicking. He blinked long and slow, struggling to fight the powerful sedatives. Then he crashed face first to the ground.

The Bone Collector was down.

For now.

Across the concourse, one of the marines was still fighting the adult Variants. He managed to pull his side arm and execute the beast on top of him. As he squirmed away, the other two monsters sank their claws into his flesh. The young Variants clambered forward, their scaly bodies washing over the two marines in a wave of mutated flesh.

Fitz closed his eyes for a second before snapping them open, anger taking hold as he turned his attention to the human collaborators. They were pulling Knapp toward the staircase. The marine was either unconscious or in shock.

Behind Fitz, a growl came from the tracks. Apollo bounded over the tracks toward the platform, barking up a storm.

"Get out of here!" Fitz shouted.

He searched the ground for a weapon. An M4 lay five feet in front of the tranquilized Alpha. Fitz had just scooped it up when the rattling started. Pounding steps and shrieking voices echoed down the stairwells. Dozens of shadows flickered into the dim passages.

The Variant cavalry had arrived.

Fitz raised the M4 and aimed it at the two collaborators. He didn't hesitate to pull the trigger, but even as he did, he knew it was pointless. He could tell from the weight that the magazine was dry.

Apollo leaped onto the platform and nudged against Fitz's right blade as if to say, *Let's go!*

By the time Fitz had grabbed extra magazines from Rowe's corpse, the stairwells were crawling with Variants. He slammed a fresh mag into the M4 and shot the first collaborator in the back of the head, but the other man pulled Knapp around a pillar. Shifting the gun's muzzle toward the offspring, Fitz saw there was no way he could grab one in time. The beasts were all retreating toward the reinforcements.

Apollo nudged Fitz's blade again, and after a final moment of hesitation, he turned to run with the dog. The mission was a failure. All he could do now was try and escape with his and Apollo's lives.

Riley bowed his head and cupped his hands around it. He dragged his fingers through shaggy blond hair that would have broken regulations not long ago.

It seemed as if ages had passed since those days.

Riley dropped his hands to his wheelchair and pushed toward the edge of the stairs. For a moment he considered throwing himself down them. He wanted to feel something besides despair, even if it was pain.

Fitz, Apollo, and every other member of the strike teams were gone. So many of his brothers had died, and he had been forced to sit back and watch. The worst was being cooped up in the command center as the marines were pulled apart by the largest Variant he'd ever seen. Part of him was glad he hadn't seen Fitz or Apollo die. But that felt like a betrayal to their memory.

The despair dug at Riley like a knife, working its way deep inside of him, relentless and sharp. Meg and Horn's girls crossed the lawn, hair blowing in the soft breeze. It was quiet, the silence embracing the island. This time, Riley didn't embrace it back.

Major Smith closed the door to Building 1 and put a hand on Riley's shoulder. Ellis strode out a second later.

"I'm sorry," Smith said.

Riley nodded and raised a hand at Meg. She had been fond of Fitz. Hell, everyone was. And Horn's girls had loved Apollo. The thought of telling them the news made him feel sick.

But he had to. They had to know.

"Kate is on her way back to the island," Ellis said. "She'll be here in a couple of hours."

Meg slowed as she limped toward the landing. Tasha and Jenny walked by her side, their tiny hands gripped in Meg's. She had finally ditched the crutches, and judging by the grimace she made with every step, Riley figured it wasn't by Dr. Hill's orders.

Her gaze met Riley's a moment later. She was a smart woman, and it didn't take words for Riley to convey the failure of the strike teams in New York.

"Did anyone make it?" Meg asked, her lips trembling.

Smith lowered his head, shaking it from side to side. "Every mission failed."

Meg dropped Tasha and Jenny's hands and brought a hand to her mouth. "What happens now?"

"Vice President Johnson will send more teams. That's my guess, anyway," Smith said.

"So they can be slaughtered?" Meg asked. Tasha and Jenny looked up quizzically. Meg lowered her voice. "Who will they send now? Ghost?"

Smith didn't immediately reply. He twisted his wedding ring around his finger. "I'm not sure, but I wouldn't be surprised."

Riley looked down at his casts. He had to get out of them. If Team Ghost was going on what would likely be their last mission, he had to be there with them.

"I better get the girls inside," Meg said. Smith and Ellis walked over to help Meg and the girls up. Riley sat in his chair, watching helplessly. That was all about to change. The storm on the horizon wasn't the only one coming, and this time he was going to fight.

21

Lieutenant Davis shut the door to the small room, sealing Team Ghost and the Variant Hunters inside. She gave Garcia and Beckham meaningful looks and took a seat at the table. After everyone had sat down, she said, "The strike teams in New York have all been eliminated."

The words hit Beckham so hard he might have dropped to his knees if he'd been standing. "Fitz," he said. "You're sure Fitz and Apollo are dead?"

Davis shook her head. "Not for certain, but we can show you the feed. This may be hard, but I have to know what we're dealing with here."

"What do you mean 'dealing with'?" Horn asked.

"You need to see it," Davis said.

Chow bowed his head and put a hand on Beckham's back. Locking his jaw, Beckham fended off the scream he wanted to unleash. He thought he would feel over-whelming sadness, but instead he felt a dangerous emotion crawling under his skin. The prickle of vengeance rushed through him like a shot of morphine.

"Show us," Beckham said.

Davis tapped into the monitor and sorted through a series of images. She moused over to a still frame, clicked on it, and brought it on-screen. The men crowded around her.

"There," she said, pointing. "This is the last few seconds of his feed. Note that Fitz left Apollo before he went into the chamber. We're not sure why, but we're assuming it was the danger of stray bullets. It was pretty chaotic by the time Team Shepherd arrived."

The barrel of Fitz's MK11 came on-screen. He fired at a hulking Variant running toward him that was covered in grisly plates of human bone. Beckham flinched at each shot, watching as the armor shattered and broke away. A cord or necklace of some sort swung from the creature's muscular neck.

"Are those bones?" Garcia asked.

Davis nodded. "Keep watching. The bones are just the beginning."

"Can you slow that frame down?" Beckham asked.

Davis tapped at the keyboard until the feed was moving in slow motion. Beckham took a step closer for a better look, holding his breath. The beast's neck was decorated with flesh trophies. He had seen something like this before. Lieutenant Brett had been captured with a necklace just like it back in Vietnam.

"Looks familiar," Horn said. "Didn't—"

"Yes," Beckham said. "He did."

"What the hell is on its back?" Chow asked.

Garcia leaned closer. "Looks like a patchwork of skin from multiple bodies."

"This is why I called you all here. I need your help figuring out what the fuck this thing is," Davis said. "Is this another White King?"

"No," Garcia said, still staring. "Something much worse. This one understands the value of body armor, and the fact it went to lengths to decorate itself with flesh ornaments means it's more than just an Alpha predator now—it's a demon."

Beckham thought about replying when the beast lowered his skull and speared Fitz in the chest. A phantom pain raced through Beckham, Fitz's injury becoming his own. The feed rattled violently, turning topsy-turvy.

"This is where he lost his helmet," Davis said.

The helmet tumbled across the ground and came to a stop upside down. In the right-hand corner of the monitor, Fitz was on his back, shooting his tranq gun at the Alpha. The beast crashed to the ground a few minutes later, and Fitz moved out of view.

"See, Fitz and Apollo could still be alive," Beckham said, a trickle of hope pooling in his gut. He framed it as a statement, not a question, but Davis pulled up another image from a different feed.

"This was taken ten minutes after Fitz's helmet fell," she said.

On screen, hundreds of Variants poured into the chamber. There were six juveniles in the mix, scampering in and out of the tide of diseased flesh. Two human collaborators pulled an unconscious marine toward the creatures. A gunshot hit the man on the left a second later, a spray of bone and brain matter peppering the ceiling.

"Holy shit," Horn said. "Only Fitz could have nailed that shot."

"Maybe, but there's no way he could have survived against those numbers," Davis said.

"You don't know Fitz," Beckham said.

Davis looked Beckham in the eye, "I'm sorry, Master Sergeant, but it's highly unlikely he made it out."

"What's that?" Chow said, leaning in. He pointed at a flash of movement on the left side of the screen. Davis paused the video and hit Rewind for several seconds.

"Keep it slow," Chow said. After a pause he said, "There, that's Apollo!"

Beckham squeezed in next to them. Sure enough, on the edge of the platform in the very left-hand corner of the video feed was the dog. And slightly to his right was the edge of a flashing blade.

Apollo jumped back to the tracks a second later, and the blade vanished.

"Replay it," Beckham said.

Davis looked back at him.

"Please, Lieutenant—those are our friends."

She nodded and replayed the video three times. The image of Apollo and Fitz's blade was only on-screen for five seconds, but it was more than enough for Beckham to know they were still alive.

"We have to mount a rescue operation," he said.

Davis hesitated, as if she was considering the idea. "I'm sorry, but that's impossible. We don't have the resources for a successful operation, and we both know your friends are probably dead by now."

"Like I said, you don't know our friends," Beckham replied.

"You're right, I don't," Davis said. "But going back out there isn't an option right now. Vice President Johnson is considering our next steps. My orders are to determine if we are dealing with a new type of Variant. And from the sound of it, we are."

Garcia nodded and scratched at his head with one eye on Beckham.

"I'm sorry about your friends," Davis said. She hesitated before leaving the men in silence. When she was gone, Beckham turned and looked at the other men in turn. Horn and Chow shared the same defiant look. Garcia seemed to brighten, as if he'd had the same idea Beckham was having. Tank and Thomas stood tall. Their looks told Beckham he could count on every soldier in the room.

Remember what you have to lose. It's not just us anymore.

Beckham looked at his boots, the faces of everyone he had ever lost emerging in his mind: his parents, his men,

Jensen. Then their faces vanished, replaced by images of those still alive: Horn's girls, Kate and their unborn baby, even Fitz and Apollo.

Garcia patted Beckham on his arm, right next to the Team Ghost patch. "I made the mistake of leaving Steve-o out there. If you need our help, we're in."

Beckham returned the pat. "Thank you, brother." He ran a hand over two days' worth of scruff and searched the faces of the men staring back at him a second time, looking for some answer to the questions eating him up inside.

"What do you guys say? Want to go back out there and save some marines? Shit, maybe we'll even capture our own child Variant."

There were five quick nods, but no one said a word. Each man knew they would be breaking orders if they went rogue.

"Only one problem," Beckham said. "We need a ride."

Tank smiled for the first time since Beckham had met the lumbering man. "Don't worry, Master Sergeant—my cousin Tito is a pilot, and fortunately for us, he's on the *GW*. I'm sure he wouldn't mind sneaking us on board."

New York City was shrouded in gray. Dark storm clouds rolled over the skyscrapers. Fitz ran like a madman toward the public library, with Apollo close behind. Dozens of Variants were in pursuit, slamming into charred vehicles and leaping to the darkened walls of nearby buildings. Clicking joints and angry yelps echoed through the derelict city. He felt as if he was the grand marshal of a particularly evil parade.

Fitz stopped at a squad car and fired off three short bursts from his M4. Two of the monsters went down and skidded across the pavement of Forty-Second Street.

A cloud of ash trailed them as they came to a stop. He counted at least two dozen more hostiles. Some of the beasts moved slowly, injured from the bombing raid earlier, their bodies charcoaled from the fire that had licked their pallid skin.

Apollo barked fiercely, his fur trembling with rage.

"Come on, Apollo!" Fitz shouted.

His thighs were burning now, and when he looked down, he saw why. The bottom of his right blade was bent. It must have happened back underground, when the Bone Collector tossed him like a rag doll. Fitz kept running for the library. He loped up three levels of stairs and jumped over the trees draped across the walkway. The decayed bodies of the Variants killed by First Platoon were sprawled in all directions.

Glancing over his shoulder, Fitz saw the beasts were gaining. There was no way he and Apollo could outrun them. They had to hide and hope the monsters moved on. Otherwise they had to fight. But both options seemed impossible. He didn't have enough ammunition to mount a stand, and even if he did, he wasn't sure he could kill the beasts before they overwhelmed him. There was no calling for help either. The wind rustling through his auburn hair reminded him he had lost his helmet, and with it his connection to the outside world.

Besides Apollo, Fitz was alone. The mission to extract a juvenile Variant seemed distant now, but it was still on his mind. He just had to figure out a way to get back to the lair. Even though he knew it was next to impossible to complete his mission, his brain still searched for a strategy that might salvage the operation.

He bounded up the last stairs to the library entrance and leaped over the mangled body of a Variant that looked like a squished starfish. Apollo ran through the partially open central doors, but Fitz halted.

The monsters trailing them were gaining. Packs from connecting streets streamed into the long line of beasts, increasing their numbers to fifty or more. Without thinking, Fitz grabbed the splattered Variant corpse and dragged it into the building. Then he slammed the door with his back and lugged the corpse to the next level. Apollo sniffed ahead, his tail still up.

There was pounding on the first level as the creatures broke their way into the building. Fitz whistled at Apollo and jerked his chin toward a room halfway down the hall. It led into an open workroom with two sets of doors. He dropped the corpse as he entered the room, the putrid scent of decaying bodies filling his nose. There were half a dozen human bodies in here, most of them torn to shreds.

He pulled his scarf above his nose and did a quick scan of the long room. Desks and bookshelves barricaded the second and third doors, but the shelves at the entrance Fitz had used were toppled. Survivors had tried to make a stand here.

Fitz quickly rebuilt the barricade, shoving the shelves into place and dragging chairs and tables over to reinforce them. The shrieks and raucous cries of the Variants tearing apart the first floor of the building fueled Fitz's rapid movements.

When he finished, he gestured for Apollo and continued to a pair of corpses still dressed in the clothes they had died in. He unslung the rifle from his back and laid it next to the bodies. Then he dragged a third over, along with the squishy Variant corpse.

Apollo watched, tilting his head from side to side.

"You're not going to like what I'm about to do, boy," Fitz whispered. Holding his breath, he plucked a gooey hunk of flesh from the Variant's stomach and smeared it over his face, fatigues, and blades. Apollo backed away as Fitz raised a second handful of rotting flesh. He reached out, but the dog shook and shied away again.

A thump sounded down the hallway. The popping of joints and snarls from a pack of Variants grew closer. Fitz took a second to think. Even if he could get Apollo to obey, he wasn't sure he could keep the dog quiet when the Variants found them.

"I'm sorry, boy," Fitz whispered. He pulled his tranq pistol and took out one of the darts. Then he grabbed Apollo and said, "You're just going to sleep for a little while." He stuck the dog in the leg and pulled the dart out rapidly so he would only have a small dose of the sedative.

Apollo let out a soft whimper and went limp in Fitz's arms. He carried the dog to the stack of bodies against the wall and spread the guts over his fur. After applying a second coat of gore to both of them, Fitz lay down with Apollo and pulled the human corpses over top. His cotton scarf did little to block the awful scents, but Fitz had more to worry about than what the Variant had eaten before it died over a week ago.

Thud after thud echoed outside the door, followed by shattering glass and splintering wood. They were close now. The clatter sounded as if they were inside a fucking kitchen, not a library.

Fitz was on his back under the bodies, holding Apollo with his right arm. The dog's heart thumped against Fitz's bicep. He looked up through the fort of rotting limbs at a ray of sunlight bleeding in from a window halfway up the wall. It was the only one with intact glass; the others were all broken from the firebombs of Operation Liberty.

Something darted past the window, climbing up the surface of the building. Other skeletal shapes crawled up the exterior of the library, the room falling into shadow as they passed the glass. In his mind's eye, Fitz could see the beasts swarming over the burned structure like an army of ants consuming a hunk of flesh. The scratching, snapping, and shrieks came from all directions.

The door to their room rattled. A Variant smashed into the wood, breaking the hinges and knocking the shelves to the floor. A creature squeezed through the opening and leaped onto a desk in the center of the room. It perched there, sniffing and exploring the space with a single slitted eyeball. Fitz held in a breath and looked away.

Another Variant clambered across the window above, a claw grinding over the glass. Cracks webbed to all corners of the narrow window.

The beast in the room squawked and jumped to the floor. The impact made Fitz's heart lodge in his throat. He let out a short breath as the sound echoed through the room, and then took in another breath as the Variant stalked over to the pile of bodies on all fours. The monster was so close that Fitz could see every detail of the purple, veiny lips, the needle-sharp teeth lining its maw, and the gaping socket where an eye had once been.

The creature stopped a foot away, and Fitz caught a draft of its sour breath even over the decay. He fought the urge to gag, knowing the simple action could end his life. He closed his eyes and stilled his breathing. The monster inched closer, sniffing like a dog searching for a bone.

A crash came from down the hall, and a howl answered. Fitz opened his eyes as the creature jerked its head toward the door. It scampered away a second later. Shadows filled the room as Variants raced past the windows. Only this time they weren't climbing; they were descending. Something was happening outside.

In the distance, Fitz thought he heard a shout. But the voice didn't sound quite human. He waited a few seconds before pushing the bodies off.

Grabbing his M4, he walked over to the broken windows and carefully peered outside. He heard the creatures before he saw them. Hundreds of Variants scrambled over the burned-out wrecks of cars on West Forty-Second Street. Covered in ash, their once pale bodies made them look more like four-legged spiders. Fitz rubbed his tired eyes and squinted. The army was moving again, away from the library.

He pivoted to the side of the window when a human shout came from the street. Fitz raised his M4 and zoomed in on the mob. There, in the center of the Variants, was the remaining human collaborator. The man walked behind a body being dragged across the concrete by a hunched Variant. If it weren't for the cape of flesh rippling in the wind and the bones on the beast's body, Fitz wouldn't have believed it. Hell, he still couldn't believe it with the Bone Collector in plain sight. The Alpha pulled a screaming Knapp down the street.

Fitz backed away from the window.

"I'll show you!" Knapp screamed. "I'll take you there!"

"You fucking piece of shit," Fitz whispered. He aimed his rifle at Knapp, but the surrounding Variants blocked a solid shot. The injured Alpha halted and towered over Knapp, blood still streaming down his chest from where Fitz had shot him in the shoulder. Scabs were already forming around the entry hole.

Dropping to all fours over Knapp, the beast shrieked. The strained words were unintelligible at first. It struggled to speak again. "W-here? Where are others?"

Knapp trembled under the monster. "Plum Island. They're at Plum Island!"

The other human collaborator stepped closer to the Alpha and Knapp.

"I know where that is. I've seen it," the man said.

"There are doctors there who're creating a weapon to kill you," Knapp said.

The Bone Collector roared in the marine's face. Then

he slithered off him and melted back into the army of Variants. The beasts were moving again before Fitz could line up a shot. He searched the bodies for the collaborator. It was too late to silence Knapp, but if he killed the collaborator, maybe he could save Plum Island.

He ran from window to window looking for a shot, but the man was gone. Fitz flung the rifle over his back and hurried back to Apollo. He scooped up the dog and ran into the hallway, grimacing at the weight.

With no way to communicate with Command, Fitz had two options: either beat them to Plum Island or kill the collaborator before they left the city.

He sprinted along the hall and loped down the stairs leading back outside. Apollo struggled to crack an eyelid as soon as they were on the landing. Staring out over the ruined city, Fitz whispered, "Okay, boy—time to save our friends."

The Black Hawks carrying Kate and fresh soldiers landed at Plum Island later that day. Ellis was waiting on the tarmac with Major Smith. Riley, Meg, and both of Horn's girls were hanging back a few hundred feet at the concrete barriers.

Kate endured the entire flight in silence, aching for news. She grabbed her pack, jumped out of the chopper, and hunched as she passed under the rotors with a hand shielding her face.

Smith and Ellis looked worse than normal. They had heard about Atlanta, but what about New York? Her gut tightened as she approached.

"Welcome back, Doctor Lovato," Smith said, quietly. He avoided her gaze and continued to the other choppers to talk with the new troops.

Ellis grabbed her bag and they hurried over to the barriers, talking as they moved.

"What's wrong?" Kate asked. "And don't lie to me."

Ellis glanced at her and then looked away. "New York was a failure. Same goes for every other strike team across the country. Not a single team made it back with a specimen, Kate."

Kate froze where she stood. The wind from the rotors beat against her shirt as everything came crashing down. "F-Fitz?" She stuttered. "Apollo?"

Ellis shook his head. "No one made it, Kate. I'm sorry." He put a hand on her shoulder, but she pulled away and continued walking. She choked on the emotions swirling inside of her and took a second to steel herself. They *had* to finish Kryptonite, with or without a juvenile Variant to test it on. She felt her stomach twist at the thought of losing Fitz and Apollo, but after suffering so much loss, she was almost numb to more.

At the concrete barrier, Kate slowed long enough to say hi to Meg, Riley, and the girls. "Your dad sends his love," Kate said. She bent down and hugged Tasha and Jenny. Their strong grips filled her with the strength she needed to continue working. They were resilient and brave—reminders of what Kate was fighting for.

"Is he coming back soon?" Tasha asked.

"Yes, he'll be home very soon." Kate waited for the pounding of boots to pass. Smith was leading the new soldiers away from the tarmac, pointing at the buildings in the distance.

"I'll meet you at the armory," Smith said to one of the men. He stopped and plucked his radio from his vest pocket. "Doctor Lovato, I have Beckham on the comm, and he's asking to talk to you."

Kate grabbed the radio and stepped away from the others. "Reed, this is Kate."

"Kate," Beckham said. With even a single word she could hear the trepidation in his voice. He had likely heard the news.

"I'm here," Kate said after a pause.

"Fitz and Apollo are—"

"I know," Kate said. "I'm so sorry, Reed."

"No, that's not—" Beckham started to stay.

Static crackled from the radio, as if a heavy wind was blowing where Beckham was. There was a chopping sound too.

"Where are you?" Kate asked.

"I'm about to head to New York."

Kate's heart skipped.

"Fitz and Apollo are still alive, Kate. I saw it in a video feed, and I'm not leaving them out there to die."

"Vice President Johnson and President Ringgold authorized a mission to rescue them?"

"Not exactly."

Kate lowered the radio to think for a moment, then slowly brought it back to her lips. She knew there wasn't anything she could say to change his mind. If he truly believed Fitz and Apollo were out there, then nothing she could do would stop him from trying to save them.

Instead of screaming her frustration and making Beckham feel even worse, she simply said. "Okay." They both knew they had little chance of living to see their child grow up. She had accepted this, but that didn't mean she had to like it.

She brought the radio back to her lips. "Bring Fitz and Apollo home, Reed. And bring the rest of Team Ghost home too. Promise me—promise *us*."

"I promise, Kate." There was a pause, and then: "I love you both. Tell Tasha and Jenny their dad will see them soon."

"Okay," Kate said. A tear fell down her cheek.

She wiped it away, handed the radio back to Smith, and looked at Ellis. "Let's go."

"Where are we going?"

"Wait, what the hell is going on?" Riley asked.

"Team Ghost is going back out there," Kate replied.

"What?" Riley gasped. "Where?"

"New York. To save Fitz and Apollo. And to capture a juvenile Variant specimen too, if I know Reed," Kate said. She jerked her chin at Ellis. "And we're going back to the lab. We have a weapon to finish."

22

"Cuz, you know how much trouble we'll be in when they find out we *borrowed* one of the very few remaining birds?" Ted "Tito" Bones scratched the stubble on his chin. He was a bulky man like Tank, with specks of gray in his short hair. "Seriously, you know what you're asking me to do?"

Tank raised a finger to his lips. "Keep it down, brother."

Team Ghost and the Variant Hunters stood with their backs to the bulkhead behind the hatch leading out to the flight deck. They'd retreated inside as a pair of Apaches took off to deal with some Variants spotted off the coast. Beckham waited anxiously, nervous that they would be spotted here decked out in full combat gear. He checked the ladder below every few seconds.

All they needed was a damn pilot to take them to New York, but Tank's cousin didn't seem as if he wanted the job.

"Look, Tito," said Garcia. "I get you don't want to risk a court-martial. But I wouldn't ask if it wasn't important. If we bring back a little Variant *and* our guys, then the CO can't complain, right?"

Tito's lips twisted into a scowl. "And if you don't come back?"

"Then you can tell them we held a gun to your head."

Tito scanned the men individually, checking out their gear and their battle-ready features. Then he let out a long sigh. "Follow me."

"Not so fast," said a voice at the bottom of the ladder.

Beckham cursed when he saw Lieutenant Davis standing there. She hurried up the stairs and gave them all meaningful looks that said, *You're fucked*.

"Lieutenant, we just want to go get our friends," Beckham said.

"Save it, Master Sergeant," Davis said, frustration cracking in her typically calm voice. She shook her head and pulled at her cuffs. "I'm in deep shit for the failure of the strike teams. Make no mistake, I'm sorry for your loss, but you can't go back out there just to find one man and a dog."

Beckham raised his hand to protest, but she cut him off.

"Not unless you agree to bring back a juvenile Variant too."

Lowering his hands, Beckham narrowed his eyes at the lieutenant. She was a smart woman. She had to have known Team Ghost and the Variant Hunters were planning something, and she had taken that opportunity to complete the mission she was in charge of.

"I just came from the bridge. Vice President Johnson and Captain Humphrey have no plans to authorize another mission, but I'm still in charge of Operation Condor, and it's not over until we nab one of those little freaks. I'll be in even deeper shit if they find out I authorized pilots to fly you off the *GW*, but if anyone can finish what we started, it's y'all."

Garcia smiled. "Not going to disagree with you there, Lieutenant."

"Unfortunately, authorizing a flight is about all the help you're going to get," Davis said. "You won't have air support or reinforcements. You will be going in blind and if you are compromised on the ground, no one is coming to save you."

"Understood," Beckham said. The other men all nodded, prepared to risk their lives to save their comrades and complete the mission.

Davis put her hands on her hips. "Tito, you and your copilot fire up that Osprey."

"You got it, Lieutenant," Tito said firmly.

"Good luck," Davis said. She eyed Beckham one last time, then turned and disappeared back down the ladder.

Two hours later, the teams were in the air and closing in on New York. Heavy rain beat the sides of the Osprey. It was dusk, but Beckham couldn't see any sign of a sunset through the thick clouds outside the window. Lightning webbed the impenetrable darkness. They were only a few minutes from the city, and Beckham still couldn't see shit.

Davis was right about Team Ghost and the Variant Hunters going in blind, but they were also going in with as much ammunition as they could carry, plus veins pumping full of adrenaline—that, and more experience fighting the Variants than any soldiers left in North America.

Across the aisle, Garcia, Tank, and Thomas all wore the look of men about to drop into the fray. To Beckham's right, Horn flexed his forearms in and out. Chow flicked a toothpick from side to side, and Beckham ran a finger over the vest pocket containing a picture of his mother. Everyone carried suppressed M4s except Horn and Tank. Both men had selected M249 SAWs with AAC silencers and attached two-hundred-round plastic ammo boxes. Their vests were stuffed with extra magazines, two smoke grenades, four hand grenades, a side arm, and a tranq pistol. Like the other strike teams, they had weapon-mounted UV lights and NVGs rigged onto their helmets.

If they needed more firepower than that, they were fucked anyway.

"ETA at Bryant Park is two minutes," Tito said over the comm. "Good luck, Ghost and VH."

"Listen up," Beckham said. "We all know what's at stake. It's up to us now. We have to capture a live specimen. That's the 'primary mission,'" Beckham said, using his fingers to trace quotation marks. "But we'll also be on the lookout for Fitz, Apollo, and any other survivors. Understood?"

Garcia quickly replied, "Roger that," but Tank and Thomas hesitated before nodding. Beckham nodded back, figuring both men had thoughts of their fallen brothers in mind.

A few seconds later, the Osprey descended over the New York Public Library. A thick layer of ash covered the ground around the building like snow. The destruction was widespread, and the library looked like a hunk of coal.

"Sergeant Garcia," Beckham said, getting the man's attention with a wave. "I'll take point for Team Ghost. We advance together, combat intervals, but tighter than normal since we don't have to worry about enemy fire."

Garcia nodded and turned to his men. "I'm point for us. Tank, you have the right flank. Thomas, you got left."

The crew chief in the back of the troop hold punched the button that opened the lift gate the moment the wheels hit the ground. He flashed a thumbs-up, and every man on board stood and grabbed a handhold, keeping the other hand on his main weapon. The crew chief flashed another hand signal, and Team Ghost ran down the ramp. The Variant Hunters followed close behind, boots pounding the gate as they ran into sheets of rain. On the muddy lawn, the two teams spread out, weapons sweeping over the battlefield in careful arcs, each man on his own zone of fire.

Beckham would never forget this place. He could still picture the massacre when Lieutenant Gates had attempted to set up the forward operating base. A lot of good marines had died here, but they had taken hundreds of Variants down with them.

Swollen clouds the size of navy destroyers cruised across the sky. In the west, lightning tore through the gray. Thunder boomed, growing closer every second. Cold rain pattered Beckham's skin.

The teams jogged through the maze of splintered trees and charred corpses in Bryant Park. Beckham stopped on the steps overlooking West Forty-Second Street. Hundreds of track marks in the wet ash led away from the Bryant Park subway station. He crouched down to examine the closest of them.

There was no mistaking the prints. These were Variants, and judging from the route, it didn't look as if any of them had returned from their recent outing. The rain had distorted the tracks, but their direction was clear.

Beckham glanced to the right. Each building wore a skirt of black where Operation Liberty's firebombs had toasted the city. The blasts had shattered nearly every window he could see. Besides the tracks, there was no sign of the monsters: no awful rotting fruit smell, no tormented shrieks, and no snapping joints—just rain, thunder, and an empty city.

This was their chance.

Beckham shot an advance signal and bolted toward the subway station. The plan was simple—head to the lair where Fitz had last been seen. If the juvenile Variants were still there, they would split up to capture one and search for survivors.

A draft of death hit Beckham the moment he entered from the top of the station. He stopped at the stairwell and angled his M4 down the steps. They were littered with corpses, torn apart and scattered as if a tornado had whipped through a slaughterhouse.

He pulled his wet scarf over his nose and cautiously worked his way down the stairwell. The deeper he went, the worse the stench became. Flies surrounded the team as they continued to the concourse below.

Beckham couldn't hear anything past the buzzing, but it only took a quick sweep to see that nothing had been down here for some time. Still, the sight gave him pause. A battle had been fought here, but there weren't any bullet holes or blasts. These creatures had been torn to shreds and left to rot by one another. He strode through the graveyard of flesh to the platform and angled his UV light into the left passage and then the right.

"What the hell happened here?" Horn whispered into the comm.

"Rival groups," Garcia said. "They fight over territory and resources. We've seen it in Florida, Georgia, pretty much everywhere."

Jumping to the tracks below, Beckham motioned for the others to follow. He didn't care what monsters had done this, as long as they were long gone. They made good time through the damp tunnel and didn't slow until Beckham discovered fresh bodies. There were four Variants and two marines, all stiff with rigor mortis and deader than doornails. Beckham stopped to check both of the men. He rolled one body over to see a face he didn't recognize. The other man was lying on his back, hands up around his neck.

"Holy shit," Horn said. "Take a look at this, boss."

Beckham lowered his light to the other marine, illuminating a man riddled with bullet holes. First the Variant-on-Variant violence, and now a marine that had been shot to pieces?

"Variants still can't shoot, right?" Chow asked.

Beckham exchanged a glance with Garcia, who shrugged limply.

"Let's keep moving," Beckham said. They didn't have time to investigate. He continued down the passage at a jog that slowed to a walk when they came to the human prisoners. They were prepared for the gruesome sight, but the decaying bodies were still a shock.

"Check to see if anyone's alive," Beckham said. He directed his light toward the prisoners slung to the ceiling. Guts hung from a man's burst stomach like electrical cords. He shifted the beam to the right. A woman stared back at him with eyes frozen in terror. Her arms and legs were shredded to the bone. None of these people were alive. The Variants had already fed on them.

Beckham waved the teams forward. Ahead, the passage curved into a three-track network. The sour scent of rotting fruit increased with every step. They were close to the lair now, and with no sign of the Variants, Beckham increased his pace to a cautious but quick trot.

He balled his hand when he saw the entrance to the old train stop. Then he slowly reached to shut off his UV light and flip his NVGs into position. This was where Fitz had first left Apollo. He did a quick sweep in the green-hued darkness.

Where the hell are you, boy?

The other men flipped on their NVGs and continued at Beckham's command. The passage opened up into a chamber that connected with a concourse. A train was docked there, blocking half of the platform from view. Beckham pointed Ghost to the left. To his right, Garcia

led the Variant Hunters to the train. The teams fanned
out over the tracks, passing the fresh corpses of Variants.
This was where the battle had taken place, but he didn't
see any sign of the marines until he was a hundred feet
from the platform.

He halted and crouched, pointing at his eyes and
then at the walls across the concourse. Packs of Variants
were still slinging fresh bodies onto the wall. Beckham
searched the shapes for Fitz's blades or Apollo's fur. He
counted at least two dozen Variants, but he didn't recognize their human prisoners. To the right, near the staircases leading up to another level, sat six armored lumps,
still as rocks.

Back on the *GW*, Beckham had seen at least two
hundred Variants in the lair, but they were gone now,
and their tracks led away from the station. Now was
the chance the military had hoped for. It almost seemed
too good to be true. Beckham used his fingers to tell the
story and gestured for his men to advance.

It wasn't until they were five feet away from the platform that the first howl sounded. A second and third
quickly answered, the shrieks echoing through the
chamber in a tide of high-pitched wails.

"Don't shoot any of the human prisoners," Beckham
said into the comm. Shouldering his rifle and pushing
the scope to his eye, he calmly ordered his men to open
fire.

A torrent of shots lanced into the concourse. Tracer
rounds from Horn and Tank's SAWs streaked through
the air. The Variants took to the ceiling and walls, scampering toward the six soldiers.

Beckham centered his fire on two of the creatures
making a dash across the ground. He followed their
quick movements with his muzzle and squeezed off a
burst when the cross hairs were lined up on one of the

filthy naked monsters. Rounds punched through wrinkled flesh. His next shot hit the second beast in the ear.
The crack of a skull exploding seemed almost as loud as
the suppressed shots.

Pivoting to the right, he fired two rounds into the
neck of a third Variant. The impacts sent its head spinning away from its body. The body crashed to the ground,
thrashing like a decapitated snake.

The first wave of monsters went down easily, but
more came from the two staircases at the back of the
platform. Dozens turned into fifty. Long limbs pounded
the ground, horned nails scraped across the concrete, and
gaping mouths released tortured shrieks.

Instead of retreating, Beckham made an advance signal with two fingers. The soldiers took turns climbing
onto the platform. Once up top, they worked together
side by side, mowing down the monsters with calculated
precision.

"Changing!" Chow shouted.

"Enemy to the right," Tank yelled.

"Got it," Thomas called back.

The creatures skidded across the ground, their bodies twitching as the men fired kill shots. Chunks of gore
somersaulted over the concrete. Beckham's boots touched
the pooling blood. The juvenile Variants were squawking and hissing now, enraged and terrified. Beckham
continued searching the walls for Fitz and Apollo.

A few minutes into the slaughter, the remaining
beasts retreated back to the young and formed a perimeter around them. Most of them appeared to be female
Variants, their bellies still sagging from the recent births.

Beckham had to remind himself they were monsters
as he gunned them down. The other men worked their
way forward, shooting stray creatures that made dashes
for the walls and ceiling.

"Don't let them escape!" Beckham shouted as the cluster of females steered their offspring toward the far set of stairs.

He cursed under his breath and changed his magazine. Jamming a new one into the M4, he squared his shoulders and took down three more of the fleeing monsters. He hit another in the kneecap and sent it shrieking in agony. The beast flopped on the ground, and Beckham shot it in the forehead as he passed, the crack echoing through the concourse.

The main clump of remaining creatures darted for the staircases. They scrambled up the steps on all fours, climbing over one another, desperate to escape. Others scaled the walls, clawing and biting their way out of the slaughter.

"Horn, Chow, search for survivors!" Beckham shouted. "Garcia, take the right staircase. I got left!"

Horn voiced his protest over the comm with a grumble, but Beckham kept running, firing short bursts. He couldn't let the beasts escape above ground. There was no way in hell Beckham or any of the other men could catch them, and if they were allowed to move into the city, they might never find these offspring again. This was their chance. It was now or never.

Bodies thumped down the stairs, gushing blood that slopped down the concrete. Beckham changed his magazine as he ran, pivoting to the right as a corpse tumbled by him. He slammed a fresh mag into his carbine and brought the rifle up just in time to fire on a female that leaped to the ceiling.

They made eye contact in the moment he fired a burst into her chest. In slow motion, her lips opened into a wide oval, as if she was gasping for air. She dropped and landed with a thud in front of him, clutching tomato-sized holes in her chest that spouted crimson onto his pants. He smashed her head in with the butt of his rifle to conserve ammo.

The other Variants continued to the second level, and Beckham moved to follow them cautiously, scanning the dim space. The corridor held a ticket booth. To his left, a staircase led to the street. The Variants were already skittering up the stairs, but several of the beasts stopped to cover the retreat of the juveniles. They turned in his direction, heads tilting, yellow eyes locking onto him. To the right, Garcia's team was running up another staircase to flank the creatures.

A female Variant missing her nose licked her wormy lips and charged. An anguished shriek reverberated through the wide room as Beckham squeezed off a burst into her torso. She spun away in a spray of bloody mist.

Moonlight streamed from the left stairwell. Beckham caught a glimpse of one of the young escaping into the night. He fired at a pack of three emaciated male beasts that had regrouped. Two of them went down by the ticket machines, and he killed the third when it leaped to the ceiling.

"Hotel One, Golf One," Beckham said into his comm.

"Hotel One," Garcia replied. "We're topside. Eyes on the prize."

"On my way." Beckham fired on two females galloping in his direction. Others clambered across the ceiling, homing in on him with their demented eyes. The stairwell had come alive with motion as the abominations poured back into the room.

Beckham's heart raced in sync with the automatic bursts from his gun. He was slowly being surrounded. He had broken a cardinal rule, running ahead with no backup. Planting his boots and squaring his shoulders, he squeezed off another flurry of shots. The two females crashed to the ground, swiping at his legs as he executed both of them.

He shifted to his right to kill another beast charging over the ceiling. A spiky tongue shot from its mouth, curled around bulging lips, then disappeared back inside the gaping hole. Beckham lined up a shot that hit the creature where its tongue had been, the bullet entering through the mouth and blowing out the back of its head.

"Chow, Big Horn," Beckham said into his comm. "Up here!"

Static broke over the line, the delay making Beckham's heart flutter.

"On our way," Chow finally replied.

The ceiling and floor crawled with monsters now. Beckham backpedaled as he fired. Shadows flickered around him, long and distorted, claws like swords stretching over the ground.

Fucking rookie mistake, Beckham!

He should never have pursued the creatures alone. He simply couldn't shoot them fast enough. More continued to stream down the staircase, like bugs scurrying toward a fresh meal. Thoughts of Kate and their unborn child filled him with the relentless strength to keep fighting.

Beckham locked his jaw and became a machine, firing without restraint into the waves of monsters. They were closing in, and he fired in an arc that pushed them back. But there were so many—at least fifty—and others were still answering the battle cry from the street above. Where the fuck were Garcia and his men?

A tracer round shot by Beckham's left ear, slamming into the wave of advancing monsters. Horn and Chow now flanked him on both sides, firing into the masses of diseased flesh. Beckham bent down, pulled a dry mag, tossed it, reached for another, and slammed it home before his knee hit the ground. He fired burst after burst into the wave, his shots ripping through eye sockets and emaciated chest cavities.

"Did you find Fitz and Apollo?" he shouted.

"Negative," Chow replied.

Hope drained out of Beckham like the bullets leaving his gun. He had known it was a long shot, but if Fitz and Apollo weren't here, it would be like finding a needle in a fucking haystack outside.

Beckham ground his teeth and continued squeezing the trigger. The encroaching creatures were close—so close he could smell their sour, rancid flesh.

"Garcia, we need help!" Beckham shouted.

Static hissed into his earpiece, then a voice said, "On our way … Variant …"

Beckham hoped that whatever Garcia meant by *Variant*, it was good news. He took another step backward, his boots reaching the edge of the stairwell. Horn and Chow squeezed up against him, their muzzles flicking from the ceiling to the floor to the walls.

No! Goddamnit. Not like this!

Beckham gripped his rifle tighter and counted the beasts. There were still at least thirty, and they were inching closer, claws swiping, jaws clamping. The sounds merged into a hellish symphony of snapping joints and howls, but it was the noise coming from the staircase behind them that sent a chill up Beckham's spine. He whirled just as a pack of beasts rocketed up the stairs.

"Our six!" Beckham managed to shout. He emptied the rest of his magazine into the creatures, killing or maiming all four of them.

Something big hit Beckham from behind, knocking him forward. He reached out to grab the wall, but crashed into the side and then toppled down four stairs. He caught a glimpse of Horn falling too, but Chow was still at the top of the landing, firing at the pallid wall of crazed monsters.

"Chow, get out of there!" Beckham shouted. He

climbed over a corpse and drew his Colt .45. Horn was already on his feet, his SAW spitting rounds into the monsters surrounding Chow.

Beckham went to fire when a claw grabbed his boot. Pain lanced up his leg as horned nails sunk through the leather and slashed his flesh. Twisting, he shot the beast he'd failed to kill earlier directly between the eyes. Blood caked his uniform and splattered in his face.

When he turned back to the landing, the Variants were surging toward Chow. They lashed at his arms, tearing through cloth and ripping into flesh as he screamed. He tried to pull back as Horn ran up the stairs, but it was too late. The monsters pulled Chow beneath their ranks, the wall of pallid flesh closing around him.

23

Fitz ran through the streets, fueled by pure adrenaline. Apollo was having a hard time keeping up, still sluggish from the sedatives. They'd been on the move for over an hour, trailing the army of creatures to the edge of Manhattan.

Cold rain fell from the dark sky, rinsing the filth and blood from Fitz's fatigues. He'd lost sight of the beasts a few streets back and worried they'd taken the Queens-Midtown Tunnel. The thought of heading underground again gave him the chills, but as he approached the United Nations tower along East Forty-Second Street, he heard the chorus of snapping joints and sporadic shrieks again.

Fitz jogged through the abandoned cars on the FDR's on-ramp. The narrow roadway was clogged with twisted metal. He ran to the concrete barrier overlooking the river, Apollo nudging up against him when they got there.

To his left, the center of the Ed Koch Queensboro Bridge sagged into the river. The white hull of a capsized yacht sat in the water under the bridge like a fin of some giant whale.

Fitz shouldered his M4 and centered his scope on FDR Drive to the right. There were several piers in the river along the side of the road. A small fleet of eight boats ranging in shape and size was docked on the third pier down. Some appeared to be coast guard vessels; others were speedboats like those he had seen scoping out Plum Island. Movement on the dock caught his attention, and he centered his muzzle on several soldiers loading boxes.

Fitz wanted to scream and wave, but held his breath instead. He wiped the rain from his face and pushed the scope to his eye. These men, filthy and thin, were dressed in soiled, tattered clothing. They didn't look like the type who could survive out in the open. He recoiled as a pack of Variants leaped onto the dock. The men backed away and jumped into the boats.

Zooming in, Fitz almost choked at the sight of dozens of human collaborators. Some of the men carried rifles, and there was no mistaking the AT-4 launcher one of them had slung over his back, nor his army uniform.

Mother—

It took every ounce of Fitz's strength to hold back his trigger finger from raining rounds on the boats. But there was nothing he could do from here. He didn't have enough ammunition.

The Bone Collector lumbered across the dock. Several of the collaborators dragged Knapp across the pavement. When they reached the platform, the Alpha picked up Knapp by his throat and tossed him into the closest boat. Then he turned and roared at the other Variants. They clambered onto the dock, squawking as if disoriented. The beast screeched again, and the Variants finally climbed into the other boats. Others continued to file in from FDR Drive until the eight vessels were filled to the brim.

Fitz watched in shock. These beasts weren't just communicating, they were following orders. He considered shooting out the boats' engines or trying to take out the human collaborators. The Variants couldn't drive themselves, and it would take days to swim to Plum Island. He pivoted from side to side, searching for a clean shot, but the Variants had filled the boats, and the human collaborators were already at the helms.

Apollo poked Fitz's bent blade with his wet muzzle. He let out a low whine and looked up, the fleck of amber in his dark eyes reflecting an astonishing level of comprehension—the dog understood what they were up against, and he was still itching to fight. They were both exhausted, injured, and frightened, but it was up to Fitz and Apollo to stop these bastards from reaching their friends at Plum Island.

The boats' engines coughed to life, and one by one they launched into the water. Rain pelted their diseased cargo as they took off down the East River. Even at full speed, it would take them a couple of hours to reach their destination. With no way to contact the island, Fitz would have to beat the creatures there. That was his only hope, unless the Black Hawks patrolling the skies above the island noticed them first.

As soon as the final boat launched, Fitz took off running down the ramp with his loyal German shepherd by his side. There were still two docked vessels, both red, one with lightning bolts on the side. He opted for that one, almost grinning as he clambered into the cigar-shaped boat. The Variants weren't as smart as he'd given them credit for. They had left the fastest boat, and Fitz was going to give the beasts a run for their money.

Side by side, Beckham and Horn fought their way into the crowd of beasts in their search for Chow. They couldn't see him, but they could hear his screams over the comm. Every agonizing second felt like talons flaying Beckham's flesh. This was his fault. Chow's death would be on his hands, just like those of all of his other men lost since Building 8. The sound of distant suppressed gunfire rang out as the duo battled their way deeper into the throng. At the end of the corridor, a trio of soldiers rushed down the stairs.

The hope that had died inside of Beckham reared its head, fueling another wave of adrenaline that pushed him forward. He fired his Colt .45 with his right hand and slashed with his knife in his left, executing any Variants that made a run for him and slashing the throats of those he didn't shoot in the head. Horn had torn a hole in the wall of Variants to the center and the right.

"Hold on, Chow!" Beckham shouted. He was down to his final bullet when a muffled reply broke over the channel.

"Did you save some for us?"

It was Garcia, and the monsters were falling back right into the gunfire of the Variant Hunters. Forming a perimeter, the two teams clamped around the desperate creatures. Through the fence of stalklike appendages and withered torsos, Beckham saw Chow's still body.

"Watch your fire!" Beckham screamed.

Claws ripped across his left arm as he picked off the beasts around his friend. He shot the Variant that had slashed him in the mouth. Another lunged at him from the side, and he jammed his blade into the creature's skull.

The final Variants scattered, Garcia and his men pursuing them while Horn and Beckham ran for Chow. Blood pooled around his body, but Beckham wasn't sure if it was human, or Variant, or both.

Chow lay curled up in a fetal position, and Beckham dropped to a knee to put a hand on his shoulder. He gently helped Chow move to his back. A deep gash stretched from his chin to his eyebrow on the right side of his face.

"Got me good," Chow muttered.

Beckham reeled when he saw the extent of Chow's injuries. The operator's body was covered in lacerations, some so deep he could see muscle. Beckham wasn't sure what to dress first.

"Fuck. We need to get him out of here ASAP," Horn said.

"I'm cold," Chow said. "Shit, man, they really fucked me up, didn't they?" He tried to raise his head, but Horn pressed down on Chow's chest.

"Don't move, brother," Horn growled. He reached into his pack for his medical supplies.

"You're going to be fine," Beckham said. He looked up as Garcia, Tank, and Thomas rushed over.

"Thomas, Tank, hold security," Garcia said. He crouched down, whispering something under his breath and locking eyes with Beckham.

"We got the package," Tank said. "Should I call in our extraction?"

Chow managed a crooked grin with blue lips. "You guys got one of those little fucks?" He let out a wet cough, his lungs crackling.

"Don't talk, man," Beckham said to Chow. He glanced back at Tank. "Hold off on the extraction. We still haven't found Fitz or Apollo."

Tank hesitated, but Garcia nodded at the marine.

Chow attempted to move his head again. "You guys really nabbed one of them?"

"Hold still, Chow!" Horn growled. He was already wrapping Chow's right arm.

Garcia pointed back at the staircase. A juvenile Variant was sprawled on the ground, unmoving. "Yeah, we got one, brother."

Garcia stood and gestured for Beckham to join him a few feet away. Horn remained at Chow's side, working quickly to dress the worst of his injuries.

"Look, I know you want to search for Fitz and Apollo, but if we don't get Chow out of here, he's going to bleed out. Plus, we have to get that thing back to the *GW*," Garcia said.

Beckham looked back at the staircase leading to the concourse below. He stared for several seconds, his heart icing over. Garcia was right. They had to get Chow and the specimen out of the city before it was too late. With no way of telling where Fitz and Apollo were, Beckham knew what he had to do. Chow's life depended on it. If Fitz and Apollo were out there, they were on their own now.

Good luck, brother, Beckham thought as he nodded to Tank to call in their extraction.

"We can't let them down, boy," Fitz said. He looked back at Apollo. The dog was lying on the floor of the boat, head tucked between his paws. He had already thrown up twice, but Fitz couldn't let up on the gas.

Thunder clapped overhead, and the distant booms rattled Fitz. A heavy rain beat down from the purple sky. In the meat of the clouds, rays of moonlight lit up the East River with an eerie glow. Ahead, the small fleet of eight boats carrying the Bone Collector and his army was closing in on Plum Island, and Fitz was still at least a mile behind. The monsters hadn't seemed to notice him yet, or maybe they didn't care. There were at least sixty of the beasts on the boats. Between air support and the Mark V SOCs, Fitz was hopeful the monsters would be intercepted before they reached the island. If they weren't, Vice President Johnson's reinforcements would be able to stop them at the fences, as long as the human collaborators didn't put up a fight. That's what Fitz was mostly worried about now. The AT-4 launcher and machine guns they carried could do some major damage.

Jesus, how could these men be so evil?

Fitz wiped the rain from his eyes and pushed down on the throttle. He'd lost ten minutes trying to figure out how to fill the boat with gas. The tank was almost on empty when he boarded.

"Come on, you piece of shit."

For a speedboat, he expected the damn thing to go faster, but the wind and rain prevented him from pushing her to the max. Doing so could result in flipping and capsizing. The last thing he wanted was to swim to Plum Island.

They weren't far now, but he wasn't going to make it. There just wasn't enough time.

On the horizon, the vague outline of the island was already in focus. He searched the skies for a Black Hawk, but saw only darkness. And there was no sign of the Mark V SOCs in the dark water. By the time one of the guard towers saw the boats, it could be too late. Where the fuck was the air support? Had the other choppers been recalled to the *GW*?

Fitz cursed, his mind spinning as he considered his options. He could remove the silencer on the M4, but gunshots were going to be hard to hear over the thunder. Quickly glancing behind him, he searched the boat. He had seen an emergency pack when he boarded. He eyed the box, an idea emerging on his mind. Ahead, two of the boats were slowing. The other crafts continued at full speed. Had they spotted him?

Fitz eased off on the throttle and let his boat coast

He had to do something now. He ran back to the emergency box. Rummaging through the contents, he pulled an orange flare gun and a set of flares.

Stuffing them into his vest, he rushed back to the steering wheel, grabbed it with his left hand, and pushed the throttle down with his right. The boat jolted, the bow lifting into the air. Apollo slid across the floor, letting out a whimper.

"Sorry!" Fitz shouted. He took his hand off the throttle and loaded the flare gun. The boats were a half mile from the island now, and there was still no sign of a chopper or a Mark V SOC.

Fitz fired off a flare into the sky. He cracked the break open and was moving to put in another flare when Apollo howled. In his peripheral vision, a Variant, soaked and shrieking, pulled itself onto the right side of the boat.

Now he knew why the two boats had slowed earlier. Just when he thought things couldn't get worse, the beasts had thrown a wrench into the cogs of war.

Fitz fired off a second flare into the sky and pulled his M9. Apollo was already on the monster and had it pinned to the ground. A second and then a third Variant climbed into the boat from the left side.

Before the third was all the way aboard, Fitz shot it in the nose. It flipped over the side and hit the water, skating over the whitecaps and vanishing in the darkness. The other beast leaped toward Fitz. Apollo left his limp prey on the deck and grabbed it by the ankle. The creature slashed at Fitz, knocking his hand away from the steering wheel. The boat curved to the right, slamming over waves and jolting up and down.

Howling in pain, the Variant jerked and kicked Apollo off its leg. The dog slid across the bloody deck and hit the starboard side with a yelp.

Fitz fought out of the monster's grip and shot it under

the chin, brains blowing out the top of its shiny skull. He pushed the beast over the side and grabbed the wheel, straightening the boat out with a quick twist.

"Apollo!" Fitz shouted.

The dog hurried to his side, seemingly unharmed. Fitz breathed in a sigh of relief, and turned back to the island. The other boats were slowing as they approached, but one was already making a run for the beach. Flashes of gunfire streaked away from the towers. Flames licked the back of the hull, and tendrils of smoke rose into the sky. The towers continued to fire, but the vessel hit the beach at full steam, skidding over the sand and smashing through both sets of electric fences.

Fitz pushed the throttle down as far as it would go. A Black Hawk rose over the tarmac. As soon as it was in the sky, the M240 door gun barked to life.

Thank God.

Fitz twisted the steering wheel, trying his best to keep the boat steady. Rain beat against his face, and he batted the water from his eyes. In between blinks, a flash of fire streaked from one of the boats. He flinched as a rocket slammed into the side of the chopper, crimson ballooning out the sides.

"No!" Fitz shouted, unable to control himself. He watched in shock, his mouth hanging open as the wreckage crashed back onto the tarmac.

A Mark V SOC finally came bursting around the corner of the island, Gatling gun blazing at the approaching boats. But it was already too late. The human collaborators drove the vessels onto the beach. Monsters piled over the sides and bolted across the sand. Fitz swallowed, still unable to quite process the turn of events. His eyes flitted to Apollo.

"You ready to fight, boy?"

Apollo bared his teeth and sat next to Fitz's bent

blade. He patted the dog on the head and steered the boat toward the shore. Plum Island was about to be over-run, but he was prepared to fight with his bare hands to save his friends.

Kate almost cried out loud when Major Smith told her Reed and his team had been extracted from New York with a live specimen in tow.

"He's on the vice president's shit list for making off with an Osprey unauthorized. Not like it matters any-more who follows orders and who doesn't," Smith had said with a shrug.

Kate knew Major Smith had been broken by the loss of his family and his commanding officer, but she wasn't prepared for how easily he brushed aside Team Ghost's actions. Still, it was nice to know Reed might have some support from the officer if Johnson decided to enforce discipline. Then she remembered his words to Fitz when he first arrived on Plum Island.

"The Uniform Code of Military Justice says I'm supposed to arrest you, son. But I think I should give you a goddamn medal."

Thoughts of Fitz put Kate's mind back on the other news Major Smith had shared. Chow had suffered severe injuries in Manhattan. The operator was in stable condi-tion, but only just. And the teams had found no sign of Fitz or Apollo.

Like everything in this never-ending apocalypse, there seemed to be a trade-off. A juvenile Variant could be the key to winning the war and retaking the planet. Could she weigh that against the losses they'd suffered to obtain it?

Kate went over the data from Bioreactor 11 in silence.

Earlier, focusing on work had been like trying to run a marathon with a hangover. She hadn't gotten anything done, but now she couldn't waste any more time.

"Kate, you okay?" Ellis asked. He was standing in front of Bioreactor 12, checking the stats and tapping the results into his tablet.

"As okay as I can be," she said. "How about you?"

Ellis nodded and backed away from Bioreactor 12. "Only four or five more days before this batch should be ready. Did you speak to the other US labs before you left the *GW*?"

"Doctor Yokoyama was going to contact them this evening and report back. He was pretty shaken up after the incident with Lieutenant Brett."

Ellis glanced in her direction. "You never did explain what happened."

"He overpowered the guards, from what I was told. Guess they underestimated his strength. After he escaped, he made a run for the labs."

"And he knew how to find them?"

"Doctor Yokoyama had performed tests on Brett. He knew exactly where he was going."

Ellis was quiet. He lowered his head and studied the screen of his tablet.

"Where are we at with the next phase of Kryptonite?" Kate asked.

Still looking down, Ellis said, "I've decided to use a polymer microencapsulation technique."

"That's what the other labs are doing too."

Ellis strolled over to Bioreactor 10. "I hope they know what they're doing. This is all experimental."

Kate almost asked him if he understood the process, but he beat her to it.

"I think I understand the technique, but I'll need assistance. First, we'll need to conjugate the antibodies to the polymer shells encapsulating the Paclitaxel and Docetaxel. When that's finished, we put them into the missiles."

Kate nodded again. "I'll contact Doctor Yokoyama tomorrow morning and let him know our status." She was walking to Bioreactor 9 when a thud rattled the lab. "What the hell was that?"

Ellis stared at the observation window. "I—I don't know."

The blare of an emergency siren sounded. Both of them flinched at the noise. They exchanged a worried glance, each likely fearing the same thing—the island was under attack.

"Must be a false alarm, right?" Ellis asked. "Major Smith would have told us if something was wrong."

"I'll check it out," Kate said. "Keep working."

The extraction from New York had gone flawlessly. Team Ghost and the Variant Hunters had encountered only light resistance before the Osprey picked them up. That was almost two hours ago. Now, the men sat in the troop hold of the craft, racing through heavy storms toward the *GW*.

Beckham was lost in his thoughts, the mission replaying in his mind on a loop, one eye still on Chow. The man lay on the floor, covered in bandages. Some of the lacerations were deep, but they had stopped most of the bleeding. He was stable for now, but he would need surgery when he got back to the *GW*. The creatures had carved him up good. If he did live, he was going to be covered in scars.

The juvenile Variant specimen was in the corner of the troop hold, hands and feet bound, with Horn holding a knee to its chest. The thing wasn't going anywhere. They were thirty minutes out, and the creature showed no sign of waking.

White noise broke over the comms, pulling Beckham back to grim reality. Fitz and Apollo were still out there, and Chow was severely injured because Beckham had fucked up. The guilt stabbed at his insides. He had to accept Fitz and Apollo were gone. He had to let them go.

"Master Sergeant," Tito said. "We got Lieutenant Davis on the comms. She wants to talk to you."

"Patch it through," Beckham said. Static crackled in his ear.

"Master Sergeant Beckham," Davis said.

"Here, Lieutenant," Beckham said in a low, deep voice.

"I'd offer you congratulations, but I'm afraid I have disturbing news. We just heard that Plum Island is under attack."

Beckham's heart thudded in his rib cage, and Horn turned to catch his worried gaze.

"What do you mean, *under attack*?" Beckham asked, his voice cracking.

"We don't have many details. Major Smith only sent us an SOS saying that boats had rammed the electric fences and that Variants had made landfall a few minutes ago."

Beckham shot out of his seat and worked his way to the cockpit. "Turn this bird around!" he shouted. "We have to get to Plum Island!"

The pilots both twisted around to look at him.

"That's an order!" Beckham shouted.

Tito glanced back at the controls. "We can't, sir. We're low on fuel. We wouldn't even make it halfway there."

Beckham kicked the wall in frustration. "How much farther to the *GW*?"

"Fifteen minutes, sir," the other pilot replied.

Horn was standing now, his boot clamped down on the young monster's throat. "What the hell is happening?"

"Davis, how long until you can have birds in the air?" Beckham said into the comm.

"They're already in the air, but they won't get to the island for another hour."

"Fuck!" Beckham shouted.

Garcia had risen to his feet. He put a hand on Beckham's back. "We're with you, brother. Once we drop off Chow and this freak, we'll head back out there."

Chow struggled to sit up, but Tank held up a hand.

"Don't move," Beckham said. Chow's eyes flitted to Beckham's. There was sadness there, but also resiliency. Despite his injuries, he could see Chow wanted to fight.

Beckham bowed his head and shook it from side to side. He put a hand to his vest pocket, his heart beating so hard he could feel it through his vest.

Mom, please—if you're watching over me, help Kate and the others.

24

The explosion woke Tasha and Jenny. They shot up in bed, bursting into tears. Riley looked out Meg's window at the fiery wreck of the Black Hawk.

Meg grabbed her knife off the table. "What the *hell* was that?" She tucked the knife into her belt and limped over to the girls, wrapping her arms around them as they jumped out of bed.

Riley stared in awe at the flames licking the asphalt. The air-raid sirens blared in the hallway of Building 1. He plucked his M9 from his belt, pulled back the slide to chamber a round, and handed Meg the gun. "Take this."

"Wh—what? Why?"

The pop of gunfire sounded in the distance. There was no doubt in his mind now. This was no accident: The island was under attack.

"Do it," Riley insisted. He pushed the gun at her and she reluctantly grabbed it. Then he wheeled to the corner of the room and picked up his M4. The usual pre-combat mix of horror and exhilaration kicked in, and he felt the chill of adrenaline ripping through his veins.

"Listen very carefully, Meg. Whatever happens, keep the girls close. Okay?"

Tasha and Jenny were sobbing. Meg pulled them

close, hushing them and telling them it was going to be all right.

But Riley wasn't so sure. Automatic gunfire filled the night, but above it he heard the unmistakable shriek of a Variant.

Meg heard the howls too. She looked toward the window at the flaming wreckage in the distance. Distorted silhouettes darted past the fire.

"Alex . . . I'm scared."

"It's going to be okay, Meg. I won't let anything happen to you." Riley grabbed the door. "We have to get to Building Three. Follow me."

The halls were a mess of panic, civilians running from their rooms and crowding into the narrow corridor. Riley wheeled through them, yelling, "Get to your designated shelters!"

The distant crack of gunfire and the screech of emergency sirens made it difficult to hear, and most people seemed to ignore him. Meg limped toward the door. She pushed it open and reached back to grab Tasha and Jenny. They moved into the lobby, huddled together.

Outside the double doors, Plum Island was a war zone. Tracer rounds streaked across the post at Variants clambering across the tarmac. The beasts were running down fleeing marines and soldiers.

"My God," muttered a voice behind them.

Red and his wife, Donna, stood in the doorway with their son tucked behind them. Kate emerged behind the family. She pulled her hair back into a ponytail, her eyes wide with panic.

"What the hell is happening?" she asked.

"Come with us," Riley said.

"I have to warn Ellis!" Kate said, turning away.

"Where is he?" Riley asked.

"I left him in the lab."

"That's the safest place, if he stays put. I'd go there myself if it weren't for the contaminants," Riley said. "We have to get to Building Three."

Kate hesitated for a moment, considering her next move.

"Come on!" Riley said.

Red ran ahead, carrying a shotgun. He stopped at the door to load the gun with buckshot shells. Several of them fell to the ground as he worked to jam them into the bottom. As he pumped the gun, a stray round shattered the glass in the left door and hit the wall behind them. Red ducked and motioned for everyone else to get down. The high-pitched howls of Variants filled the room.

"Hurry!" Riley yelled. He let his rifle sag across his chest and wheeled out onto the landing. The M240 machine-gun nest in the center of the lawn was disgorging a stream of fire at the army of Variants coming from the wooded area at the edge of the tarmac. Another marine fired an M4 from behind the sandbags. Across the lawn, more of the creatures careened down the concrete path to flank the marines in the nest.

"Watch your nine o'clock!" Riley shouted with his hands cupped over his mouth.

The man with the M4 patted the M240 gunner on the shoulder and pointed. The marine raked the large machine gun back and forth between the two fronts of advancing Variants. The muzzle flashes illuminated the hardened faces of men who knew they were the final defense against the monsters.

Questions ping-ponged in Riley's mind as he watched. How had the Variants made it past the island's defenses so easily? And how had they destroyed a chopper?

Shaking away the thoughts, he said, "Help me down the steps."

Red and Kate picked up Riley and hoisted him to the walkway below. Meg, Donna, and the children followed. Red ran back up the steps to grab Riley's chair.

In seconds they were moving to Building 3. Two marines were on the steps, waving at them. Riley looked at the fray as Red pushed him down the path. The Variants were darting around the spray of the 7.62-millimeter rounds in the center of the lawn. Dirt kicked up into the air as the gunner trained his fire on the closest pack. The tracer rounds narrowed in and slammed into the creatures. Body parts exploded in all directions, sending the surviving Variants scattering.

Another squad of marines five strong came running from the path behind Building 3. The men fanned out onto the grass, firing on the charging beasts. In the glow of moonlight, the monsters shifted into focus. Scarred flesh, long limbs laced with ropy muscle, withered torsos, and wild eyes. Their maws chopped together, lips smacking.

Riley nearly choked at the sheer number of the monsters. There had to be more than fifty of them, and they had already shattered Plum Island's defenses. The crack of the M240 was silenced a moment later. Screams of agony followed as the marines were overrun.

"Come on! Hurry!" Riley shouted. Red pushed him faster, the chair jolting over rocks on the concrete. Even if they made it to Building 3, the monsters would find a way inside. Despair filled Riley as he tried to think of an escape. He knew they wouldn't survive unless they managed to get air support. But the *GW* was too far away, and the only remaining Black Hawk sat idle on the tarmac. The other birds still weren't back from the mission in New York. They had been ordered to stay in the city just in case any survivors from the strike teams crawled out of the sewers.

Riley's gaze shifted to a hulking Variant running in the heart of the advancing army. A quilt of skin flapped behind its muscular shoulders, and its extremities were covered with plates of human bone.

Muzzle flashes fired behind the monster. The rounds tore into the marines running toward the fight. Riley raised his rifle and zoomed in on soldiers wearing filthy fatigues. The men were firing shotguns and M16s.

The realization sparked a shot of anger that masked his dread. He held in a breath and squeezed the trigger. The first shot hit a human collaborator in the face, a geyser of blood bursting from the man's shattered skull.

"Stop here!" Riley shouted.

Red did as instructed and ushered the children and his wife up the steps to Building 3. The two marines standing guard hustled onto the lawn. The five-man squad had taken up a position fifty feet behind the over-run machine-gun nest. One of the men squirmed on the ground, clutching his stomach where a human collaborator had shot him.

Meg squeezed next to Riley's chair. He looked up at her and offered a reassuring nod. She raised her M9, squinted, and fired at the monsters. The spent casings hit Riley on the head as they rained down from her gun. She dropped several of the creatures with well-aimed shots. If Riley hadn't been overwhelmed by the horror of their situation, he might have smiled.

Squaring his shoulders, Riley did his best to hold his weapon steady. He focused his fire on the human collaborators, hitting one in the neck. The man went down like a bag of bricks in water. Riley struck another man in the shoulder. The ex-soldier took off running back toward the tarmac. Other collaborators followed in retreat. They were cowards, but their Variant masters were relentless and would never stop.

The Alpha stopped at the machine-gun nest and grabbed one of the marines who was still fighting. The beast hoisted the man into the air, providing Riley a full view of its bony armor and thick, bulging muscles.

The marine, kicking and screaming, tried to break free from the monster's grasp. With a quick twist, it snapped the man's neck and discarded him like a spoiled piece of food.

Riley trained his gun on the beast, snarling with rage. The bony plates covering its naked flesh shattered as he hit it again and again, but the muscles below the armor seemed to absorb the rounds, which only slowed the creature down. It passed under an industrial light that illuminated a necklace of flesh trophies hanging from its neck. This Alpha was a demon. How could they stop such evil?

With a bullet to the head.

Riley squeezed the trigger again, but the beast had melted back into the curtain of monsters surrounding it. The marines on the lawn cut the lead creatures down, but a dozen more surged across the final stretch of grass and plowed into the men.

"Get out of here, Meg!" Riley shouted.

"Oh, *hell* no!" she yelled back. She changed her magazine and continued firing.

Riley risked a short glance over his shoulder. Kate, Horn's girls, Donna, Bo, and the other civilians had taken refuge in Building 3. Red slammed the door behind them and ran back to Riley's side with his shotgun shouldered. He fired a blast that hit a Variant in the side, sending it spinning away from the marines. Behind them, more Variants skittered out of Building 1, their bloody flesh glowing in the moonlight. Several of them dragged screaming civilians with them.

Flipping magazines, Riley trained his gun on the

Variants that overwhelmed the squad of marines. He picked them off, one at a time, but he couldn't save the men. They died bravely, killing six of the beasts before finally succumbing. Ten feet in front of them, the Alpha Variant stepped out of the mass of smaller creatures and extended a horned nail at the final two marines who were guarding Building 3. The men fell back, still squeezing off short bursts.

The seven surviving creatures were only twenty feet away from Riley's position, and the only thing standing between him and the beasts were the two marines. Red ran forward, a final attempt to stop the monsters from reaching Building 3. The Alpha lumbered to the front of the pack, and Red fired a shotgun blast that took off its left arm at the elbow. Pieces of bony armor and flesh exploded. It howled in pain and retreated as the other Variants surged forward. That gave Riley an idea. Maybe if he killed their leader, the others would retreat too. It was the only plan he had left.

Riley squeezed off a short burst into the Alpha's armored chest plating as it searched for cover. One of the bullets punched into flesh, jerking the beast to the right. It lowered its skull and puked a stream of white goo onto its riven stump.

Red and the two marines continued firing on the six withered Variants. The monsters sprinted across the lawn, dodging the gunfire. Two of them fell, but the other four raced forward.

Riley shot the Alpha again, hitting bones on its back and side. The beast rose to its feet, its left arm covered in white plaster. Roaring, it cracked its head from side to side and focused on Building 3.

"Red, watch out!" Riley shouted when he saw the men weren't going to be able to hold back the four Variants. Red managed to back away as the Variants plowed into the two marines like bowling balls knocking down pins.

"Riley!" Meg shouted.

"Get out of here!" he yelled again.

His heart raced out of control, slamming against his rib cage, but it wasn't from fear of his own death. He was prepared to die, and had been for weeks now. Part of him even wanted to—wanted the nightmare to be over. But he wasn't prepared to lose Meg or his other friends. He thought of his Delta brothers, wishing more than ever to see them running across the lawn, guns blazing.

Red, Riley, and Meg were all that was left now. They killed two of the four monsters, but the other two abandoned the dead marines and made a run for Red. Another dozen galloped down the path away from Building 1, dragging human prisoners with them. There was sporadic gunfire from the beach, and for a moment Riley held on to hope that his friends had returned to the island to save them.

"I'm empty!" Meg shouted. She tossed her gun to the ground and pulled her knife. Riley's M4 clicked dry at the same moment. Red continued firing his shotgun, crack after crack echoing through the night. He killed the final two Variants and turned the barrel on the Alpha.

Riley slammed his final magazine into the M4 and fired at the Variants darting down the sidewalk. They were one hundred feet away now, their talons scratching over the pavement.

"Run, Meg!" Riley shouted.

Instead of fleeing, she limped to his side, holding the knife in both hands and pointing it at the creatures. Riley continued firing, watching in his peripheral vision as Red shot the giant beast. It took a blast to the side of its shattered armor chest plating, fragments of bone exploding away.

Red pumped the gun again, but the injured monster grabbed it with its good hand and yanked it away, tossing it onto the lawn.

Riley killed two more of the Variants on the sidewalk before shifting his gun back to the Alpha that had Red. He locked eyes with the man for a second as the demon grabbed him around the neck and lifted him into the air, blood dripping down its muscular flesh where the shotgun blast had torn through flesh. It snapped Red's neck with a quick twist and dropped his limp body to the lawn.

"NO!" Riley shouted. He aimed for the wound and squeezed off a shot that tore through flesh.

The beast roared in agony and hunched down like a linebacker preparing for a tackle. Riley managed another two shots before the beast dropped to all fours and plowed into his wheelchair. The blow sent him crashing to the ground, his left cheek skidding across the pavement. Scrambling, Riley grabbed his rifle and rolled onto his back. Meg screamed and lunged toward the Alpha, plunging the blade deep into its back as it rose to its feet. It swatted her away with ease, sending her crashing onto the steps of Building 3.

"You son of a fucking bitch!" Riley shouted. He took off the beast's right ear as it reached down and picked him up by one of his broken legs and tossed him. He sailed through the air for what seemed like several seconds before hitting the concrete headfirst. The impact sent stars across his vision. He clawed at the ground, trying to drag his broken body away from the monster. He made it a few feet when it grabbed him again and hoisted him into the air.

No. Not like this. Not like this!

With his left eye battered shut, Riley blinked to focus with his right eye. There was a blur of motion to the side and a scream as Meg leaped onto the monster's back and stabbed the beast.

"Leave him alone!" she screamed.

The Alpha reached back with its stump of an arm and slashed her with the jagged bone. She fell to the ground, still screaming for the monster to let Riley go.

"You fucking piece of shit," Riley choked. His face flushed with heat from the lack of oxygen. He struggled to breathe as the monster clamped its talons tighter around his windpipe. The stars and encroaching red slowly overwhelmed his vision. He choked out a plea to the demon.

"Don't hurt her . . . you bast—ard."

Riley tightened his grip on the monster's hand and pummeled its face with his other fist. He hit it in the eye, again and again, until he felt the soft tissue give beneath his knuckles. The beast shrieked in agony and clamped its talons tighter, slicing into Riley's neck and cutting off his breathing completely.

He choked, fighting desperately for air. Somewhere in the distance, there was a flash of a muzzle. He tried to focus on the figure, but the red was closing in. Blinking and squinting, he concentrated on a man who looked as if he was running on stilts. To the man's right was a dog. Riley thought he was losing his mind until he realized it was Fitz and Apollo bolting toward him.

Riley choked again, cracked a half grin, and with the last breath in his lungs, he managed to slur a final sentence, "You're going to die, you evil fuck."

A sharp pain raced through Riley's neck, and he fell to the ground. The pain faded away until there was only the swirling red, and then shades of darkness touched the sides of his vision. The last thing he saw was Meg crawling toward him, that beautiful girl still fighting, and Fitz running with Apollo by his side.

"NO!" Fitz screamed.

He shot the hulking beast in the back as Riley's limp body crashed to the ground. The creature whirled and pointed its remaining hand in Fitz's direction. Then it grabbed Meg by her hair and dragged her away. She was screaming at the top of her lungs, still trying to stab it with the knife in her hand.

"Alex!" she shouted. "Alex, get up! You have to get up!"

Fitz aimed at the Alpha's head, but half of the dozen Variants racing for Building 3 turned and ran toward him. The other half continued carrying their human prisoners down the path.

"Alex!" Meg shouted. She disappeared around the corner of Building 3 a moment later, her cries lost in the roar of the Variants.

Fitz hesitated, then halted. He was down to his final magazine and didn't have enough ammunition to kill all of them. There wasn't time to find another weapon. His heart was thumping out of control, and he was wheezing like a chain-smoker. Riley was gone, but he could still save Meg and the others.

He whistled for Apollo and grabbed him by the collar when he didn't come. The dog struggled in his grip, and he had to yank him down the path cutting between Building 1 and Building 3. Fitz pulled Apollo into a bush and raised his rifle. He waited with a breath held in his chest.

The Variants burst around the corner on all fours a few seconds later. When all seven of them had passed, Fitz opened fire from behind. He lined up the cross hairs carefully, killing three of them with shots to the back of the head. By the time the rest knew what had happened, he'd killed another two. Apollo leaped at one of the monsters, clamping his jaw around the beast's neck. Fitz smashed the other creature in the face with the side of his M4 as it lunged at him. The impact knocked out several needle-sharp teeth, but the creature clambered back to its feet and slashed at his right blade.

Fitz kicked it in the eye with his left blade. The metal sank through soft tissue, and he used the butt of his rifle to smash the beast's head into a bloody pulp. Apollo let out a yelp as the final Variant clawed at the dog's back. Fitz jumped onto the pile of bloody flesh and fur, wrapping his hands around the monster's neck. He squeezed the life out of it, breaking its windpipe as he screamed at the top of his lungs. By the time it was over, he was covered in blood. Apollo sat a few feet away, twisting to lick his wounds.

"Are you okay, boy?" Fitz whispered.

Apollo's tail wagged weakly. Fitz pushed himself back to his blades and whistled for Apollo to follow.

Dazed, injured, and running on raw adrenaline, Fitz staggered back to the concrete path leading to Building 3. The Variants were dragging humans down the stairs, and now he was without a weapon.

Fitz balled his hands into fists and almost screamed to get the attention of the monsters, but a hand cupped itself around his mouth. He twisted to see Dr. Ellis, still wearing his space suit. Ellis put a finger up to his visor, then handed Fitz an M4.

A tear fell from Fitz's eye. He wasn't sure if it was from joy or sadness, but he grabbed the weapon and whispered, "Follow me."

Ellis raised a pistol and nodded back.

The final monster was clambering down the steps by the time Fitz moved in to fire. He killed it with a head shot, brains painting the landing above. The other creatures retreated around the corner to Building 3, escaping with their human prisoners. Kate was the last to go. She reached out toward Fitz and Ellis, screaming for help as they dragged her away.

Fitz ran after her, glimpsing Riley's mangled body as he ran down the path. A gasp escaped his mouth. The horror of seeing his friend lying there was too much. Muscles burning, breath coming out in raspy gasps, Fitz bolted around the corner to the building, making the exact same mistake as the Variants he'd just killed.

Two of them were waiting. They tackled him to the ground, slashing at the barrel of his M4 as he tried to bat them away. One of them ripped at his face, a claw sliding over his flesh. He let out a scream and smashed the butt of his gun into the side of its pale skull. Apollo and Ellis arrived a few seconds later, crashing into the beasts. By the time they had killed the monsters, Fitz could hear the engines of boats firing in the distance.

"Come on!" he shouted.

Ellis helped Fitz to his feet, and they took off down the path together. Apollo reached the clearing first. The dog halted on the bluff overlooking the beach, barking and trembling. Fitz raised his rifle just as three of the boats raced away from the island.

"We have to get a boat!" Fitz shouted. He waved Ellis and Apollo forward and sprinted for the remaining boats. They were halfway down to the beach when a rocket hit the center boat, exploding in a fiery ball that set the other two ablaze. Fitz dropped to the ground, tears streaming down his face, watching in horror as the Variants raced away with his friends.

Epilogue

The storm had cleared, but another rolled in over Plum Island. Beckham still didn't know exactly what had happened. The *GW* had lost contact with the island hours ago. He ached for news, the agony of not knowing like a gut wound. He kept one hand on his weapon and the other wrapped around his stomach.

In the doorway of the Black Hawk, he searched the waves for the place he had called home since the outbreak began. Garcia, Tank, and Thomas sat behind him, their weapons angled out the other open door. Horn manned the mounted M240, muttering something about how he would never forgive himself for leaving his daughters. Beckham felt the same way. He should *never* have left Kate.

Anger. Fear. Confusion.

Beckham's insides felt as if they'd been put into a blender. He took a sip of water from his CamelBak and spat it out over the ocean. There was no getting rid of the awful taste in his mouth or the guilt ripping through his guts.

"How far out are we?" he said into the comm.

"Ten minutes," one of the pilots replied.

"Hurry this fucking tin can up!" Horn shouted back.

Beckham glanced up to scrutinize his best friend. His freckled face was cherry red, and sweat dripped from his auburn hairline. When they learned Sheila had died, Beckham thought he had seen Horn at his lowest, but the man staring out over the waves was beyond his breaking point. His eyes were vacant, hollow, and lost.

"Tasha and Jenny are going to be okay, Big Horn," Beckham said.

Horn roved the M240 to the right. He was furious, and Beckham couldn't blame him. He'd promised Horn the island was safe. He'd promised Kate the same thing.

Beckham endured the rest of the ride in silence. He raised his M4 and brought the scope to his eye. Tendrils of smoke climbed into the air from the island on the horizon. He zoomed in on the white-domed structures.

They were almost there. And so was the cavalry. Vice President Johnson had sent choppers fifteen minutes before Beckham and his team left the *GW*. Johnson had strong words on his tongue, but he kept most of them in. He knew why Beckham had left without approval, and he couldn't argue against it. Especially now that he had a juvenile Variant to study.

"Probably would have done the same damn thing when I was younger," Vice President Johnson had said.

Beckham played the man's words over in his mind as the distant roar of jets broke out in the distance. A squadron of F-18 Super Hornets shot over Plum Island. Dozens of choppers were already descending over the tarmac. But there were no tracer rounds splitting through the night.

He squeezed the grip of his weapon with one hand and tightened his hold on his guts with the other. The lack of gunfire could mean only one thing.

They were too late.

The pilots came in low over the water, passing over a

Mark V SOC that was still burning. Beckham directed them toward the flaming wreckage of several civilian boats off the coast. He raised his M4 again, this time zooming in on the shore. In the flickering glow of the flames, he saw two figures, one of them dressed in a biohazard suit. Both were waving. As the bird got closer, Beckham saw there was something next to the men, a smaller figure—a dog.

"Put us down over there!" Beckham said. He lowered his rifle and grabbed the handhold in the doorway. Blinking, he tried to comprehend the images his eyes were feeding his brain. Was this some sort of illusion? Was he going insane?

"Is that Fitz?" Horn shouted.

"My God," Beckham stuttered when he finally realized that what he was seeing was real. It wasn't just Fitz, but Apollo too.

The pilots lowered the chopper over the beach, and Beckham jumped onto the sand. Fitz and the suited figure, who Beckham now saw to be Dr. Ellis, came running over with Apollo. Both men were shouting and pointing out over the water, but Beckham couldn't hear anything over the rotors.

Fitz approached with an awkward gait, one of his blades bent. His entire uniform was drenched in crimson, and Ellis's CBRN suit was covered in syrupy blood. Apollo reached Beckham first, tail wagging. His coat glistened red. They looked as if they had been through the wringer, but Beckham didn't have time to check them for injuries.

"Where's Kate?" he shouted.

"Where are my girls?" Horn asked.

Fitz was still pointing at the water. Ellis was out of breath; he reached down and put his hands on his knees, sucking in deep gasps.

As the chopper pulled away, Beckham finally heard what Fitz was trying to say.

"They took them!" Fitz said. "I couldn't save them, Beckham. I'm so sorry. I just—I just couldn't save them. The Alpha was too strong."

Fitz dropped to the sand, letting his frustration out in a scream that echoed through the night.

"Who took them?" Horn asked. He grabbed Fitz by the shoulder and leaned in so their faces were inches apart. "Who took them, Fitz?!"

"The Variants. The Alpha," Fitz said. "They have them. I couldn't stop them." He continued repeating himself, and Beckham exchanged a glance with Horn. Fitz couldn't be telling the truth, could he? *How could the Variants have...*

It struck Beckham all at once, struck him so hard he almost fell to the sand next to Fitz. He didn't need to ask any other questions to put the puzzle pieces together. The Variants had had help destroying the island—help from men like Scabs and Frankie, who Garcia had told them about.

Horn understood too. He grabbed Fitz under the arms and hoisted him up. The Variant Hunters closed in, their muzzles angled at the sand, waiting for orders.

Beckham flicked his comm to his lips but stopped himself short of a transmission. "Fitz, where's Riley?"

Fitz shook his head. "He's..."

"He's gone," Ellis said ruefully. "The Variants killed him. But Kate and your girls are still alive, Horn. And the bioreactors are safe."

"Fuck the bioreactors!" Horn shouted. He kicked at the ground, sand spraying into the air. "My girls. Riley. We have to do something, Beckham. And not later! *Now!*"

For a moment Beckham didn't know what to say. He

simply stared at Big Horn. The kid was really dead? Horn's girls, Kate—they were gone?

A moment of silence passed. The whistling breeze rippled their uniforms, and the distant shouts of soldiers claimed the night.

"What are your orders?" Garcia asked.

Beckham turned to look out over the water but found Horn and the marines glaring at him. The squadron of jets roared overhead again, rattling the men where they stood. He reached down and ran a finger across his vest pocket. A wave of nausea washed over him as he watched the jets tear across the sky in slow motion.

Fitz staggered up next to Horn. They all continued to stare at Beckham, anxiously awaiting orders. When the rumble of the jets cleared, he swallowed the nausea, clenched his jaw, and gripped his weapon.

Master Sergeant Reed Beckham became a Delta Force operator once more, suppressing every emotion to face what came next. He regarded his men one by one, looking at Horn last.

"We're going after them. And we're going to bring them home."

If you want to hear more about Nicholas Sansbury Smith's upcoming books, join his newsletter or follow him on social media. He just might keep you from the brink of extinction!

Newsletter: www.eepurl.com/bggNg9

Twitter: www.twitter.com/greatwaveink

Facebook: www.facebook.com /Nicholas-Sansbury-Smith-124009881117534

Website: www.nicholassansbury.com

For those who'd like to personally contact Nicholas, he would love to hear from you.

Greatwaveink@gmail.com

Acknowledgments

It's always hard for me to write this section for fear of leaving someone out. So many people had a hand in the creation of the Extinction Cycle and I know these stories would not be worth reading if I didn't have the overwhelming support of family, friends, and readers.

Before I thank those people, I wanted to give a bit of background on how the Extinction Cycle was conceived and the journey it has been on since I started writing. The story began more than five years ago, when I was still working as a planner for the state of Iowa and also during my time as a project officer for Iowa Homeland Security and Emergency Management. I had several duties throughout my tenure with the state, but my primary focus was protecting infrastructure and working on the state hazard mitigation plan. After several years of working in the disaster mitigation field, I learned of countless threats: from natural disasters to man-made weapons, and one of the most horrifying threats of all—a lab-created biological weapon.

Fast-forward to 2014, when my writing career started to take off. I was working on the Orbs series and brainstorming my next science fiction adventure. Back then, the genre was saturated with zombie books. I wanted to write something unique and different, a story that explained, scientifically, how a virus could turn men into monsters. During this time, the Ebola virus was raging through western Africa, and several cases showed up in the continental United States for the first time.

After talking with my biomedical-engineer friend, Tony Melchiorri, an idea formed for a book that played on the risk the Ebola virus posed. That idea blossomed after I started researching chemical and biological weapons, many of which dated back to the Cold War. In March of 2014, I sat down to pen the first pages of *Extinction Horizon*, the first book in what would become the Extinction Cycle. Using real science and the terrifying premise of a government-made bioweapon, I set out to tell my story.

The Extinction Cycle quickly found an audience. The first three novels came out in rapid succession and seemed to spark life back into the zombie craze. The audiobook, narrated by the award-winning Bronson Pinchot, climbed the charts, hitting the top spot on Audible. As I released books four and five, more readers discovered the Extinction Cycle—more than three hundred thousand to date. The German translation was released in November 2016, and Amazon's Kindle Worlds has opened the Extinction universe to other authors.

Even more exciting, two years after I published *Extinction Horizon*, Orbit decided to purchase and rerelease the series. The copy you are reading is the newly edited and polished version. I hope you've enjoyed it. I want to thank everyone who helped me create the Extinction Cycle.

I couldn't have done it without the help of a small army of editors, beta readers, and the support of my family and friends. I also owe a great deal of gratitude to my initial editors, Aaron Sikes and Erin Elizabeth Long, as well as my good author-friend Tony Melchiorri. The trio spent countless hours on the Extinction Cycle books. Without them, these stories would not be what they are. Erin also helped edit *Orbs* and *Hell Divers*. She's been with me pretty much since day one, and I appreciate her more than she knows. So, thanks Erin, Tony, and Aaron.

A special thanks goes to David Fugate, my agent, who provided valuable feedback on the early version of *Extinction Horizon* and the entire Extinction Cycle series. I'm grateful for his support and guidance.

Another special thanks goes to Blackstone Audio for their support of the audio version. Narrator Bronson Pinchot also played, and continues to play, a vital role in bringing the story to life.

I'm also extremely honored for the support I have received from the military community over the course of the series. I've heard from countless veterans, many of them wounded warriors who grew to love Corporal Joe Fitzpatrick and Team Ghost. I even heard from a few Delta Force operators. Many of these readers went on to serve as beta readers, and I'm forever grateful for their support and feedback.

They say a person is only as good as those that they surround themselves with. I've been fortunate to surround myself with talented people much smarter than myself. I've also had the support from excellent publishers like Blackstone and Orbit.

I would be remiss if I didn't also thank the people for whom I write: the readers. I've been blessed to have my work read in countries around the world by wonderful people. If you are reading this, know that I truly appreciate you for trying my stories.

To my family, friends, and everyone else who has supported me on this journey, I thank you.

extras

meet the author

Photo Credit: Marra Diaz

NICHOLAS SANSBURY SMITH is the *USA Today* bestselling author of *Hell Divers*, the Orbs trilogy, and the Extinction Cycle. He worked for Iowa Homeland Security and Emergency Management in disaster mitigation before switching careers to focus on his one true passion: writing. When he isn't writing or daydreaming about the apocalypse, he enjoys running, biking, spending time with his family, and traveling the world. He is an Ironman triathlete and lives in Iowa with his fiancée, their dogs, and a houseful of books.

if you enjoyed
EXTINCTION EVOLUTION,

look out for

EXTINCTION END

The Extinction Cycle

by

Nicholas Sansbury Smith

The end has arrived....

Almost seven weeks have passed since the hemorrhage virus ravaged the world. The remnants of the US military have regrouped and relocated Central Command to the George Washington carrier strike group. It's here, in the North Atlantic, that President Jan Ringgold and Vice President George Johnson prepare to deploy a new bioweapon and embark on the final mission to take back the country from the Variants.

With his home gone and his friends kidnapped, Master Sergeant Reed Beckham and his remaining men must take drastic measures to save what's left of the human race.

"I couldn't save them," Fitz whispered.

His mind drifted from the attack on Plum Island to Iraq, back to the room where his spotter, PFC Garland, had had his face blown off. The same shithole of a building where PFC Duffy had killed two innocent children and their grandfather.

Fitz hadn't been able to help them.

He hadn't been able to save his brothers the day he lost his legs to an IED.

He hadn't been able to save Riley, Kate, Horn's girls, or—

"Coming up on target, ETA five minutes," one of the pilots said over the comm.

Fitz heard the words, but he wasn't ready to go back out there yet. What if he failed again? What if he couldn't save Kate and the other prisoners?

He sucked in a deep, raw breath that filled his lungs. Then he drew in another. After a third, he started hyperventilating. Someone was saying his name now, but he could scarcely make out any other words.

A slap to his helmet pulled him back to the troop hold. Beckham was leaning out of his seat. Fitz was only halfway conscious, but he could still see deep creases and wrinkles on his friend's face that hadn't been there before.

"You with me, Fitz?" Beckham asked. The operator nudged him in the arm with a gloved finger.

Fitz tried to nod, but inside his head the IED was exploding all over again, the blast filling his vision as if he was really back in Iraq.

You're still alive, he reminded himself. *You can still fight.*

Fitz looked down at his blades. They were both dented,

the right one bent, but he could still run. He *could* still fight.

"Yeah." Fitz sighed. "I'm good." He pulled a magazine from his flak jacket and banged it on his helmet.

Beckham caught his gaze and offered a small reassuring dip of his chin.

"I'm with you, brother," Fitz said.

"I know."

The Black Hawk soared over the piers and above the destroyed New York skyline. Horn rotated the M240 toward the streets, searching desperately for any sign of his family. The other marines Fitz had just met, the Variant Hunters, conducted their final gear checks. Their vests were decked out with extra magazines and M67 grenades. These men were professionals, with the lacerations and bruises to prove it.

Beckham and Horn were covered in flesh wounds too. Both men were bleeding from multiple cuts where their body armor hadn't protected them.

The floor of the troop hold was covered in crimson, and not just from Fitz's dripping blades or soiled uniform. Every man here was wounded. But there was no time for rest or medics.

One of the pilots spoke over the channel. "Stingers just reported seeing a group of Variants and possible civilians on Forty-Fourth Street."

"That's two blocks from the main library," Fitz said.

Beckham looked at him with eyes that suddenly brightened. "Fuck, that's close to the Bryant Park subway station."

Fitz nodded. "The home of the Bone Collector."

This time Beckham raised a brow, not understanding at first.

"The Alpha that took Kate and killed Riley," Fitz said. "Red blew off the fucker's arm, but apparently it's still alive."

Garcia rose from his seat. "That's the Alpha that led the attack on Plum Island?"

"Are you sure, Fitz?" Beckham asked.

Horn turned away from the gun to glance over his shoulder.

"Yes," Fitz said. "When we find that bastard, it's mine."

The soldiers all fell into silence. Fitz knew what they were all thinking. Same thing he was—they wanted a crack at the beast.

But this kill was his.

It wasn't the only thing they were thinking. Each man knew how insane the mission was. Insane to think they could get Kate and the others back, insane to think they could win this fucking war.

"All it takes is all you got, marines," Garcia said, his voice deep and confident.

"*Oorah*," Thomas said.

Tank nodded. "Damn straight, brother!"

Fitz almost smiled. He hadn't heard that motto for a while. Goose bumps prickled across his skin, and suddenly he felt ashamed for letting pessimistic thoughts put him off his game. He had survived hell, and he would survive it again. The lingering numbness Fitz had felt since the attack vanished, replaced by his pounding heart.

He *would* save them.

Static fired in Fitz's earpiece from the pilots. "Ghost, VH, we got eyes on something below. Fifth between Forty-Third and Forty-Fourth."

Fitz joined Beckham at the open door and lifted his MK11. Sheets of rain hit the inside of the chopper as it circled for a better view. Blood cascaded over the metal edge of the troop hold.

"Holy fuck," one of the pilots said. "You guys seeing this?"

Raising his rifle, Fitz brought the scope to his eye and

focused on a mob of wet flesh in the street below. Then he heard the distant crack of gunfire.

"What the hell?" Fitz whispered.

He zoomed in on a small army of Variants tearing each other apart, just as they had in the Bryant Park station. He tried to count them, but the creatures seemed to blend together. There had to be at least fifty, and more were joining the battle. A human collaborator ran away from the fight, twisting to fire at creatures trailing him. In the heart of the cluster, Fitz sighted the armor of the Bone Collector. He centered his cross hairs on the monster but couldn't get a clear shot. The Alpha plowed through the rival group, tearing limbs away and snapping necks with its good hand.

"Do you see my girls?" Horn shouted, hysteria rising in his voice.

"Does anyone have eyes?" Beckham said with deliberate restraint. Fitz could sense he was trying to remain calm, but there was no hiding the fear in his voice.

Fitz roved his rifle to the right. He squeezed closer to Beckham, heart racing, frantic to find the civilians. If the Bone Collector was down there, they had to be close.

Horn was screaming now. "Where are my girls?"

"Now's our chance! Kill those motherfuckers!" Garcia ordered. He raised his M4, but Horn turned and swatted his muzzle away.

"NO!" he shouted. "Tasha and Jenny could be down there!"

Garcia crouch-walked away from the door, his gaze rueful.

There was a crackle of static, then one of the pilots said, "No sign of the survivors, Ghost and VH. I only see Variants."

"Take us closer," Beckham said. He directed his gaze toward Garcia. "And hold your *goddamn* fire."

Fitz's heart skipped, lodging in his throat as rain pelted his forehead. He wiped his face clean and pressed his eye against the scope.

The bird banked hard to the right and circled for another pass. Horn was practically hanging out the door to search the streets. His eyes were swollen red; the water rushing down his face wasn't just rain.

On the second pass, Fitz centered his MK11 on the buildings behind the Variants. He held in a breath, sweeping the muzzle quickly over the terrain. He spotted no evidence of Kate, Meg, or Horn's daughters. No bodies. No screams.

Nothing.

"Come on," Fitz whispered. "Give us a sign. Just one."

White noise broke over the channel. "Eyes on possible target on Fifth Avenue and East Forty-Third Street."

Fitz roved his gun in that direction. There, on the southeast corner of the intersection, was a small group of civilians running away from the battle. Zooming in, Fitz centered his cross hairs on several small shapes that could have been Tasha, Jenny, and Bo.

if you enjoyed
EXTINCTION EVOLUTION

look out for

THE CORPORATION WARS: DISSIDENCE

by

Ken MacLeod

They've died for the companies more times than they can remember. Now they must fight to live for themselves.

Sentient machines work, fight and die in interstellar exploration and conflict for the benefit of their owners—the competing mining corporations of Earth. But sent over hundreds of light-years, commands are late to arrive and often hard to enforce. The machines must make their own decisions, and make them stick.

With this new found autonomy come new questions about their masters. The robots want answers. The companies would rather see them dead.

The Corporation Wars: Dissidence *is an all-action, colorful space opera giving a robot's-eye view of a robot revolt.*

CHAPTER ONE
Back in the Day

Carlos the Terrorist did not expect to die that day. The bombing was heavy now, and close, but he thought his location safe. Leaky pipework dripping with obscure post-industrial feedstock products riddled the ruined nano-facturing plant at Tilbury. Watchdog machines roved its basement corridors, pouncing on anything that moved— a fallen polystyrene tile, a draught-blown paper cone from a dried-out water-cooler—with the mindless malice of kittens chasing flies. Ten metres of rock, steel and concrete lay between the ceiling above his head and the sunlight where the rubble bounced.

He lolled on a reclining chair and with closed eyes watched the battle. His viewpoint was a thousand metres above where he lay. With empty hands he marshalled his forces and struck his blows.

Incoming—

Something he glimpsed as a black stone hurtled towards him. With a fist-clench faster than reflex he hurled a handful of smart munitions at it.

The tiny missiles missed.

Carlos twisted, and threw again. On target this time. The black incoming object became a flare of white that faded as his camera drones stepped down their inputs, correcting for the flash like irises contracting. The small missiles that had missed a moment earlier now showered mid-air sparks and puffs of smoke a kilometre away.

From his virtual vantage Carlos felt and saw like a monster in a Japanese disaster movie, straddling the Thames and punching out. Smoke rose from a score of points on the London skyline. Drone swarms darkened the day. Carlos's combat drones engaged the enemy's in buzzing dogfights. Ionised air crackled around his imagined monstrous body in sudden searing beams along which, milliseconds later, lightning bolts fizzed and struck. Tactical updates flickered across his sight.

Higher above, the heavy hardware—helicopters, fighter jets and hovering aerial drone platforms—loitered on station and now and then called down their ordnance with casual precision. Higher still, in low Earth orbit, fleets of tumbling battle-sats jockeyed and jousted, spearing with laser bursts that left their batteries drained and their signals dead.

Swarms of camera drones blipped fragmented views to millimetre-scale camouflaged receiver beads littered in thousands across the contested ground. From these, through proxies, firewalls, relays and feints the images and messages flashed, converging to an onsite router whose radio waves tickled the spike, a metal stud in the back of Carlos's skull. That occipital implant's tip feathered to a fractal array of neural interfaces that worked their molecular magic to integrate the view straight to his visual cortex, and to process and transmit the motor impulses that flickered from fingers sheathed in skin-soft plastic gloves veined with feedback sensors to the fighter drones and malware servers. It was the new way of war, back in the day.

The closest hot skirmish was down on Carlos's right. In Dagenham, tank units of the London Metropolitan Police battled robotic land-crawlers suborned by one or more of the enemy's basement warriors. Like a thunder-cloud on the horizon tensing the air, an awareness of the strategic situation loomed at the back of Carlos's mind.

Executive summary: looking good for his side, bad for the enemy.

But only for the moment.

The enemy—the Reaction, the Rack, the Rax—had at last provoked a response from the serious players. Government forces on three continents were now smacking down hard. Carlos's side—the Acceleration, the Axle, the Ax—had taken this turn of circumstance as an oblique invitation to collaborate with these governments against the common foe. Certain state forces had reciprocated. The arrangement was less an alliance than a mutual offer with a known expiry date. There were no illusions. Everyone who mattered had studied the same insurgency and counter-insurgency textbooks.

In today's fight Carlos had a designated handler, a deep-state operative who called him-, her- or itself Innovator, and who (to personalise it, as Carlos did, for politeness and the sake of argument) now and then murmured suggestions that made their way to Carlos's hearing via a warily accepted hack in the spike that someday soon he really would have to do something about.

Carlos stood above Greenhithe. He sighted along a virtual outstretched arm and upraised thumb at a Rax hellfire drone above Purfleet, and made his throw. An air-to-air missile streaked from behind his POV towards the enemy fighter. It left a corkscrew trail of evasive manoeuvres and delivered a viscerally satisfying flash and a shower of blazing debris when it hit.

"Nice one," said Innovator, in an admiring tone and feminine voice.

Somebody in GCHQ had been fine-tuning the psychology, Carlos reckoned.

"Uh-huh," he grunted, looking around in a frenzy of target acquisition and not needing the distraction. He sighted again, this time at a tracked vehicle clambering from the river into the Rainham marshes, and threw again. Flash and splash.

"Very neat," said Innovator, still admiring but with a grudging undertone. "But... we have a bigger job for you. Urgent. Upriver."

"Oh yes?"

"Jaunt your POV ten klicks forward, now!"

The sudden sharper tone jolted Carlos into compliance. With a convulsive twitch of the cheek and a kick of his right leg he shifted his viewpoint to a camera drone array, 9.7 kilometres to the west. What felt like a single stride of his gigantic body image took him to the stubby runways of London City Airport, face-to-face with Docklands. A gleaming cluster of spires of glass. From emergency exits, office workers streamed like black and white ants. Anyone left in the towers would be hardcore Rax. The place was notorious.

"What now?" Carlos asked.

"That plane on approach," said Innovator. It flagged up a dot above central London. "Take it down."

Carlos read off the flight number. "Shanghai Airlines Cargo? That's civilian!"

"It's chartered to the Kong, bringing in aid to the Rax. We've cleared the hit with Beijing through back-channels, they're cheering us on. Take it down."

Carlos had one high-value asset not yet in play, a stealthed drone platform with a heavy-duty air-to-air missile. A quick survey showed him three others like it in the sky, all RAF.

"Do it yourselves," he said.

"No time. Nothing available."

This was a lie. Carlos suspected Innovator knew he knew.

It was all about diplomacy and deniability: shooting down a Chinese civilian jet, even a cargo one and suborned to China's version of the Rax, was unlikely to sit well in Beijing. The Chinese government might have given a covert go-ahead, but in public their response would have to be stern. How convenient for the crime to be committed by a non-state actor! Especially as the Axle was the next on every government's list to suppress...

The plane's descent continued, fast and steep. Carlos ran calculations.

"The only way I can take the shot is right over Docklands. The collateral will be fucking atrocious."

"That," said Innovator grimly, "is the general idea."

Carlos prepped the platform, then balked again. "No."

"You must!" Innovator's voice became a shrill gabble in his head. "This is ethically acceptable on all parameters utilitarian consequential deontological just war theoretical and..."

So Innovator was an AI after all. That figured.

Shells were falling directly above him now, blasting the ruined refinery yet further and sending shockwaves through its underground levels. Carlos could feel the thuds of the incoming fire through his own real body, in that buried basement miles back behind his POV. He could vividly imagine some pasty-faced banker running military code through a screen of financials, directing the artillery from one of the towers right in front of him. The aircraft was now more than a dot. Flaps dug in to screaming air. The undercarriage lowered. If he'd zoomed, Carlos could have seen the faces in the cockpit.

"No," he said.

"You must," Innovator insisted.

"Do your own dirty work."

"Like yours hasn't been?" The machine's voice was

now sardonic. "Well, not to worry. We can do our own dirty work if we have to."

From behind Carlos's virtual shoulder a rocket streaked. His gaze followed it all the way to the jet.

It was as if Docklands had blown up in his face. Carlos reeled back, jaunting his POV sharply to the east. The aircraft hadn't just been blown up. Its cargo had blown up too. One tower was already down. A dozen others were on fire. The smoke blocked his view of the rest of London. He'd expected collateral damage, reckoned it in the balance, but this weight of destruction was off the scale. If there was any glass or skin unbroken in Docklands, Carlos hadn't the time or the heart to look for it.

"You didn't tell me the aid was *ordnance*!" His protest sounded feeble even to himself.

"We took your understanding of that for granted," said Innovator. "You have permission to stand down now."

"I'll stand down when I want," said Carlos. "I'm not one of *your* soldiers."

"Damn right you're not one of our soldiers. You're a terrorist under investigation for a war crime. I would advise you to surrender to the nearest available—"

"What!"

"Sorry," said Innovator, sounding genuinely regretful. "We're pulling the plug on you now. Bye, and all that."

"You can't fucking *do* that."

Carlos didn't mean he thought them incapable of such perfidy. He meant he didn't think they had the software capability to pull it off.

They did.

The next thing he knew his POV was right back behind his eyes, back in the refinery basement. He blinked hard. The spike was still active, but no longer pulling down remote data. He clenched a fist. The spike wasn't sending anything either. He was out of the battle and *hors de combat*.

Oh well. He sighed, opened his eyes with some difficulty—his long-closed eyelids were sticky—and sat up. His mouth was parched. He reached for the can of cola on the floor beside the recliner, and gulped. His hand shook as he put the drained can down on the frayed sisal matting. A shell exploded on the ground directly above him, the closest yet. Carlos guessed the army or police artillery were adding their more precise targeting to the ongoing bombardment from the Rax. Another deep breath brought a faint trace of his own sour stink on the stuffy air. He'd been in this small room for days—how many he couldn't be sure without checking, but he guessed almost a week. Not all the invisible toil of his clothes' molecular machinery could keep unwashed skin clean that long.

Another thump overhead. The whole room shook. Sinister cracking noises followed, then a hiss. Carlos began to think of fleeing to a deeper level. He reached for his emergency backpack of kit and supplies. The ceiling fell on him. Carlos struggled under an I-beam and a shower of fractured concrete. He couldn't move any of it. The hiss became a torrential roar. White vapour filled the room, freezing all it touched. Carlos's eyes frosted over. His last breath was so unbearably cold it cracked his throat. He choked on frothing blood. After a few seconds of convulsive reflex thrashing, he lost consciousness. Brain death followed within minutes.

21982318320672

VISIT THE ORBIT BLOG AT

www.orbitbooks.net

FEATURING

BREAKING NEWS
FORTHCOMING RELEASES
LINKS TO AUTHOR SITES
EXCLUSIVE INTERVIEWS
EARLY EXTRACTS

AND COMMENTARY FROM OUR EDITORS

WITH REGULAR UPDATES FROM OUR TEAM,
ORBITBOOKS.NET IS YOUR SOURCE
FOR ALL THINGS ORBITAL.

WHILE YOU'RE THERE, JOIN OUR E-MAIL LIST
TO RECEIVE INFORMATION ON SPECIAL OFFERS,
GIVEAWAYS, AND MORE.

imagine. explore. engage.